The Navigator

*Apollo Stone Trilogy
Book 1*

by

P.M. Johnson

The Navigator by P.M. Johnson

Copyright © 2016 by P.M. Johnson

All rights reserved. No part of this book may be used, reproduced or transmitted in any form or by any means, electronic or mechanical, including photocopying, recording, or by any information storage or retrieval system, without the written permission of the author, except were permitted by law, or in the case of brief quotations embodied in reviews or critical articles.

This is a work of fiction. Names, characters, places, organizations, and incidents are the product of the author's imagination or are used fictitiously. Any resemblance to actual events, locales, or persons, living or dead, is entirely coincidental.

This book is licensed for your personal enjoyment only. This book may not be re-sold.

Cover design © 2016 by Joel Artz.

Edited by Robert Helle.

For more information about this book and the author, please follow me on Twitter at PM Johnson@pmjohnson003 or visit www.apollostonetrilogy.com

This book is for
Gisele, Lukas, and Blake.

Chapter 1

Arthur Chambers looked back at the shop just as the lights above the entrance went dark. He heard the deadbolt slide into place as he scanned the dark street as casually as possible, noting the handful of pedestrians hurrying home now that the restaurants and shops were closing down. To his right was the dark blue sedan which had followed him from his apartment. He had driven around town for the better part of an hour in an attempt to throw them off his trail, and at one point he believed he had succeeded, but there it was again, the same blue sedan. He cursed his stupidity for having thought he could elude them.

Chambers walked across the street, still wet from the rain, toward a small gray Victory automobile parked on the opposite side. He opened the door and squeezed his tall lanky frame into the driver's seat. He inserted the key into the ignition.

"Damn it!" he whispered to himself.

Chambers turned the key, but it refused to start. He frowned and shook his head. *We have fighter planes that exploit extra-dimensional gravitational differences but we still can't build a decent car.* Chambers took a deep breath and followed the usual ritual of pumping the gas twice and counting to five. Then he rotated the key once more. The Victory coughed and rattled in protest, but it finally started. He turned on the headlights, looked in his side mirror, and pulled away from the curb.

As he drove away, Chambers looked in his rear view mirror and saw a man exit a coffee shop and step into the passenger side of the dark blue sedan. The headlights turned on and the car quickly pulled into the street behind Chambers. He turned left and then right. The blue sedan did the same. His heart began to pound as his anxiety grew. A thousand questions raced through his mind. Would they retrace his footsteps? Would they question the shop owner who had promised to mail the hastily conceived note? He felt a sudden pang of terror surge through his body. He'd made a terrible mistake. He needed to retrieve it; undo what he had done.

Chambers approached a sharp bend in the road. He looked in his rear view mirror, and when he was out of sight of the blue sedan, he gunned the Victory's engine and sped down the hill toward the five way intersection at the bottom. At the last moment, he pulled the steering wheel sharply to the right. The tires screamed their warning, but he ignored them. He clenched his teeth and kept his foot on the gas pedal, trying to turn onto the little street that ran along the river.

Then he heard a popping sound and the left front tire suddenly turned perpendicular to the car frame. The little Victory spun out of control and slammed head first into a cement block at the foot of a bridge.

Moments later a man in a dark blue overcoat ran up to the car. He pulled hard on the door, but it refused to open. He pulled again and again until it finally yielded. The man crouched down and looked at Chambers, who was pressed tightly against the steering wheel. Blood flowed freely from a head wound.

Chamber's eyes were closed, and he breathed in small gasps as his punctured lungs quickly filled with blood. "Don't touch it," he rasped. "Don't use it." He opened his eyes and looked at the man's face. He struggled to focus on his features, then with his last breath he whispered, "Fool."

Chapter 2

The sun was just beginning to rise above the tree tops when Logan returned from his run. He entered the code into the apartment's keypad and went in. He walked into the small kitchen and poured himself a tall glass of water from the faucet and gulped it down. Then he prepared a pot of coffee. As the pot filled with steaming dark liquid, a door in the small living room next to the kitchen opened.

"Hey, Cap" Logan said to the blond haired young man who entered the kitchen.

"Hey," replied Cap, squinting at the morning light filtering through the window shades. He sat on a stool at the kitchen bar and leaned forward, resting his torso on the counter and moaning softly. Then he stretched his arms out and said, "Need coffee…brain…hurting."

"You stayed out past your bedtime, Cap" said Logan.

"I did," replied Cap. With eyes half open, he lifted his head and rubbed his temples with his fingertips.

"Drink this, you'll feel better," said Logan as he handed Cap a cup of black coffee.

Cap tried a sip. "This coffee tastes like a sweaty gym sock."

"Drink up. It'll put steam in your stride," said Logan as he walked toward his bedroom door.

An hour later the two men, now shaved and showered, exited the apartment building. Both wore dark blue pants, black shoes, white dress shirts, and blue waist length jackets. Each had a bag slung over his shoulder. They joined a stream of identically dressed young men and women walking toward a group of buildings two blocks away. As they crossed the street they passed a large boulder with a brass plaque on it. It read, *Malcom Weller Military Academy for Science and Engineering.*

Walking on bright green grass, Logan breathed in the fresh spring air. Tall trees provided a brilliant display of blossoms in the bright morning light. At the center of the park was a large bronze statue of a man standing on a stone pedestal. The statue's eyes looked boldly toward the horizon. His overcoat was open, flowing behind him as if he faced a strong wind. His right arm was raised and his large hand pointed forward. His left arm was at his side, the hand clenched into a fist. The name "Malcom Weller" was carved into the pedestal.

They walked past the statue and entered a building on the far side of the park. As they climbed the steps to the second floor, they were joined by an attractive young woman with shoulder length dark hair and dark brown eyes.

"Hey Lena," said Cap. "I missed you last night at The Cave."

"You didn't miss me. I had no intention of being there," she replied coolly. "I have two finals today. One of which you're also taking, Caparelli."

"What? I have a final today?" said Cap in mock surprise.

She ignored Cap's theatrics and turned her attention to Logan. "You ready for the fluid mechanics final?"

"We'll find out tomorrow," Logan responded. Logan had received the highest score on the midterm, but Lena's project had won Professor Bouchet's greatest praise. The final exam would probably decide who would receive the highest overall grade.

"Well, good luck," she said. She turned to her right and walked down the hall.

After Lena disappeared in a crowd of cadets, Cap looked at Logan. "By 'good luck' I think she means 'I hope you fail miserably'."

"Probably," agreed Logan. Lena Moreau was hyper competitive by any standard, and she excelled at everything from academics to close-quarters combat. Logan clapped Cap on the back. "Good luck with that systems design final."

"Thanks, but I just need to pass," said Cap as he started to walk in the same direction Lena had gone in. "Maybe I'll sit next to Lena. She digs me, I can tell."

Logan shook his head and smiled. "Yeah, she *digs* you. Have a *groovy* day."

Logan entered a small lecture hall. There were about fifteen students already in the room but the class had not yet started. At the front of the room there was a large view screen behind a wooden lectern. Facing the lectern were four rows of seats, a continuous curving bench running along each row. Logan ascended several steps and walked down the second row, taking the seat next to a man with short black hair.

"Phillip," said Logan, deepening his voice and nodding his head in feigned formality.

"Logan," answered Phillip, also slightly nodding his head. Then he smiled and said, "Did you catch any of last night's Re-ded match-ups?"

"Some," answered Logan. "Looks like Samarak will win gold for sword and guard. And I don't think anyone is going to beat Muthu's time in the triathlon."

"Yeah," said Phillip. "That guy's inhuman. A beast. Who's your pick for the big one, the banner race?"

"I don't know," answered Logan as he watched a few more cadets file into the room. "Vorsek probably. He's won twice already and looked good in the prelims." Looking back at Phillip he asked, "More importantly, how many banner thieves will get run down this year?"

Phillip shrugged his shoulders. "Hard to say. How many was it last year? Two? Plus another four injured? There are rumors the SPD will crack down on it this year."

Logan shook his head and said, "No way. People would take to the streets if they kept the thieves out. Watching them jump out and try to steal banners is more popular than the race itself. And as long as the bookies keep paying anyone who can steal a banner, the thieves will keep trying. I hear they get a fully loaded black buy card if they get one."

"I doubt that," scoffed Phillip. "They get cash, but the SPD can trace a card through its bio-encryption. They'd just invalidate it."

"The SPD already looks the other way by letting the thieves in the race. Why would they care about a couple cards? And you never hear about a crackdown on the bookies."

"I hope you're right," said Phillip. "I've got fifty bucks riding on Vorsek to run someone down, and another twenty-five it'll be fatal. You?"

"Not me," said Logan, hands raised. "I don't have cash lying around to give away to bookies."

"Too bad we can't use buy cards like cash," said Phillip with a grin. "I'd put five hundred down on Vorsek."

Logan laughed. "Yeah, right. People would blow their allowances on booze and bookies."

"Money well spent," said Phillip. "Damn, I hope I win. I need the cash. I still have one year until graduation, and I can't make it on a cadet's green buy card."

"Maybe you should jump the fence and grab a banner," suggested Logan. "With a loaded black card you could get a nice apartment, eat at the best restaurants. You could buy new car. Might even get bumped to the front of the waiting list."

"Maybe you should do it. You could buy a new PDD," said Phillip pointing at Logan's battered personal data device.

"Don't need a new one," said Logan. "I'll be going on full active duty right after graduation. Don't need a PDD to fire an M-35 or march in a straight line."

Phillip grinned and shook his head. "You? Fire a weapon? March around? They won't waste your talent on that."

Logan smiled and looked toward the front of the room. "Who knows what plans the Guardians have for any of us?" he said in a mock philosophical tone.

Their conversation was interrupted when a tall thin black man wearing khaki pants, a dark green dress shirt, and a brown jacket entered the room. He walked to the lectern and placed a folder filled with paper on the nearby table.

"Good morning everyone," he said.

"Good morning, Professor Garrison," murmured a few students.

Pointing at the folder, Professor Garrison said. "As you can see I have printed out and graded your final papers. I will return them to you at the end of the class."

He looked around the room and smiled at the students. "I am holding your papers hostage because I know some of you will be tempted to leave as soon as you know your grade. Not everyone will be happy with the results, but if you have questions about your grade we can discuss them after today's class or during my office hours on Wednesday."

"Okay," said Garrison as he clapped his hands. "Your grades are determined, but our conversation is not over. For today's topic, our final topic, I wanted to dig a little deeper into the influences on early colonial society that led to a shift in perspective. I'm not talking about the proximate causes for the revolution, namely the British crown's oppressive mercantilist policies combined with counter-productive individualism in the colonies. I want to discuss why the people's collective consciousness had advanced to a point where they identified more with each other than with the interests of the crown. Who has a theory? Who wants to begin?"

A woman with short brown hair sitting behind Logan raised her hand. "Professor Garrison?"

"Yes, Ms. Becker," said Garrison with a smile. "Please get us started."

"According to Larrent's *Roots of a Revolution*, the colonists' view of themselves as a distinct people began with the Seven Years War. It was the first time colonists had to fight for their homes in a meaningful way."

"Great," said Garrison. "That's what Larrent thinks. What do the rest of you think?"

The question prompted several cadets to raise their hands and an animated discussion followed. Some cadets argued that the seed of colonial separateness was formed very early, before the Seven Years War. Some believed the feeling of a separate identity formed at least fifty years prior to the war due to the crown's prohibitions against the colonies developing certain industries or producing manufactured goods. Then there was a heated debate about the deep divide within pre-Revolution society between those who wanted independence and those who supported the crown both during and after the war. Phillip argued the divide was fueled by the wealthy merchants who would benefit from freer trade versus merchants and landowners who benefited from the status quo. Logan argued that whatever the causes of the war the split in society was deepened once it started because most people followed their convictions. It wasn't just about wealth, manufacturing, and trade; ideas truly mattered.

The debate continued until the bell rang, after which Professor Garrison called out each student's name and returned their final paper as they walked by. Logan's name was the last to be called. When he received his paper, he turned to the final page to see the grade. Ninety-seven. Maybe not the highest score, but enough to ensure he'd get an A for the course. He thanked Professor Garrison for teaching the class and walked toward the door.

"Mr. Brandt," said Garrison.

"Yes?" he said, turning around to face the professor.

"I thought you made some interesting points in your paper. However, I noted a few threads of thought that were, how shall I put it, unsupported by leading scholars of pre-Impact society."

"I see," said Logan.

"Look," continued Garrison after a pause. "I understand that there are some theories out there that can be attractive to young people, but you need to guard against undedicated modes of thinking. It probably doesn't matter too much for ancient, medieval or even early American history, but as you approach the period immediately preceding Impact, I recommend you stick to the authorized histories."

"Yes sir," said Logan. "Thank you for the advice."

Garrison smiled and continued. "Personally, I don't think it's harmful to discuss these things in a properly supervised environment, such as our classroom. I said many times throughout the semester that I welcome all well-reasoned discussion. But you will be leaving academia soon and things will be different. You'll need to watch your step."

Logan nodded. "Thanks Professor Garrison. I'll keep that in mind."

Garrison placed a hand on Logan's shoulder and looked him in the eye. "I hope you know that you can trust me."

Logan nodded his head and said, "Yes sir. Thanks."

Logan left the classroom and exited the building. He walked across a small square toward a three-story glass building. He went inside and entered a large open room. There were a few rows of books, but the majority of the space was devoted to individual study stations equipped with large transparent view screens and docking stations. Wooden tables arranged in rows occupied the center. Students sat at the tables, quietly studying alone or in small groups.

He found an unoccupied study station and docked his PDD. The view screen flickered and then icons of various software programs, textbooks, and other files appeared. Logan touched the icon of a textbook entitled *Advanced Propulsion.* The view screen showed the table of contents. He touched on one of the chapters and the screen opened a page with text and equations. He pulled up the notes file on his PDD and inserted a portion of them next to the textbook file so he could simultaneously view the text and his class notes. Touching the screen, he flicked through the pages of notes until he found the relevant information.

He read something that didn't make sense to him. What he'd written down in class did not seem to agree with what the text was saying. He opened up the lab simulator program, and using his finger as a stylus, he wrote out a series of equations. He touched the image of a green "GO" button and the simulator program converted his equations into charts and graphs. The screen displayed a 3D image of how his model would function. He adjusted some of the variables, such as fuel purity, mass, and environmental conditions. He frowned at what he saw. Frustrated, he sat back, unconsciously running his fingers through his wavy brown hair. Then a thought occurred to him. He made some adjustments to his equations and hit "GO". This time he smiled when he saw the results.

He stopped studying at 11:45 and went to the cafeteria to get some lunch. He took a tray from the top of a stack and pushed it along a metal shelf. He indicated what food he wanted and one of the dozen or so cafeteria staff workers placed it on his tray. He looked around the large crowded room and saw Cap and another student sitting at a table.

"How'd your systems final go?" asked Logan as he sat down next to Cap.

"About usual," said Cap unenthusiastically. "I didn't light it up but I didn't crash and burn either."

The student sitting across the table took his heavy-rimmed glasses off and started cleaning them with a small cloth. "Systems design with Fowler is a joke," said the other student. "Try taking it from Van Horn. The man's a sociopath."

"No thanks, Hamza." replied Cap. "Fowler was crazy enough for me. Did you know he sings to himself when he writes on the view screen? What a cube."

"Strange," agreed Logan. He looked at Hamza. "What about you? How are exams going?"

Hamza held his glasses up to the ceiling lights, gave them a final wipe, and placed them on his nose. "I had three last week and two more this week. Then I'm a free man." He looked around the cafeteria. "Free from this fucking bullshit gulag."

"Free?" replied Cap. "Your active duty station is Peoria. *Peoria!* That's the goddamn frontier, boy. Shithole central."

Logan and Cap laughed. Agitated, Hamza adjusted his glasses and said rather defensively, "That's where they need civil and agricultural engineers. I'm good at both, so they're sending me where the work needs to be done. At least I'll be doing work that makes a difference, makes us one people, one nation."

Logan smiled. Then he said, "You better be good with an M-35, too. The clans raid out there at least once a week."

"Shit," said Cap. "Hamza will be too busy pissing his pants to get a shot off."

Hamza mimicked Cap. "*Hamza will be too busy pissing his pants to get a shot off.*" He leaned across the table toward Cap, "I can hit a fly's eye at two hundred meters."

Cap coughed on his food as he laughed. He swallowed and said, "Look at you! You're blind as a bat. You couldn't hit your mama's fat ass at ten meters."

Hamza tightened his lips and said, "Meet me at the range tonight, and I'll show you how it's done, asshole."

Cap grinned. "A challenge from the lady in the spectacles!" he said in a ringmaster's tone of voice. "I accept. I'll see you at the range at nineteen hundred hours. M-35 and 9mm. One clip per person."

"You're on, fly boy bird turd," said Hamza. He stood up to leave. As he walked away he said over his shoulder, "Bring some money. No buy card bullshit. Cold cash. I want to make it interesting."

"I'm going to enjoy this," said Cap after Hamza had gone. "Easy money."

"I wouldn't get too cocky," cautioned Logan. "Hamza looks like a geek but he was walking foot patrols west of Chicago during last summer's active duty. It's wild out there so I'm pretty sure he fired his weapon in anger a few times."

"Not concerned," said Cap. "I did a lot of shooting during last summer's AD, too."

Logan shook his head and chuckled. "You flew F31 patrol missions. You're a fly boy, a stick jock. You played with expensive toys all day and got tucked into your warm bed at night."

Cap waved a hand, dismissively. "You're backing up Hamza because you're both infantry. Flat Foots, ground pounders."

Logan shrugged. "We'll continue this discussion tonight when you get back from the range. And don't bullshit me. I'm going to verify every detail with Hamza tomorrow."

Logan took a final bite of green mush on his plate and stood. "Time to meet my fluids study group."

"Have fun with your fluids," said Cap. "Tell lovely Lena I said hi."

"I will not. She thinks you're an egotistical idiot."

"Just one of my many charming qualities," replied Cap.

Ten minutes later Logan entered a library study room and sat at a table with four other cadets, including Lena.

"Cap says hi," he said to her.

"Caparelli?" she said without looking up from her PDD. "That boy's an idiot."

Chapter 3

That evening Logan was sitting at the apartment kitchen table in front of a small view screen docking station. A 3D video was depicting how waves interact when they collide with other waves. Logan paused the simulation and opened up the equation screen. He scrolled through pages of numbers and symbols until he found the spot that interested him. He changed several of the numbers and was about to return to the simulator to judge the results of his adjustments when the door buzzer sounded.

Irritated by the interruption, he got up from his chair and walked to the door. He looked at the video screen next to the door. A man with a flat nose and a square jaw wearing a light blue coat stood outside. He wore a military style cap with a small badge above the visor. On the badge was an image of an eagle clutching a shield in one talon and lightning bolts in another. The letters "SPD" were sewn on his coat collar.

Logan stiffened and clenched his jaw muscles. He looked back at the kitchen table, then at the door to his bedroom. He was about to walk to his room when the buzzer sounded again. Logan took a breath and opened the door.

"Logan Brandt?" said the man.

"That's right," replied Logan noting that under his long blue coat, the man wore a gray shirt and blue trousers, which disappeared into calf-high black leather boots. A black stripe ran down the length of the trousers.

The officer smiled and said, "I'm Lieutenant Fischer from the State Protection Directorate of the National Security Ministry. May I come in?"

Logan stepped out of the way and extended his hand toward the apartment's interior. Lieutenant Fischer walked past Logan and into the small living room. He removed his hat, tucked it under his left arm, and turned to face Logan.

"Please sit down," offered Logan.

"I'll stand," replied Fischer. "This shouldn't take long."

"What can I do for you lieutenant?" asked Logan.

Lieutenant Fischer didn't answer the question. He looked around the room and said, "You have a very nice apartment," he observed. "They take good care of you here at the Weller Academy."

"Yes they do," agreed Logan.

Fischer walked toward a shelf and glanced through the cheaply bound books. He pulled one from the shelf, looked at it for a moment, and returned it to its place. He walked toward Logan's bedroom and peered through the open door. Then the SPD officer returned his attention to Logan and smiled.

"Don't misunderstand me," continued the SPD officer. "Unlike some, I do not begrudge another's successes. In fact, I'm glad that you are well cared for. After all, you and your fellow students are our future leaders. You will be defenders of the People's Republic of America and should be given every opportunity to excel."

Logan smiled but said nothing.

"I was wondering if I could ask you a few questions about your recently deceased grandfather, Dr. Arthur Chambers."

"Okay," said Logan, hoping the SPD officer did not notice the hint of tension in his voice.

"When was the last time you heard from your grandfather?"

"Let me think," said Logan. "It would have been about one week before he died."

"So just three weeks ago?" said Lieutenant Fischer. "What did you talk about?"

"We didn't talk. I received a congratulations card from him. I'm due to graduate from the academy this Saturday."

"How very nice," said Fischer, his mouth stretching into a smile, revealing crooked yellow teeth. "He must have been very proud of you. Do you still have the card?"

"I think so."

"May I see it?"

"Sure, just a second." Logan went into his bedroom and searched through some clutter on his dresser top. He found the card and brought it into the living room. "Here you go."

Lieutenant Fischer read the card. "It's a nice card. I see he wrote you some riddles. Did he often do that?"

"Sometimes," replied Logan. "When I was a kid."

"Interesting. May I scan the card?" he asked as he pulled out a personal data device. Without waiting for Logan's response he laid the card on the table. A red cone of light shone from his PDD. The light rotated a few times and then flashed brightly. When he had finished, Fischer looked up and smiled. "Where would we be without these PDDs?"

Logan smiled. "Yes. They're very useful," he said, although he was unfamiliar with the scanning function on the SPD officer's device. Clearly, theirs came with added features.

"Do you still have the envelope in which the card arrived?"

"Not anymore."

"What happened to it?"

"I threw it away."

Lieutenant Fischer frowned when he heard the response, but then he said, "Oh well. That's understandable. Do you recall what the return address was?"

"No, I don't."

"Don't recall?" asked Lieutenant Fischer. "Was it his home address? Some other place?"

"I don't think I bothered to look," said Logan.

Lieutenant Fischer tapped the nail of his index finger on the PDD and stared at Logan for several heartbeats. At last he said, "You're probably wondering why I'm asking about your grandfather."

"I suppose you have good reasons," said Logan as he eyed the man's PDD. "Keeping the Republic safe must require you to investigate many things."

"That is true. The price of safety is constant vigilance, I always say. In this case I can tell you that whenever a high ranking person or prominent citizen, such as your grandfather, dies we at the SPD conduct a thorough investigation. Better safe than sorry, right?"

Logan nodded. "Agreed. No harm double checking things."

"I'm so happy you understand. Terrorists from the Southern Union, The Pacific Federation, and the Waste grow bolder by the day," said Fischer.

"I know," said Logan.

"You know? What do you know?" asked Lieutenant Fischer, as a faint smile played across his lips.

The question startled Logan. "Nothing special," he muttered. "Just what you see on the news. There are always reports of some clan raid or the discovery of some spy ring."

Lieutenant Fischer nodded his head. "Yes. The news is full of these stories." He tapped his PDD. "So, returning to the subject of your grandfather, the last communication you received from him was the card. When was the last time you two actually spoke?"

Logan took a deep breath and thought for a moment. "I guess that would have been during winter break. He came to visit us for a couple of days."

"When you say 'us' you mean you and your mother, correct?"

"Yes."

"Your father died when you were young, right?" asked Fischer. "He was stationed on the frontier and died during a reconnaissance-in-force mission near Indianapolis, though the record contains a few contradictions." He smiled slightly, noting Logan's discomfort. "Forgive me, but I conducted a little research before coming to visit you."

Logan shook his head. "It's okay. Yes, that's how he died."

"Did you ever talk about your father with your grandfather?"

"Not really," said Logan. "Dr. Chambers was my grandfather on my mother's side, so there really wasn't any reason to talk about my father."

Lieutenant Fischer nodded and asked, "During your grandfather's winter visit, do you recall any conversations that seemed strange?"

"Strange in what way?" asked Logan.

"Did he seem nervous? Did he mention any person or persons who might have wanted to harm him?"

"No. Just the normal stuff."

"Just the normal stuff. Good." Fischer paused for a moment then he placed his hat on his head and said, "Well, I've kept you from your studies long enough. If you remember anything about Dr. Chambers that seems out of the ordinary, please contact me at this number."

He handed Logan a business card and smiled. "I'll show myself out."

Logan didn't move after Lieutenant Fischer left the apartment until he heard the faint thud of the stairwell door closing. Then he walked to the apartment door and looked at the monitor screen. The hallway was empty. He walked into his room and opened the top drawer of his dresser. He reached in and searched under some T-shirts until he found an envelope. He pulled it out and tilted the open end until a small flat medallion about the size and shape of a large coin rolled into his cupped hand.

He held the medallion up to the light and examined it. Etched in white against a black background was an image of a man holding a torch. He was standing in a chariot pulled by several horses. To the man's right was what appeared to be an arrow or comet shooting upward toward a small dot. Logan turned the medallion over to the other side. It was covered in a silver metal lined with thousands of tiny swirling grooves.

His grandfather had written a note and taped it to the medallion. Logan pulled it out of the drawer and read it. *Logan, please keep this for me. I will retrieve it soon. It's important that you keep it safe.*

Below this request, his grandfather had written something else. *Wanderer, if you come to Sparta, tell them there you have seen us lying here, obedient to their laws.*

Logan returned the medallion to the dresser drawer and closed it. He took the note and envelope into the kitchen. Lighting a wooden match, he set fire to both of them and washed the ashes down the sink.

Chapter 4

Cap closed the apartment door behind him and pressed a button on the control pad. The dead bolt slip into place with a click. He went into the apartment and saw Logan sitting at the kitchen bar. Cap could see his roommate was deeply engrossed in his studies, so he quietly walked behind Logan's chair toward his bedroom.

"How'd the shooting match go?" asked Logan without looking up.

"Hm? Oh yeah," replied Cap. "It went okay."

"Just okay?" Logan looked at Cap and smiled. "Something tells me Hamza's pocket has some of your money in it."

Cap raised his arms slightly, palms up, and said, "I was out of my rhythm. Any other night I would have won."

Without giving Logan a chance to reply, Cap asked, "How's the studying coming? Ready for your fluids final tomorrow?"

"I think so," Logan said, returning his attention to the PDD and view screen.

Cap continued walking toward his bedroom when Logan asked, "What is the center of gravity?"

Cap stopped in the doorway and turned around. "Excuse me?"

"It's a riddle my grandfather sent me before he died."

"You're grandfather sent you a riddle before he died?" asked Cap. "Weird."

"He sent me a congratulations card since he would not be able to attend the graduation ceremony. He included a few riddles in the card."

"I see. How many?"

"Three. I've figured out the first two, but I don't understand the one about the center of gravity."

"What are the first two?"

Logan looked at the card and read aloud. "'You can cut me and put me on the table but never eat me.' I think that one is flowers."

Cap nodded his head in agreement.

"The second one is, 'Why is a beating heart like a writing desk?' Edgar Allen Poe wrote on both of them."

"I would never have gotten that one," admitted Cap. "But I think you're right."

"That leaves the one about the center of gravity, which I can't figure out."

19

"Why the sudden interest in these riddles on the night before a final?"

Logan put his hands behind his head, laced his fingers, and leaned back. He looked at the ceiling for a moment. Then he said, "My sudden interest was sparked by a visit from Lieutenant Fischer of the State Protection Directorate. He came here to ask about my grandfather. He found the riddles interesting and scanned an image of the card they were written on."

Cap sat down at the table. "The SPD? Really? Why would they care about your grandfather's death?"

"I don't know. He died in a car accident, but they apparently check into any deaths involving anyone significant. Anyway, that's what Fischer said." Logan handed the officer's card to Cap.

"Was your grandfather 'significant'?" asked Cap, handing back the card after reading it. "I remember seeing him a couple of times a year at your house when we were kids, but I didn't get the impression he was a heavyweight worthy of SPD attention."

"Yeah," said Logan. "He was a pretty well-known physicist, but I don't think he was influential outside his professional circles. And even if he was, I don't know if the SPD is investigating as a matter of routine or if they're onto something suspicious."

"Maybe they don't believe the car accident was an accident," offered Cap.

"That's what I was thinking, but all I have to go on is these riddles. That's why I've been wasting valuable study time trying to figure out what the 'center of gravity' is."

"What happens when you solve it?" asked Cap.

Logan hesitated for a moment. Then he stood and went into his bedroom. When he returned, he laid the medallion on the counter. "My grandfather sent me this and asked that I keep it safe."

Cap picked it up and examined it. "Interesting. What did Fischer say about it?"

"I didn't tell him."

Cap raised an eyebrow. "Did he ask?"

"Not directly. He asked if my grandfather had communicated with me. I showed him the congratulations card he sent."

"But you didn't show him this." Cap turned it over and ran his thumb over the swirling grooves on the back. "You don't think showing it to the SPD is what your grandfather would have wanted? It wouldn't be safe?"

"I don't know. Something in my gut held me back." Logan scratched his head. "Probably not too smart to have kept this to myself."

Cap raised an eyebrow and said, "It's never smart to play around with the SPD. I'd rethink this if I were you and give Lieutenant Fischer a call. Tell him you suddenly remembered the medallion."

"You think he'd believe that?" asked Logan, incredulously.

"No, but then you'd be done with it. Think big picture. You'll be at the National Defense Research Center soon, one of the best active duty postings you can get coming out of Weller Academy. Your grandfather's career is over; yours is just starting."

Logan nodded. "I get it. Let the dead bury the dead."

Cap raised a thumb. "Right on."

Logan smiled and shook his head. "Nobody says that kind of stuff anymore. You know that, right?"

Cap shrugged and walked away.

Chapter 5

"Here comes Bouchet," said Logan to Lena, who was sitting in the row behind him.

She looked up from reading some notes and saw the professor. "Right on time, as usual."

A short man entered the lecture hall. His head was bald, except for a horseshoe of dyed black hair that ran around the back of his head. He wore a blue double-breasted pinstriped suit, white shirt, and a red bow tie with yellow stripes.

"Someone needs to tell him he dresses like a clown," mumbled Lena.

"Watch your tone. He graduated at the top of his class at Clown College," replied Logan.

"Okay, everyone. Let's get started," said the professor in a loud but rather high pitched voice.

He handed a stack of papers to an assistant and said, "Please distribute these to the students, face down."

Logan heard Lena popping her knuckles. He turned around and saw she was feverishly reading a page on the small screen of her PDD. He looked down and saw she was unconsciously bouncing her leg under the bench.

"Relax, Lena," he said.

"I am relaxed," she replied.

"You have to let your mind focus on something else, even for just thirty seconds. Believe me, it helps."

She waved the back of her hand at him, fingers down. "Be gone," she said in a mock imperious tone.

"You've got thirty seconds before the final begins," said Logan. "How much do you think you're going to learn in thirty seconds?"

Lena did not respond.

"Hey, I've got a riddle for you," said Logan. "What's the center of gravity?"

"V," she said without hesitation.

"What?"

"The center of gravity is 'v'. It's a kids' riddle. Now leave me alone."

Logan considered her answer and smiled. "Oh yeah. Makes sense."

At the front of the auditorium, Professor Bouchet cleared his throat and spoke. "Ladies and gentlemen, please quiet down. Take your seats if you have not already done so." He waited until everyone's attention was on him.

"Welcome to your fluid dynamics final," he said with a broad smile. "As with the midterm, this is an open-book exam, or, more precisely stated, an open PDD exam. You may refer to your PDD textbook and any notes that are of your own making."

He walked along the front row of students and surveyed the faces directed toward him.

"However," he continued, "as you no doubt realized while taking the midterm, your PDD and your notes won't do you any good if you do not understand the material. My advice is to do your best on each question and *move on*. Don't get bogged down. Maintain your pace. You can go back and revisit your answers when you have finished all the questions, although it's unlikely you will have much time to do so."

He saw a hand go up. He half closed his eyes and said, "And yes, you may use your PDD's simware, but understand you won't have time to program anything."

The hand went down.

When the tests had been distributed, Professor Bouchet pressed a button on a controller and the number two followed by a colon and two zeros appeared on the room's view screen. "You will have two hours to complete the exam. You may begin." The view screen started counting down.

The students turned the exams over and began working. Logan had done a good job anticipating the first few questions and breezed through them. The next two questions were complicated, but once he had sorted out the irrelevant information, he developed a solution that he was confident would work. He looked up at the clock. An hour had already passed.

Logan looked down again and started to read the next question. As he read, his left hand began to twitch. He ignored it. A moment later it twitched again and he felt an aching sensation in his left thumb. He looked at his hand. *Shit!* He thought. *Not now. Not now!* His hand began to twitch more frequently. He put it on his lap but the twitching continued. With a sigh, he set down his pencil and closed his eyes. Soon he lost awareness of the classroom, the people around him, and the fact that he was taking a final exam. Everything turned black.

Professor Bouchet sat on a chair at the front of the class. He had a PDD in his hands, which displayed a news article. *Clan Attack on Border Town Kills 20, Injures 33*. He shook his head slowly as he read the details of how armed members of a border clan had attacked a small frontier town without warning or provocation. They looted it for food and fuel, killing anyone they could find, even the innocents. The attackers had retreated across the Mississippi before local military units could arrive on the scene.

Another article entitled, *Anarchist Cell Uprooted in Louisville - Visa Controls Tightened*, described how SPD tactical security units found bomb-making materials in several apartments of an abandoned building in Louisville. Five people were arrested, including a local government official. They were suspected to have caused several explosions near government buildings over the preceding year and would face an SPD tribunal within the month. The article discussed the additional measures the SPD was taking to improve public safety, including expanding travel restrictions around Louisville to visa holders only. A spokeswoman was quoted as saying the SPD also needed the assistance of the citizenry to identify strangers or strange behavior and report it to their local SPD office.

Professor Bouchet shook his head and looked up. "Barbarians," he muttered. He scanned the faces of the students, stopping when he saw Logan. The young man was staring vacantly into the space in front of him. His left hand was aimlessly fidgeting on his lap and his cheeks were bright red.

Bouchet stood and quickly went up the stairs to Logan's desk row. Slipping behind two students' chairs to reach him, he leaned down and noted that Logan was clenching and unclenching his jaw muscles.

He whispered, "Are you all right, Mr. Brandt?"

He placed a hand on Logan's shoulder and gently squeezed. Logan did not respond; he continued to look into the distance, his jaw muscles flexing. Bouchet looked down and saw Logan's left hand repeatedly pulling at his trousers at the knee, as though picking away pieces of lint. Some of the students had noticed the commotion and watched Bouchet and Logan. Lena looked up from her exam and saw the professor in the row in front of her leaning close to Logan. Bouchet looked left and right and took a deep breath.

"Class," he said loudly. "Continue with your exams. Mind the clock."

With that announcement, even those who had not noticed Logan and Professor Bouchet looked up. Bouchet repeated himself more forcefully. "Continue with your exams." Most complied with the instruction, but a few continued to watch the strange scene unfold.

Bouchet signaled for his assistant to come to him. "Something is wrong. We need to call a doctor," said Bouchet to the young woman when she arrived.

Just then, Logan blinked and looked up at the professor.

"Are you all right, Mr. Brandt?" asked Bouchet with a nervous smile.

"I'm fine," replied Logan, but his words were a bit slurred. He rubbed his face with his hands and took a deep breath. "I'm fine, I'm fine."

Bouchet patted him on the back and asked, "Are you sure?"

"Yes. Thanks." Logan looked around the classroom to see a number of cadets were staring at him.

Bouchet nodded his head. He and the assistant returned to the front of the auditorium.

Logan picked up his pencil and tried to focus on the next question, but the words did not make sense to him. A minute or two passed before he could get back into a rhythm and regain his focus.

Bouchet sat down and continued to read his PDD. He periodically looked at Logan and searched for further signs of unusual behavior but saw none. When the countdown reached zero he called out in a loud voice, "Stop work. Turn your exams over."

Logan turned over his exam. He had just finished the final question, but he had rushed through it and wasn't confident that he had provided a complete answer. He took a deep breath and slowly let it out. He hadn't failed the exam, but he knew he no longer had a shot at the top grade.

"You feeling all right?" asked Lena as they walked out of the lecture hall.

"I'm fine," he said. "I just zoned out, I guess. Thanks for asking."

"Sure thing," she said.

Lena smiled at him, but Logan thought he detected a hint of silent jubilation behind her dark brown eyes.

"I've got close-quarters combat training now," she said, and patted him on his shoulder. "See you later."

Logan watched as she turned left and quickly descended a flight of steps. A thought flashed across his mind. *There goes our class valedictorian.*

Chapter 6

Logan entered the apartment that evening and found Cap and two classmates watching a martial arts competition on the wall-mounted view screen. They were drinking beer and cheering.

"Heeeyyyyy, Logan's back from the last final of his life!" yelled Cap. "His *final* final! We've been waiting for you. The Re-Ded mixed martial arts finals are on – come watch. Then we're all going out." He pointed at the two cadets sitting on the couch and then at Logan. "All of us. You're coming, too. No excuses!"

Logan smiled and put his hands up. "Sounds good, but first I'm going for a run." He turned and walked to his room.

Cap followed him and stood in the doorway. "I know what you're up to and it isn't going to work."

"What are you talking about?" asked Logan without looking at Cap.

"You're going on a twenty-kilometer run with no intention of going out tonight." He stepped forward and patted him on the back. "But not this time, my friend. We're done with Weller Academy. We're going our separate ways soon and who knows if and when we'll see each other again. I mean these guys." He pointed toward the living room with his thumb just as the two cadets let out loud cheers as one of the martial arts combatants landed a series of powerful blows. "You and I grew up together so you're stuck with me for life."

Logan's smile faded and he looked at Cap. "I had an episode," he said. "I had a seizure right in the middle of the final. Barely finished in time."

Cap folded his arms and leaned against the door frame. "Shit. I thought the meds were supposed to stop those."

"I guess not." replied Logan. "If Bouchet reports this up the chain, they'll reevaluate me. They gave me the all-clear three years ago, and I haven't had a seizure for five, but if this gets out there's no way the army will trust me with anything more dangerous than a pencil."

"So what?" said Cap in an encouraging voice. "You'll just be a regular Flat Foot infantryman. No big deal."

"Do you think they'll give an infantryman who suffers seizures a weapon? Not likely." Logan threw his book bag on his bed. He sat down on the corner of the mattress and ran his hands through his hair. "Damn it!"

After a moment, he looked up at Cap. "I don't care about being able to drive a tank or shoot a rifle, but I don't want to be separated from everyone else. I don't want to be the guy who spends his active duty years riding an office chair with 'unfit for combat' written on the top of his personnel file."

"What are you talking about?" said Cap dismissively. "You won't be in an office. You're slated for National Defense Center. You probably won't even be required to serve in a combat unit. You're a research and development guy."

"Thanks, Cap, but you know that's bullshit. Everyone who's fit does at least one year in a combat unit. And if I don't do that one year, what are my chances for advancement? Even at the NDC. They'll always look at me as being somehow deficient."

After a few moments Cap said, "Fuck it. They won't find out. As far as Bouchet knows, you just zoned out. Now get changed. We're going out."

"I'd rather not," said Logan. "I need go for a run, clear my head. And besides, it's a Tuesday night."

"So what?" asked Cap. "You're done with finals. Take my advice for once and live a little."

Chapter 7

Cap handed everyone a shot of whiskey, then he placed four glasses of beer on the table in front of them. Raising his glass to eye level, he looked at each of his companions in the eye and said, "Logan, Ben, Hector - a toast to the end of school and the beginning of our lives."

The others raised their glasses and gulped down their whiskey. Cap coughed after he swallowed. "Damn it, Mick!" he yelled at the bartender. "*Wash* the bathtub before you make the whiskey!"

An attractive young woman standing behind the bar shrugged and said, "We make the whiskey in a bucket. The gin is made in a bathtub, fly boy. And if you don't like it you can get the hell out of here."

Cap winked at her and smiled, but she turned away to pour a beer for a balding man in a rumpled brown suit.

Ben passed around the glasses of beer. "Gentlemen," he said. "Here's something to wash down that suspect whiskey."

"Thanks, Ben," said Cap. He took a long drink and smiled. "Better," he said, smacking his lips. "Better get another one."

"So why'd you insist on coming to this stinking hole of a bar?" asked Hector, a short stocky man with curly dark hair. "It should be closed down as a threat to public health."

"Simple," said Cap in a voice loud enough for Mick to hear him. "Mick is in love with me, and I wanted to give her a goodbye kiss before going on active duty."

Mick was pouring a beer from the tap. "You never give up, do you." She handed the beer to an overweight man in a collared shirt a size too small. She looked at Logan and said, "Why don't you introduce me to your handsome friend?"

"Who? Logan? He's not your type," said Cap.

"Tall, strong, and handsome is exactly my type," she said, allowing her eyes to linger on Logan for a moment before she turned and walked toward the other end of the bar.

Cap looked at Logan and said. "She's too much woman for a boy of your tender disposition. She'd only break your innocent heart."

"Thanks for protecting me," said Logan with a smile. Then he looked at Hector. "Where's your active duty station, squid?"

"Charleston," he answered with a smile. "Warm weather and beautiful girls."

"And scrubbing floors in the hold of a fifty-year-old coastal cutter," added Ben, a skinny man with a weak chin and a thin beard.

"Like hell," Hector responded. "I'm assigned to a new destroyer, *Hampton*, and lieutenant JGs don't scrub deck floors."

Logan looked at Cap and Ben. "Why is it that whenever you talk to a lieutenant junior grade they always shorten it to 'JG'?"

"They're compensating for something," said Cap. "Let's just call him junior."

"To junior," said Ben, raising his beer.

Logan and Cap raised their glasses and repeated, "To junior!"

Hector shook his head. "Two ground pounders and a bird turd. You boys are not navy material, that's for sure."

As they took a drink, Logan noticed a view screen mounted in a corner was showing images of burning homes, cars, and shops. He walked toward the screen, and the others followed. The repetitive, pounding music coming out of the bar's speakers was too loud for them to hear what was being said, so they read the news script running along the bottom of the screen.

Ben shook his head. "More clan raids on the frontier," he said. "When are we going to put a stop to this shit?"

"It's getting pretty bad," agreed Cap. "Things have just settled down on the southern border and now this is flaring up. We can't catch a break."

"You would think we could handle these clans," said Hector. "But they just keep raiding and we keep letting them get away."

"Is that all there is to it?" asked Logan. "Just clan raids?"

"What do you mean?" asked Ben, a little annoyed.

"I'm just asking," replied Logan. "If we're so much better organized and better equipped than they are, why can't we prevent the raids?"

"The border's too porous," said Ben. "We need to tighten it up."

Hector nodded his head. "Agreed. These frontier territories joined the Republic about...what... fifteen years ago? Obviously, they're better off now than they were, but they need stability to really get going. More troops on the border would help."

"More troops?" asked Logan. "We've got troops all along the frontier."

"What are you getting at?" asked Ben.

"Nothing," said Logan. "I'm just saying we're hearing how these disorganized clans from the Waste are somehow sneaking thirty, fifty, a hundred kilometers into our territory, raiding small towns, burning a few barns, and then running back. Sometimes we get them, but usually we don't. Why is it so hard for us to put a stop to it?"

"They blend in with the population," said Hector. "We can't tell who's who."

"I don't know about that," said Logan. "Seriously – why can't we locate and destroy a bunch rifle-toting goat herders dragging loot fifty klicks back to the far side of the Mississippi?"

"They know the area like the backs of their hands," said Cap. "They probably have a lot of secret paths in and out."

Logan shrugged. "All I'm saying is either the clans are a lot more sophisticated than we give them credit for, or we are not as effective as we think we are."

"I get what you're saying," said Hector. "It's too easy for them to move in and out of PRA territory. The SPD needs to tighten internal controls.

Ben nodded. "I hear they're deploying Republican Special Forces in the frontier territories to help the SPD."

"That should help," said Hector. "Of course we need to get at the real problem, the so-called League of Free Cities out there in the Waste. They're supplying and controlling the clans."

Looking at Cap, Hector said, "I hear the League's scraped together some kind of air force. You ready for a little action out west?"

"I'm always ready," said Cap with a grin.

"What about you, Logan?" asked Hector. "You ready to put some hurt on the League and their clan cronies west of the river?"

"Sure," replied Logan. "But I think we should figure what's going on in the frontier before we go marching across the Mississippi."

"I just told you," said Hector. "The League and their clan minions are the source of the problem. Take care of the League, and we take care of the clan raids."

"What if the clan raiders aren't really getting away across the Mississippi?" Logan asked. "What if they're staying on this side of the river?"

Ben scoffed. "You mean PRA citizens? Why would they do that? After joining the PRA their lives got a hell of a lot better. Steady food supply and clean water. Education for their kids. They would have no reason to be raiding."

"They haven't been citizens that long," said Logan. "Maybe they need time to see the benefits of life under the Guardians."

"I don't want to hear any shit like that," said Hector, noting the sarcasm in Logan's voice. "We're trying to pull this country back together again after a hundred years of chaos. We're not going to let the

League or a few raggedy-ass clans stop us. I think it's time we put the boot down on the League, the clans, and maybe even the fuckin' frontier territories." He took a quick drink of beer and looked away, his face flushed red. He swallowed and raised a finger at Logan. "One people, one nation."

"One plus one equals one," agreed Ben, nodding his head.

"Hector's right Logan," said Cap. "We're going to pull the country together again. That'll put an end to the raids." He clapped Logan on the shoulder. "Tell Hector he's right."

Logan looked into Hector's eyes and saw the anger boiling beneath the surface. Then he smiled and said, "Yeah. Of course Hector's right. We need to pull the country back together. That's what they're training us for, right?"

"Right," said Cap. "Let's have another beer."

Ben and Hector left after drinking the next beer. They embraced Cap and clasped hands with Logan but without great enthusiasm. As soon as they were gone Cap looked at Logan. "What the hell was all that about?"

"What?" asked Logan, his eyebrows raised in surprise.

"All that fifth column, enemy within bullshit," said Cap. "You know that Hector's brother was killed chasing down clan raiders, right?"

"No. I didn't," said Logan.

"It happened last year. They ambushed his company someplace near Nashville," said Cap.

"They ambushed his *company*?" asked Logan. "That's a hundred fifty or two hundred troops. Clan raiders ambushed that many PRA soldiers? Inside the PRA?"

"Let it go," said Cap. "You're letting this get too personal."

Logan didn't answer right away. Then he nodded. "You got to move, right? Move on."

"That's the first intelligent thing you've said all night," said Cap. "Let's get out of here. I hear they've got a good rev band playing at the Billy Goat."

"Asynchronous reverberation and growling lyrics. Can't wait," said Logan unenthusiastically.

"There will be women there," said Cap encouragingly as he pushed Logan toward the door. "Lots of beautiful crazed dancing women."

Chapter 8

Professor Garrison heard a light knock on his office door and looked up from the hard cover book he was reading to see Logan standing in the doorway.

He removed his reading glasses and said, "Mr. Brandt, come in."

Logan smiled and entered. It was a small windowless room just large enough for a desk, two chairs, and a filing cabinet. There were a couple of framed prints of colorful impressionist paintings hanging on the wall, but the room was otherwise a uniform shade of beige. Logan sat down in one of the chairs.

"I know I said I'd have office hours today, but I have to say I'm surprised to get a visitor now that everyone has their grade. Pleasantly surprised, though," he added, smiling. "What can I do for you?"

"I wanted to show you something and get your opinion about it," said Logan as he reached into his pocket. He removed the medallion his grandfather had sent him and placed it on Professor Garrison's desk. "It's a family heirloom that my grandfather passed down to me."

Garrison put on his reading glasses and picked it up to examine it.

Logan continued. "I've already looked this up on the net, and I'm pretty sure the man on the chariot with the torch is supposed to represent the Greek god Apollo, but I wasn't able to find any references to the arrow pointing up or the dot its flying toward."

"I see. You could try the academy's reserve hardcover collection," replied the professor as he held the medallion under the light of his desk lamp, turning it to see it from different angles.

"I was just there. Nothing," replied Logan.

"Not surprising, considering we don't teach art or ancient history here," said Garrison.

The professor held the medallion at an angle. "I agree the man with the torch is supposed to represent the Greek god Apollo, but I don't know if this is an arrow flying toward the dot. It might be a shooting star or a comet." He rubbed his thumb over the intricate swirling design on the other side. "What are these grooves for, I wonder," he said, half to himself.

"I don't know," said Logan. "They're definitely a different artistic style than the image of Apollo."

"Hmm," said Garrison.

Garrison handed the medallion back to Logan. He removed his reading glasses and leaned back in his chair. "Your family heirloom certainly predates the Impact, but I'm sure you've already guessed that."

Logan nodded his head.

Garrison thought for a moment, tapping his glasses against his open hand. Then he said, "Logan, please close the door."

Logan looked a little surprised but did as the professor asked.

After Logan sat down again, Garrison said, "As I said, I agree the man on the chariot is probably Apollo, the Greek god of the sun, healing, prophecy, and a number of other things. As for the other images, the flaming arrow or comet and the dot, I think they may refer to something that is not often discussed these days. In fact it's quite taboo."

He dropped his glasses on the desk, laced his fingers together, and rested them on his stomach, his elbows on the chair's arms. He stared at Logan for a few moments. Then he shrugged and tilted his head a bit, as though answering a silent question.

"As you know," said Garrison, "In 2031 a series of asteroids crashed into the planet. Not only was there significant damage at the impact sites, but the debris thrown into the atmosphere darkened the skies for many months. This led to the Long Winter, worldwide crop failures, and radically different weather patterns, which persisted for many years, even to today. You're familiar with the turmoil that followed."

"I'm familiar with it. Everyone's familiar with it," said Logan, surprised at his own terseness.

Garrison held up a hand and said, "Please. Be patient." He cleared his throat and continued. "The social fabric was shredded. Soon after Impact there were the resource wars, the breakup of the United States, the Tyranny of the Nine, and so on. Finally, under the leadership of Malcom Weller the eastern part of the former United States regained some semblance of order and power was restored to the people and the Congress of Representatives. And of course we can't forget the Guardian Council, which carries out the will of the people and enforces the laws passed by Congress. That's all familiar territory for you."

Logan nodded and added, "After the Impact, the western region formed the Pacific Federation and the south formed the Southern Union. The rest of the world experienced similar political and social upheaval and environmental pressures."

Professor Garrison nodded. "As for here in the former United States, the Midwest was hit by several massive direct impacts and descended into complete chaos. We're told it's still mostly ruins and rain-starved scorched lands. The few people living there now have begun to reoccupy the ruined former cities, but politically speaking, they're just a bunch of warring clans. A few cities have recently made a claim for legitimacy, calling themselves the League of Free Cities. But, we are informed their land can't support even their modest population, so they are forced to raid our frontier towns for food and supplies."

"The Midwaste," said Logan.

"Exactly," said Garrison. "Now, Congressional leadership and the Guardians assure us that we here in the People's Republic of America have regained, and even surpassed, the quality of life enjoyed by citizens of the United States prior to Impact."

Garrison looked into Logan's eyes and said, "Now, before I continue, let me emphasize that as a professor of history, I am simply informing you of a minor line of academic theory. A *very* minor line. I do not personally agree with this theory."

Logan nodded his head. "I understand."

Garrison shifted in his chair and paused to collect his thoughts before speaking. After several moments he said, "There is a very small minority of fringe thinkers who believe pre-Impact society was much further advanced in certain aspects than ours. Orthodox teaching about pre-Impact society emphasizes street crime, injustice, income disparity, and the immoral self-indulgence of a rich ruling class. But the fringe scholars I mentioned think this view is overstated."

Hearing footsteps in the hallway outside his door, Garrison stopped speaking. The footsteps stopped. After a few seconds there was a knock on his door. Garrison leaned forward and placed his hand over the medallion. He gave Logan a cautioning look and said, "Come in."

The door swung open and a man with swept back white hair wearing a blue blazer and blue trousers stepped into the office. Under his blazer he wore a blue button-down shirt. A narrow red and green striped tie hung from his neck, running over the curvature of his round stomach and terminating slightly above his belt. "Excuse me, Professor Garrison," said the man. "I didn't realize you were in a meeting."

"Not at all, Professor Ferrin," said Garrison in a warm tone. "We were just discussing Mr. Brandt's grade."

"I prefer *doctor* Ferrin."

"Of course," said Garrison. "My apologies."

"No matter. I try not to take these things too seriously, but it's better to be accurate." Dr. Ferrin smiled at Garrison and then looked at Logan.

"Discussing grades, eh? I hope you weren't too hard on our dedicated citizen, Mr. Brandt," he said to Garrison with a wink.

"Not too hard," said Garrison.

"I must say I'm a little disappointed Mr. Brandt didn't accept my invitation to take my course, Roots of Authority to Govern," said Dr. Ferrin. "I think he would have found it stimulating, and his insights would no doubt have elevated our class discussions."

Sensing Ferrin was waiting for him to speak, Logan said, "There are so many good courses and so little time."

Ferrin smiled and lifted a hand. "Don't worry. I'm not offended. I know you needed to prepare yourself for a lifetime of important military service. Advanced political theory is for politicians, not warriors, eh?"

Ferrin turned his attention to Garrison. "Can we expect to see you at the faculty meeting this evening? We'll be discussing new initiatives for next year's freshman class."

"Of course," said Garrison. "I'll be there."

"Great, great," said Ferrin. He looked at Logan and then back to Garrison. "Well, I'll leave you to your conversation about grades." He flashed them a smile and closed the door.

Garrison stared at the door and listened to the sound of Ferrin's fading footfalls. "As I was saying," he continued, "one of the threads of this fringe theory includes a belief that society had achieved spaceflight. And not just spaceflight, that humans had visited the moon."

Garrison leaned back in his chair and pointed at the medallion on the desk. "I believe your family heirloom refers to something called the 'Apollo' moon landing. I have seen some of the symbols these fringe believers have used over time, and the image on that medallion reminds me one used long ago."

Logan looked at the medallion again, excited by the possibility that humans had overcome the engineering challenges and visited Earth's ancient satellite. Returning his attention to Garrison, he said, "Okay, so the medallion pre-dates the Impact and might be evidence of a belief that we have sent ships into space and perhaps even to the moon, but if it were true why would Congress or the Guardians not want that known? If someone told me that pre-Impact society had done all of this, I would be inspired to try and match or exceed the achievement."

Garrison smiled and nodded his head. He held his index finger up and said, "Yes, if it were true. *If* it were true, the story could serve to inspire not just you, but many people to push the boundaries of our understanding."

Then Garrison dropped his smile. He leaned forward and rested his folded hands on the desk. "But consider this," he said in a serious tone. "Since the Impact, we have been through a lot. By many estimates, four-fifths or more of the world's population died from the Impact and the natural disasters and crop failures that followed the Impact. The resource wars here and elsewhere in the world that followed killed even more. It has only been about forty years, just two generations, since we have enjoyed much stability here in the PRA. And that stability is due largely to the fact that a strong government emerged and created order out of chaos. Now that..."

Logan interrupted, "But can you imagine how excited people would be if they knew how much we had achieved before Impact and how much more we could be doing now?"

"Excited or angered by the gap that still exists?" asked Garrison. He leaned back in his chair. "I think you'll find that whether people are content or not depends on how they see themselves compared to others around them. Neighbors envy neighbors for the slightest perceived disparity in wealth or privilege. They don't care that they are no longer starving to death like people did after the Impact. People are not intrinsically happy, they are only comparatively happy. That's just human nature. Now imagine if they knew that our supposedly great society is a mere shadow of pre-Impact society? That would only serve to upset social harmony."

Logan shook his head, "People's happiness depends on more than what their neighbors are up to. I think that's narrow thinking."

"To you it is, Logan. But if you're in charge of running a government, don't you think you'd prefer to have an obedient and relatively content society instead of a volatile one? Wouldn't you prefer to govern a society whose attention is occupied by frequent military parades, so-called just wars, and the Rededication Games? Or would you prefer to govern a society that is constantly pressing for change because it is reminded of the superior achievements of the past?"

"I think I'd prefer to have a government that holds out examples of great achievements and inspires people to exceed them. If the Congress of Representatives or the Guardians are afraid to do that, we need a change in leadership."

Garrison held up both hands and said in a low voice, "I wouldn't repeat that anywhere outside of this room."

Logan realized he had gone too far, much farther than he had ever openly stated before. He had contradicted sacred doctrine which had been ground into him since he was a small boy. He'd been told again and again that the only thing standing between social order and the chaos of the past, the chaos that still gripped the middle of the continent, was a strong government and a unified people. To cut at the roots of this great social compact was to risk everything that had been achieved since the founding of the People's Republic. How many times had he repeated the final line of the national pledge, *we are one people, one nation?* Probably every day since he was six.

Garrison silently observed Logan for a few heartbeats. Then he said, "Everything I have said is pure speculation, you understand. It's a fringe theory. But if you want to explore this further, there is just one approved text that I am aware of. It was published about fifteen years ago but has not been digitized so you can't get it off the net. However, the Central Library has a hardcopy in the reserve section.

Garrison opened his drawer and retrieved a pen and pad of paper. "The book's author goes to great lengths to disprove the truth of the Apollo flight stories, but at least you will be able to read some of the fringe arguments that have been advanced."

Garrison wrote down the name of the book and the author. "Go to the reserve librarian's desk and ask for this title," said the professor as he handed Logan the note. "You can't check it out, but they'll let you read it in the library."

"Thanks," said Logan as he looked at the note. It read *Social Organizational Theory in Pre-Impact Society* by Miguel Velasquez. He folded it and put it in his pocket, along with the medallion. Then he stood up to leave.

"And Logan," said Garrison before Logan opened the office door. "I wouldn't show that medallion to anyone you don't trust. It's an unusual thing to have these days."

Chapter 9

An hour after leaving Professor Garrison's office, Logan ascended the marble steps of the hulking Capitol District Central Library. He looked up at the massive stone walls and giant bronze doors. It had been one of his favorite places to go when he was a youth. He'd always marveled at the monumental inspiring building. On each side of the great bronze doors was a huge statue, also of bronze. On the left was the image of a man in coveralls with his shirt sleeves rolled up. He clutched a hammer in his right hand and looked confidently into the distance. The statue on the right was of a soldier standing guard, a rifle at his side. His handsome young face wore an expression of fearless determination.

Logan walked through the doors and into the long hall, the walls of which were decorated with a series of paintings depicting the history of the People's Republic of America. The first image showed the devastation the Impact had caused. People lay on the ground, reaching to the skies as streaks of fire rained down. The next image showed the people's misery as they starved or fought for scraps of food. This was followed by a scene depicting the collapse of the United States and the failure of the weak successor state to feed the people or maintain rule of law as people rioted for food, clean water, and shelter. The next image depicted the Tyranny of the Nine, a time when mass protests were mercilessly put down by force of arms.

After these scenes of misery came a bright optimistic painting showing a figure on a hill with large crowds looking up to him, arms outstretched. It was Malcom Weller gathering the people together, uniting them to overthrow the Nine. This was followed by a painting representing the War against the Nine, which finally shattered the nation and split the country apart, resulting in the three successor states plus the ungovernable Midwest.

The next image depicted the death of Malcom Weller soon after he founded the People's Republic of America. It was followed by a painting showing the struggle for power after Malcom Weller's death as those loyal to the Nine tried to reassert their control over the PRA. Then came an image showing the people in triumph as they defeated the resurgent but secret forces of the Nine during the Rededication. The final panel depicted a peaceful scene where farmers, laborers, scholars, and soldiers stood shoulder to shoulder, facing a rising sun.

Logan passed by the final panel and entered the large reading room. The ceiling was very high, almost two stories. A balcony ran along all four walls of the central hall. Behind the balcony were many narrow hallways containing thousands of hardcopy books on metal shelves. At the back of the reading room was a semi-circular desk. A sign above it said "Reserve Books".

Logan approached the thin man standing behind the desk and said, "I'm looking for a book and I was told there might be a copy in the reserve selection."

"What is the title and author?" asked the man in a tired tone, slipping an index finger behind the lens of his wireframe glasses to rub his right eye.

Logan read him the information from the note Professor Garrison had given him.

The man entered the information into the computer in front of him. "Here we are. *Social Organizational Theory in Pre-Impact Society* by Miguel Velasquez. It's only in hardcopy. I'll be right back." He turned and walked into the dimly lit warren of bookshelves behind him.

After a minute, the man returned with a book in his hand. "Here you go. I'll need your ID. You can use one of the tables over there." He pointed at a row of five long wooden tables.

Logan accepted the book and handed him his identification card. He walked past several tables where people sat reading various reserve books and found an empty one next to a wall near the reserve shelves. A sign on the end of each shelf said *Reserve Section : Staff Only*.

He opened the text and read the table of contents. It contained twelve chapters, each dealing with what the author considered to be a pre-Impact fringe theory. Two of the chapters dealt with technology that might include the space flight theory. Logan looked at the index in the back for the word "Apollo". He found several entries concerning an alleged pre-Impact space program. The author went into some detail regarding a few of the space flight theories, dismissing them one by one. In some cases, he went so far as to question the mental and emotional state of the space theorists, arguing their "undedicated" ideas bordered on madness and sedition. With regard to the moon landing theory, Velasquez dismissed it as technologically impossible as well as strategically and politically pointless.

Logan leafed through the chapter and stopped at a page that contained a drawing. He removed the medallion from his pocket and laid it next to the image. They were very similar. Both showed the Greek god Apollo bearing a torch and driving a chariot. Both had what appeared to be a flaming arrow or comet and dot above Apollo's head. Logan read the caption under the image. It said "Symbol of Apollo Society". Velasquez described the society as a group of discredited scientists and social misfits that had been disbanded during the Rededication.

Logan heard a thump and spun around in his chair. Behind him was a thin female librarian loading a cart with books. "Oh, I'm sorry," she said, pushing a few loose strands of black hair behind her ear as she stooped to load more books onto the cart. "Didn't mean to surprise you."

"It's all right," said Logan. He returned his attention to the book.

"That's an interesting piece," said the woman leaning over the empty chair next to Logan. He placed his hand over the medallion, which was resting next to the book. She looked at the book. "I think I've seen some other books on this sort of pre-Impact thing. If you're interested, I can show you."

"Maybe," said Logan.

"May I see it?" she asked, eyeing his hand covering the medallion.

"I'd prefer not," replied Logan.

"Okay," she said with a shrug. "But come with me. There's one book in particular you should look at."

She led him into the rows of reserve bookshelves. The stacks were very tall, blocking the ceiling lights from neighboring aisles and casting shadows over most of the shelves and the floor. Logan followed the woman as she wove her way through row after row of dark passages. Finally, they reached a spot in what Logan thought must be the back of the library. She reached up, pulled a book off the shelf, and handed it to Logan. It was entitled *The National Aeronautics and Space Agency. A History*.

Logan turned the book over in his hands. On the front cover was an image of a tall rocket lifting off from the ground, a great ball of fire and smoke erupting from its engines. He looked at the spine. Then he opened the book to the first page.

"There's no bar code or stamp," he said.

"No, there isn't," said the woman. "Don't take this back to your table. Read it right here. When you're done, put it back on the shelf." She walked away, and quickly disappeared around a corner.

Logan opened the book and began to read.

Chapter 10

Thirty minutes later, Logan was outside the library. It was a sunny warm spring afternoon. The Central Library was located in the heart of the Capitol District, and although there was a nearby bus stop where he could catch a bus that would take him back to Weller Academy, he decided to enjoy the weather and walk a few blocks to the next stop.

The sidewalk was full of pedestrians as the warm sunlight drew people out into the open air. The road was busy too as people on bicycles and motor scooters hurriedly wove their way around each other. A few small Victory and Unity cars sputtered through traffic, occasionally honking their tinny horns at indifferent co-commuters.

Looking at a sign hanging from a crate at a fruit stand, Logan noted it was blue shopping day. Those with blue buy cards were out in large numbers buying groceries and other essentials. The fruit was rather expensive, probably imported from Florida, thought Logan, but people were glad to have fresh produce to eat so early in the year and the vendor had nearly sold through his quota.

As he walked, Logan thought about what he had learned in the library. He had skimmed each chapter of the book the woman had shown him and was intrigued by what he had read. The book had contained detailed accounts of a variety of space programs: Gemini, Mercury, Apollo, Skylab, Space Shuttle, and Orion, not to mention numerous unmanned probes and satellites. The book was broad in scope, and it contained such convincing details that Logan found it difficult to dismiss.

He returned the smile of two young women passing in the opposite direction. One of them reminded him of the woman he'd met in the library. Clearly, her appearance was not a coincidence. She didn't just happen to find him researching the topic of pre-Impact spaceflight. She didn't just happen to know of another book that contained a wealth of information on the topic. And she didn't just happen to know the exact spot where it was located in the book stacks. Also arguing against a serendipitous encounter was the fact that the book didn't appear to belong to the library; it had lacked a barcode, stamp, or other indication that the library owned it.

Logan arrived at the bus stop. As he waited for the bus, he looked at people sitting at sidewalk tables of nearby cafés and restaurants. They were in high spirits, enjoying the arrival of warm sunny weather after the long harsh winter. A pair of women at an Italian restaurant laughed loudly and pressed wine glasses to their lips. A well-dressed young man sat at a table behind them, smiling and trying to get their attention. The women were indifferent to his overtures until one of them saw the black buy card between his index and middle finger. She momentarily locked eyes with his and granted him the hint of a smile.

When the bus arrived, Logan took a deep breath, taking in the sweet smells of thousands of nearby blossoms, and smiled. As he boarded, Logan looked to his left and saw something that made his heart skip a beat. On the passenger side of a small blue Victory sat a man with a tan face and short-cropped black hair. Logan only caught a glimpse of his face, but he was quite certain he'd seen him at the library sitting at one of the tables.

Logan was tempted to go to the back of the bus and look at the car through the rear window but he didn't dare. He decided he would get off the bus at a stop just before the Weller Academy campus. If he saw the man in the blue Victory he would know it was not a coincidence.

During the twenty-minute bus ride, Logan weighed his options. If he was being followed, it was probably an SPD officer, which meant Lieutenant Fischer had ordered that he be put under surveillance. If Lieutenant Fischer was having him followed, Logan thought perhaps he should come clean. Telling the SPD the full story was the prudent thing to do. What did he hope to accomplish by withholding information anyway? His grandfather had asked him to keep the medallion safe until he could retrieve it. But now that he was dead, did Logan owe him anything? He thought about his promising career, what his mother expected of him, what his father would have advised him to do if he were alive. He shook his head and looked out the window.

A few minutes later, the bus arrived at his stop near the academy. As Logan stepped onto the sidewalk, he looked to his right and searched the street and surrounding area. No blue car. No strangers watching him. In fact, the street was empty. He looked at his watch. Sword and shield training was at 4 p.m. and it was already 3:40. Logan broke into a run, arriving at his apartment five minutes later. After changing into his exercise gear, he placed the medallion in his dresser drawer and headed for the door. He turned the handle, but then he paused. He turned around, went back into his bedroom, and retrieved the medallion. He put it in his pocket and left the apartment.

Chapter 11

"As always, the SPD appreciates your vigilance and assistance," said Lieutenant Fischer as he made a few final notes in his PDD.

"Not at all," replied Dr. Ferrin, smiling broadly from behind his desk. "Any way I can be of service, please let me know." He watched the SPD officer type into his PDD. After a few moments, he cleared his throat, which prompted Lieutenant Fischer to look up.

"Yes?"

Dr. Ferrin took a breath. "I wonder if I can introduce one final topic to our meeting agenda."

"Certainly, doctor," said Lieutenant Fischer, smiling but only thinly masking his annoyance. "What would you like to discuss?"

"Logan Brandt."

Lieutenant Fischer's smile lingered but his eyes hardened. He rested his PDD on edge of the desk and leaned back. "What do you want to say about Logan Brandt?" he asked.

Something about the way the SPD officer replied gave Dr. Ferrin pause. He removed his stylish, nonprescription glasses and cleaned the lenses with a small cloth he took from his breast pocket. "I should preface my comments with the fact that he is a very accomplished student. I'm told he's good with a sword, too."

"Is that what you want to tell me about Mr. Brandt?" asked Lieutenant Fisher.

"No, of course not," said Dr. Ferrin, straightening his shoulders and putting his glasses back on. "He hasn't given me or any other faculty member any serious cause for concern. But I feel compelled to say I'm not sure he will be a good leader."

"And why is that?" asked Fischer.

"Despite his talents, I do not have the impression he is particularly motivated to serve the people. He's quite introverted and seems to be happiest when working alone on a difficult math or science problem."

Lieutenant Fischer folded his hands on his lap. "Not everyone is a leader," he said. "The Guardians value the contributions of our scientists and scholars." He said the last word with a smile and a nod of recognition to Dr. Ferrin, who returned the smile.

"Yes," said Dr. Ferrin. "I see your point, but with him I sense there is something more at work. I sometimes sense a reticence when talking with him. He seems somewhat…guarded, as though he is holding something back that he'd very much like to share but fears the repercussions that would follow."

"Undedicated?" asked Fischer.

"No, no," replied Dr. Ferrin. "Nothing so concerning as that."

"I see. But you believe he's holding something back?" asked Lieutenant Fischer, eyebrows raised.

"Yes. And although this may be nothing," continued Dr. Ferrin, "I did happen to find Mr. Brandt talking with Professor Garrison in the professor's office."

"Garrison," said Lieutenant Fischer in a rather more serious tone. "I see. Do you know what they discussed?"

"Unfortunately I do not. They said they were talking about Mr. Brandt's grade for a course Garrison taught, but I know they were discussing something else. They seemed to be uncomfortable in my presence."

Lieutenant Fischer nodded his head. "Perhaps it was due to your well-known devotion to the proper education of these students."

"Perhaps," said Dr. Ferrin, the corner of his mouth turned up in a smile. "But I am concerned. I believe he is the sort of person who needs added attention; at least until he is a little older and his career path is firmly established."

Lieutenant Fischer nodded. Then he took a deep breath and stood up, placing his PDD in his coat's inner pocket. Dr. Ferrin also stood.

"Thank you for your thoughts, Dr. Ferrin," said Lieutenant Fischer. "Your many contributions are greatly appreciated. We will take your concerns about Mr. Brandt into consideration."

Lieutenant Fischer smiled and placed his SPD officer's cap on his head, adjusting the rim to be just above his eyes. He opened the office door but turned before exiting. He looked at Dr. Ferrin and said, "Keep in touch."

Dr. Ferrin smiled and nodded.

Chapter 12

Logan ran across the academy's campus, arriving at the training facility just after Sergeant Major Mojeski called everyone to attention. Breathing heavily but trying to mask it, Logan slipped into the line next to Cap.

"Glad you could join us, Cadet Brandt," barked the sergeant major as he walked along the formation. "Please give me twenty pushups."

Mojeski put his hands on his hips as he watched Logan drop to the ground and begin doing the pushups. "Slow down cadet," said the sergeant major. "I want you to enjoy each one."

Logan slowed his pace but maintained perfect form. Mojeski nodded his head with satisfaction as he watched Logan perform his assigned task. Then he started to slowly walk along the formation, looking at each face as he went by.

"Cadets," said Mojeski as he walked, "this will be the last of our little get-togethers. After graduation you will transition from reserve status to full-time active duty. Congratulations. It goes without saying that you will never be able to repay the considerable investment in time and resources the People's Republic of America has made in you these past four years, but you can show your gratitude by defending her to the utmost of your ability. And if you're lucky enough, you will be afforded the opportunity to kill the enemy. You may die in the process, but you will have done your duty. And there is satisfaction in that."

The sergeant major walked to the center of the room and faced the group, hands folded behind his back, feet shoulder width apart. "The time will come for all of you to demonstrate your value to your platoon, your company, your battalion, your corps. You're all aware of the rise in atrocities these Waste clans are committing on the frontier. Towns raided, farm developments burned, defenseless citizens slaughtered. You're all aware that the so-called League of Free Cities incites these clans into committing these crimes."

He raised his right hand and said in a loud voice, "But have faith! The Guardians are no doubt planning an appropriate response." He nodded his head and looked at the young faces in front of him. "They are not going to sit back and watch a few wild clans destroy what we have achieved. You know and I know that the order will come. They will send our beloved armed forces into action to right these wrongs! To punish those responsible. To bring freedom and prosperity to the oppressed. You have spent the past four years training your minds and bodies for one thing, to defeat the enemy. When the order comes I know you will do your duty. You will not disappoint."

Mojeski slowly walked to his right. "We've got the best military this world has ever seen, pre-and post-Impact. Not only have we risen from the rubble, but we have surpassed the achievements of our ancestors. We have achieved this because we have a purpose which our predecessors, trapped in their meaningless decadence, lacked. That purpose is to unify this continent. The People's Republic of America has great plans for this land, and each and every one of you will play your part in bringing those plans to fruition."

Mojeski waited for Logan to finish his last pushup and join the formation. Then he yelled, *"One people! One nation!"*

"One people! One nation!" echoed the cadets.

"That's right. But we will not achieve this lofty goal with talk," said the sergeant major. "We will achieve it with rifles, swords, and shields. Now fall out, collect your blade and bracer, and get into training formation."

Everyone quickly crossed the training room to a row of compartments, each containing a sword and a bracer. Each sword had a slightly curved blade and was about as long as a man's arm. The bracers were about half a meter long and contained a loop at each end. The cadets slipped their non-dominant hand through the loops until the bracer covered their arms from the top of their hand to their elbow.

"Activate your guards."

The cadets snapped their wrists, and long rectangular guards consisting of thin curved sheets of interlocking metal plates shot out from their bracers and enveloped their forearms like a metal sleeve. After the guards had locked into position, the sergeant major yelled, "Activate antiballistic shields!"

They all pressed buttons located on their bracers where they covered the heels of their hands. A wave of refracted white light emerged from the bracer and swept over their bodies. Once fully activated, the shield was invisible except for an occasional shimmer of light.

"Everyone in your standard fighting position," said the sergeant major. "Let's warm up. First, we will practice ripostes, transitioning from defense to counterattack . The first riposte we will practice is over your opponent's sword arm. Ten times. Begin."

The cadets went through the motions of blocking an imaginary strike with their guards and counterattacking with a lunge over the imaginary attacker's sword arm.

"Don't get caught flat footed. Stay on the balls of your feet and strike quickly." He walked between the rows of cadets who repeatedly blocked and lunged. "Okay, next riposte is under the sword arm. Ten times. Go!"

The cadets altered their counterstrike to an upward thrust. "Good, good." He stopped in front of a young man. "Akira, you're dropping your guard arm on your counter strike." He walked a few paces and looked across the room. "Krieger, loosen up. Use all the available space."

After twenty minutes of similar drills, the sergeant major yelled, "Stop! Go get your helmets and sparring belts!"

They stopped their blocking and counterstrike exercises and quickly retrieved helmets with transparent face protection from hooks on the wall. Once they were back in their training positions, the sergeant major yelled, "Ready stance!"

Helmets on, they raised their guards in front of their chests. Their blades were at their sides but pointing forward, and their legs were slightly bent.

"First and third rows, about face!"

The first and third rows of cadets turned around to face the second and fourth rows. "Meet your sparring partners. Pick a sparring ring and turn on your counters. Remember, arms and legs are worth one point. Torso is worth three. Head is worth five. Low score wins."

The cadets paired with the person opposite and went to one of the rings painted on the floor. Logan found himself matched against a young black man. "Well, well, well, if it isn't my old friend Logan Brandt," said the man as he went into a ready stance.

"Roberts, nice to see you," said Logan without enthusiasm.

Roberts took three quick swipes at Logan, who blocked them with his arm guard, then countered with a lunge to Roberts' torso. Roberts easily deflected the attack with his blade and moved to his left. Logan lunged forward and swung low when Roberts was mid-step, striking his shin. A red light on Roberts' belt blinked.

Roberts shook his head and cursed as he went into his ready position for round two. Logan took two quick steps forward, hoping to surprise his opponent but Roberts spun to his right, swinging as he moved. Logan blocked the attack with his guard and continued his pursuit with a flurry of strikes. Roberts was stepping backward, using both blade and guard to block Logan's attacks. Suddenly, Roberts stepped forward, raised his guard above his head to block Logan's downward thrust, and drove his own blade forward into Logan's exposed chest. Logan's sparring belt light blinked three times.

As they went back to their ready stance, Roberts smiled and said, "You have to cover up, my friend."

Logan rubbed the spot where Roberts had struck him. Even with the dull sparring blades, it had been a hard hit and would no doubt leave a bruise. He looked across the room to see Cap sparring with Lena. She scored a point with a lightning fast strike to his sword arm, causing his belt to blink. Logan grinned as he heard Cap cursing.

Sergeant Major Mojeski was slowly walking around the room, giving advice here and there. After a few minutes he said in a loud voice, "A glancing blow might score you a point in practice, but unless it's hard and precise it will bounce off in a real fight. Remember, your opponent will likely be wearing battle armor, which can be pierced with a well-placed strike, but it's very hard to do. Forget about points. Aim for where the armor is not – lower abdomen, groin, arm, shoulder and leg joints, the neck; even the back if you can turn your opponent."

Logan and Roberts continued their sparring. Logan evened the score with two strikes to Robert's limbs. The first was to the sword arm as Roberts failed to deflect Logan's attack. The second was to Roberts' leg as he swung high at Logan's head. With the score tied, the two young men carefully circled each other, searching for an opening.

"You ladies having a nice dance?" asked Mojeski as he passed by their sparring circle. Seeing the numbers on their belts, he remarked, "Oh, I see. We're all tied up and too scared to attack. That's no good. It's not about points. It's about practicing what you've been taught."

He looked around the room. "There are no ties in combat!" he yelled. "We're out of time now so if you're not tied, put down your blades. If you're tied, make your move!"

Except for three groups, the cadets stopped their sparring and gathered around the remaining matches, cheering and urging the combatants to attack. Cap and Lena joined the group around Logan's sparring circle. Logan and Roberts continued their probing feints and thrusts.

"Let's go, Logan!" yelled Cap. His belt had the number seven on it. Lena's was blank. "Take him out!" he said.

As the other two remaining fights resolved in a clear winner, more cadets joined the group around Logan and Roberts. They cheered loudly, chanting the names of the combatants. Roberts suddenly attacked with a combination of feints and slashes that put Logan on his heels, but he successfully blocked them using blade and guard. He countered with several thrusts, but Roberts defended well. They circled each other for a few moments, the crowd yelling louder and louder.

Logan took two quick steps, swinging at Roberts' head, but the other man had anticipated the attack and crouched low and swung upward under Logan's guard arm. The tip of Roberts' blade pushed into Logan's stomach, causing Logan's belt to blink three times. The crowd cheered and clapped their hands.

"Well done, Roberts," said Mojeski as the cheers subsided. A group of students was congratulating Roberts, but he broke away and shook Logan's hand.

"Good job," said Logan.

"I thought you were gonna take my head off," said Roberts, smiling.

Logan laughed. "That was the plan."

Sergeant Major Mojeski called Logan over to him. "Let me see your shield settings."

Logan showed him his antiballistic shield controls on his guard's inner wrist covering.

"You've got it set too high," said Mojeski. "Higher settings give you more protection against projectiles, but if you go too high the shield becomes less flexible. It slows you down. Take it down ten percent. Bullets still won't penetrate, and you'll move faster."

Logan nodded. "Thank you, Sergeant Major Mojeski. I'll do that."

"You're cautious, Cadet Brandt," said the sergeant major. "That's good, but sometimes you have to be bold."

"Yes Sergeant Major."

Mojeski nodded and turned his attention to the class. "All right, all right, cut the chatter and fall in!" he yelled as he walked toward the center of the room. After the cadets had lined up he continued. "I saw a lot of good sparring, but I saw some sloppiness, too. Remember that when you attack you expose yourself, but if you don't attack you'll eventually be cut down. Use your guards to cover up as you attack. Blade and guard should work together. Your guard is not an afterthought when you attack; it is part of your attack."

He walked a few paces down the line. "Now, as I've told you before, we've broken from standard training procedures. Over the past four years we've combined standard sword and guard training with a variety of martial arts techniques and straight up gouge 'em in the eye street fighting. You might catch flak from others for your unorthodox style, but I can tell you with one hundred percent confidence that you're the best trained cadets to ever graduate from Malcom Weller Academy. What I've taught you could save your life someday, so remember it."

He looked at their faces. "All right, fall out. Turn in your equipment. Guardians' address is in one hour. See you in the assembly hall. Congratulations on graduating and good luck at your AD station."

Chapter 13

Logan and Cap left the training facility and hurried back toward their apartment. "Shit!" said Cap. "I'd forgotten about the Guardians' address tonight."

"Some cadet you are," said Logan. "This speech is the highlight of the year. Something every little girl and boy looks forward to."

"Sarcasm is undedicated," said Cap.

Thirty minutes later they were shaved, showered, and in their dress blue uniforms, which were identical except Cap's had a yellow shoulder braid, indicating he was an air defense cadet, and Logan's was red, indicating he was an infantry cadet.

"You ready ground pounder?" asked Cap as he finished giving his black dress shoes a spit shine.

"Ready bird turd," answered Logan.

They quickly walked across the campus to the assembly hall, where other cadets were streaming toward its doors, causing a logjam at the entrance. Logan and Cap exchanged a few greetings with classmates as the crowd slowly inched forward. They all wore the same blue dress uniform and most had red shoulder braids, but there were a few yellow air defense braids and blue navy ones.

Several professors were also arriving. Many wore the uniform of the service they continued to serve in as reservists, often with colorful ribbon racks indicating what engagements or campaigns they'd served in. Logan spotted the academy's dean. He was wearing a simple dark suit, but on his breast pocket he wore a large silver medal that hung at the end of a red and white ribbon.

Cap nodded toward the dean. "Nice medal, eh? The Protector of the People has only been awarded three times."

Logan took a long look at the dean. In a low tone he said, "Hamza told me Dean Walsh received the award fifteen years ago during the Rededication when he was a colonel in the Republican Special Forces. He was stationed somewhere out west."

"That's great. I'm happy for him. What's your point?" asked Cap.

"Think about it," said Logan. "The Rededication."

Cap said, "Yes…the Rededication."

"Do you need me to spell this out for you?"

"I guess so," said Cap, a perplexed look on his face.

"During a one-month span fifteen years ago, a bunch of frontier clan territories are added in a sudden push along the entire eastern border; the uprising that followed in those new territories is then put down over the next few months. Secret followers of the Nine Tyrants were blamed for inciting the people in the new territories to violence. Then, in the middle of it all, Grand Guardian Cordivan is pushed out and replaced by Guardian Harken. And what is Harken's first move? He purges the army's leadership of suspected supporters of the Nine and 'rededicates' the country to the vision of Malcom Weller, including reunifying the former United States."

"I've heard a version of this in high school civics," said Cap. "And I should point out that according to our teachers, Cordivan stepped down for health reasons."

"Yeah, it was no longer healthy to be Grand Guardian," said Logan.

"What's this got to do with Dean Walsh?" asked Cap.

Logan glanced around to make sure no one was listening, and then continued. "During the purge, officers were disappearing or being executed for supposedly supporting the Nine, but not Walsh. Instead, he gets the Protector of the People medal. And a few years later he's appointed to a cushy job as dean of the most prestigious military academy in the country."

"So this conversation isn't about Dean Walsh, this is about your father," said Cap.

Logan shrugged. "My father and others get a firing squad and Walsh gets a medal. Maybe he didn't pull the trigger but he was rewarded for a reason."

Cap pulled Logan out of the crowd and said in a hushed tone, "I know you want someone to be pissed at. That's normal. But what good will it do you? You're lucky to have been admitted to the academy given everything that happened during the Rededication. They know who you are. They know who your father was. They could have rejected your application based on that alone, but they didn't."

Logan tensed as he listened to Cap and tried to interrupt, but Cap wouldn't let him.

"You need to make the best of this opportunity," said Cap. "Because what's the alternative? Work as a minor faceless bureaucrat in some massive agency? Make toasters in a production development? Pull a plow on the frontier?"

Logan slowly shook his head and stared at Walsh as he disappeared into the assembly hall. Then he closed his eyes and said, "You're right.

I'm lucky to be here. And I'm lucky to have you as a friend. I should look to the future, not dwell in the past."

Cap smiled and clapped Logan on the back. "That's more like it."

The two young men made their way through the crowd then walked to their assigned positions inside the great hall. They stood shoulder to shoulder with three thousand classmates on the main floor of the assembly hall. School officials, political leaders, and honored guests sat in the surrounding seats closest to the main view screen, which currently showed the People's Republic of America seal, an eagle clutching arrows in one talon and lightning bolts in the other. The remaining seats were filled with cadets' family members, schoolchildren, members of various civic societies, and the general public.

A series of chimes silenced the crowed and the academy's sergeant at arms called out, *"Attention!"*

The cadets came to full attention, each one stamping his or her right foot at once to create a great booming sound. Patriotic music played over the loudspeakers. The audience members stood and put their right hands to their hearts. Cadets saluted. After a few notes had played, they all sang the national anthem, after which the audience sat down. The image of the national seal on the main view screen and the smaller ones stationed throughout the hall was replaced by the image of a tall thin man standing behind a lectern. He had clear blue eyes and white hair, which was combed straight back. He wore a dark suit and a red tie. Three colorful ribbons and several medals adorned his suit breast pocket. Behind him, a large PRA national seal covered the wall.

"Good evening, citizens of the People's Republic of America," he said in a strong voice that belied his thin frame and advanced years. "I am Grand Guardian Harken, and I am honored to once again stand before you to celebrate another year's achievements."

Thundering applause reverberated throughout the auditorium where the Grand Guardian was speaking. The camera view switched to show a huge audience full of smiling people enthusiastically clapping, including the full membership of the Congress of Representatives, who occupied the first few rows. The people in the Weller Academy hall also applauded. Grand Guardian Harken held up his hand for silence and continued.

"The PRA continues to be the world's shining light when there is still so much darkness. The world looks to us to lead it though the continuing challenges flowing from the Impact and to help it regain the glory and unity of the pre-Impact era. The world sees what we have achieved here in the PRA and the world's people are inspired. They see that we now enjoy a quality of life superior to that of pre-Impact society and continue to build on our achievements, year after year. The world sees we are one people, one nation."

"One people! One nation!" shouted the audience as they clapped and cheered.

Grand Guardian Harken continued after a moment. "As you well know, the peace and stability we have secured has not been easily won. Indeed, it has been secured at great cost, including the ultimate price in many cases. But our sacrifices have produced astounding results. We enjoy higher manufacturing production, higher crop yields, and longer life spans. Our years of unwavering dedication and toil have provided us with stability and prosperity."

The people again applauded and cheered.

"I am proud to report that in the past year crop yields are up four percent; production of consumer goods is up three percent; and our all-important military production capability has increased by an astounding seventeen percent. These great leaps forward are due in large part to our commitment to rapid reindustrialization and the successful military campaign to recover Detroit with its ancient but still robust industrial might. We are one people, one nation."

"One people! One nation!"

"And we will build on the success of the Detroit campaign," said Grand Guardian Harken. "We are a shining beacon of hope to the people still living in darkness. We are the liberators of those enslaved by petty warlords and bickering clans. We are the steadfast foes of tyrannical governments which prefer the violence and chaos of disunity over the peace and order of one people, one nation."

"One people! One nation!"

"We have achieved much, but there is much more to do and the road ahead is a difficult one, for our success is also our commitment to the people of the world. To them I say, we who stand in the light of prosperity have heard your calls from the dark wilderness. We have seen how you suffer under the yoke of tyranny. To these desperate people, I say be strong. To those who oppress them, I say the time of reckoning is at hand. We are coming, and we will not give up the fight until we are all once again one people, one nation."

"One people! One nation!"

"To our nation's mothers and fathers I say, continue to raise your children in the spirit of our great visionary redeemer, Malcom Weller. Continue to encourage their growth and commitment to our great cause. And do not weep when they are called to protect what we have achieved. Do not fear when they are called upon to grapple with our foes. For it is their strength of arms, their zeal, their unwavering dedication to our great cause that will secure ultimate victory and a lasting, permanent peace. They are our shield and our sword. Our hopes rest on the strong shoulders of this generation and on as many generations to come as may be required until we are once again one people, one nation."

"One people! One nation!"

After a few more moments of applause, the Grand Guardian said, "And now I invite Guardian Castell to speak a few words."

He nodded his head and raised his left hand to someone off camera. A tall heavy-set man in his fifties with dark wavy hair took Harken's right hand in both of his and gave a slight bow, smiling as he looked into Harken's eyes. The man then stepped forward to the lectern as Harken walked out of the camera's view.

"Thank you, Grand Guardian Harken, for your inspiring words," he said after the cheering had subsided. "Our great thanks to you and your enduring leadership and guidance."

He folded his hands on the lectern and looked into the camera. "Citizens of the People's Republic of America, I am Guardian Castell and I will speak to you about the state of the nation's security. As Grand Guardian Harken so eloquently stated, we enjoyed outstanding successes in the past year. We not only strengthened the security of our borders against the tyrannical rulers to the north and south, but we also brought Detroit and its industrial might back into the embrace of the People's Republic of America."

He paused as the audience enthusiastically cheered.

"But we must be ever vigilant," he warned. "Our successes are the envy of many. The very fact we exist is a danger to our enemies' iron grip on their suffering people. Yet, whispers and rumors of our achievements filter through our enemies' false propaganda and reach the ears of the oppressed. Our promise of unity and freedom beckons them to our doors. Defections to our great nation are commonplace, and of course we welcome them. We welcome the oppressed, the weary, and the disheartened into our community, for we are one people, one nation."

"One people! One nation!"

"But as Grand Guardian Harken said, we have a long and hard road ahead of us. We have heard his challenge and we are prepared to meet it. We will continue to expand our borders to the west and northwest. Last year we recaptured Detroit. Two years ago it was Chicago. Three years before that it was Nashville. We will continue until we have reached the great Mississippi River and beyond, for we are one people, one nation."

"One people! One nation!"

"We have achieved great victories on our borders, but let us not forget the danger within our borders. A free community such as ours is strong because of our freedoms, but it also leaves us vulnerable. Vulnerable to saboteurs. Vulnerable to enemy agents sent to sow discord among us. Vulnerable to the rot of undedicated thinking. Our visa travel rules and other protective measures have inoculated us against the worst of such efforts, but we must remember that security and safety is everyone's duty. Be vigilant. Be ready. For we are one people, one nation."

"One people! One nation!"

Logan's mind began to drift as Guardian Castell continued to talk about border security, new defensive and offensive weapons systems in development, and so on. Now and again his attention snapped back to the speeches when he and the others enthusiastically chanted the mantra of *"One people! One nation!"*

After Guardian Castell finished his speech, he introduced Guardian Bishop, the Justice Guardian, who spoke for twenty minutes about internal security, expanding on what Guardian Castell had said regarding visa controls and increased SPD presence. He read through statistics indicating general crime rates were at record lows but that there was a troubling uptick in the number of terrorist cells the SPD had rooted out. He promised to redouble the efforts of the Justice Ministry to ensure the nation's security and asked for everyone's support and cooperation in achieving that great goal.

Guardian Bishop was followed by Commerce and Industry Guardian Hoffman, who talked at length about increased industrial production, crop yields and consumer goods. He lamented the terrible loss of life and reduced energy production cause by the recent Appalachian coal mine collapse. He vowed to continue to work with Guardian Bishop's Special Investigators to capture all of the perpetrators, many of whom were already in custody or dead. He promised a public trial and swift execution for the ringleaders of the horrific attack.

Commerce and Industry Guardian Hoffman was followed by Information and Public Affairs Guardian Hyatt and Health & Wellness Guardian Feldman, each of whom spoke for only five minutes and largely echoed what had already been said.

When Guardian Feldman was finished, Grand Guardian Harken returned to the lectern. He smiled at the faces in the audience. "We have achieved more than anyone could have possibly imagined in the years since the Impact, but there is much more to do. And make no mistake, we will all be put to the test. Each and every one of us. Every morning you must look in the mirror and ask yourself, 'Am I prepared? Am I ready?'"

He looked into eye of the camera. "You see, we all play important roles in our great community. Everyone from the tough and dedicated farmers and workers in developments sprinkled across this great land all the way up to our highest military and civic leaders. We must all do our duty. Myself included. For I have the greatest duty of all, the duty of service to each of you. But it is a calling which I accept with a cheerful heart.

Harken looked at the crowd and smiled. "Now let us stand side by side, arm in arm, and bravely march forward. A new dawn awaits us, for we are one people, one nation!"

"One people! One nation!"

Grand Guardian Harken nodded and stood back from the lectern. The people in the auditorium chanted the phrase again and again. The camera swept across thousands of adoring faces. Many of them were weeping as they all chanted. *"One people! One nation!"*

The camera view changed to show the entire stage and all of the Guardians standing in a line, waving to the crowd. Then a new location was shown on the view screen. It was a large auditorium full of people in some other city. They all cheered and waved at the camera. Other similar gatherings popped onto the view screens.

Logan looked at the large light above the main view screen in the academy hall. It began to flash yellow and then it turned green. The crowd around him suddenly screamed in ecstasy. They waved at the camera, their delighted faces beaming with joy in the realization that they were appearing on the view screen. A few moments later, the light turned red. The cheering continued, but after thirty seconds it began to dwindle. They heard a chime. Music began to play and they sang the national anthem one more time. After they'd finished singing, the sergeant at arms dismissed the cadets. The crowd filed out of the assembly hall, excitedly discussing what the Guardians had said.

Chapter 14

Lena joined Logan and Cap as they exited the auditorium. "What did you think of the speeches?" she asked.

"Time well spent," said Logan.

"I'm still giddy," added Cap.

Lena knit her brow but did not pursue the subject. Then she asked Logan, "When do you have to report to your active duty station?"

"Next Wednesday, but Cap and I have to be out of the apartment by Sunday at midnight."

"So you have to wait seven days before reporting, but you'll be homeless in just four days. That's well coordinated. Will you go home after Saturday's graduation ceremony?"

"Maybe, but I might go straight to my duty station at the National Defense Research Center. They'll accept early arrivals."

Cap asked, "What about you, Lena? You going straight to your AD station?"

"Not sure," she said as she adjusted her red shoulder braid. "I have two weeks before I have to report. I might go to New York and visit my cousins."

"You'd better decide fast," replied Cap. "I hear it's getting very hard to get nonessential travel visas."

She shrugged her shoulders, and then she looked at Cap. "What about you? When are you supposed to report?"

"I've got about two weeks. Then it's advanced flight training for six months."

"You're that good?" she said.

"He's better than good," said Logan. "During AD last summer they had him testing the Phantom 2. Fastest thing we've got. He's the only cadet they would let near it."

"It's a thing of beauty," said Cap. "New everything. Heads up-controls, anti-missile defenses, fire-control, all radically different from anything we've had before. And fast. The engines combine traditional thrusters with a gravity dampener, making the plane fifteen percent lighter and twenty percent faster."

Lena raised her eyebrows. "Gravity dampeners are already in production? I knew they had worked out the theoretical kinks, but I thought they still faced big engineering challenges."

Cap shrugged his shoulders and said, "I don't know how they got it done, but it's fun to fly."

"I suppose we'll be using them against the Southern Union," she said. "They stuck it to us last year at Lake Seminole."

"Two divisions pinned down with their backs against the water and no air cover to support," said Logan. "What a catastrophe."

"I wouldn't talk about it too loudly," said Cap. "The official word is that it was a hard-fought stalemate against a vastly superior force."

"In another year they'll be saying it was a stunning victory," said Logan. He looked at Lena to see if he'd gone too far, but she didn't seem perturbed.

"You guys interested in getting a drink or a bite to eat?" asked Lena.

"Sure," said Cap without hesitation.

"Great," she said. "Where should we meet?"

"Just come over to our place," answered Cap. "You know the building. Unit 205."

"Sounds great." Lena smiled and turned to walk down a sidewalk toward her dormitory room.

"See you in a few," said Cap.

When they'd walked a little farther and were out of earshot, Cap said with a grin, "She's coming around to my charm."

Logan laughed and shook his head. "She takes things too seriously, and you don't take anything seriously. You're incompatible."

Cap waved his hand dismissively and shook his head. "Not a big deal," he said.

"In the four years we've been here, have you ever known her to have a single drink or go to one party?" asked Logan. "In that same time, have you ever missed an opportunity to have a drink or go to a party?"

Cap was undeterred. "She's a good student, and I respect that. But now that school is behind us, it's time for her to start having some fun."

"And you're the one who's going show her how?"

"I am," said Cap. "I'm a passionate man. She's a reserved woman. We're like yin and yang. We balance each other out perfectly."

Logan chuckled and shook his head. "More like oil and water, but your enthusiasm in the face of such poor odds is truly inspiring."

"Dig it," replied Cap."

"But you'd better lose the ancient hippy talk if you want to win her,"

"Maybe that's what she likes about me," replied Cap. "Don't mess with the formula."

Chapter 15

SPD Colonel Alexander Linsky sat behind his desk with his hands resting on the arms of his high backed chair. He had a slender build with a thin nose and high cheekbones. His light brown hair was cut short and combed straight back, and his blue uniform made his light blue eyes seem to glow.

"And you interviewed the accident witnesses again?" asked Linsky.

"Yes sir," said Lieutenant Fischer, who stood facing the desk.

"Nothing new emerged? No fresh recollections?"

"No sir. I don't think the old woman saw much of anything. It was dark. It had just stopped raining. She heard the screech of tires on the road, looked up, and saw Chambers' car pile into the bridge's right suspension anchor."

"What about the couple that reported the accident? Anything new?"

"No, sir."

"And we've thoroughly investigated the woman and the young couple?" asked Linsky as he stood. He walked over to a window where several potted plants rested on the sill. He plucked off a few brown leaves from one of them and watered it out of a small cup.

"The woman is an eighty-three-year-old grandmother," said Lieutenant Fischer. "No indications of anything unorthodox. The young man and his wife also checked out okay."

"And the car?" asked Linsky. "You've reviewed the reports again?"

"Yes," said Fischer. "I also talked to the investigators. They still think it was bad luck. The connection between the tie rod and the left wheel was heavily rusted. It just broke and he lost control."

"What about suicide?" asked Linsky.

"Can't rule it out completely," said Lieutenant Fischer. "But we double checked Chambers' annual psych evals and interviewed the doctors. There's never been anything to suggest he was suicidal."

"No evidence of unauthorized communications? Was he talking to anyone?"

"Only colleagues and friends. All known. All vetted."

"What about the grandson?" asked Colonel Linsky. "What did you learn from him?"

Lieutenant Fischer consulted his PDD. "Smart as hell. Big guy. Good athlete. But mostly keeps to himself. A professor at his school thinks he wanders outside the lines a little. Asked me to keep an eye on him, but nothing concrete to go on."

"I read your scan of the note Chambers sent him," said Linsky. "Don't you find it strange that he included childish riddles in a note to someone about to graduate from Weller Academy?"

"A little," replied Fischer.

"Yes, a little strange," agreed Linsky. "And let's not forget the boy's father supported the Nine and paid the price. The acorn does not fall far from the tree."

"He was just a kid then. Thousands of kids lost mothers and fathers in those days and have never made an issue out of it."

"Hmm," said Linsky to himself as he examined some spots on the plant's leaves.

"I also read his academy admission evaluation," said Fischer. "There were no red flags."

Linsky turned from the window and the plants on the sill to look at Lieutenant Fischer. "Being evaluated for academic value to the PRA is not the same as being evaluated as a suspect in an official investigation. And let's not be too quick to discount the manner of his father's death. Hatred's embers burn long. What about the mother?"

"She's a dedicated citizen," said Lieutenant Fischer. "Eager to cooperate, but I don't think she knows anything useful. I get the impression neither Chambers nor her boy was in the habit of telling her much."

"Because they were hiding something?" asked Linsky.

Fischer shook his head. "Because she's a gossip."

Colonel Linsky returned to his chair and sat down. He smoothed back his hair with his right hand. "So, barring any new evidence, we're left with our initial conclusion. Accidental death."

"I think so, sir."

Linsky laced his fingers together and placed them on the desk in front of him, momentarily lost in thought. Then he looked up at Lieutenant Fischer. "The most pivotal person in the most significant effort of our time smashes his car into a bridge just before his work is completed. Just when he is needed most," said Linsky. "I refuse to accept that as coincidental. There's more to it."

"We'll keep digging," offered Lieutenant Fischer.

"Do that. Pay attention to every possible lead. I receive daily inquiries on this matter and I don't want to disappoint."

"Understood, sir."

Fischer turned and walked toward the door.

"And lieutenant," said Colonel Linsky. "Look deeper into the grandson's connection. Check his apartment door monitor, his buy card history, public transportation records, city safety cameras. The full treatment. I think there's more going on here than meets the eye."

"Yes sir."

Chapter 16

Lena arrived at the apartment a few minutes after Logan and Cap.

"That was fast," said Logan as he held the door open for her to enter.

"Really?" she said. "Or are you two just slow?"

"I guess we like to look our best," he replied with a smile. He led her into the small living room and turned on the view screen hanging on the wall. He handed her the remote control.

"Feel free to help yourself to whatever is in the fridge," he said as he went into his room to finish getting ready.

"There's no way I'm eating anything that comes out of a bachelor's fridge," she said as she sat down in front of the view screen. She cycled through a few channels showing the usual mix of sporting events, comedies, and dramas. She stopped when she found the news channel.

A young well-dressed male reporter was providing the latest information about a clan raid. "The Defense Ministry has released new footage of the atrocity, which occurred in the predawn hours this morning on the frontier west of Nashville." Images of dark-clad armed militants wearing red scarves across their faces appeared on the screen. They were running and shooting indiscriminately at fleeing men, women and children.

The reporter continued. "This large raiding party is believed to have crossed the Mississippi two days ago near Memphis and quickly slipped deep into the frontier territories. They attacked the town of Bixby and looted a food convoy destined for Chicago as well as a nearby farm development."

The view screen showed footage of a half dozen burning convoy trucks on a two lane road. In the distance, black smoke rose from a small town.

"There is still no report on the number of casualties," said the reporter, "but we have been assured the situation is now fully under control. A strike force is in pursuit of the clan raiders, but advanced anti-aircraft and other weaponry provided by both the Pacific Federation and the so-called League of Free Cities has limited the PRA military's ability to kill or capture the raiders. There are also unconfirmed reports the raiders downed two pursuing Bering Class helicopters."

"The Congress of Representatives passed a resolution this afternoon calling upon the Guardians to direct the military to take all measures necessary to fully and completely secure the frontier. The Guardians and military leadership are now in closed door discussions regarding how to address this rapidly escalating conflict on the frontier. Here is Guardian Helen Hyatt, who spoke to us just moments ago prior to joining her colleagues in this critical meeting."

Guardian Hyatt appeared on the view screen. "This is intolerable. We have heard the calls of the people struggling to bring the frontier region under control, and we will answer that call."

She looked directly into the camera. "These good people have labored and tilled the soil to make the frontier fruitful once again, but clan raiders and their foreign backers are destroying everything they've worked for and filling their hearts with fear. But rest assured, the People's Republic of America will not let this aggression go unanswered. We will bring peace, prosperity, and security to the frontier. Now, if you'll excuse me, I'm needed inside." She smiled and walked toward a large wooden door. An armed guard standing next to the door opened it for her.

"Strong words from Guardian Hyatt," said the reporter as the image switched back to him standing at the scene of the attack. "But what about the views of those directly impacted by the raids? I have with me Yolanda Perez, who awoke before dawn this morning to the sound of gunfire outside her home. A home which has been reduced to ashes."

The camera panned to a young woman holding a small child in her arms. The child was sobbing into her shoulder. They were both covered in soot. "Someone has to do something," she said to the reporter, her eyes flashing with anger. "Why do the Guardians tolerate this? I know they want to resolve all of this peacefully, but they're burning our homes and stealing our food. They're murdering us! It's time to fight back!"

"More trouble on the frontier," said Cap, who had come into the living room to hear the report. "What the hell's going on out there?"

"Judging from the news, it looks like the Waste clans are getting bolder and bolder," said Lena.

Cap went to the view screen and tapped a few controls in the lower right corner. The image changed from the news channel to a peaceful scene of ocean waves rolling gently onto a sunny beach. "We're going to hear plenty about the frontier, the clans, the League of Free Cities, and all the rest when AD starts. For now, let's listen to some music and relax." Cap pressed a button on the controller.

Lena was silent for a moment as she listened to the music. "What's this? It's...unusual."

"Louis Armstrong, *Mack the Knife,*" said Cap. "Listen to it. I think you'll dig it."

"*Dig it?*" she said with a chuckle. "You're in a world of your own, Caparelli."

"Give it a try," he said as he walked toward his room. He stole a glance over his shoulder before going through the doorway and saw Lena looking at book titles on the bookshelf. He smiled when he saw her hand tapping her hip to the beat of the music.

Chapter 17

Cap woke to the sound of someone pounding on his bedroom door. "What?" he croaked, his face half buried in his pillow.

"Let's go!" Logan yelled through the door. "Lena's here. We're waiting on you."

Cap pulled himself out of bed and threw on an old blue bathrobe. He opened the door and blinked, bleary eyed, at Logan.

"Nice bed hair," observed Lena, who appeared from the kitchen. "Get ready. Let's go."

"What are you guys talking about? Where are we going?"

"To solve the riddles, my friend," said Logan. "Lena thinks she's cracked the code. Remember the answers? Flowers, Edgar Allen Poe, the letter V?"

"What?" asked Cap, trying to catch up to the conversation.

"I think it's a place," said Lena. "My piano instructor teaches out of her home on Poe Avenue and there's a flower shop on the five hundred block. You know V is the Roman numeral for five, right? Anyway, I go by the shop once a week on the bus."

"You play piano?" asked Cap.

"And the clarinet," she said in a matter-of-fact tone. "If you want to come with us, you'd better get dressed."

"But don't we want to watch the banner race? You know, top ten racers from around the country...banner thieves," his voice trailed off. "C'mon, I've got money riding on it."

"No," said Lena without hesitation. "Get dressed."

Cap looked at her as if to argue, then said, "Okay, okay. Give me a minute. Someone make some coffee."

"Will do," said Logan. "Now get moving. Unhitch the plow."

Cap closed his eyes and slowly shook his head. "Did I just hear you say 'unhitch the plow'? I didn't know you spoke hillbilly." Then he closed his bedroom door.

Forty-five minutes later, the three of them were stepping off a city bus on Poe Avenue. It was a warm sunny day and the sidewalk was full of people on their way to the banner racecourse, which wound its way around the Capitol District.

"Finally," said Cap with an approving smile as he looked at a pair of women walking together and laughing. "It's finally warm enough for women to wear dresses."

"You're a classy guy, Caparelli," said Lena. Then she pointed and said, "It's a couple blocks up this way."

They wove their way through the pedestrian traffic, which was walking in the opposite direction toward a fenced-off section of the racetrack two blocks away. There was already a sizeable crowd lined up along the fence. As they walked along, Lena occasionally stopped to look at something in a shop or to talk to street vendors selling everything from pretzels to jewelry. Logan tried to hide his impatience with her uncharacteristically relaxed pace. He'd been wondering about the unusual note his grandfather had sent him for several days now and was anxious to solve the mystery. Lena's theory that the riddles were clues about a place made sense to him and he was eager to find out if she was right.

"What are we supposed to be looking for at this flower shop anyway?" asked Cap as they crossed the street to the five hundred block of Poe Avenue.

"I don't know," said Logan. "I guess we'll know it when we see it."

"That's very helpful," replied Cap. "Maybe you can buy me some flowers."

"It's not like we have any place to be now that our finals are over," said Lena as she looked at the people on the opposite side of the busy street. "The graduation ceremony isn't until tomorrow."

"Speak for yourself," said Cap. "I was happily sleeping away the day before you two came banging on my door."

They reached a store with a display of flowers and bouquets in the window. The brightly painted sign hanging from a wrought iron bracket above the door read "Wallflowers and Early Bloomers".

"I guess this is it," said Cap as he stared at the sign.

"You don't miss a thing, Caparelli," said Lena. She opened the door and entered.

Logan looked at Cap and smiled. "Has she fallen under the spell of your charm yet?"

Cap shook his head. "She's playing hard to get."

Logan chuckled. Holding the door open for Cap to enter, he said, "Yes. Very hard to get."

The flower shop was small. Along one wall was a line of refrigerators with glass doors containing various flower arrangements in vases. On the floor around the main counter and along its side were buckets filled with different kinds of flowers. At the back of the store were decorative vases and other containers for displaying plants and flowers, and an assortment of knickknacks and figurines filled several shelves on the back wall.

"Can I help you?" asked a young man from behind the counter.

"We're just looking around," said Cap as he strolled toward the refrigerators, hands clasped behind his back.

"Okay. Please let me know if you need anything," replied the man. He returned his attention to the bouquet he was arranging at the end of the counter.

Logan looked at the displays and along the walls, hoping to find some new clue. He was surprised by the number of gnomes, fairies, angels, and unicorns displayed in the back of the shop and on the shelves. But if they stock them, there must be demand for them he told himself.

Cap wandered over to Logan and whispered, "Any luck? Or are you just looking to add to your gnome collection?"

Logan shook his head. "Funny guy," he said. He looked from display to display and sighed. "Maybe this is a waste of time."

"You think?" asked Cap in a sarcastic tone.

Lena joined them. "See anything, Logan?" she asked. "Anything trigger any thoughts?"

"Nothing," he said. "Maybe we should…" He stopped speaking mid-sentence and stared at the top shelf. "Look up there. See the bust?"

"Yes," said Lena as she looked up to see several white plaster statues of angels, fairies, and the like. In the midst of them was a bust of a man wearing a helmet.

"My grandfather wrote me a note that included a line from an ancient poem," said Logan.

"You didn't mention a note or a poem," said Lena. "Just the card you showed the SPD officer."

"Must have slipped my mind," Logan replied without looking at her. He repeated the line. "Wanderer, if you come to Sparta, tell them there you have seen us lying here, obedient to their laws."

"That's a nice poem," said Cap. "Cheerful. What does it mean?"

"See the bust of the man?" asked Logan, pointing at a bust of a bearded man wearing a helmet. "I'm guessing that's Leonidas, the Spartan king who said those words twenty-five hundred years ago."

Cap raised his eyebrows and looked at Lena, whose gaze was locked on the bust. Then he nodded his head and said in a confident tone, "I agree. It's Leonidas."

"Don't pretend you know who Leonidas was," said Lena without looking at him.

"Of course I know who he was," said Cap. "He was the bushy bearded king of the Spartans."

Logan turned and walked to the counter. "Excuse me," he said to the clerk. "How much is it for that bust up there?"

The clerk disappeared into a back room and returned with a step ladder. He placed it near the back wall and retrieved the bust from the top shelf. Once back on the ground, he examined it with a puzzled expression on his face. "Strange," he said. "There's no tag on it."

He turned it around in his hands a few times, looking at it from different angles. "Let me call the owner. He's at home today."

"I'll give you twenty dollars," said Logan, immediately chastising himself for sounding too eager.

The clerk looked at him for a moment and said, "I'm not sure how much it costs, and without a price tag and code I wouldn't even be able to ring it up. Your buy card wouldn't work."

"I'll pay cash," said Logan. "It's a gift for my mother. It's her birthday today and I need something right away."

"Well, something like this is a cash-approved item," said the clerk. "But I should probably call the owner, he'd..."

Logan interrupted. "Fifty dollars. You'd be doing me a huge favor."

The clerk hesitated. Logan dug in his pocket and pulled out thirty dollars. It was all he had. He looked at Lena and Cap. "A little help would be appreciated."

Lena had ten dollars, which she gave to Logan. He looked at Cap, who slowly shook his head and produced his money clip. He pulled out two five-dollar bills and reluctantly handed them to Logan, who handed the cash to the clerk.

The clerk was about to say something, but then reconsidered. "Would you like it giftwrapped?"

"No thanks," said Logan as he took the bust from the clerk's hands and handed it to Lena to put in the small backpack she had brought. "We're in a rush."

Chapter 18

Logan used his buy card to purchase a cup of coffee for each of them at a nearby café. Cap had suggested that they sit at one of the sidewalk tables, but Logan insisted on sitting inside. Once they were seated and had their coffee, Logan pulled the bust out of Lena's backpack and placed it in the middle of the table.

"So, what's the deal with this head, and why did I buy a twenty-percent stake in it?" asked Cap.

Logan looked at the bust and rubbed his chin. "I don't know, but I can't believe all of this, the riddles, the flower shop, the poem, and the bust, are not somehow connected."

Looking at Lena, Cap said, "For Lena's benefit, can you explain who Leonidas was?"

She shook her head look and said, "Oh, please."

"He was a Greek king of Sparta," said Logan as he rotated the bust, examining it.

Lena jumped in. "Twenty-five hundred years ago, Leonidas and three hundred of his men held off a horde of Persians at a narrow pass, buying time for the other Greek cities to prepare their defenses."

Cap took a sip of coffee. He made a face and added a generous amount of sugar. "I knew that. Are there any more riddles? Any more clues about what to do with the head?"

"It's a bust. Not a head," said Lena. "Logan, you have to tell us everything your grandfather wrote to you. We're obviously missing something."

Logan took a deep breath. "Okay, you know about the riddles. You know about the line from Leonidas. The only other thing he wrote me was a request."

Lena leaned forward. "What kind of request?"

"He asked that I keep something safe until he could retrieve it."

"Keep what safe?" said Lena.

Logan sipped his coffee but didn't respond.

Cap looked at him and said, "Maybe you should tell Lena about your visit."

"What visit?" she asked, looking back and forth between the two young men.

Logan leaned back in his chair and looked at Lena. "An SPD officer stopped by a couple of nights ago."

"The SPD? What did he want?" she asked.

"He was interested in my grandfather and whether we had talked. He wanted to know if he had given me anything or if we had spoken near the time of his death."

"What did you say?" asked Lena.

"I told them about the graduation card with the riddles he had sent me, but not about the other note."

"Or the medallion," said Cap as he sipped his coffee.

"What medallion?" asked Lena.

Logan shot Cap an angry look, but then he took the medallion out of his pants pocket and handed it to her. She looked at it for a few moments, carefully tracing her index finger along the image of Apollo in his chariot and the horses that pulled it. She turned it over and examined the intricate design of swirling grooves on the back.

"It's beautiful," she said as she handed it back to him. "But you can't tell the SPD about the medallion or the bust."

Logan looked at her, surprised that she didn't recommend total disclosure. "Why not?"

"Despite your grandfather's warning to keep it safe, I don't think the medallion or the bust is of interest to the SPD. But now that you've started down this road, it's best to keep quiet," she said. "You'll never explain to the SPD's satisfaction why you didn't tell them about everything right away. You'll always be under a cloud of suspicion."

"I'm not so sure that's a good idea," said Cap as he placed his coffee mug on the table. "Just tell them you found the second note and the medallion when you were packing for AD. They might ask you a few more questions, but nothing has happened that you can't explain away. In fact, they might thank you for figuring out the riddles and getting the bust."

Logan looked at the coffee shop door as two men entered. They sat at a table near the window. One of them flashed a quick look at Logan as the waiter handed each of them a menu.

Cap leaned forward and got Logan's attention. "Logan. You've got a great career ahead of you. You'll do five years active duty, then you'll get a nice research job at one of the ministries or an academy, maybe even Malcom Weller." He pointed a finger at the bust. "Don't blow it over a couple riddles and a cheap hunk of plaster."

Logan didn't respond. He looked again at the two men at the table. Then he relaxed when two women entered and joined them. The men stood and welcomed them with a kiss on the cheek. They laughed at some joke one of the men said and sat down.

"Why is this decision hard for you to make?" asked Cap, exasperated.

Logan looked at Cap. "You know why," he said in a low voice.

Cap shook his head and sat back. "Just last night you agreed that you shouldn't dwell on the past. That you should look to the future and not squander your opportunities."

"Maybe I changed my mind," said Logan. "Maybe I wasn't being honest with myself when I said that."

Lena looked at Logan. She studied his face but asked nothing. They finished their coffee in silence and left the café.

Chapter 19

When they reached the bus stop they saw that the schedule had been suspended until after the banner race. "They've shut down all traffic around the course, so they must be getting ready to start," said Cap as he smiled at a group of young women passing by.

Noting the direction of Cap's gaze, Lena folded her arms and shot him a disapproving look. "You really are full of yourself," she said. "Do you come on to every woman you see?"

"Just about. And why shouldn't I?" he replied unapologetically. "There's nothing wrong in acknowledging a woman's beauty. Although you might be the exception to the rule, women like it when I compliment them. And they come on to me, too."

Lena chuckled. "You've got to be kidding me. You? What woman in her right mind would come on to you?"

Cap looked over his left shoulder. "What about those two?" he said. "They were staring at me the whole time we were at the café and here they are again."

Logan looked in the direction Cap indicated. He saw two young women, one with short brown hair and the other with straight blonde hair pulled back in a ponytail. They were smiling and talking with each other, but when ponytail shot him a quick glance he saw something in her eye that seemed harsh and calculating.

"Let's get out of here," he said.

Cap looked at him and laughed. "The visit from the SPD has made you paranoid. Those two are not spying on us."

"You think the SPD only employs thugs in jackboots and uniforms?" asked Logan.

"No," said Cap. "I'm just saying those two beautiful young women are not SPD operatives. I'll prove it. I'll go talk to them."

"That's a brilliant plan," said Lena sarcastically.

"I've got a better idea," said Logan. "Let's walk around a little and see if they're still following us. And this way Cap gets to see the banner race. Everybody's happy."

"It's better watching it on a view screen," Cap mumbled. "But I won't say no."

They walked toward the crowd control barrier on the raceway, then turned left and continued along the edge of the quickly growing crowd of men, women, and children of all ages. Many carried pennants with their favorite rider's name and number. A few held up homemade signs with the names of the most famous banner thieves.

As they wove their way through the crowd, Logan resisted the urge to look back, focusing instead on the spectators' growing excitement and looking for an open spot to slip in and watch the elaborately designed motorcycles race by. To their right, Logan saw a number of tall strangely shaped towers in the middle of the raceway. Originally designed to throw various obstacles, ramps, or other challenges in the way of the racers, the towers had become favorite places for so-called banner thieves to hide behind so they could leap out at the racers as they roared by. The practice had started about twelve years earlier when three people jumped over the crowd barrier and dared drivers to run them down. One was severely injured but only after she had snatched the rider's fluttering banner from the back of his bike. In the years that followed, the spectators had grown to love the unexpected and deadly thrill these banner thieves added to the race and cheered loudly whenever someone dodged a racer. They cheered even louder when a racer hit a thief.

Within a few years following the advent of the first banner thieves, certain informal rules had developed. The thieves' goal was to dodge racers, and, if possible, steal the racers' numbered flags affixed to the backs of their motorcycles. For their part, the racers were allowed to hit the runners, but they risked losing control of their machines if they did so. Therefore, to keep the thieves at bay, they threw blunt darts at them, using small atlatls to propel them at blinding speeds. Though they weren't sharp, the darts could cause considerable pain, even crack bones.

Most racers enjoyed the competition with the banner thieves and painted their motorcycles with elaborate animal-inspired designs celebrating the deadly contest. The most famous of these was the image of a fierce bull's head, complete with slightly protruding horns, which adorned the front fairing of the very successful and dangerous racer, Nicolaus Vorsek. Other racers' designs included shark heads, birds of prey, charging horses, and venomous serpents.

None of this was officially condoned by the government, and race officials warned against the practice every year, but no serious effort was made to stop it. At most, authorities simply kept it from becoming unmanageable. For example, no more than twenty banner thieves were ever allowed to jump the barrier in one race.

Logan pointed at an opening in the crowd near a large oak tree. "There," he said. "Move quickly. We'll mix in with the crowd and hide behind the tree."

They trotted down a grassy hill and got behind the trunk of a tree near the raceway. Logan looked around the tree trunk to see if the two women had followed them. He didn't see them after carefully searching the sea of faces. A few moments later, he looked at Cap and Lena and said, "I guess I am a little paranoid."

Just then they heard the sound of a cannon going off. The crowd all around them and behind the barrier on the opposite side of the road cheered, waved flags, and raised cups of beer into the air. Then they heard the high-pitched whine of motorcycle engines in the distance. They grew louder and louder as the motorcycles rapidly approached.

As they waited for the racers to come around the bend, Cap caught Logan's attention and nodded toward the top of a little hill behind them. Logan peaked around the tree and saw the two women from the café as well as a tan dark-haired man in a black leather jacket. Logan recognized him as the same man who had followed him from the library. They were slowly scanning the crowd. The man's eyes stopped when he saw the oak tree. He spoke to the two women, who nodded and started walking toward the tree. The man stayed where he was and spoke into a small device he held in his hand. He nodded and then followed the women toward the tree.

Logan leaned his head toward Lena and Cap and said in a loud voice so he could be heard above the sound of the oncoming racers, "We need to get out of here. Now!"

They turned to their left but saw two uniformed SPD officers quickly making their way toward them. Looking to his right, he saw the two women were angling toward them in order to block any possible escape in that direction. Suddenly, a man dressed all in black pushed past the two SPD officers. They tried to grab hold of him but failed as he placed his hands on the top of the fence and deftly swung himself over. He dashed toward a tower in the middle of the raceway just as the first motorcycle came around the bend. The officers leaned against the fence and yelled for the man to return to the spectators' side of the raceway, but he ignored their commands and quickly donned black gloves and a black knit cap.

Logan looked back toward the hill and saw that the two women and the man in the leather jacket were quickly moving toward the three cadets. Then, when they were about twenty meters away, Logan saw the man reach into his coat.

"I have to get out of here!" yelled Logan to the others above the sound of screaming engines as the motorcycles whizzed by. Looking at the other two he said, "We have to split up. Get away from here. They're not interested in either of you."

He quickly turned Lena around and pulled the backpack containing the bust off her shoulders and slipped it onto his back. He placed his hands on the top of the fence, hopped over, and ran for the protection of the tower in the middle of the raceway just as two straggling racers came around the bend. As they roared by, he felt the breeze of something fly near his left ear, then he heard the ringing clatter of metal darts as they struck the obstacle tower.

When he reached the tower, the man in black who had also jumped the fence was surprised to see him. "Most banner thieves don't bring their lunch with them," he said, pointing at Logan's backpack.

"Believe me, I would rather not be here," replied Logan. He looked back at the SPD officers, who appeared perplexed by the appearance of the second banner thief. Ten meters to their right were the two women and the man in the leather jacket. He could not see any sign of Cap or Lena and hoped they had slipped away unnoticed.

"I have to get to the other side," said Logan. He looked for SPD officers on the other side, but all he saw were hundreds of screaming half-drunk faces. He was about to make his move when he saw an SPD crowd-control van pull into view behind the spectators with its blue lights flashing.

"Did you pay the SPD boltheads their fee to jump the fence?" asked the banner thief.

"What?" asked Logan. "No, I just jumped it."

"Me either," said the thief. "It takes away from the virtue of the challenge, the authenticity of the ritual." He eyed the two SPD officers he had eluded as they pushed their way through the crowd. One of them was talking into a small PDD. "They're going to try and pull us in. We have to get to the next tower before the racers come by again."

The banner thief turned and ran toward the next tower fifty meters farther up the course. Without thinking, Logan followed him as quickly as he could. By all accounts, Logan was strong and fast, but the thief moved with the grace, power, and speed of a tiger, and the distance between the two runners rapidly increased. When he reached the tower the thief was already there waiting. He pointed at the SPD crowd-control van trying to push its way through the mass of cheering spectators, but it was making slow progress.

"See that?" he said with a grin. "They won't catch us."

Logan searched for the SPD vehicle but was distracted when the crowd suddenly let out a wild cheer. Logan followed their gaze to see a large view screen on the wall of a nearby building. It was showing a slow-motion replay of two people at another location of the course attempting to steal a racer's banner. A dart struck the first thief in the head as he tried to dodge a motorcycle, causing him to collapse to the ground where he lay motionless. But the second thief ran straight toward the front of the last racer and vaulted into the air at the last second. The racer threw his dart at the thief but missed just before she flew over his head and grabbed hold of his banner, pulling it from the back of the machine. She tucked herself into a ball and somersaulted in the air before landing on her feet and rolling to a stop. Triumphant, she jumped up and held the banner high for the cheering crowd to see.

Logan heard the high-pitched sound of motorcycle engines approaching and looked toward the curve from where the racers would soon appear. He looked at the banner thief and said, "You don't understand. I really don't want to be here. I need to get to the other side of the fence."

The thief looked at him and raised an eyebrow. "I see," he said. He pointed at the tree where Logan had jumped the barrier. "So there's someone on that side that made you want to get to this side." Then he spotted the man in the leather jacket push his way up to the fence and place his hands on top, preparing to jump.

"Who's that?" asked the thief. "SPD?"

"I don't know," said Logan.

"All right," said the thief. "Get behind the tower and make your run when I go for the banner. The tower is going to throw an obstacle into the race this lap, so be ready to adjust."

Logan looked the banner thief in the eye. Then he asked, "Why are you helping me?"

"Shouldn't I be?" replied the man.

Just then a group of motorcycles came around the bend with Vorsek's painted bull leading the pack. As the racers approached the first tower two arms quickly swung down. When the arms were close to the pavement, interlocking plates shot out at a thirty-degree angle, forming small ramps. Vorsek and the others responded by rising somewhat in their seats just before their bikes launched into the air. But while the others slowed somewhat as they approached, Vorsek hit the ramp and landed his machine without breaking pace.

Then the pillar behind which Logan and the man were hiding made a clicking sound. An arm suddenly lowered to block the side of the race track to which Logan needed to run. The racers guided their motorcycles toward the left side of the pillar, causing the man in the leather jacket to think twice about getting onto the raceway.

Logan peered around the edge of the pillar to see Vorsek was in front but had three racers right behind him. The remaining six motorcycles were just approaching the first tower and its ramp. Looking back at Vorsek, Logan saw he was holding a thin metal rod in his hand, which he lowered to the side of his cycle. When he raised his hand, there was a dart attached to the end of the rod. Then one of the racers behind Vorsek launched his dart at Logan, barely missing his left eye.

As Logan pulled his head back, he saw the banner thief was crouching low behind the tower. Then he launched himself across the path of the onrushing motorcycles. Logan watched, fascinated by the man's seeming disregard for danger as he flew through the air with his body and arms outstretched. Two darts struck the thief, one in the shoulder and the other in the chest, just as Vorsek passed under him. Yet, despite being struck twice, the thief lowered his arm and reached for Vorsek's banner, his fingertips touching the small mast to which the flag was attached. But the thief could not close his hand quickly enough, and the banner slipped through his fingers. The thief crashed to the ground and rolled awkwardly several times until he slammed against the crowd barrier.

SPD officers reached over the barrier and pulled the semi-conscious thief to his feet. One of the officers looked at Logan and pointed a finger at him. "You!" screamed the officer. "Come here! Now!"

Logan turned and ran toward the opposite side. As he dashed across the course, a racer launched a dart at him, hitting him in the back of his shoulder. He cried out in pain but kept running for the barrier. The cheering crowd parted for him as he clambered over the fence. He moved as quickly as he could through the mass of people, who occasionally patted him on the back but also chided him for not attempting to grab a banner.

"Get back out there, thief," said one very drunk man with greasy hair and a three day old beard. "Don't puss out on us."

"Get out there yourself, you fat fuck," yelled a nearby woman.

A scuffle broke out as more people got involved in the argument. Logan continued to push through the throng until he reached the back edge and slipped into a large group of beer drinking, singing revelers as they staggered through the street.

Chapter 20

Logan was in his bedroom packing his clothes as quickly as possible when he heard someone entering the code into the apartment door's keypad. He walked to his bedroom door and opened it slightly, peering through the crack. He heard the door close shut and saw Cap step into the living room.

"Damn," said Cap when Logan opened his door. "That's the craziest thing I've ever seen you do. Glad you made it out of there alive."

Logan had already turned around to continue packing. "I've gotta get out of here," he said.

"Where to?" asked Cap.

"I'm heading straight to active duty," he replied. "I don't know who was after us. If it was SPD, they'll just pick me up when I report. But if it was someone else, maybe they won't be able to get me."

"Yeah," said Cap. "I think I'll do the same. Time to get the hell out of this place."

"Where's Lena?" asked Logan as he threw some shirts into a duffle bag.

"We split up right away," said Cap. "I swung by her place but no one answered the door."

"I'm sure she got away," said Logan. "She's smart, fast, and tough as shit."

"Yeah," said Cap. "I feel sorry for the poor bastard who tangles with her." Despite what he said, Logan could tell his friend had lingering concerns but he didn't press it.

"Do you still have the bust?" asked Cap.

"Yeah," said Logan as he pointed with his thumb at the backpack on his bed.

Twenty minutes later, Logan and Cap had finished packing and had stacked their bags against the wall. They were doing a final walkthrough of the apartment when they heard the keypad on the apartment door beep and then click. They turned toward the now open door and saw Lieutenant Fischer and another SPD officer standing in the doorway.

"Good evening, Mr. Brandt," said the SPD man as he placed his PDD in his inner coat pocket. "Mr. Caparelli," he added with the nod of his head to Cap.

"Hello," said Logan guardedly.

Stepping past the two young men and into the apartment's living room, Lieutenant Fischer said, "It appears that you have completed your studies and are preparing for the next chapter in your lives."

"That's right," said Logan.

"I congratulate you, but before you go we would like to have another conversation about your grandfather," said Fischer.

"Okay," responded Logan. He shot Cap a quick look. Then he said to Fischer, "Please have a seat."

"Not here," said Fischer. "There is someone I'd like you to meet. Please come with us." He pointed toward the door with an open hand.

Logan hesitated.

"Don't be concerned, Mr. Brandt. This will be a very informal conversation. And your friend Mr. Caparelli is invited as well, so you won't be alone."

Cap raised his eyebrows but kept quiet.

"That won't be necessary," said Logan. "I'm happy to come along. Cap can stay here."

The Lieutenant shook his head. "No. I am quite sure Mr. Caparelli's presence will be required." He pointed toward the door again. "There is a chill in the air this evening. You will need your coats."

The second SPD officer pulled their coats from the closet near the door and threw them at the young men. They put them on and walked out of the apartment, followed by the SPD officer. Alone in the apartment, Lieutenant Fischer glanced at the packed bags they had lined up against a nearby wall. Among them was the backpack Logan had been wearing earlier that day. Fischer walked into Logan's room and quickly cast his eyes over the dresser, armchair and bed. He did the same to Cap's room. Then he walked toward the door, giving the small apartment a final look before exiting.

The two young men were sitting in the back of the SPD patrol car when Fischer seated himself in the front passenger seat.

"Go," he said to the driver.

They drove about three blocks when Logan saw two vans with SPD painted on the fronts and sides pass by in the opposite direction. He turned his head to see where they were going.

Fischer noticed Logan's interest. He smiled and said, "We're going to take an inventory of the contents of your apartment. Nothing to worry about, I'm sure." Although he continued to show his crooked yellow-toothed smile, the SPD officer did not try to hide the malice in his eyes.

Chapter 21

SPD Colonel Linsky looked up from reading his personal data device. "Ah. Mr. Brandt. Mr. Caparelli. Please sit." He indicated two chairs on the other side of his desk.

The young men sat down as instructed. They had been searched prior to entering the building and an SPD officer placed the contents of their pockets in front of each of them. The two piles consisted of keys, identification cards, buy cards, Cap's money clip, and, in front of Logan, the medallion.

"You are no doubt curious about why we've invited you here to talk," said Colonel Linsky. He looked at Logan and winked. "Don't worry. It's not about your little adventure at today's banner race. I hope your shoulder was not severely injured."

Logan shook his head slightly but didn't say anything.

"Good," said Linsky. Then he took a deep breath and slowly exhaled. "As you know we are investigating your grandfather's death. You see, Arthur Chambers was not only a renowned physicist, but he was also quite highly regarded in government circles for his many contributions to the defense of this nation. Were you aware of these contributions, Mr. Brandt?"

Logan shrugged and said, "I knew that he worked in a government lab, but I was not aware of the details of his work."

"Understandable, quite understandable," replied Linsky. "I had the honor of working with him the last few years of his life. He was brilliant in many ways, but his true genius lay in his ability to take concepts that are quite abstract and find practical applications for them. Many of his breakthroughs have helped ward off considerable threats to the People's Republic of America. His untimely death in a fluke car crash was a terrible blow to this nation and its people, worse than you could ever know."

Colonel Linsky stood and walked over to a large view screen attached to a wall. "Given the significance of his work, we have been carefully investigating the cause of the crash, and although that work continues, you will be relieved to know that we have found no evidence suggesting his car was tampered with. It appears there was some sort of malfunction.

He lost control while turning a corner and crashed into a bridge support. It's the sort of thing that happens every day, unfortunately."

Linsky looked at each of his guests and said, "We never know when our time will come, eh?" He smiled at the two young men, but their faces remained expressionless.

"But we are not here to discuss life's precariousness. I asked you to come here so I could get your opinion on something quite unusual we recently observed while reviewing security footage of the lab where Dr. Chambers worked. I'd like you to look at this recording from a safety camera in the late doctor's office."

Colonel Linsky nodded toward Lieutenant Fischer, who clicked a button on a view screen controller. A video feed appeared on the screen depicting a desk, a bookshelf, some cabinets and a few chairs. As the video played, Logan saw his grandfather busily packing his briefcase, apparently preparing to go home for the night. Chambers turned his back to the camera as he made final preparations. Then he turned and walked out the door and out of camera view.

"Did you see that, Mr. Brandt?" asked Linsky, slightly excited.

Logan looked confused. "I don't know what you mean."

Linsky walked over to Lieutenant Fischer and took the controller. He reversed the footage and ran it again. "Look at this right here." He pointed at a spot on the view screen. "Do you see this object on the bookshelf?"

Logan had seen it and knew exactly what it was. "Yes, I see it."

"This bust moves!" He zoomed in on the bust on the shelf and pressed the play button. They could see that before Chambers turned his back to the camera and obscured the view of the bust, it was facing straight out from the shelf. When Chambers turned around and left his office, the bust came back into view, but it was facing slightly to the right.

"I'm not sure I understand," said Logan.

"Allow me to add some more information, which I think will shed some light on all of this." Linsky folded his arms over his chest. "When Dr. Chambers arrived at the laboratory that morning, his bag was unusually heavy, according to security data we recently reviewed. It was also quite heavy when he left. We interviewed the morning and evening security details. The morning detail recalled inspecting the bag and the bust. Apparently, Chambers said he was bringing in the bust to decorate his office. The evening detail also examined the bust and found nothing unusual about it, though records indicate it was heavier than it had been that morning. Chambers explained to the evening security guard that he was bringing it home and planned to give it to a friend as a gift."

Logan said nothing.

Linsky tapped the view screen controller in his open palm. Then he said, "Mr. Brandt, do you know why your grandfather brought a duplicate bust to the laboratory, switched it with the one on his shelf, and took it out of the building?"

He ran the video again to emphasize his point. "Do you know where this bust is now, Mr. Brandt?"

Logan looked Linsky in the eye and said, "No. I don't know."

Linsky locked eyes with Logan for a few moments and said, "Did he mention his plan for the bust when you two had lunch together last month?"

Logan's heart skipped a beat, but he maintained his composure.

Colonel Linsky smiled and continued. "Recordings from a nearby safety camera show you met at a restaurant near Veterans Park last month. April third, to be precise. Your cautious grandfather sat with his back to the street, but the camera caught your handsome face just as clear as day. You each ordered something, ate your lunch, and one hour and seventeen minutes later you departed."

Logan swallowed involuntarily but remained silent.

"Did you two hatch a plan involving the bust during that lunch?" asked Linsky.

Logan opened his mouth but quickly closed it. His cheeks and neck grew red.

"Why did Chambers switch the bust?" asked Linsky in a loud voice. He bent down and screamed in Logan's ear. "Where is the bust!"

Logan clenched his jaw muscles and stared straight ahead, but refused to speak. Linsky stepped back and slapped Logan across the face. Surprised but not hurt by the blow, Logan slowly raised his eyes and glared at Linsky. Then he leaned forward and rested his elbows on his knees. He folded his hands together and looked at the floor.

Linsky leaned against his desk and looked at Logan. Then he smiled. "I found Chambers' switching of the bust interesting, but I must say your behavior is even more so. We're just following up on something we found puzzling. There could be an innocent explanation for all of this. If you don't know anything about the bust, just say so."

"No," said Logan, still looking at the floor. "That's not how it works. No matter what I say, you're going to grill me until you've poked your nose into every facet of my life. You know it. I know it."

Linsky shrugged his shoulders. "Very well. I can see you need some time to consider your responses. We will continue this conversation later."

Looking at Lieutenant Fischer, Linsky said, "Please escort Mr. Brandt to the holding facility for further questioning. As for Mr. Caparelli, take him back to the apartment. We'll decide what to do with him after we've completed the inventory." He looked at Logan and shook his head. "You're throwing away a promising career, a life many people would kill for," he said to the defiant young man. Then he said to Fischer, "I think he has the bust. Go find it."

"Yes sir," said Fischer. He opened the door and motioned for two SPD guards to come in.

As one guard locked manacles around Logan and Cap's hands, Linsky picked the medallion up off his desk. "Be sure to bring Mr. Brandt's personal effects to the detention center." He dropped the medallion into the second guard's hand and said, "I'd like to learn more about this ornament. It's quite intriguing."

The guards led the two young men down the hall to a stairwell. They descended several flights and entered a parking garage. There was a variety of vehicles parked in different sections. Most were patrol cars, but there were also a number of armored trucks with machine guns and water cannons mounted on top.

The guards placed Logan in the back seat of one patrol car and Cap in the back seat of the car next to it. The two young men gazed through their windows at each other for a moment, stunned by what was happening. Then Logan's vehicle sped away toward the exit.

Chapter 22

Lieutenant Fischer sat in the front passenger seat of the second patrol car. He turned and looked at Cap. "You'd better hope we find what we're looking for. Your friend is stubborn. He has a hard road ahead of him, but you might be okay. It all depends on whether you fully cooperate."

Ten minutes later, the patrol car pulled in front of the apartment building and parked behind the SPD vehicles they had seen earlier. The driver turned off the headlights and was preparing to get out, but Lieutenant Fischer told him to stay with Cap in the car while he went in to check on the progress of the inventory.

Just before Lieutenant Fischer closed his door, he looked at Cap and said, "Think carefully about your next move. You'll get your chance to help in a minute. Your decision will determine your future."

Cap watched Fischer disappear into the building. He looked to the right and saw the face of a woman peering through the curtains of a first-floor window. Seeing Cap in the back seat of the patrol car, she quickly pulled the curtain shut. Cap looked around and saw there was no one on the street or the sidewalk. He felt a slight breeze as the driver rolled down his window to let in the fresh but chilly night air. Cap sunk into the car seat, took in a deep breath and slowly exhaled. He closed his eyes for a moment, then opened them again to look out the window next to him.

Suddenly a dark shadow glided by Cap's door. He saw a long metal rod reach into the driver's window. As soon as the tip of the rod touched the unsuspecting SPD officer's neck, sparks shot out of the end causing the man to go into convulsions. A moment later, the SPD officer was unconscious. The rod was pulled back out the window and Cap's door swung open. Cap was stunned when he saw who was crouching by the open car door.

"Lena?"

"Where have they taken Logan?" she asked in an urgent but hushed voice. Cap tried to respond, but his thoughts were jumbled as his mind sought to process what was happening.

She repeated the question with greater emphasis. *"Where have they taken Logan?"*

"They, they, uh," Cap struggled to remember. "They took him to a detention facility. Not sure where it is."

"I do," she said as she pulled out a small PDD. "What kind of vehicle did they take him in?"

"A patrol car like this one," Cap said. Then he added, "It had a five in the number painted on the side. I don't remember the rest. Wait...it was a letter then two five. D twenty-five!"

She pressed a few buttons on the PDD screen. A woman's voice said, "Yes."

Lena pressed the device to her ear. "He's in a patrol car. Number D twenty-five. They're headed for the detention center. We need to move fast."

Cap heard a muffled voice through the PDD. Lena nodded. "Yes," she said, looking at Cap.

The voice said something. Then it was silent. Cap could see that Lena was reluctant to answer. The voice repeated itself. "I understand," said Lena.

Cap looked at Lena as she ended the transmission. "I don't like that look in your eyes," he said.

She took a moment to consider what she was going to say. Then she looked Cap in the eye and said, "Cap, I need to know where you stand. I could leave you here and you could take your chances with the SPD, but they'll want to know what happened, and I don't think you would withstand interrogation. Nobody does."

"I'd give them a false description," he said. "Buy you some time to get away."

"Here's the problem with that," she said. "I don't plan on getting away. I plan on staying. They'll keep working on you until you've told them everything you know, including what you know about me."

Cap pulled his eyes away from Lena's and saw the grip of a pistol sticking out of a shoulder holster under her jacket. "But there's another option you're considering. One that ensures I won't say anything."

"I'm not going to choose that one."

"So there's a third option," said Cap. "Let me help you free Logan and escape with him."

She nodded her head. "The odds are stacked high against us. And if we somehow pull it off you'd be on the run, forever. You'd have to leave the Capitol District, get out of the country. And if they ever catch you, we're both dead."

Cap smiled. "They won't catch me. Don't stand a chance." He twisted his body slightly to reveal his handcuffs behind his back. "Now get me out of these things."

Chapter 23

Colonel Linsky stood next to his desk, a small PDD pressed to his ear. His face was expressionless as he listened to the person speaking on the other end of the line. At length, he said, "I understand, Guardian Bishop. I will take immediate action. We will be back on track very soon."

He ended the call and dropped the device on his desk. He walked to the door, flung it open and yelled, "Get me Komatsu! Now!"

He walked to the filing cabinet behind his desk. He pulled a ring of keys from his pocket and unlocked a drawer. He removed one of the files, marked "QA" and sat at his desk to read it. A few minutes later there was a light rapping on his door.

"Enter!" he said loudly.

An older man with thick disheveled graying hair wearing a white lab coat entered the room. Linsky looked up from the QA report and stared at the man for a moment. Then he said, "I've been reviewing recent test results from the quality assurance department, and I must say I am extremely concerned with what I am seeing."

Komatsu started to speak, but Linsky held up his hand to silence him.

"Dr. Komatsu, you were Dr. Chambers' lead assistant. Together you made remarkable strides forward, but since his death and your elevation to project manager all progress has ground to a halt. Furthermore, the quality assurance team has been unable to reproduce *any* of the results from prior experiments. Something is very wrong, Dr. Komatsu, and I need you to find out what it is, immediately."

Dr. Komatsu nervously scratched the black and gray stubble on his chin. "Colonel Linsky, my team and I are working round the clock to determine what is wrong," he offered, his voice thin and uncertain. "We share your concern about the lack of progress and with the difficulties the QA department is experiencing. But I must say if they have followed the protocols to the letter, there should be no reason why the tests should fail."

Linsky dropped the report onto his desk and leaned forward. "Dr. Komatsu. I don't think you comprehend the gravity of the situation." He tapped the report with his right index finger. "This project is of the highest significance. We have a schedule to maintain and it cannot be extended. As you are aware, there are many interdependencies between this and other efforts, and our failure to deliver a fully functional product on time will lead to a cascade of failures of massive proportions. Lives are at stake, doctor. The survival of our nation is at stake."

"Y-Yes, I understand," stammered Komatsu.

Linsky pointed his finger at the scientist. "I certainly hope so," he said, through clenched teeth. "Because if you fail to complete this project you'll be lucky to be swinging a pick in a mining development. It's more likely you'll spend your final days in a dark cell, in a dark prison, awaiting a dark fate."

Komatsu's face grew pale. He swallowed. Then, after a moment he said, "May I offer a suggestion?"

"You may."

"I think we should examine the item."

"That's been done," replied Linsky.

"We haven't taken it out of the chamber and physically examined it," responded Komatsu. "We've only checked it with diagnostic systems."

"You're suggesting we take it out of the suspension chamber? That hasn't been done in years. What if it engages unexpectedly and we lose it?"

Komatsu leaned forward and placed his hands on the edge of the colonel's desk. "But it's the only variable which has not been triple checked. If you want to deliver our product on time, I fear we must take that risk."

Linsky threw Komatsu a threatening look. The scientist removed his hands from the desk and took a step back. Then the SPD colonel leaned back and looked at the ceiling as he considered Komatsu's recommendation. Time was running short, and he knew that if the project failed he would be in the cell next to Komatsu's.

"Very well," he said, returning his attention to the scientist. "How much time do you need?"

"Not much. Two hours at the most."

"Do it. Report back as soon as you know anything."

"Yes sir."

Komatsu spun on his heel and quickly exited the office.

Chapter 24

The delivery truck raced through the red light and smashed into the rear quarter panel of the SPD patrol car, sending it spinning toward the far curb. Before the car came to rest, a woman and two men jumped out of the truck and ran toward the car, pistols held out in front of them. When they reached the car they tried to open the doors, but they were locked. The woman peered through the driver's window and saw that the driver and the passengers were disoriented but moving. She signaled to one of the men, who placed a small device on the handle of the right rear door. The explosion that followed was small but sufficient to cause the door to open.

One of the men reached in and pulled Logan out of the car. Logan looked around him, confused. His head felt like it was spinning and he had trouble maintaining his balance. One of the men unlocked his handcuffs and guided him through the intersection toward the delivery truck. Logan looked to his right and saw the traffic had stopped and people were gawking at the events unfolding at the crash scene.

When they got to the delivery truck, the woman said to one of the men, "Get him in the back."

Logan shook his head. "No, wait," he said. "We need to get something from the guard who sat next to me."

"What is it?" she asked.

"A medallion. I need it."

"Why? Why do you need it?" she asked urgently.

"I don't know yet, but I'm sure I need it." He looked at the woman, recognizing her from the library.

The woman looked back at the patrol car. A fire had started in the engine. The guard who had been seated next to Logan stumbled out of his seat, dazed, and slowly drew his pistol.

"Too late," said the woman. "Let's go."

Logan pushed the woman aside and bolted toward the patrol car. The SPD officer fired two shots at Logan as he raced forward. The officer was about to shoot a third time but a bullet from the woman's gun found its mark. He fell to his knees, then slumped to the ground.

Logan ran to the dying man, who clutched his chest in a vain attempt to stop the bleeding. Logan looked in his eyes and saw the terror. He reached into the man's coat pocket and pulled out the medallion. The man grabbed hold of Logan's arm and tried to prevent him from getting away, but his strength had left him. Logan pulled himself free and ran back to the truck. As they drove away, the SPD driver stepped out of the burning vehicle and fired a few shots, hitting the back of the truck but doing no serious damage.

"After you drop us off, take the truck to the river and leave it there," said the woman to the driver. "No time to hide it."

Logan looked at the woman sitting in the front passenger seat. "I remember you from the library. You showed me the book in the reserve section."

She nodded.

"What's your name?" he asked.

"You can call me Attika," she replied. Then she said in a cold, measured tone. "Now that introductions are over, if I tell you to do something, you'd better make goddamn sure you do it. I just shot a man because you failed to listen to me. Never, ever do that again."

Logan returned Attika's stare for a moment, then turned to the dark-haired man sitting next to him. The man looked at him, stone faced. "I recognize you from the banner race," said Logan. "What happened to your two lady friends?"

"You don't need to talk to him," said Attika.

Logan shrugged and looked forward, but the man continued to watch Logan, his hand resting on the grip of an automatic pistol.

The driver made a sharp turn, nearly overturning the unwieldy truck. He made several more turns until they had left the main roads and ducked into a residential neighborhood of squat gray apartment buildings. He brought the truck to a sudden stop, and Attika, Logan and the other man got out. The driver stepped on the gas and drove away just as Attika slammed her door shut.

"This way," said Attika. She ran toward a cluster of trees on the edge of a small grassy area. As they approached, a parked car flashed its lights twice. She veered toward the car, opened the back door and indicated for Logan and the other man to get in. Then she got in the front passenger seat.

Attika looked in the back seat and then at Lena, who was sitting behind the steering wheel. "I see we've picked up an unexpected guest," she said, nodding her head at Cap who was already in the back seat. "You weren't supposed to pick this one up."

"I'll vouch for him," said Lena, shooting Cap a warning look in the rearview mirror as she spoke. She put the car in gear and pulled away from the curb.

Attika looked at Cap as she spoke to Lena. "Okay, but he's your problem if this all goes to shit."

"Who are you people?" demanded Logan. "Where the hell are you taking us?"

Attika looked out the front windshield and replied, "Isn't it enough that you're not on your way to a detention center and months of interrogation, followed by a lifetime of working on a frontier development?"

"No, it's not enough. What's going on?" demanded Logan.

Attika turned and looked at the two young men sitting in the back seat. "You may not like it but you're going to have to trust me. We're trying to get you out of the Capitol District to somewhere safe. I know you have a million questions, but here is the main thing you need to focus on. You are fucked. And not just a little bit fucked. You're massively fucked. And you already know why. You asked questions you weren't supposed to ask, and you learned things you weren't supposed to know. It's as simple as that."

Logan scoffed and was about to reply when Lena suddenly slowed down and pulled over to the side of the road as an SPD patrol car came up from behind. It raced by, lights flashing but no siren. Lena checked that no more patrol cars were coming and proceeded down the road.

Attika watched as the flashing blue lights disappeared ahead of them and continued speaking. "Those guys in the patrol car are looking for you so they can take you to a detention center outside the wall. And I can guarantee you that it would be just the first stop on a long string of unpleasant destinations."

She turned her attention to Cap and said, "And although I wouldn't have invited you along, you're lucky you're here."

"I don't feel very lucky," replied Cap.

"Well, you are. Your association with Brandt would have been a permanent black mark on your record. You would have spent the rest of your life on the margins, an outsider looking in. No more piloting advanced fighters for you. Your future would have consisted of recurring surprise background checks, denied security clearances, and no advancement. By age forty, you'd have settled into a comfortable rut pushing a broom in some old garage and drinking cheap liquor."

"I see Lena has briefed you on me and Cap," said Logan. "That's what you say our future would have been if you hadn't intervened, and maybe you're right. But how are you going to help keep it from happening, and, more importantly, *why* are you going to help?"

Attika looked out the front window again and scanned for SPD vehicles as she responded. "Good questions, but I don't have any answers. I've got instructions to get you out at all costs. You can ask why later, if you make it out alive."

"Who gave you the instructions?" asked Cap.

Attika didn't respond.

Logan considered what Attika had said. He knew his reluctance to cooperate had put him on a collision course with the SPD. He hadn't intended to make trouble, but something in his brain just refused to happily go along with whatever the SPD demanded. This was not a new phenomenon. While growing up, his mother often chastised him for being willful and stubborn, often to his own detriment. She'd say despite all his "smarts" he had a few loose wires that needed fixing. Maybe she was right – maybe he had a fatal flaw that kept him from getting with the program. Cap recognized it too. He recalled what his friend had said in the café. What rational adult sabotages a promising career over some riddles and a plaster bust?

Logan looked at Cap, who was sitting next to him. He felt a pang of guilt at the thought of Cap not being able to live his dream of flying fighter jets. It's all he'd wanted to do since he was a kid. He'd suffered through four years of academy education just so he could get in the cockpit of a fast plane. Now it was all gone.

Logan's thoughts were interrupted by the sound of multiple sirens in the distance.

"They'll be putting up roadblocks at major intersections," Attika said to Lena. "Get off this street."

Lena turned off the wide boulevard and picked her way along a roughly parallel course on narrow side streets.

After a few minutes, Attika asked Lena, "Did you bring it?"

Lena nodded. "Just before they got there. It was close, but no one saw me."

Suddenly an SPD patrol car raced across the intersection in front of them, blue lights flashing. Lena hit the brakes. The patrol car honked its horn and swerved to avoid colliding with them.

"That was too close," said Lena. She exhaled and drove on, resisting the urge to speed.

After a few more minutes, they turned into a dark alley that ran between a series of three- and four-story brick buildings. Lena parked the car behind a large garbage bin and they all got out.

Speaking to the dark-haired man, Attika said, "I'll take it from here. Get out of sight and be careful."

The short but powerfully built man nodded. Then he gave Logan and Cap a warning look and held up a cautionary finger. "Don't get this woman killed or I'll come for you and cut your throats." He turned and jogged down the alley into the darkness.

Attika pounded on the metal door next to the garbage bin. Nothing happened. She pounded again. Still no response. She prepared to pound again when the door flew open. A short, fat, balding man peered out at them from the threshold.

"Stop making so much fuckin' noise and get in here!" he said. He looked up and down the alleyway as they filed passed him. Once inside, they waited for the man, who closed the door behind them and slid the heavy bolt into place.

"This way," he breathed as he squeezed his bulk past them.

They followed him until they reached a room that had probably been a kitchen at one time but was now some kind of workshop. They gathered around a table in the middle of the room.

"You didn't tell me the SPD would be on your ass," said the fat man in a voice equal parts anger and fear. Logan raised an eyebrow when the scent of alcohol reached his nose.

"Risks of the trade," responded Attika. "We'll need two more visas now, plus IDs. I'll pay triple the agreed price."

Attika looked at Lena, who was clearly surprised by what she had heard. The older woman said, "You too. It's time you got out."

The man placed both hands on top of his head and pulled his sparse greasy hair. "*Three* visas? *Three* fucking visas? It's hard enough to do one in the time you're giving me, but three? The IDs I can do, but not the visas. Not possible. Not fucking possible!"

Attika looked at her watch. "You've got forty-five minutes."

"No. I won't do it," said the man, folding his arms across his chest. "I'm not a magician. It can't be done, so you'd better get the hell out of here. Figure some other way to get out of the District."

"I thought you were the best," said Attika.

"I am," replied the man. "But there are limits. I'd have to cut a lot of corners to finish three IDs with visas in forty-five minutes. And that means the chances of these three zits being caught go up, way up. And how long do you think these pussy-ass pole suckers will stand up to SPD interrogation? About a nanosecond. Then it's bye-bye freedom, hello firing squad for yours truly."

Attika pulled a pistol out of her coat pocket and placed it on the table with the barrel pointed toward the man. "You will give me three visas and you will do it in forty-five minutes."

"Or what?" he asked. "You'll shoot me? You're not the shooting kind."

She stared into the man's eyes for a moment. "Don't cross me on this one. You're doing this job, even if I have to put a slug in your leg."

The forger looked at Attika and then at the gun. "All right. Fuck it, I'll do it. Under fucking protest, but I'll do it. But they're not going to get past a close check." He looked at the three young people. "Avoid visa officers, okay kiddies? Their scanners will pick these fakes out right away. Try to limit any inspections to visual only."

"Do your best," Attika said as she returned the gun to her pocket.

"Okay," said the forger as he clapped his hands together and rubbed them. "Which of you little shits is first?"

Chapter 25

Linsky slammed the phone down, his face red with rage. Brandt had been freed, Caparelli was missing, and the bust Chambers had gone to so much effort to smuggle out of the lab had not been located at the apartment.

A knot began to form in his stomach. He picked up the phone and dialed a number. "Komatsu, what's the status on the item?"

"I was just about to call you." Komatsu spoke in a quivering voice, "It's a fake. I don't know how it happened, but there's no doubt."

"Fake? Impossible!" insisted Linsky. "It's been locked in the containment field and kept in isolated suspension for years. No one could have touched it without setting off every alarm in the building."

"As I said, I don't know how it happened, but there's no escaping the truth," said Komatsu. "The Apollo Stone is gone."

"I want a full report of your findings within the hour. I'm sending Security Chief Kassick down to the lab. I want to know who did it, how it was done, and when!"

He hung up and immediately dialed a number. "This is Colonel Linsky. Instruct C-Comm to implement a full lockdown of the Capitol District until further notice. We are looking for two highly dangerous foreign agents. Logan Brandt and Michael Caparelli. I will transmit their details shortly. No one gets in or out of the city without explicit SPD approval."

He hung up and placed the phone on his desk. He stood and paced a few times across the room, angrily and loudly cursing Chambers and Brandt. After venting his anger somewhat, he stopped and looked at the phone. He had to make one more phone call before going to C-Comm to assume control of the search for the fugitives. He dialed a number. After a moment he said, "This is Colonel Linsky. Put me through to Guardian Bishop."

Chapter 26

The forger had gone into one of the side rooms to prepare the documents, cursing loudly and freely as he worked. Lena went out to the car and returned with the backpack from the banner race. She pulled the bust out and placed it in the middle of the table.

"How did you get the backpack out of the apartment?" asked Logan in a surprised voice.

"I took it after the SPD arrested you but before their search crew arrived," she responded.

"But how did you get into the apartment?" asked Cap. "You didn't know the code."

Lena looked at him, raised an eyebrow and said, "I'm resourceful."

Attika's PDD buzzed and she stepped into another room to answer the call.

"I don't get it," said Logan, looking at the bust. "What is so special about this thing?" He leaned in and carefully examined the bust's features. He looked for seams, unusual marks, hidden compartments, but there was nothing.

"I have an idea," said Cap. He disappeared into the shadows of the workshop and returned with a hammer. He handed it to Logan.

Logan looked at the hammer and said, "Time to cut the Gordian Knot?"

"I don't know what that means," said Cap. "But I think the bust is either a worthless piece of plaster or there's something inside. Worst-case scenario, you broke a fake present to your mom."

Logan shrugged and raised the hammer. "She never cared much for history anyway."

When Lena saw Logan lift the hammer she raised a cautionary hand and started to say something, but Logan ignored her. He swiftly brought the hammer down. Plaster chips flew in all directions. He repeated the action again and again, shooting large and small chips around the room. On the fifth blow, he hit something hard. He brushed away the dust and debris and saw bronze-colored metal.

Attika reentered the room with an alarmed expression on her face, still holding the phone to her ear. She watched Logan smash the bust. "Understood," she said into the phone then hung up. "What the hell's going on here?" she asked, but no one responded as they watched Logan continue to destroy the bust.

After a half dozen more blows, Logan had exposed the top half of a small metal sphere about the size of a tennis ball. He worked to break away the remaining material until the sphere was freed of its plaster prison. He picked up the metal object and held it close to the lightbulb hanging from the ceiling, slowly rotating it in the dim light.

"What is that?" asked Cap.

"I don't know," said Logan. "But my grandfather thought it was important enough to smuggle out of a top-secret laboratory."

"And don't forget Colonel Linsky is also interested in getting his hands on it," said Lena.

They heard a door in the hallway open. Logan quickly slipped the sphere into his coat pocket. A moment later, the forger appeared in the room carrying three documents in his hand. He laid them on the table.

Attika looked at each travel visa and ID. She raised her brow. "They'll probably do for a casual check," she said. "But they won't get past a scanner."

"I already told you that!" snapped the forger. "It's the best I could do in forty-five minutes."

Attika eyed the forger. He tried to return her stare, but was soon compelled to look away. She reached into her coat pocket and pulled out an envelope of cash and handed it to him.

"And a word of advice," she said to the forger as she and the others headed down the narrow passage toward the alley door. "Keep your head down. The shit has hit the fan. They'll be rounding up everyone they can think of, and I assume your name is on several lists."

"Thanks for the warning," said the forger sarcastically. "Let's never do business again."

The alley door slammed shut behind them. Logan heard the bolt slide into place. Attika took the car keys from Lena and told the others to get in. She started the engine and drove down the alley.

"Now where are we going?" asked Logan.

"We're going to try and get you out of the Capitol District. There's a train leaving for Pittsburgh in about twenty minutes."

"Why are we going to Pittsburgh?" asked Cap.

"You're not," responded Attika. "You're getting off at the first checkpoint, Frederick. From there, make your way to Point of Rocks, about fifty kilometers south of Frederick on the Potomac River. Stay there until you're met by a man."

"Until we're met by a man?" asked Cap. "What man? How will we know him?"

Attika navigated the car down a dark residential street. "You'll know he's your contact by a scar around his wrist."

After several minutes, they came to an intersection. Logan saw the train station a few blocks away.

"Good," said Attika. "The SPD is shutting everything down, but it looks like they haven't gotten here yet. Here's some money." She handed each one a buy card. "Buy round-trip tickets to avoid suspicion."

"But won't they trace the buy card record?" asked Cap.

"Yes, but we don't have an option because train tickets are not cash-approved items. These are blind cards, so they won't be able to trace them for a while."

She guided the car to a parking spot in the back of the station's parking lot. It was ten p.m. and there was very little foot traffic. She pointed at the dimly lit ticket booth across the parking lot. "Remember," she said. "Buy round-trip tickets."

Everyone got out of the car and started walking toward the ticket booth. Lena stopped and looked back at the car for a moment. She saw Attika's smiling face looking at her through the windshield. Lena returned the smile then turned toward the station.

The ticket booth stood next to the locked station gate. A weary-looking old woman behind a thick glass partition spoke through a microphone. "May I help you?"

Lena stepped closer. "One ticket to Pittsburgh."

"One way or round trip?"

"Round trip."

The woman opened a small slot under the protective glass and Lena pushed her buy card through it.

"Your ID and travel visa, please," said the woman in a flat tone.

Lena slid her documents through the opening. The woman examined each. She looked at the photo on the visa and then at Lena. She scratched the visa foil's surface with her thumbnail. Then she shrugged and handed it back to Lena. "Next."

Logan and Cap purchased their tickets in the same manner. Then, one by one, they inserted their tickets into a thin slot next to the gate. A scanner read the code embedded in each ticket and opened the gate, returning the ticket as it did so. The tall metal gate swung shut with a thud after each person passed through.

Once inside the station, they looked at the large screen on the wall showing train arrival and departure information. The train for Pittsburgh was scheduled to depart from track one in five minutes. It was the last train scheduled to leave that night. They boarded together, but to reduce the chances of being discovered they decided to sit in separate compartments.

Lena sat in the last car. Cap sat in the car in front of her, and Logan sat in the one immediately behind the big diesel engine. Logan was happy to see that the train was moderately full. He'd been concerned that they would be the only passengers on board, making them more conspicuous. He found a seat next to a window and slouched low. After five minutes, he looked at the large clock on the station wall. The train was supposed to have already left the station.

As the minutes ticked by, Logan grew increasingly impatient. He looked down the aisle toward the back of the train and wondered what was causing the delay. Then he looked out his window and felt a shot of adrenalin suddenly surge through his heart. An SPD patrol car had screeched to a halt in front of the station gate and three men got out. Just behind it was an SPD van containing two K-9 units, each consisting of a German Shepherd and two officers. The officers and their dogs trotted to the ticket window. The booth attendant opened the gate and they entered the station. One of the SPD officers instructed a K-9 unit to search the train's undercarriage while the other searched around the train station. He gave an order to the two remaining officers and pointed to the back of the train. They walked to the last car and boarded while he remained on the platform, pacing back and forth with an eye on the station gate.

Logan swore under his breath. Risking another look down the aisle, he could see movement several cars back. He saw Lena casually walking forward. She was looking at her ticket and the seat numbers as though she was searching for an assigned seat. Then Logan saw Cap stand up and follow her. Soon they were in his car and sitting in the seats across the aisle from him.

"They're doing a sweep, checking everyone's visa," said Cap in a hushed but terrified voice. "We're cooked."

Logan glanced out the window and saw the lead SPD officer still pacing. He periodically turned his head to look around the station.

"Well," Logan whispered. "We've run out of train to hide in and we can't get off without being spotted." Then he looked at Cap and Lena. "They're looking for two young men fitting my and Cap's descriptions, but they might not be looking for a young woman." Looking at Lena he said, "And I have noticed you have certain hidden qualities."

"Really," she said, a hint of curiosity in her voice.

A minute later the two SPD officers entered the railcar just behind the engine. They requested visas from the handful of passengers near the door through which they had entered. They carefully reviewed the documents, occasionally scanning the visas with a device that emitted a flashing red light. They arrived at the front of the railcar and opened the sliding door that led into the space between the railcar and the engine. The taller officer closed the sliding door and turned to see a woman exiting the bathroom. Though startled, he quickly regained his composure and said, "ID, travel visa, and ticket, please."

Lena retrieved the documents from her coat pocket and handed them to the officer. He gave them a cursory review and passed them to his partner, a stocky man with short thick fingers and no neck. The tall guard watched her with emotionless eyes while his partner closely reviewed the visa, exposing it to red scanner light.

Lena did her best to return the tall SPD officer's gaze even as she fought to calm her pounding heart. The second officer tapped the taller one on the arm and pointed to something in the corner of Lena's ID. The tall one looked at it for a moment then his eyes widened.

"Forgive us," said the tall one as he stood a little straighter. "We didn't expect to see a Special Investigator on the train. We're looking for two young men, aged twenty-one. One is big, about one point nine meters tall with curly brown hair. The other is average height with short blond hair." He showed Lena images of Logan and Cap on his PDD. "Have you seen them on the train?"

Lena accepted her documents back from the stocky officer. "No. I haven't seen them. Now how much longer will this take? I have urgent business in Pittsburgh."

"Just a few more minutes," said the tall guard.

They touched the visors of their hats and went on to search the engineering compartment. Moments later they joined the guard and the K-9 units standing on the platform. The lead SPD officer heard their reports. He turned and stood looking at the train for about ten seconds. As he considered his next move, the officer tapped the buckle of his pistol belt with his right thumb. Then he waved for the train engineer to pull out of the station.

In the parked car outside, Attika placed the pistol back in her pocket as she watched the train slowly emerge from the station. She started the car and drove away, periodically checking her rearview mirror.

Inside the train, Lena knocked on the restroom door. "All clear," she said. Cap and Logan unlocked the door and happily stepped out from the cramped space.

"We heard the whole thing," said Cap admiringly. "I don't know how you stayed so cool, but you did it. You saved our butts."

Logan smiled. "Like I said, you have hidden qualities."

"Piece of cake," said Lena with a smile, though her voice was a little shaky.

They returned to their separate seats, still wary of drawing unwanted attention to themselves. As the train passed through the District on its elevated tracks, Logan looked at the brightly illuminated monuments. The great dome of the Capitol building, Union Square with its towering statue of The People in Victory, the obelisk, and many other public works defied the night's darkness with daggers of white light. Yet, as the train got farther from the heart of the District, the city seemed to grow lifeless, empty. There were very few cars on the streets, mostly due to fuel restrictions. Public transportation was readily available and buses ran until midnight, but few people wanted to be out after ten-thirty when the restaurants, theaters, and bars were required to close their doors.

Soon, the train curved to the northeast, passing through residential neighborhoods of low cement apartment buildings and row upon row of small single-level homes. Then the train shot into a tunnel that passed through the Capitol District wall. When it emerged on the other side, Logan could see the searchlights of the safety towers on top of the barrier flashing back and forth both inside and outside the thick ten-meter-high wall. Within fifteen minutes of passing through the wall, the city lights were mere pinpricks in a black tapestry and the countryside a vast expanse of darkness.

With nothing to see through his window, Logan's mind began to drift. Not for the first time, he wondered what his grandfather had been working on that prompted him to steal the sphere, to commit treason. He thought about their last conversation, when he and his grandfather had met at Veterans Park. Logan knew then that his grandfather had changed. Gone was the strident supporter of expansion and reunification. That fire breather had been replaced by a sullen suspicious old man who spoke in vague terms about betrayals of trust and past sins in need of atonement. Logan had sensed then that his grandfather was on the brink of doing something unexpected. He was therefore not completely surprised when he received the medallion and the cryptic note instructing him to keep it safe.

Logan drifted off to sleep, but was soon awakened by the feeling that the train was slowing down. After a few seconds he was sure the train was gradually decelerating as it approached the Frederick checkpoint. He pulled out his visa and looked at it. He was unsure if it was good enough to pass the imminent inspection and took several long deep breaths to suppress a wave of anxiety that coursed through him. Lena's ID and visa had survived the SPD officer's inspection, but hers had the Special Investigator symbol on it. Logan wondered if the SPD officers had given her documents less scrutiny out of respect or perhaps fear.

Logan lurched forward as the engineer suddenly applied the brakes. The wheels screeched in protest but the conductor did not let up and soon the train came to a stop. Logan looked out the window, but he knew they were still far outside of the town of Frederick. The other passengers in his compartment looked around as well, curious about why they had stopped short of the train station. Logan looked back down the aisle and saw Lena and Cap standing in the railcar behind him. She waved for him to join them.

When he got there, Lena closed the doors separating the two railcars and said, "I don't like this. We're not supposed to stop here. I think something's wrong."

"Yeah," agreed Logan. "It doesn't feel right."

Cap looked through the window in the north-facing door and said, "Have a look at this."

The other two looked through the window and saw the headlights of several vehicles racing toward them.

"Damn it!" said Lena. "We have to get off this train." She stepped to the opposite side of the train and looked for a button or lever that would open the door on that side.

"You need a key to open it," said Cap. "Unless the engineer opens all of the doors, which he's not going to do."

Lena looked through the north-facing window again. The lights of the approaching vehicles grew brighter and brighter as they closed the distance to the train. Reaching into her jacket, she pulled the pistol from its holster and quickly screwed a silencer onto to the end.

"Cover your faces."

She pointed the barrel at the window of the south-facing door and blasted three holes through the thick glass. It didn't shatter, but the bullets caused it to crack into large pieces. Logan grabbed a fire extinguisher near the restroom door and smashed the cracked window, forcing the pieces out of the frame. He ran the extinguisher along the window seal to knock out any remaining shards of glass. Cap removed his jacket and laid it across the bottom of the frame to protect them as they climbed though the opening.

Lena took one last look out the north-facing window as she removed the silencer and holstered the gun. There were four vehicles pulling up to the side of the track.

"Let's go!" she said.

Cap was the last one through the opening. When he landed on the ground, he retrieved his jacket and joined the other two, who had quickly disappeared into the darkness. He found them crouched low behind some bushes about fifty meters south of the train. Looking back, they could see men with flashlights searching the area.

"It won't take them long to find the broken window," said Logan. "We've got to move." He started running. The others leapt up to follow.

"Where to?" asked Cap as they jogged through the uneven terrain.

"Point of Rocks, remember?" said Lena. "It's about fifteen klicks south of here."

"Fifteen klicks?" Cap said, irritated. "Are we supposed to run the whole way?"

"If necessary," replied Lena.

"Remember your training, cadet," said Logan over his shoulder. "Adapt and overcome. Adapt and overcome."

"Is that what they were saying?" asked Cap. "They always told me *Shut up and get it done! Shut up and get it done.* Followed by *drop and give me twenty!*"

"Some cadets require more encouragement than others," said Lena as she jumped over a half-buried boulder.

Behind them, they could hear the sound of shouting voices. Two vehicles drove over the train tracks and headed into the darkness after them. A spotlight shone on the ground to their right. They could hear powerful engines revving as the vehicles climbed over hills and rocks. Moments later, the light swept across the ground in front of them.

"It's just a matter of time before they spot us. We have to get out of this open country," said Logan as he increased the pace.

"There!" said Cap. "See those houses? See the light?"

"They'll search there," said Lena.

"Yes, but it looks like there's a ravine before the road. That'll slow them down. We'll hide in the woods behind the houses."

It was their only option, so Logan veered toward the houses. They reached the ravine and splashed through the knee-deep water. They scrambled up the bank on the other side and pulled themselves over the retaining wall and onto the road.

The houses were all dark. The light they had seen was coming from a fire burning behind the middle one. They sprinted across the road. Logan stopped near the corner of the house farthest to the left and peered around the corner. Three men with long hair and thick beards warmed themselves at the fire. Two women sat across from them. There were several rough-looking backpacks stacked in a line near a tree at the edge of the firelight.

Logan eased back from the house's edge and whispered to the others. "Three men. Two women. Looks like they're passing through and stopped here for the night."

They all turned at the sound of a revving truck engine near the ravine. The group around the campfire heard it, too. They sat stone silent, heads cocked, and listened for more noise. Then came the sound of slamming doors and shouting voices. One of the bearded men got to his feet and kicked dirt onto the fire. Within seconds, the fire was out and darkness descended. Logan saw the outlines of the five people quickly put on their large packs and run for the trees. Behind him, the sound of voices grew louder as men climbed up the ravine and onto the road.

Logan, Cap, and Lena ran toward the break in the trees into which the five backpacks had disappeared. In seconds, they were inside the dark forest, barely able to see. Logan was able to make out the faint line of a trail in front of them, which he followed as quickly as he dared. Cap and Lena were right behind him.

Spurred on by the clanking sound of loose items on one of the backpacks ahead of them, Logan trotted along the trail, occasionally stumbling on a root or rock, but never slackening the pace. The clanking sound seemed to be getting farther away. Assuming the backpackers knew the best escape route, Logan increased his speed in order to keep up with them.

Suddenly, three dark figures leapt out from behind some trees on their left and crashed into them. The attackers carried long sticks and used them to push Logan, Cap, and Lena off of the trail and down a hill on the right side. They rolled for a few meters before coming to a stop. Logan fought to get up, but one of the figures struck him in the head with a staff, knocking him back down. Logan looked up to see a man with a thick black beard standing over him. He held the tip of his walking staff above Logan's head, ready to strike.

Logan held up his hands. "Wait, wait," he said. "We're just trying to get away from those men."

"I can see that," said the man with a slight twang in his voice. "And that's exactly why you need to get the hell off this trail and strike out a different way. We don't want no trouble with them Red Legs, and I'd sooner smash in your skull and let them find your body than have you leading them to us." He raised the staff and made some quick jabbing motions toward Logan's face.

Logan turned his head and saw Lena and Cap were also on their backs, a man standing over each of them. One of the men was pointing what appeared to be an old revolver at Cap. The other had a thick staff ready to strike Lena. Logan looked at Lena and their eyes locked. She made a slight gesture with her right index finger. He saw the pummel of her gun in its holster under her jacket. He shook his head slightly.

A light clanking sound drew Logan's attention up the trail. He saw a woman approaching.

"Stop talking like that, Hugh," she said to the man standing over Logan. "If the Red Legs is after these young folks then we should help 'em. That's the Traveler Code."

"They ain't Travelers," replied Hugh, disdain in his voice. "Look at their clothes, Claire. No food, no packs, no boots."

Claire cut him off. "The Traveler Code ain't just for Travelers. It's for everyone. Now let them up, and if they mean no harm then they can travel in peace." She reached to the side of her pack and tucked a loose metal cup hanging from a string into a pocket.

The man named Hugh paused for a moment. Then he lowered his staff and took a step back. "Search 'em," he said to the other woman who was half hiding behind a tree. She came forward and quickly went through their pockets. She found their documents and train tickets. She also found Lena's gun and the metal sphere, but she missed the medallion inside Logan's pocket.

Hugh looked at the pistol and silencer. "Well, well. This is a fancy rig. I think I'll hold on to it for a while." He grinned at Lena and tucked the gun into his belt. "And what the hell is this thing?" he asked, holding the bronze-colored sphere in front of him. "A little cannon ball?"

He looked at Logan, who said nothing.

Hugh squinted one eye shut and said, "So yer the silent type. Maybe I'll hold on to this for a while, too."

They heard voices from the direction they had come and saw flashlights illuminate the trees. "Come on," said Hugh. "Let's git."

He darted up the hill and ran down the trail. Two of the Travelers followed, but not Claire or the man with the revolver. Claire looked at the young people's faces and said, "We need to git movin'. They found the trail entrance and will be on us before you can spit."

She turned and ran after Hugh and the others. The man with the revolver signaled for the three of them to stand up and follow the group. They complied and soon caught up with Claire.

They all trotted down the trail as quickly and silently as possible, but their unburdened pursuers were gaining ground. They came to a fork and Hugh veered to the right down a gentle slope. The group followed him down the trail, winding their way between trees and bushes. Logan had no idea how many pursuers were behind them, but he hoped that at least a few of them would take the wrong turn on the trail.

As he ducked under a tree branch, Logan recalled Hugh's description of their pursuers. *Red Legs.* He must have meant Republican Special Forces, an elite fighting force within the Republican Guard whose field uniforms included burgundy-colored leggings. But it couldn't be RSF because they were prohibited by law from operating anywhere inside the nation's borders. They were strictly for border protection and special operations in foreign conflicts.

His thoughts were interrupted when he saw Claire trip over a root. She stumbled a couple of steps and struggled to regain her balance, but her heavy backpack caused her to lurch out of control toward the right. She crashed to the ground and slid to a stop five meters down the hill.

Logan immediately ran down the slope to help her get to her feet. Cap was close behind. The man with the revolver, who was the last in the group, stopped and quickly assessed the situation. Then he stepped behind a tree and pointed his weapon back along the trail in the direction they had come from.

Hugh trotted back to the group and looked at Claire as she climbed back up to the trail, Logan and Cap assisting on either side. Hugh's eyes filled with panic. He looked at his companion with the revolver, then got behind a large tree trunk. He stared grim-faced up the trail, Lena's pistol at the ready.

When they were all back on the trail, Logan heard a voice call out from higher up the trail. "This way!"

Flashlights illuminated the trees around the little group. The man with the revolver was preparing to fire a shot at one of the lights, but Logan placed his hand on the man's arm and gently pulled the weapon down.

Logan turned and whispered to everyone. "You folks aren't going to die tonight. They're after us and if we give ourselves up, they'll leave you alone. But only if you give me back that sphere. They want that more than anything else."

The Travelers looked at each other. Hugh nodded and handed Logan the sphere, which he slipped into his coat pocket. Then he offered Lena her pistol.

Lena shook her head. "Keep it. You might need it sometime."

Hugh leaned toward her and said in a low voice, "Red Legs kill Travelers." He held the gun out again for her to take it.

"No," said Logan. "We'd never win a shootout. And they want to capture us alive."

"Maybe," said Hugh. "But what happens after that?"

Not waiting for a response, Hugh turned and said in a low voice to the other Travelers, "Let's go."

Claire hesitated and looked at the three young people.

"*Claire.*" Hugh gripped her by the arm and pulled her away.

The Red Legs came around a bend in the trail just as the Travelers disappeared behind a large boulder.

"Hands where I can see them," barked a man in a camouflage uniform holding an urban combat version of the M-35 assault gun.

Logan, Cap and Lena raised their hands above their heads. "Now get down on the ground. Face down." The three of them complied with the command.

Three more Red Leg soldiers arrived, weapons drawn. "Secure their hands," said one of the Red Legs. Logan looked up from the ground and saw the soldier was a sergeant in the Republican Special Forces.

One of the soldiers knelt down and placed his knee between Logan's shoulder blades. He pulled Logan's hands behind his back and bound them with a plastic cord. He repeated the process with Cap and Lena.

"Private Sands," said the Red Leg sergeant as he looked down the trail at the boulder. "Take a look down there and make sure it's clear."

The Red Leg private dashed down the trail until he reached the boulder. He peered around it. Then he raised his M-35 and fired three quick bursts.

After a few moments, the sergeant called for him to return.

"Hit anything?"

"Maybe," said the private. "Thought I saw some Travelers. They won't bother us."

They searched all three prisoners and discovered the sphere in Logan's coat pocket and the medallion in another pocket. The sergeant looked at the sphere with mild curiosity, then put it in the thigh pocket of his camo pants. He put the medallion in a breast pocket. They pulled the three prisoners to their feet and marched them back up the trail toward the road. The sergeant and Private Sands were in the lead, followed by Logan, Cap, and Lena. The two remaining soldiers were behind Lena.

Walking behind the sergeant, Logan could see his battle pack had seen a lot of use. There were scrapes and gashes near the opening of the slot into which the M34 was tucked. Its stock pointed out the bottom of the pack, allowing the soldier to reach back and pull it out with ease. A sword handle extended from the top of the pack behind the sergeant's right shoulder.

"Private Sands, take point. Twenty meters up," said the sergeant.

"Yes, sergeant," said the soldier in front. He trotted ahead, using his flashlight to scan the surrounding trees.

"Where are you taking us, Sergeant Red Legs?" asked Cap.

"Where I'm told to take you," replied the sergeant.

"Alive, I hope," said Cap.

"If possible, but my orders are a little vague on the subject."

Lena cleared her throat. "Shouldn't you be at the border? I mean, it's strange that the RSF was mobilized to chase us down. Usually a job for the SPD, isn't it?"

The sergeant said nothing.

"Must have been a nuisance when the order came to hunt for a few runaways," she continued. "You were probably done for the day, relaxing, drinking a beer."

"Private Miller," said the sergeant.

"Yes, Sergeant Lezad," answered the soldier behind Lena.

"Instruct the prisoner to remain quiet. If the prisoner speaks again you have permission to silence her."

The soldier said, "Yes, sergeant." He struck Lena in the back of her head with the butt of his M-35 and yelled, "The prisoner will remain quiet!"

The unexpected blow caused Lena to stumble forward a few steps and crash into Cap's back, but she managed to stay on her feet.

"Is that standard RSF training?" asked Logan, his throat tight with anger.

The sergeant stopped in his tracks. He turned and stood toe to toe with Logan. "Listen up, prisoner. Your mama clearly nursed you too long, so allow me to explain how shit works."

He gave Logan a swift punch in the solar plexus, knocking the wind out of his lungs and causing him to double over. Logan dropped to one knee and gasped for breath.

Lezad put his hands on his hips and addressed all three prisoners. "Now, I am being exceedingly patient with you because I need you three to be in good enough condition to walk out of these woods. However, your behavior will determine how well you will be treated when we have reached our vehicle. You are enemies of the Republic. You've got no rights and I can do whatever the hell I want to you. Remember that."

He nudged Logan with his boot. "Get to your feet, Nancy."

As Logan stood up, Lezad said, "I believe I've made myself clear on this subject. Now let's move."

They walked in silence for another ten minutes until they emerged from the tree line behind the abandoned homes and still-smoldering fire pit. "Private Sands, why haven't you started the MPV?" asked Lezad in a tired voice.

Private Sands, who was seated behind the wheel of an armored vehicle, leaned out the open door and yelled, "Won't start, sergeant."

"Shit," said Lezad. "Private Sands, radio for backup, then get up on the 50 cal. Keep an eye out for Travelers. Lee and Miller, keep an eye on these three pieces of shit."

The sergeant walked to the MPV and unlatched the heavy clasps holding down the hood. He lifted the hood and propped it open. Using his flashlight, he examined the engine. After a moment he saw the problem; the fuel pump relay was disconnected. He reattached it and closed the hood. Then he walked to the driver's seat and hit the ignition button. The MPV started with a deep rumbling sound.

Lezad turned toward the tree line and slowly scanned it for threats. Then he said, "Private Miller, load the prisoners."

Just as he finished speaking, he heard a whistling sound as something flew out of the woods and over his head. It hit something with a dull thud. He turned to see Private Sands gripping an arrow protruding from his chest. Sands struggled to remove it for a moment, then slumped forward over the 50 caliber gun. A second arrow hit Private Lee's thigh. He dropped to the ground screaming.

"*Shields!*" yelled Sergeant Lezad as he pressed a button on his bracer to activate his antiballistic shield. Miller did the same and ran to the side of the MPV, dropping to one knee and pointing his weapon toward the trees.

Caught between the Red Legs and whoever was firing the arrows from the trees, Logan, Lena and Cap dropped to the ground and lay flat.

"They're using arrows," said Lezad. "Set your shields high. It'll slow your reaction time, but at least you won't have a stick in your guts."

"Yes, Sergeant," said Miller.

Another arrow flew out of the woods and struck Lezad in the ribs. He felt a slight pressure at the point of impact, but the arrow failed to penetrate the soldier's shield. With an effort, he raised his M-35 and fired a burst into the trees where he thought the arrow had come from.

"Miller, get on the 50-cal and light these woods up!"

Before Private Miller could comply with the order, a dark figure in a long black coat emerged from the shadows of the forest, a sword in one hand and a long dagger in the other. Both soldiers opened fire on the figure, but the slugs were deflected. Seeing the occasional light shimmering of their opponent's shield as each bullet struck, Lezad dropped his M-35 and reduced his shield's rigidity back to its normal setting. Miller followed his example.

"Well fuck me with electricity," said Lezad. "A Traveler with a sword and shield. What dead soldier did you pull those off of?"

The sergeant slipped his M-35 into its slot in his battle pack. Then he reached his right hand over his shoulder and drew his sword. He swung the blade in front of him a few times then pointed a taunting finger at the stranger. He snapped his left hand and a guard emerged from the bracer, its thin metal plates quickly locking into place around his forearm and top of his hand.

Still lying on the ground, Logan turned his head toward the woods. The man in the long black coat slowly approached the Red Leg soldiers, passing by Logan and the others without looking at them. From his position on the ground, Logan could not see the man's face very well, but he seemed to be grinning, like a wolf approaching easy prey.

Logan looked back at the two Red Legs still standing. The sergeant seemed to have decided that the stranger was more formidable than he had first thought. He approached with a veteran's recognition of potential danger. By contrast, Miller was a little unnerved by the stranger's demeanor and bounced his sword up and down as he walked forward.

When they were within a few steps from each other, the stranger made a feint toward Lezad, then turned toward Miller and swung his sword. Miller blocked the attack with his blade, but he was too slow to block the man's dagger, which sliced his sword arm below the shoulder.

Miller cried out and fell back just as Lezad attacked with a series of rapid strikes, which the stranger parried while retreating. The two men paused, each assessing the other's ability. The stranger took a step forward and thrust with his sword. The sergeant deflected the blade, but the stranger's attack was followed by another and another. He kept attacking using quick slices and thrusts, never slowing down, never giving Lezad a chance to counterattack. Finally, the stranger's sword hit its mark, slicing Lezad's leg, causing him to collapse to the ground.

As Lezad was falling, Miller attacked from behind with his sword upraised. The stranger blocked the downward stroke with his dagger and slammed the pummel of his sword into Miller's face, causing him to fall backward to the ground. The stranger took two steps toward the stunned private and slammed his boot into his head, knocking him unconscious.

The stranger then turned to face Lezad, who had gotten to his feet but was not putting much weight on his wounded leg. The stranger held out his sword, pointing the tip at Lezad's eyes, and slowly advanced.

"I won't surrender," said Lezad defiantly.

"No one's asking you to," replied the stranger.

Lezad struck the stranger's extended blade to the side and lunged for his stomach, but the stranger blocked the attack with his sword. Stepping to his left, he drove his dagger deep into Lezad's side between his ribs. Lezad attempted a final swing at the stranger but fell to the ground instead. He coughed up some blood then was silent.

The stranger walked toward the three prisoners, who had gotten to their feet. They backed away, uncertain of what would happen next. He reached out and caught Lena's arm. Then he cut her restraints. He did the same for Logan and Cap.

"Leave the battle packs but get the weapons, including swords and bracers," said the stranger. "You'll probably need them."

"Who are you?" asked Logan.

"You can call me Kane," said the man as he retrieved a small compound bow and a quiver of arrows from behind a tree. "Now let's get going. And don't forget the sergeant has a few things of yours in his pockets."

Logan looked at the other two and then at Kane as he walked away. "Where are we going?"

"Point of Rocks for starters," said Kane as he climbed into the MPV's driver seat.

Logan, Lena and Cap looked at Kane. Cap whispered, "How do we know this is the guy Attika said we were supposed to meet?"

"Attika said he would have a scar around his wrist." said Lena. She was about to say something to Kane when Cap cut her off.

"Lena, who are these people we're mixed up with?" he asked. "I'm here to help Logan, but I'm not here to kill Republican Special Forces soldiers. I'm not a traitor."

Lena took a step forward and looked Cap in the eye. "What if helping Logan makes you a traitor? What if they're the same thing? You made your choice when I got you out of that SPD patrol car. I said you'd be on the run." She poked a finger in his chest. "Well, now we're on the run. This is what it's like."

Cap stepped back and held up his hands. "Easy, easy," he said. "All I know is my world has gone to shit. One day I'm on track to be a fighter pilot. The next day I'm running for my life because Logan didn't want to cooperate with the SPD."

He looked at Logan. "Don't get me wrong. I'm with you one hundred percent. I just want to know why we're doing this. If it's worth the risk."

Logan waited a moment before replying. Then he said, "I want to know too. Each of us has a lot of questions that need answers. But for now, we need to focus on staying alive."

Cap looked into the distance, thinking about what Logan and Lena had said. Then he looked at Logan. "I had a lot of shitty foster parents growing up," he said. "You know that, Logan. But Mrs. B was a good woman. I got lucky when I landed in her house down the block from you and your mom. She put up with a lot of crap from me. And I guess I didn't listen to her as often as I should have. But one thing she used to say has always stuck with me. *You pays your money and you takes your chances.*"

Cap's voice broke when he recalled the words, though he smiled. "I never understood what she meant, but now I think I do. You don't know what will happen in life, but you've got to decide what you stand for and put your money down. Decide and then live with it."

Cap looked at Logan and then Lena. After a few heartbeats, he said, "I'm in. For whatever's coming, I'm in. But we have to stick together. Us first, always. We have to agree to that."

"Agreed," said Logan. "We stick together."

Cap looked at Lena. "Agreed?"

"Agreed," she said, nodding her head and smiling.

Logan walked to Sergeant Lezad's body to retrieve the sphere and medallion. He pulled the sphere out of the side pocket of the soldier's camo fatigues. Then he searched his breast pockets for the medallion. He pulled open the Velcro flaps and probed with this fingers. As he searched, Lezad's dead eyes seem to stare right into Logan's. Logan looked away but kept searching until he found the medallion and pulled it out. He stood and joined the others at the MPV. Kane had gotten out and was leaning against the grill, arms folded.

"You children have a nice chat?" asked Kane when Logan arrived.

Logan looked at Kane for a moment, taking in the man's features. Logan guessed he was in his mid-thirties, but his weather-worn face and a few strands of gray hair mixed in with the thick tangled black made him seem older. He was a little shorter than Logan, and though he wasn't powerfully built, Logan knew from watching him defeat the Red Legs that he was strong and athletic.

"Show us your wrist," said Logan. Cap and Lena, who were on either side of Logan, each took a step forward.

A hint of a smile touched Kane's lips. He raised his right arm and pulled his coat sleeve up to reveal a thick scar around his wrist. He held his hand high for everyone to see.

"Now that I've established my bona fides," said Kane to Logan, "you can help me get this body out of the truck. One of you other two children needs to tie up those two soldiers. Or finish them off."

No one spoke for a moment, uncertain how to respond. Then Cap said, "I'll tie them up." He shot Lena a concerned look.

"Good. Here's some rope. Don't forget their feet. Don't want them hoppin' up and runnin' back home."

Cap caught the rope Kane threw at him and walked to the two soldiers. Miller was still unconscious. Lee was awake, but the pain caused by the arrow embedded deep in his leg had nearly knocked him out. Cap checked their wounds to make sure they were not bleeding too severely and dragged them behind the nearest house. Cap tied their hands and feet and returned to the MPV. As soon as Cap was in the vehicle, Kane gunned the engine and headed south down the road.

"Don't you think we're a little conspicuous driving in a Special Forces multi-purpose vehicle?" asked Logan. "It won't be long before someone sees us."

"Would you prefer we left it on the side of the road?" asked Kane. "We'll hide it in Point of Rocks. It's just a few klicks south of here."

"And the tracking system?" asked Lena. "They'll find us pretty fast once they know we have this MPV."

Kane reached between the driver and passenger seats and pulled up a small black box with four severed wires coming out one end. "I think we'll be okay." He dropped the box and said, "I'm more worried about high-altitude recon, but we've got friends jamming their signals, at least for a few hours."

After a few minutes Lena asked, "How did you know where to find us?"

"Word travels fast," he responded. "They've mobilized everyone in uniform across all agencies, so communications weren't coded. Wasn't hard to figure out where you were from all the chatter."

A few minutes later, Kane turned off the main road and drove down a narrow dirt lane. Soon they reached a cluster of houses. Solitary flickering lights shone through a few windows but as the MPV approached, they went black. Kane pulled up to an empty garage and parked the vehicle inside. They got out and he swung the wooden garage doors shut.

"Let's walk," he said.

Kane led them farther down the dirt road past the little houses of Point of Rocks to a barn about half a kilometer away. He pulled open the large half-rotted door and led them inside. Inside the barn there were a dozen or so empty wooden stalls and some badly rusted farm equipment in the far corner. Half of the hayloft had collapsed to the ground, and Logan could see a few large holes in the roof.

"What, no horses?" asked Cap with a grin.

"Not unless you're hiding one somewhere," replied Kane as he entered one of the empty stalls. He returned with a pack on his back. He had slid his sword and dagger between two straps on the side of the pack.

"Go get your packs," he said.

They looked in the empty horse stall and saw three packs. Each person picked one and slid their swords under straps on the sides.

"Where are we headed?" asked Logan as he adjusted the shoulder straps on his pack.

"Deep Pool. It's about seventy-five klicks northwest of here on the Potomac. We'll walk by night using Traveler trails. We've got about five more hours of darkness left, so let's make the best of it." Kane started walking. Lena fell in behind him, followed by Cap and Logan.

"What's in Deep Pool?" asked Lena.

"Not what, who," replied Kane. "We're meeting someone."

"Okay then, who?" she said.

"A man named Ravenwood."

"Why are we meeting him?" asked Logan.

Kane didn't respond. He held his hand up and listened. Logan thought he heard the revving of a distant engine, but he couldn't be sure.

Kane motioned for them to follow. They quickly crossed a grassy field behind the cluster of houses that made up Point of Rocks and soon came to a line of trees. Kane led them through a dense growth of brush and thorns. They struggled through the thicket for about twenty steps until they found a narrow path. Kane turned to his right and walked up the trail with the others in tow.

"Not much of a trail," observed Cap as he pushed aside yet another low-hanging tree branch.

"It's a deer trail," said Kane. "They crisscross these forests. Travelers use them to move unseen by SPD visa patrols. But don't worry, the trails up ahead will be broader and easier on your tender feet."

"Just keep walking," said Cap, annoyed. "Don't worry about us. We'll be right behind you."

"Sure thing, tenderfoot," said Kane.

"A minute ago, you mentioned someone named Ravenwood," said Logan. "Who's that?"

"Hard to say exactly who Ravenwood is," replied Kane. "I suppose he's a kind of emissary. He travels from place to place, city to city, talking to people, trying to prepare everyone."

"Prepare for what?" asked Lena.

"For war," said Kane.

"Because of the trouble on the frontier?" asked Cap. "Is the People's Republic making a move to get the clans under control?"

Kane scoffed. "Those so-called clans are just unfortunate folks who happened to be living between the Alleghenies and the Ohio River Basin when the PRA decided to push its borders west. That was fifteen years ago, and they've been trying to get rid of you ever since."

"That's not how the story is told where we come from," said Logan. "If you ask anyone in the PRA they'll tell you those areas had been part of the PRA when Malcom Weller was in charge. After his death, the clans infiltrated the population and encouraged the people to rebel. Those lands were simply being reincorporated into the PRA when the Guardians initiated the Rededication."

"That's a nice story. Now they're all back in the loving embrace of Guardian Harken, right? One happy family," said Kane. "And you can add the people of Chicago and Detroit to Harken's list of reluctant fellow citizens. Now he wants to reach across the Mississippi."

"That doesn't make sense," objected Cap. "I understand why Harken wants to reunite the land east of the Mississippi. But why cross the river? Why invade the Waste? There's nothing there worth having."

"Grand Guardian Harken wants to reunify the entire former U.S.," said Kane. "Isn't that the point of the Rededication?"

"The Rededication is his excuse to maintain a tight grip on the country," said Lena with a bitterness in her voice Logan had never heard before. "It's a control mechanism. People will put up with a lot of abuse as long as they feel they're part of a grand vision, one that gives them hope. And visions don't get more grand than reclaiming the glory and territory of a past great power."

Kane held up his hand. They all stopped and listened. Logan heard the sound of distant engines for a few moments. Then all was silent.

"They're at Point of Rocks," said Kane. "We have to pick up the pace. Stay close." He turned and walked swiftly along the barely visible deer trail. With his long legs, Logan was able to maintain the pace, but Lena and Cap had to occasionally break into a trot to keep up. After they had walked twenty minutes, Logan reached his hand into his coat's inner breast pocket to feel the sphere's cold metal, making sure it was still there. It was already costing people their lives. How many more, he wondered, and would his or his friends be among the tally?

"How did you know the Red Leg sergeant had the sphere?" he asked Kane.

"Because I watched him take it from you," replied Kane in a matter-of-fact tone.

Logan thought for a moment about the sergeant's accusing dead-eye stare. It reminded him of the fearful gaze of the SPD officer from whom Logan had retrieved the medallion a few hours earlier.

"Do you know what the sphere is?" asked Logan.

"I know what it might be," answered Kane.

"What might it be?"

"I have my suspicions, but Ravenwood will know more. He usually does."

"What if he's not in Deep Pool?" asked Lena. "What if there are SPD or Red Leg patrols and it's not safe for him to stay there?"

"Then we will press on," answered Kane.

"To where?" asked Cap.

"Across the Mississippi to the League of Free Cities."

Cap scoffed. "I still don't see how running away to a handful of squabbling, ruined cities, each one surrounded by kilometers of useless desert, is supposed to help us."

"Unfortunately for you three, it's your only option," said Kane. "But that's enough talk for now. Your Red Leg friends are on our heels, so keep your mouths shut and your ears open."

Except for the occasional curse from Cap as he swatted away a tree branch or mosquito, they walked in silence. Kane led them through a network of hardly visibly trails, but always northwest toward Deep Pool. From time to time there was a break in the trees, and they could see they were walking along a line of bluffs overlooking the Potomac River. The moon was half full and it illuminated much of the river valley below as well as the forest on the opposite side of the channel.

After an hour and a half of walking, they took a brief rest and drank some water from the canteens attached to the sides of their packs. Kane said he estimated they would arrive in Deep Pool the following evening, but they had to keep up a good pace.

A few minutes later, they stood and put on their packs. They'd walked a hundred meters when they were surprised by the thunder of a helicopter passing low over their heads, its searchlight flashing through the forest. They instinctively ducked and watched it as it flew down to the river valley, where it swung south, periodically hovering to thoroughly search a spot. Then it disappeared.

"You three are popular," observed Kane. "We were lucky they didn't see us with their night vision equipment."

"Are we going to make it to Deep Pool?" asked Lena. "I mean, what are our chances if they've got helicopters looking for us? The infrared cameras will spot us eventually. And what about high-altitude surveillance?"

"Friends are jamming their drones' signals, at least for a few more hours, but helicopters are a problem. Everyone, look in your pack for a sheet of green camouflage material," said Kane.

They did as he asked. Logan pulled out a rolled up metallic-feeling sheet.

"Keep it handy," said Kane. "If a helicopter comes near, get underneath it. It'll keep them from detecting you."

Logan partially unrolled the camouflage colored material and inspected it suspiciously. It was some kind of reflective material, no doubt. But it was very thin and looked like it would rip easily. He tested an edge, but he could not tear it. He folded and unfolded it and saw that it did not wrinkle or crease.

Kane looked at each of their faces and said, "We'll be fine if we're careful. But if they've got helicopters in the air, you can bet they've got plenty of troops on the ground, too. Best get moving. And keep it quiet."

Chapter 27

"Wake up, Mr. Schaefer."

Colonel Linsky prodded the corpulent naked man in the stomach with a standard-issue SPD nightstick, causing the man's body to gently swing back and forth. Linsky repeated himself, this time a little louder and with more encouragement from the nightstick, but there was no reaction.

"Water," said Linsky, nodding to a large bald man dressed in brown work trousers, brown boots, and a black t-shirt, which fit tightly around his muscular torso and arms.

The man reached down and removed two metal prongs from a bucket filled with water. The prongs were connected by insulated cables to a large black battery next to the bucket. He picked up the bucket and threw the water over the hanging man's head.

Dripping wet, Ronnie Schaefer slowly opened his right eye and tried to focus on his surroundings. The left eye was too swollen to open.

"Mr. Schaefer. Please wake up. This is no time to rest. We still need your assistance with our investigation," said Linsky.

A low moan arose from deep in Schaefer's throat. He twisted his bloody hands in the manacles, but they were fastened too tightly for him to get free. His toes nearly touched the ground, but the thick chain through which his handcuffs where strung kept him suspended from a hook in the cement ceiling.

"Mr. Schaefer," continued Linsky. "You were just saying how you had provided one of the insurgents with a Special Investigator's code and seal. What prompted you to do that? What are they planning to do that required one of them to be an S.I.?"

A string of bloody drool flowed from Schaefer's lower lip. "No time," he whispered. "No time."

"No time for what?"

Schaefer closed his eye and began to softly weep.

Colonel Linsky put his face close to Schaefer's and said in a loud voice, "You're not making sense, Mr. Schaefer. Stop crying and answer the question!"

Schaefer closed his right eye and tried to look away.

"We still need your help, Mr. Schaefer."

But the forger didn't respond.

"Speak!" After a moment, Linsky pointed at the battery and said, "Again."

The muscular man in the t-shirt filled the bucket with water from a nearby faucet and dipped the prongs into the bucket. After donning rubber gloves, he flipped a switch on the battery, lifted the prongs, and pressed them against Schaefer's naked back.

Schaefer convulsed as he screamed in pain.

"Why the S.I. code and seal?" screamed Linsky. "Tell me their plans!"

Schaefer whimpered. "No time for strip. No time."

Linsky said, "You had no time for the coded strip so you gave one of them the S.I. code to help them bluff their way past inspectors?"

Schaefer nodded his head almost imperceptibly.

"Tell me, Mr. Schaefer," insisted Linsky. "You must say it! Say why you created the false S.I. document!"

Schaefer drifted back into unconsciousness. Linsky repeated the demand but did not receive an answer. He smashed the nightstick into Schaefer's ribs, cracking several of them.

"Schafer!" He hit his ribs again. "Speak, you fat pig!"

No response.

Linsky looked at the muscular man and said, "Lower him. Give him thirty minutes rest and then wake him. Continue the line of questioning about their destination and intentions. And keep pressing on the S.I. code. We need to know their plans."

The man said, "Yes sir," and waved to the large mirror located on a nearby wall. Another man quickly entered the room and assisted him with moving the prisoner.

Colonel Linsky reached into his front pocket and removed a white handkerchief and wiped the sweat from his forehead. He looked at the damp cloth and returned it to his pocket. He watched for a moment as two men lifted the forger and uncuffed his hands. The wet, battered body collapsed to the floor with a thud.

Linsky looked with disgust at the unconscious man on the floor. He shook his head and exited the room. He walked down the dimly lit corridor lined with metal doors, each containing a small window near the top, until he reached a door at the end. He rapped his knuckles on the door and turned his face to the camera above. The door buzzed and he walked through. Linsky brushed passed an SPD guard without acknowledging him and hit the button to call the elevator. When it arrived, he swiped his identification card through the reader and entered a code into the keypad. The elevator doors closed and he pressed the button for the fifth floor of the detention center. Two minutes later, he was sitting at his office desk drinking a cold glass of water.

He set the glass down and dialed a number into his phone. He sat up straight. After a moment, he said, "Guardian Bishop. This is Colonel Linsky, sir."

"Well, what have you discovered?" asked Guardian Bishop.

"The forger made three visas, sir. One of them was a Special Investigator visa. We…"

Guardian Bishop interrupted him. "Why did they need an S.I. visa?"

"As I was about to say, we have no indication the S.I. visa was intended for any particular purpose. The forger had limited time, so we believe he used the S.I. code and seal in order to give the bearer the appearance of authority."

"And therefore receive only a cursory review," said Bishop, finishing Linsky's thought. "If that is the case, the strategy appears to have worked. Find out who permitted that train to leave. We must tighten our training and swiftly punish any deviation from standard procedures."

"That's already being done, sir," said Linsky.

"Fine. What else have you discovered?"

"Sir, we've confirmed the identities of the two cadets who escaped custody. We also have a description of the forger's contact, a woman named Attika."

"And the third one, the girl cadet?" asked Bishop. "Were you able to confirm your earlier suspicion?"

"Yes sir. The forger's description of her is a very close match. He destroyed his records prior to being arrested, but his description and the camera image from the train station leaves no room for doubt."

"Don't mention her identity in your report. Just say there is a third unknown female insurgent. Include everything else, the fact that Chambers was a spy employed by foreign agents, the two other cadets' identities, the relationship of Chambers and Brandt, the coordinated attack to free them, etc."

"Yes sir," said Linsky. After a pause he continued. "But if I may, sir, information provided by the Special Forces soldiers who encountered the insurgents outside Frederick will no doubt help them identify the girl."

"Yes Linsky. I realize they will eventually put the pieces together," said Guardian Bishop. "But I want to reveal her identity during the next council meeting with the Grand Guardian. The effect will help divert Harken's attention away from this embarrassing error of losing the item, *your* error."

"I understand, sir."

"I have my doubts whether you do understand, Colonel Linsky," replied Bishop angrily. "You were entrusted with managing the greatest weapons project in human history, but you allowed the top scientist to be turned by foreign agents and steal an object of incalculable value right from under your nose. If his co-conspirators successfully smuggle the item out of the country, the People's Republic of America will face the threat of annihilation. Annihilation, Linsky!"

Bishop's voice grew steadily louder as he unleashed his pent-up anger.

"The magnitude of your failure cannot be understated," continued Guardian Bishop. "Quite frankly, your familiarity with the item and the lack of time to appoint a suitable replacement are the only things keeping you in your present position. Whether you successfully retrieve the item and arrest or neutralize those responsible for its theft will figure prominently in how I decide to punish you for this debacle. Needless to say, you will never be promoted, but you may avoid a long prison term or worse if you can undo the damage you've caused."

There was a long pause before Guardian Bishop spoke again. "Now do you understand, Linsky?"

"Yes sir," said Linsky, his face pale.

"Good. Now get back to work. Update me immediately if there are any developments, no matter how small."

"Yes sir!"

Chapter 28

Colonel Dornicz ended the call and dropped the phone on the hood of the MPV. "Captain Dreyfus!" he yelled.

A woman in camo with the Republican Special Forces insignia of a red skull on the left shoulder of her uniform quickly walked to where Dornicz was standing. She saluted and said, "Yes sir!"

"Captain Dreyfus, I just got off the phone with a weasel SPD colonel named Linsky," said the Colonel. "He's on his way here to help coordinate the search for the three prisoners he lost. With all these SPD patrols running around with their panties on fire, I guess they want to make sure we don't accidently shoot any of them, not that it would be much of a loss. Captain, your task is to fully cooperate with this Linsky piece of shit when he gets here. And by 'fully cooperate' I mean keep him the hell away from me. Take him on a few helicopter rides. Make him feel like he's doing something."

"Yes sir," replied Captain Dreyfus. "I'll handle him."

"Good, now give me an update on our search."

Dreyfus placed a paper map of the surrounding area on the hood of the MPV. "Sir, we've broken the territory into five-by-five kilometer quadrants and we're searching each one with air and ground units. We've already cleared these four." She pointed at some grids that had been drawn on the map. "We're moving on to the next ones. We've also placed units at all road intersections and bridges within a twenty-kilometer radius."

"Okay," said Dornicz as he surveyed the map. "Be sure to round up as many Travelers as you can. Those field rats always know what's going on in the countryside."

"Already gave the order, sir," replied Captain Dreyfus. "We've got a dozen already. No information yet."

"Kill one of them," said Dornicz casually without looking up from his examination of the map. "Be sure the rest see it. They'll shit their filthy pants and tell us everything they know."

"Yes sir," said Dreyfus.

"Now, what about the man who's helping the prisoners?" asked Dornicz, fixing his gaze on the captain. "He killed two of my men and I want him."

"Sir, based on one of the surviving soldier's description, we think he's a terrorist known as Kane."

"Local or foreign?"

"We think he's from west of the Mississippi, but he spends a lot of time causing trouble on this side."

"Try to get him alive," said Dornicz. "But don't hesitate to put a slug in his head if you need to. Take the three fugitives alive."

"Yes sir." Captain Dreyfus saluted and went to carry out the Colonel's orders.

Chapter 29

Logan, Cap, and Lena walked in silence behind Kane. Twice, they heard the sound of a nearby helicopter, and each time they quickly got under their reflective covers. As soon as the danger passed, they pressed on, not resting until the sun lit the eastern horizon, when Kane took them off the trail and found some downed trees. They used the logs and the reflective covers to create low shelters to rest under.

"Get some sleep," said Kane. "We still have a long way to go, and you'll need your strength. There's some dried meat in your packs. Eat some of it. No one gets out of their shelter while it's light unless I say so."

Logan got under his shelter. He ate a little and closed his eyes, trying to go to sleep, but he couldn't. His mind raced with the implications of what had happened over the past few days. He placed his hand over the coat pocket containing the small sphere. His grandfather had smuggled it out of his laboratory at great risk to himself. If he had been discovered, he would have lost his position and his freedom, maybe even his life, so it was clearly a very important item. But why did he do it? What was this thing?

Logan pulled the sphere out of his pocket and looked at it closely. It was made of a perfectly round, smooth, bronze-colored metal. It fit easily into his hand, like a small apple. There were no markings of any kind on its surface. He estimated it weighed about one kilo. Rolling it around in his hand, it felt cool despite having been in his inner coat pocket during the preceding night's march. It didn't seem to warm up after he held it for a few moments, either. He wondered if there was some kind of mechanism inside moderating its temperature. If that were true, what was the purpose of keeping it cool? Logan looked at it a bit longer, then returned it to his inner coat pocket. Exhausted, he closed his eyes and soon drifted off to sleep.

A hand gently shook Logan's shoulder. He woke up and saw Lena's face. She held her finger to her lips, then pointed toward the trail. Logan slowly crawled out from under his shelter and stood up to a crouch. He saw Cap and Kane hiding behind a thick log, watching something on the slope below. Logan quietly followed Lena as she crept forward. When he reached the others, he peered over the log and through a cluster of bushes to the trail fifty meters below. He saw Red Leg soldiers in camouflage and a female SPD officer slowly walking along the trail. The SPD officer was holding a long piece of metal in one hand and methodically waiving it left and right. She stopped. Then she swung it in the direction of the fugitives.

Logan's heart skipped a beat. He looked to his right and saw Kane slowly easing his rifle to his shoulder, its barrel hidden by the surrounding brush. The woman took a few steps up the slope, pressing an earpiece with her hand while she read a display screen on the long metal instrument. She stopped and adjusted the display. Then she shook her head and pointed down the trail toward Point of Rocks. The soldiers slowly walked on, and a minute later they disappeared from sight.

Kane whispered, "Get your packs. We've got another hour before nightfall, but we can't stay here any longer."

Soon they were walking in a line behind Kane as he led them along the faintest of game trails. It took them up to the ridge line, which Kane was careful not to go over in case someone should see their silhouettes. As the sun set they reached the edge of a small clearing giving them a view of the Potomac River winding its way to the southeast. A patrol boat was slowly making its way downstream and two helicopters appeared upstream, one on each side of the river valley. They flew past the patrol boat and continued southeast, periodically hovering over a section of the river before moving on.

"What was that thing the SPD officer was holding?" asked Cap in a hushed voice.

"I'm sure it was something to detect the sphere," answered Lena. "It must give off some kind of signal or radiation."

Logan was tempted to take it out of his pocket but resisted the urge. "I was holding it this morning," he said. "It was cool. It should have warmed up a little in my hand but it didn't."

"Keep quiet and move," said Kane as he led them along the edge of the clearing, just inside the tree line.

A few hours later, Kane allowed them a brief rest. They all drank a little water and ate some dried meat.

"The forest ahead thins out and the terrain becomes open grassland," said Kane. "There are a few farms here and there – some occupied, some not. Good places for the SPD to watch for people on foot traveling west. We will need to cross the river where there's more cover."

He drank a few gulps of water and looked into the darkness, momentarily lost in thought. He wiped his whisker-stubbled chin with his hand and continued. "Deep Pool is about fifteen kilometers from here as the crow flies, but we're taking the most remote trails I can think of. If we can cross the river tonight and avoid the patrols, we'll make it to Deep Pool by midnight."

Cap shook his head. "With all of the patrols searching these hills, how can we be sure Deep Pool is safe? It seems like they have a good idea where we are. They're eventually going to corner us."

"No," said Logan. "They don't know we're here. They know we headed south from the train because they probably found the MPV in Point of Rocks. But as far as they know, we're heading southeast to the coast or southwest toward the Southern Union border. They might even think we swung north to Canada. They're pouring resources into this search and looking in every direction."

"Let's hope you're right," said Kane. "But we know they haven't been in Deep Pool. At least not yet."

"How do you know that?" asked Cap. "Been talking to the Grand Guardian?"

Kane looked at him and gave a wry smile. "No. A Traveler told me." He walked a few meters to a large boulder at the edge of the trail. "See these marks? Someone put these here less than an hour ago."

They looked at the rock where Kane was pointing. In the light of the moon, they could see that someone had scratched some symbols and numbers onto the rock. "This tells how many troops the Traveler saw, where he saw them, and which direction they were headed." Kane pointed at another set of symbols. "These tell me what path he thinks is clear and what sanctuaries should be safe."

"You can tell all that from a few marks on a rock?" asked Cap, looking closely at the symbols. "What's this one at the end?"

"That means 'safe camp', followed by the symbol for Deep Pool. But getting there is not going to be easy. We'll make for Williamsport, about two kilometers from here. There's an old bridge there we can use to cross the Potomac."

"Won't the bridge be watched?" asked Logan.

"Probably, but there's no place to ford the river for at least sixty kilometers and we don't have boats. That leaves the bridge."

He picked up his pack and started walking, touching the Traveler symbols with his hand as he passed. The others scrambled to catch up. They followed Kane until they came to a creek that flowed swiftly downhill into the Potomac River below. They followed the creek until they reached the river valley. Looking upstream, they could see the isolated lights of a few homes.

"Okay," whispered Kane, pointing at the lights. "There's Williamsport. That black shadow going across the river is the bridge." He reached into his pack and pulled out a field scanner. "I don't see anyone on the bridge, but I'll bet you all a hot meal and a cold beer that there are SPD or Red Legs hidden in the town watching the bridge. Probably a few on the other side too, just to be safe."

"I still don't understand how we're going to get across the bridge if it's being watched like you say," said Cap.

Kane smiled and said, "What's the matter? Don't you trust me?"

"Not really," said Cap.

"Good," replied Kane. "Quick to trust, quick to die. Okay, we'll be going into the water. Crouch low and make your way upstream. Your bracers and swords will be okay in the water, but your M-35s should be kept dry, so hold them above the water line. Your packs are waterproof, so they'll be okay as long as you don't let water in from the top."

He took another look at the bridge with his field scanner. "There you are, tricky bastards." He pointed to the head of the town side of the bridge. "An SPD officer just walked across the street."

"That's pretty far away," said Lena. "How do you know he's an SPD officer?"

"Because he walks like one," answered Kane. "All right, the moon has set so it's good and dark. If we keep low in the water, we'll be below the crest of the riverbank and they won't see us. Pray any SPD on the other side aren't looking this way."

Kane looked at each of their faces and smiled. "Ready children?"

Cap looked at Logan and Lena and said, "We should think about this. Are we sure we want to go this way?"

Kane didn't wait to hear what the others had to say. He stood into a crouch and crept to the river's edge, where he eased into the water and started moving upstream.

"Looks like the discussion's over," said Logan as he watched Kane. He looked at Lena, who got into a crouch and followed Kane.

Cap whispered, "*Lena!*" but she kept going. He shook his head and looked at Logan as he got into a crouch. "This just keeps getting better and better."

Logan smiled as Cap went by. Then he whispered, "Relax, Cap. What could possibly go wrong?"

"Plenty," replied Cap over his shoulder.

The three fugitives followed Kane's example and slipped into the river, holding their M-35s above the water. They all kept close enough to shore to stay below the river's raised bank and out of sight of any unfriendly eyes in Williamsport. Soon, they reached the base of the bridge. Kane climbed up the embankment and quickly walked to one of the supporting pillars. He slung his rifle over his shoulder and looked up.

He grabbed the lowest rung of a ladder embedded in the concrete pillar and started to climb.

Logan paused to look at the bridge column which rose about fifteen meters above the riverbank. Kane was already half way up the pillar. He wasn't sure what Kane hoped to accomplish by climbing up to the bridge, but he figured the man had gotten them this far and seemed to know the area. That made Kane their best hope for getting through this alive.

He followed Lena and Cap as they climbed up the riverbank. They swiftly and quietly glided to the bridge's first pillar. Lena quickly ascended the ladder to join Kane above. Even with a pack on her back and a gun slung over her shoulder, Lena moved with surprising agility and ease. Cap went next and Logan followed.

When he reached the top, Logan began to understand Kane's plan. There was a gangplank under the bridge road, probably used for maintenance purposes. The gangplank ran the length of the bridge about two meters below the surface. Kane cautioned them to move as silently as possible and started to traverse the expanse. They had taken about twenty steps when they heard something and stopped.

Logan turned his ear toward the town, but didn't dare turn completely around. He thought he could hear voices coming from one of the houses near the head of the bridge. He heard a woman's voice laughing, followed by man's voice saying, "Shhh!" The woman giggled, then a door slammed shut.

After waiting a few moments without hearing anything more, the four continued to walk along the gangplank. When they reached the other side, Kane didn't climb down. Instead, he led them up to the bridge's surface using a narrow hanging ladder. Kane reached the road and looked along the length of the bridge. He turned to the others and motioned for them to follow. Lena was watching from the top of the ladder when Kane gave the signal. She climbed the rest of the way up, and Cap and Logan followed. They quickly dashed for the tree line, but as they ran there was a sudden crashing sound emanating from the town. Logan instinctively broke to the right toward a nearby cluster of trees.

When he got into the trees, Logan stopped and leaned against a tree trunk, intently listening for more sounds from Williamsport, but all was silent. Relieved, he walked deeper into the forest at an angle he hoped would intersect with the others' path. As he adjusted the shoulder straps of his pack, he noticed something out of the corner of his eye. He turned his head to see an SPD officer standing just a couple meters away.

Shit!

The SPD officer looked at Logan and froze as though he was seeing an apparition. Neither man moved. Then the officer reached for his sidearm. Logan quickly reached over his shoulder and pulled out his sword. He lunged forward and drove the blade through the SPD officer's stomach. The man looked with disbelief at the sword projecting from his body. He tried to raise his pistol, but Logan drove his blade in deeper causing him to drop the gun. The officer fell to his knees and collapsed to the ground.

Cap came running from deeper in the forest. "Are you okay?"

He looked at the body and then at Logan, who stood as if frozen, his mouth slightly open. "You did what you had to do," he said. "Now let's get out of here."

Kane appeared, sword in hand, and quickly assessed the situation. Pulling the sword out of the body and handing it to Logan, he said, "Hide the body in that thicket and keep your eyes open. Where there's one, there's another. They rarely work alone."

Logan tried to comply but couldn't move. His mind was still adjusting to what he had just done. He'd killed a man. True, it was a man who had wanted to kill him, but that didn't lessen the magnitude of what had occurred. The thought flashed across his mind that he'd taken away everything the man was. Husband, father, brother, son. It was all over for him. One minute he's taking a piss in the woods and the next he's worm food. He looked at the sword in his hand as though for the first time.

Seeing Logan wasn't moving, Kane and Cap took the SPD officer's body by the arms and legs and carried it to an area of thick underbrush. They placed the body in the middle.

"Let's go," said Kane as he walked by Logan. "You did it and now it's done. He's dead and you're alive. Now get your head straight and let's go."

Logan nodded. "Yea, yeah," he said, more to himself than Kane. He used a large leaf to clean his blade of the SPD officer's blood. He eased the sword back into its makeshift sheath on the side of his backpack, then trotted after Kane.

Cap and Lena looked at each other for a moment. Cap was about to say something but Lena turned and trotted after Logan. Cap stood alone in the darkness watching Lena's back as she disappeared into the shadows. He looked in the direction of the bushes where they'd hastily hidden the body. Cursing under his breath, he took off after the others.

They jogged along a twisting trail for the next forty-five minutes before slowing down to a walk near a small clearing. Then Kane stopped and the others gathered around him. "Okay, those lights ahead are Deep Pool," he said. "We made good time since crossing the bridge. I had planned to rest before meeting Ravenwood, but we need to move fast.

That means you'll be pushing on tonight and maybe through tomorrow, so be prepared."

He continued along the trail with the others close behind. When they reached the outskirts of the town, he turned left and led them along the edge of the tree line, but always staying in the shadows. Through the trees they could see a cluster of about fifty houses; most were dark, but as they walked around the perimeter of the town, they saw a dimly lit white stucco building. They could hear the muffled sound of music coming from within its walls.

"This way," said Kane. "Lay down your packs, bracers, and weapons in these boxwood bushes."

They followed his instructions and he covered the equipment with additional branches. Then he walked toward the building, looking from side to side as he went. He stepped into the faint light of a small lamp mounted on the building and waved for them to follow. They quickly walked from the tree line to Kane, who was standing next to a door. He pulled it open and they entered.

Once inside, Cap's eyes widened. He grinned with delight. "I hoped this was what it sounded like."

He looked around the large dimly lit tavern they'd entered. A heavyset older woman stood behind a bar pouring beer for a few rough-looking patrons. About thirty people were gathered in front of a small stage watching a band play, dancing in time to the music. There were booths along the wall and tables in the middle of the room along the edge of the dancefloor. Three or four waitresses moved from table to table delivering food and drinks.

Cap patted his pockets and looked at Logan. "Lively place, don't you think? Do you have some money by any chance?" he asked.

Logan shook his head. "I left home rather unexpectedly and forgot to bring my wallet."

Cap looked at Lena, who shook her head. "Even if I did, I wouldn't waste it on beer."

"I'm not asking you to waste it on beer," replied Cap. "I'm asking you to give it to me so *I* can waste it on beer."

He looked at Kane. "What about you? Spare a few shekels for a thirsty Traveler?"

Kane ignored the question as he slowly turned his head, scanning the room. He stopped when he saw a particular booth. He looked at Logan and nodded toward the booth.

"This way," said Kane.

As they walked across the tavern floor, Logan looked at the band on stage. They were in their mid-twenties and wore tattered dirty work pants and t-shirts. Two women played electric guitars. There was a man playing the bass and another on the drums. A long-haired man was bobbing his head in time with the driving blues groove and heavy guitar riffs. He approached the mike stand and began to sing.

> *Well, I saw that girl,*
> *Comin' down the street.*
> *Don't move so fast,*
> *I ain't got no gas.*
> *She looked at me*
> *And shook her head.*
> *"You got nothin' to show*
> *So you can just go."*
> *I said, "Pleeeeasse baby."*
> *I said, "Pleeeeasse baby."*
> *She shook her head.*
> *And she shook her hands.*
> *She shook her hips.*
> *But not for me.*
> *No, no, not for me.*

The man in the corner booth stood when they approached. He was a tall, barrel-chested man with closely cropped gray hair, a square jaw and a rather large wide nose. Logan noted his large hands and thick fingers. To Logan he appeared to be a simple laborer or farmer, but there was something in his eyes that contrasted sharply with his plain, rough exterior. They shone with intelligence and something else, which Logan could only describe as cheerfulness.

Kane smiled as he took the other man's extended hand in his own and then embraced him. "Good to see you," he said to the man.

"And you," replied the man in a strong but raspy voice. "I see you've brought some guests with you. Welcome to Deep Pool."

"You must be Ravenwood," said Lena.

"I am. And you must be Lena, Logan, and Cap," he said with a smile as he sat down in the booth. He gestured for the others to do the same. All accepted the invitation except for Kane, who leaned close to Ravenwood and whispered something in his ear. Ravenwood nodded.

Kane looked at the three young friends and said, "I'm leaving you for a while, but we will meet again. Ravenwood will get you where you need to go." He smiled and turned toward the door.

"Where is he going?" Logan asked Ravenwood when Kane had left.

"He is returning to Williamsport to distract your pursuers."

Logan thought of the dead SPD officer they had left behind. "What if they catch him?" Logan asked Ravenwood.

The big man smiled and chuckled. "Red Legs and SPD thugs have no chance whatsoever of catching Kane. He's more at home in the woods than the cleverest fox. And besides, he will not be alone. Others will help."

"The Travelers," said Lena.

"Yes," replied Ravenwood, smiling at Lena. "The Travelers will help throw the dogs off the scent. Travelers have always disliked the SPD, visa inspectors in particular, but they have recently developed a visceral hatred for Red Legs. Republican Special Forces units have been stationed in the region for the past year or so and have caused nothing but misery for the Traveler community. Part of a stepped-up enforcement effort, it would seem."

"What do the Red Legs do to them that make the Travelers hate them?" asked Lena.

Ravenwood frowned and said, "Red Leg tactics are harsh. More than a few Travelers have died while in custody."

"What do you mean they died in custody? What happens to them?" asked Lena. Something in her voice told Logan she wanted to know the answer but was afraid of what she might hear.

"It's usually some variation of 'shot while trying to escape,'" Ravenwood answered. He looked from face to face and continued. "As I said, Travelers' already difficult lives have changed for the worse. SPD visa inspectors are usually satisfied with throwing Travelers in a cell for a few days and transporting them to the nearest farm or production development from which the Travelers could usually escape without much effort."

Ravenwood fixed his gaze on Lena. "But Red Legs are different. They don't like being policemen. It's not what they're trained for. They're soldiers, and not just ordinary soldiers. They're shock troops, trained to take on the toughest missions, to kill as many of the enemy as possible by any means possible."

"So why are they stationed here?" asked Logan. "Ever since the days of Malcom Weller, it's been forbidden for the Republican Special Forces to operate inside the country's borders. They should be on the western frontier or south along the Smokey Mountains."

"Red Legs are in those places as well, but the Guardians need them in the interior now," replied Ravenwood.

"Is the SPD losing control?" asked Cap. "Why do they need the RSF to help?"

Ravenwood slowly rubbed his large hands together and then laced his fingers. "My guess is that there is conflict among the Guardians. Guardian Bishop is the Justice Minister and therefore has jurisdiction over national law enforcement. He uses his SPD to enforce the Uniform Code of Justice, root out so-called undedicated elements of society, and conduct counter-espionage operations. Guardian Castell is Defense Minister and therefore has authority over the military, including the Republican Guard to which the Red Legs belong. I believe Bishop and Castell are encroaching on each other's jurisdictions, trying to position themselves to be the next Grand Guardian when Harken dies."

"Why now? Is Harken sick?" asked Cap, a bit suspiciously.

"Many believe old age is taking its toll on him," said Ravenwood with a shrug. "He's seventy-five, after all. No one lives forever, and there has never been a peaceful transition of power in the PRA. Seizing control and silencing your competitors is the traditional path to power."

"How do you know all of this?" asked Cap, not trying to hide his doubts. "Internal rivalries between Guardians aren't the kind of thing that's reported in the news."

Ravenwood sat back and smiled. "I know because I talk to people and I listen to what they say. But there is someone here who probably knows more than any of us about the inner workings of the Guardian Council. Wouldn't you agree, Lena?"

She narrowed her eyes and asked, "Why do you think that?"

"Because your father is the Defense Minister, Guardian Castell," answered Ravenwood.

Logan and Cap looked at her, stunned. She ignored them and leveled a cold stare at Ravenwood.

"I understand why you created your false identity of Lena Moreau," continued Ravenwood. "You didn't want people at the academy to treat you differently. And your father no doubt saw some advantages in allowing you to mask your identity. But your secret life has become difficult to maintain, and it is no longer necessary."

"So maybe the massive manhunt isn't really for Logan," said Cap, breaking the silence which followed. "Maybe they're looking for Lena."

"They're looking for all of you," said Ravenwood. "They need to find Lena because of who she is, and they need to find Logan because of what he has."

He looked at Logan and held out his hand. "May I see it?"

Logan hesitated and looked into the intense but reassuring eyes of the big man. Then he reached into his coat pocket and pulled out the sphere. He put it in Ravenwood's outstretched hand. "Do you know what it is?" Logan asked.

Ravenwood raised and lowered the sphere a few times, gauging its heft. He smiled at Logan but didn't answer his question. Then he said, "Not too heavy, eh? But it's cold."

"I think there's some kind of cooling system inside the sphere," said Logan. "But I don't know why it would need to be kept cold. I don't know what the sphere is for."

"No, I'm not surprised," said Ravenwood as he rolled the sphere in the palm of his hand. He reflected for a moment and then asked nonchalantly, "I don't suppose you have another unusual object, do you? Perhaps something your grandfather gave to you."

Logan was a little surprised by the question, though in retrospect he knew he should have anticipated it. He reached into his pants pocket and retrieved the medallion. He placed it on the table with the image of Apollo's chariot facing up. Ravenwood held the sphere in his right hand and picked up the medallion in his left.

"This way, please," he said as he stood up.

They followed him toward the tavern's back door, but instead of exiting Ravenwood gave a slight nod to the woman behind the bar. She opened a nearby door, which was concealed as a panel. Ravenwood led the group down a short flight of stairs to a stone-walled cellar. The room was empty except for some packing crates stacked along the walls. Ravenwood walked to the far corner and turned up a kerosene lamp that was hanging from the ceiling. When the others had gathered around him, he produced the sphere and medallion and set them on a stack of crates.

"Dr. Chambers was a very clever man," he said with a nod of his head. "Some called him a genius. But it was not his intelligence alone which vaulted him to the top of his profession. He could also point to innovation after innovation as proof of his superior mind. You are probably familiar with the antiballistic shield, for example. Elite fighting forces have been using them for at least twenty years now, and you have Chambers to thank for that."

Logan said, "An SPD colonel we recently met said he was talented at adapting advanced technology to practical uses. What advanced technology? What did he adapt it from?"

Ravenwood smiled. "You've been traveling in dangerous circles," he said with a wink. "But it's a good question. Sometimes it was pre-Impact technology. Early twenty-first century Earth society had achieved some considerable breakthroughs, particularly in computers and communications. Chambers researched and reintroduced many of these achievements. His work led to the PDD, advances in wireless communications, and more. But other technology he adapted was far more advanced than that of pre-Impact Earth."

"What do you mean, more advanced than pre-Impact Earth?" asked Cap.

Ravenwood took a deep breath and looked at Cap. Then he said, "Cap, I'm told you're a gifted pilot. What if someone came to you and offered you a way of improving the performance of your aircraft not by a factor of two, but of two hundred? Imagine also that the person who is offering this to you does not want anything in return except for you to assist him to get home. That would be a tempting offer, wouldn't it?"

Cap shrugged his shoulders. "I guess so."

"Of course it would be," said Ravenwood, nodding his head. "And I think you would accept the offer if you found yourself in a constant struggle with your neighboring countries. Any advantage that could tip the scales on the battlefield would be welcome."

"Maybe," replied Cap. "But what does that have to do with Dr. Chambers or us?"

Ravenwood folded his arms. "I'm going to tell you three a story that you would not have heard growing up where you did, or anywhere else for that matter. Years before the Impact, the United States was engaged in a decades-long struggle with the Soviet Union. That much you should know. One of the areas of competition was space exploration. The Soviets had scored some early victories by sending satellites and even humans into Earth's orbit, so the United States responded by announcing its intention to send humans to the moon."

Logan recalled the book Attika had shown him in the reserve section of the library. "The Apollo program," he said.

Ravenwood raised his eyebrows. "Correct, Logan. It was called the Apollo program. And they achieved their goal. They sent men to the moon, not just once but several times."

Lena's eyes lit up. "What did they find?" she asked.

"Mostly rocks," replied Ravenwood with a dismissive wave of his hand. "Rocks and dust."

He looked at each of their faces and continued. "Undeterred by these mundane results, the United States sent several additional ships to the moon, and they found more of the same. However, one of those missions is of great significance to us. I am speaking of the Apollo 14 mission, which occurred in 1971. Although long planned for, the timing of its launch was also in response to something scientists on Earth had observed occurring in space. Just two weeks before launch, listening stations on Earth detected the unmistakable sound of an explosion, which they believed originated somewhere between Mars and Jupiter. Furthermore, they heard some sort of electronic communication just before and just after the explosion. Then, after several days of silence, they heard a steady transmission coming from the moon."

Cap looked at him incredulously. "So you're saying an alien spaceship blew up somewhere between Mars and Jupiter and a piece of it landed on the moon?"

"I think he's saying survivors landed on the moon," said Lena.

"Exactly! Very good, Ms. Castell." replied Ravenwood, clapping his hands.

"So that's what the Apollo missions were about?" asked Cap.

"No, not all of them, but the United States repurposed Apollo 14's mission to discover the source of the signal. According to the reports of the time, the mission had a crew of three astronauts, but there was a fourth crew member. He secretly boarded the rocket, and while the world watched the other three play golf on the moon and plant flags in the dust, he made his way to what turned out to be an escape pod."

"How did he get to the pod? I mean, it's one thing to go to the moon, but how do you get around once you're on the surface?" asked Cap.

"He used a lunar rover, a bare-bones jeep," offered Logan. "I recall seeing an image of one in the book Attika showed me."

"Okay, so they had a vehicle," said Cap. "How did they get it home? How big was the Apollo ship?"

"You ask good practical questions, Mr. Caparelli. I admire that," said Ravenwood with a warm smile. Looking at Logan he said, "Yes, they did use the lunar rover and they did use the cargo space intended for moon materials in order to bring the small pod to Earth. But there's more. The fourth astronaut found not only the pod, but he also found a single survivor, and in that survivor's hand was this." He pointed at the sphere.

"He found a sentient alien on the moon?" asked Cap. "How is that still a secret? How could something so big be kept quiet?"

"They didn't keep it quiet," answered Ravenwood. "The story was leaked within a few weeks of the astronauts' return. But rather than deny the truth of the allegations, which would only lend it credence, the United States engaged in a massive misinformation campaign that went on for years. Reports of alien visitors, alien spacecraft, alien abductions, and so on were constantly fed into the news outlets. These stories soon acquired a life of their own. Sometimes people believed it, and sometimes not, but it didn't matter because the government had achieved its goal of masking the truth in a sea of lies."

"So what is it? What is the sphere?" asked Logan.

"The sphere?" asked Ravenwood, tapping the cold object. "This is a carrying case. It's the thing inside the sphere that interests us, and many others. Would you like to see it?"

He picked up the medallion and brought it close to the sphere. When they were nearly touching, a circular portion of the sphere the size of the medallion flattened to reveal an intricate design of ridges and valleys. Ravenwood placed the medallion into the newly formed indentation. With a click, the grooves on the reverse side of the medallion locked into the sphere's new indentation.

Logan and the others leaned closer, transfixed by what they were seeing. The top half of the sphere opened to reveal a small round object in the middle, no bigger than a child's marble. It was black, but tiny ribbons of white, yellow and red ebbed and flowed within. The object floated in the middle of the sphere, suspended in a shimmering, golden energy field.

"It's beautiful," said Lena, eyes wide. "What is it?"

"The Apollo Stone, and it is the most important item on a ship if you want to shift space."

"What do you mean 'shift space'?" asked Cap.

"Shifting space occurs when you bend space until two different points occupy the same location and then you unbend it. A ship that can shift space would begin in one place, bend space, and then appear in a different location. Any location. Instantly."

"Sounds like he's talking about an Alcubierre Drive," said Lena.

Logan shook his head. "An Alcubierre Drive is a very speculative hypothesis."

Logan looked at Ravenwood, who appeared puzzled, and said, "An Alcubierre Drive would, *hypothetically*, expand space-time behind a ship and shrink space-time in front of it to create a space-time wave which would allow the ship to essentially surf through the universe until the ship's current location and a desired destination touch. The ship doesn't really move, in the sense we're used to movement. Space moves around the ship. It's an interesting idea, but it's just a hypothesis."

"I agree it's just a hypothesis," said Lena. "But what Ravenwood is describing sounds like an Alcubierre Drive." Looking at Ravenwood, she asked, "How would you get enough power to shift space? According to the hypothesis, a ship would need a huge amount of power to bend space-time. It would have to convert something with a mass about the size of Mars into energy. You know, $E=MC^2$? There's no power source that could achieve that."

Ravenwood looked from face to face. "Well, I don't know the answer to that question, but I would say you three know more about shifting space than I do, which is welcome."

"Leaving aside the impossibility of building a functioning Alcubierre Drive," said Logan, "how was my grandfather involved with this Apollo Stone?"

"He developed the power source you say can't exist and the navigation interface that would allow a ship, a very powerful gunship called the *Blackhawk*, to use the Apollo Stone to instantly shift to any desired location."

Cap leaned forward and looked closely at the Apollo Stone. "He built an engine and navigation system to use this thing? How could he have done that without even knowing what it is?" He pointed at the Apollo Stone. "How do you go from finding it in an alien escape pod to building an Alcubierre Drive?"

"You are forgetting the survivor," said Ravenwood. "The survivor greatly accelerated the learning process."

"But you said the Apollo Stone and the survivor were found in 1971," observed Cap. "It's 2136. Is the alien still alive?"

"I believe so," said Ravenwood.

"That's a long time," said Logan. "We're talking one hundred sixty-five years."

"It is, but who's to say how long aliens live?" asked Ravenwood.

Logan took a long look at the Apollo Stone. Its beauty was calming, hypnotic. The slow swirl of colors in the midst of pure blackness filled his vision and drew him steadily in.

"How did you come to know all of this?" asked Logan, pulling his gaze away from the stone.

"I know because your grandfather told me," replied Ravenwood in a matter-of-fact tone.

"Unlikely," said Logan with a scoff. "He was a true believer. He never would have talked to you, an enemy of the People's Republic."

"Circumstances change. People change," answered Ravenwood. "He gave you the sphere and medallion, after all."

Logan frowned and shook his head. "He gave it to me, sure. But just to keep it safe. Whatever his plan was, it didn't include letting me keep it."

Ravenwood grinned. "How well do you think you really knew your grandfather?" he asked. "The SPD watched his every move, listened to his phone conversations, spied on his friends and family. He couldn't risk telling anyone what he was planning to do. Not without risking his life and perhaps the lives of others, too."

"He did give you the clues to find the sphere," said Lena. "He must have at least considered the possibility that he wouldn't be able to retrieve it."

Logan thought about the conversation with his grandfather a month earlier at Veterans Park. They had talked about Chambers' discouragement with the direction the government had been going in recent years. They even discussed Logan's father, whose denunciation and execution during the Rededication had been a taboo subject in the family since Logan was a boy. But Chambers hadn't breathed a word about the Apollo Stone or suggested in any way that he planned to commit treason. Nevertheless, Logan had definitely noticed a change in the old man.

Ravenwood held up the sphere and looked at the Apollo Stone. "Although his motives may forever be unknown, I personally think Dr. Chambers realized that what he and his colleagues were building would give the Guardians an insurmountable tactical advantage over any enemy. Don't forget Chambers' engine and navigation system were to be installed in an extremely powerful gunship, the *Blackhawk*. With the Apollo Stone guiding it, the *Blackhawk* would have been able to suddenly materialize behind enemy lines and cause massive casualties without warning."

Lena looked at Cap. "Have you heard anything about this gunship?"

"No, but I did fly the new generation Phantom fighter," he said. "It's such a huge leap ahead of previous aircraft that I wouldn't be surprised if the same technology was used to build some kind of big gunship."

Ravenwood laughed and said, "Aha! I detect a modest acceptance that what I have told you is the truth. Don't misunderstand. I'm glad you three are skeptical, but please keep your minds open to new possibilities."

He closed the sphere and returned it, as well as the medallion, to Logan. "Here," he said. "Dr. Chambers entrusted them to you, so it is your responsibility to keep them safe. But remember to keep the sphere closed. If you open it, the Apollo Stone can be detected."

Logan looked at the sphere. "Does the stone emit some kind of radiation? Should we be worried?"

"No. It doesn't emit radiation. But we don't want to risk attracting attention," replied Ravenwood. "Now, we'd better get moving. We don't have much time."

Lena cleared her throat. "Before we go walking out the door, I'd like to know the end goal," she said. "I understand we don't want it to be used in the *Blackhawk*, but what are we supposed to do with the Apollo Stone? Destroy it?"

Ravenwood shook his head. "You cannot destroy the Apollo Stone. You could hit it with a sledge hammer and it wouldn't show a scratch. And don't think for a moment that the *Blackhawk* is no longer dangerous simply because it cannot shift space without the stone. It has extremely advanced weaponry and propulsion systems. I'm told it is also capable of transporting up to two hundred and fifty troops. It is a formidable weapon in its own right."

"Okay," continued Cap. "So we can't destroy the Apollo Stone and we have to be careful about the *Blackhawk*, but what's the plan?"

Ravenwood started walking toward the steps leading up to the tavern. "The plan is to leave immediately and head for the Blue Mountain. It is the gateway into Cumberland Gap. I had hoped to skirt north of the Allegany Mountains and travel west, parallel to the Heartland Road, but I no longer think that is possible, given how intently the Guardians are searching for you."

"It sounds like the Cumberland Gap is the more direct route to the Mississippi anyway," said Logan.

They reached the top of the stairs and passed through the false door. Ravenwood nodded to the woman behind the bar and ushered the others out the tavern's back door and into the night.

As they walked toward the place where they had hidden their packs, Ravenwood replied to Logan's earlier observation. "It is true that traveling through the Cumberland Gap is the shorter route to the great river and the League of Free Cities on the far bank, but the Gap has its own perils," said Ravenwood.

Before Logan could respond, Ravenwood stopped and looked up at the stars. Muttering to himself and turning a half circle to get oriented, he pointed at several constellations, then lowered his eyes to the forest in front of him. He held out his arm in a straight line.

"This way," he said as he set off with long strides into the forest.

The others scrambled to grab their gear from where Kane had hidden it and catch up with Ravenwood as he disappeared into the night. When they had caught up to him, Ravenwood continued to speak. "As I was saying, there are dangers associated with traveling through the Gap. Chief among them is the fact that the Allegany highlands are the home of the so-called Mountaineers, a general term referring to the many loosely associated and frequently bickering peoples living there. The most powerful Mountaineer tribe is called the Greenspurs. They are led by Tamara Barrough. Calls herself the Queen of Cumberland. Queen Tamara's allegiance usually lies on the side opposite the Guardians, but one can never be sure whom she will support."

Cap laughed. "The *Queen* of Cumberland? Isn't that a little excessive?"

"Well, what is your Grand Guardian if not a king?" asked Ravenwood. "He is selected by the rather pliable Congress of Representatives and serves for life. He cannot be removed from office except by unanimous consent of the four other Guardians and the Premier Judge, and his word has the power of law."

They pushed through thick brush until they reached a well-worn trail. Ravenwood turned west and set a quick pace.

After they had walked a few minutes, Lena said, "If we're not sure about Queen Tamara's allegiance, can we get through the gap without her knowing?"

"No. The pass runs right in front of her stronghold."

"Can we go south, around the Smokey Mountains?" asked Cap.

"Perhaps, but time is too short."

They came to a three-way split in the trail. Without hesitating, Ravenwood led the group down the left path.

"What about Kane?" asked Lena. "Will he be able to find us? Does he know the route we're taking?"

"Yes," said Ravenwood. "If all goes well, we will meet him at the Blue Mountain."

Chapter 30

They had been marching in silence for several hours when Ravenwood said, "It will be light soon. There is a cave behind a waterfall not too far ahead. We will spend the day there and continue in the evening."

"How much farther to Blue Mountain?" asked Logan, who had begun to feel the effects of several days of constant walking.

"About twenty-five kilometers," answered Ravenwood. "If all goes well, we'll be there after tomorrow night's march."

They continued walking for another fifteen minutes, when they heard the sound of rushing water. Just as the sun was lighting the eastern sky, they came around a bend in the trail and entered a grassy clearing. There was a small pool and a stream running from it toward the south and into the trees. The pool was fed by a seven-meter-high waterfall. Ravenwood led them around the pool until they were next to the waterfall. He turned sideways, pressed his back against the rock, and slipped behind the tumbling water. The others followed.

It was dark in the open space behind the falls, but Ravenwood lit the area with a flashlight. He walked a few meters into the cave to escape the dampness and pointed to dry ground on which the others could sit. "We'll rest here. Try to get some sleep. The march tonight will be a long one and the ground is uneven. You will need your strength."

They were all grateful for the break. Each was in good physical condition, but they were not accustomed to walking such long distances with packs on their backs. Logan dropped his pack to the ground and lowered himself to his knees. He unfastened a side pocket to get his canteen and refill it when he noticed his left hand beginning to quiver. He grasped it with his right hand, but it didn't stop the involuntary motion.

"Damn it!" he whispered angrily.

He felt the quiver grow stronger and darkness began to fill the edges of his vision. Knowing what was coming, he sat down on the ground and waited.

Cap looked at Logan when he sat down and noticed his pained expression. "What's wrong?"

"It's happening," answered Logan.

Cap dropped his bag and went over to Logan. He crouched down and put his hand on his shoulder. Just then, Logan's eyes became vacant and his hands began fumbling with his jacket buttons. He methodically clenched and unclenched his jaw muscles.

Lena crouched next to Cap. "What's going on?" she asked, her brow furrowed.

Without taking his eyes off Logan's face, Cap said, "He's having a seizure."

"What?" she asked in a surprised voice. Then she looked again at Logan. "What can we do?"

"Nothing," replied Cap. "We just need to make sure he doesn't accidentally hurt himself. He'll snap out of it in a minute or so."

"I remember this happening to him during a final exam," she said. "I was too wrapped up in answering the questions to pay much attention."

Cap noticed Ravenwood was watching them from the other side of the cave. He looked him in the eye and said, "He'll be okay."

Ravenwood said nothing but kept watching.

After about two minutes, Logan blinked and looked around him. "What happened?" he asked, confused. He noticed that everyone was silent and wore concerned expressions.

"I see," he said as he scratched his head. "I had a seizure. I remember now."

"What kind of seizure was it?" asked Ravenwood.

"A complex partial seizure," said Logan. "I don't get them very often and they don't last long."

"But you are incapacitated when they occur?" asked Ravenwood.

"I can feel them coming, so I can take precautions."

"How often do they happen?" asked Lena.

"When I was a kid, before I started taking the medication, I had them about once every other month. They've just started to happen again. I hadn't suffered any for a long time, but this was the second one in about a week."

"Your medication is at the apartment, isn't it," said Cap.

Logan nodded.

Ravenwood could see that Logan was uncomfortable talking about the seizures. "Well, we won't discuss it any further. But please let us know when you feel one is about to happen so we can make sure you're safe. As for now, I recommend we all eat a little something and then get some rest."

Chapter 31

Attika pulled the small hypodermic needle out of her arm and grabbed the pistol off of the table. She pointed it at the door. The echoes from the burst of automatic gunfire reverberated throughout the ancient factory. Still pointing her pistol at the door, she removed the encoder card from the PDD, dropped it on the concrete floor, and crushed it with the heel of her boot. Then she launched the scrub-and-dump virus on her PDD.

There was another burst of automatic gunfire, followed by the *boom-boom* of Gregor's 10mm long-barreled pistol. More automatic gunfire. Then a scream followed by a thud. Attika stood and kicked the small pieces of the shattered encoder card into the corner then silently glided to the door. She opened it a little and peered through the crack.

Her eyes scanned the four floors of the balcony encircling the old factory work floor. There was an SPD Tactical Assault Corp unit on her floor, five officers dressed in dark blue battle armor with SPD written in large white letters on their Provex breast plates. She could hear the faint hum of their antiballistic shields as they quickly but carefully swept through the rooms on her level. Looking up to the fourth-floor balcony, she caught a glimpse of Gregor disappearing into a dark hall just as a second TAC unit appeared on the stair landing to his right.

Attika stepped away from the door and slipped her pistol into her shoulder holster. Hearing the sound of fast-approaching vehicles, she walked to the room's exterior wall and peered through the empty window frame down to the ground below. Several SPD patrol cars had just pulled up to the main doors, and half a dozen SPD officers in standard uniform quickly deployed behind the cars with their guns drawn.

She heard footsteps outside her door. In the blink of an eye, she stepped through the empty window frame onto the ledge just as a TAC officer threw open the door. She grabbed hold of the frame of an empty window in the room next door and swung herself inside. She landed in a crouch and froze, hardly daring to breathe as she listened to the TAC unit in the room she had just left.

Nothing. No sounds of alarm.

When she heard the TAC unit move to the next room, Attika quietly approached the door. Halfway there, she heard the unmistakable ringing sound of blades striking each other. It sounded as though it was coming from the fourth floor. Gregor was a Baku-trained swordsman, but Attika doubted he could hold out against two SPD TAC units in battle gear.

A woman's voice yelled, "Here! Cut him off! He's going for the stairs!"

Attika cracked the door open and peered through. She saw TAC officers running along the fourth-floor balcony toward the stairs. The TAC unit on her floor dashed for the stairs in an attempt to cut Gregor off. The sound of swords striking each other came from somewhere above. Then she heard a scream of pain.

Attika took one last look through the door, then swung it open. She took two steps straight ahead and rolled over the balcony railing. She grabbed hold of the lowest rung and swung her body toward the opening of the second-floor balcony. She rotated her body as she fell in order to face the railing, landing in a three-point stance.

"We got one down here!" yelled a nearby voice. Attika looked to her left and saw a TAC officer standing in the corner. Another one emerged from the shadows of the corner to her right and rushed toward her.

"Down on the ground!" yelled the first TAC officer with his automatic weapon pointed toward her.

Attika spun to her right and leapt through an open door into a dark room. The windows in the room were covered by rotted boards, making it difficult to see anything. A second later, the two officers appeared as silhouettes in the door. One of them pulled a small round object from his belt, pressed a button on the top, and tossed it into the room. The silhouettes stepped out of sight as the object landed with a thud and rolled toward Attika.

Attika quickly pressed the concealed button on her belt to engage her shield and dashed for the door. The stun grenade went off just as she rolled out of the room.

Though somewhat dazed, Attika quickly stood up. As she stood, she reached under her jacket to pull out two long knives from sheaths strapped to her back. The TAC officers opened fire and several of the slugs hit her. She felt the muted force of the bullets through her shield, but it was not enough to slow her down. She attacked the TAC officer on the right. He pressed a button to deploy his M-35's bayonet just in time to block Attika's blade.

The TAC officer on the left quickly slid her short M-35 urban assault gun into its slot in her battle pack and drew her sword. She sliced at Attika's neck, but Attika ducked low and quickly drove both knives into the TAC's sides between her Provex breast plate and battle pack. The woman tried to gasp, but the air in her lungs had escaped through the two wounds and she collapsed to the ground.

Attika turned her attention to her second opponent, who had secured his M-35 in his pack's slot. He drew his sword and locked his arm guard into place. She saw Gregor out of the corner of her eye. He was battling two TAC officers on the same level as Attika, desperately trying to break through to assist her. He downed one of them with a thrust to the neck and crippled the other with a vicious slice to the back of his knee.

The second TAC officer launched a deadly combination of slices and thrusts at Attika. She dropped back, desperately parrying and dodging the swinging blade. She managed to lunge forward with her left-hand knife, but the TAC used his sword to push the blade to the side. She sliced with her right blade, but her opponent blocked it with his guard. Then the TAC officer delivered a crushing blow to her jaw with his arm guard. She staggered to her right, reaching for the wall to steady herself but couldn't find it. She fell to the ground and looked up at the spinning balcony above her.

Attika's opponent was nearly on her when Gregor stepped in to block his advance, kicking him in the side of his right knee and driving his sword into his thigh. Gregor immediately spun around to deflect the blades of two TAC officers who had raced up behind him, but lost his footing and slipped. One of the TAC officers seized the opportunity and stepped forward to drive his blade deep into Gregor's back. He screamed out in pain and fell to one knee. The other officer drove his blade into his chest. Gregor gazed at Attika for a moment with eyes filled with sorrow and fell to the balcony floor.

Still lying on the ground, Attika screamed in rage and drove her right-hand blade into a TAC officer's groin. He howled in pain and collapsed as she stood and swiftly ran into the darkened room from which she had recently escaped. She dashed straight for the boarded window and threw her body at it. The dry rotten wood splintered into a hundred pieces as she burst into the morning sunlight four meters above the ground. She landed on the hood of an SPD patrol car, and rolled off it to the ground.

Lieutenant Fischer had instinctively crouched behind the patrol car when he heard the boards breaking above him, and he was still in that position when something heavy landed on the hood of the car next to him. Looking up, he found himself face to face with Attika. In the blink of an eye, she thrust her knife deep into his unprotected chest just before another SPD officer knocked her unconscious.

Fischer cursed and wrapped his hand around the knife grip. With a great heave, he pulled it out of his chest. He looked down and watched as blood gushed out of the large wound.

"You bitch!" he said to Attika's unconscious body.

Then he dropped the knife and fell face forward onto the broken pavement.

Chapter 32

In high orbit above Jupiter's moon Ganymede, repair droid KB923, brought a replacement part from the manufacturing module to the gate's power source. The droid inserted the thin disk under the poloidal coil and fused it into place. The iron, nickel and other metals that were used to create this replacement part and so many others had been mined by ZT1441 from asteroids millions of kilometers away and loaded onto a little makeshift delivery shuttle. The shuttle, which KB923 had adapted from a deep space probe found drifting in the wreckage of the mothership, was powered by a cannibalized but extremely efficient fusion ramjet rocket.

The shuttle had made the long voyage from the asteroid belt to Ganymede hundreds of times. With each delivery of raw materials, KB923 programmed the manufacturing module to create various replacement parts, which KB923 then inserted into the ancient gate.

The repairs had taken much longer than typically necessary, a consequence of the unexpected explosion of the mothership in the asteroid belt. The situation was made worse by malfunctioning companion repair droids, caused in large part by the fact that the droids had not been designed to operate independently for such long periods.

These malfunctions manifested themselves in different ways. VR779 had simply stopped its work and fired its thrusters in the direction of a distant constellation without warning or apparent purpose. Another droid, SQ224, began dismantling rather than repairing the gate. KB923 had to completely shut down SQ224 when reprogramming proved to be impossible. That left only KB923 to complete the large majority of repairs to the gate.

KB923 closed the power source's protective paneling and sealed it shut. The droid then ran a series of diagnostic tests to ensure there were no more systems failures, an exercise that had failed hundreds of times before when testing revealed some new malfunction. But not this time. When all testing was complete and no errors were detected, KB923 gave the command code for the gate to initiate loading procedures. Shortly thereafter, the space between the two massive pillars shimmered slightly as it came online.

The gate immediately began transmitting routine data to other gates in the network through the micro wormhole it had just opened. Moments later, it began receiving similar transmissions from those gates. KB923 monitored the gate's operations for some time thereafter, but it did not detect any malfunctions. After running a final series of tests, the droid powered down the manufacturing module and returned to its recharge station. It signaled ZB1441 on its distant asteroid that the gate was operational. Then KB923 went into low-power mode and awaited further instructions.

Chapter 33

"I recommend we postpone the attack," said Guardian Bishop.

Though surprised by the statement, the other Guardians did not respond. Instead, they looked at the thin figure of Grand Guardian Harken, who was seated at the head of the conference table. Harken placed his hands on the arms of his chair and looked at the Justice Guardian. Raising an eyebrow, he asked, "Why?"

Bishop looked Harken squarely in the eye and said, "Simple. Because we've lost the Apollo Stone. Without it, we will not be able to hit vital targets behind enemy lines, disrupt supply lines, or draw strength away from their river defenses. And let's not forget that after our forces cross the river, the gunship *Blackhawk* was to be used to keep up the pressure on League troops retreating to their fortress at Deep Six. None of these things are possible without the Apollo Stone."

"Grand Guardian Harken," said Defense Guardian Castell. "We don't need the *Blackhawk* to achieve our goals. Our forces are strong enough to cross the river on schedule. We have the tools and the numbers necessary to overwhelm their fixed defenses. And with the air superiority we will enjoy thanks to the Phantom 2 fighters, we are less dependent on the *Blackhawk* than previously believed."

Harken looked at the Justice Guardian. "Am I correct in assuming that your recommendation to postpone the attack indicates a lack of faith that you will soon recover the Apollo Stone? Which your people lost, I don't need to remind you."

"Of course not, sir," said Bishop. "I have complete faith we will recover it. As a matter of fact, I've just been informed that we've made a significant breakthrough in this effort. We've captured the woman who facilitated the escape of the three fugitives."

"Very good," said Harken. "I want to know every detail of her debriefing."

"Certainly," said Bishop with a slight nod. "But my recommendation to postpone the attack stands, if only for a week or two in order to recover the stone."

Castell shook his head. "One or two weeks? Can't be done. We already hit the start button. The clock is ticking."

Bishop began to speak, but Castell cut him off, repeating his words with greater emphasis. "The clock *is ticking*. The timetable for troop and supply deployment must be followed without *any* deviation whatsoever. There's no other way to effectively move hundreds of thousands of troops two thousand kilometers across the country, not to mention tanks, artillery, fuel, munitions, medical supplies, food, water, and all the rest."

"I understand your point," said Bishop, "but I don't agree."

Castell chuckled lightly and said, "You don't agree." He looked around at the other Guardians and said, "What are they going to do with the stone anyway? They don't have the navigation system. It's useless to them!"

Bishop ignored Castell and directed his attention to Harken. "Sir," he said. "I appreciate the complexities of launching this operation. Believe me, I do. But let me ask you this. What if the League and their allies were aware of our plans? What if they had detailed knowledge of our troop concentrations, points of attack, and contingency plans?"

Harken gave Bishop a sharp look. "What do you mean? How would they know any of that?"

Bishop shot a quick look at Guardian Castell and continued speaking to the Grand Guardian. "I'm afraid I must report a security breach of significant magnitude. We have confirmed that Lena Castell is the unidentified third defector. Who knows what sort of classified information she was feeding to our enemies before she fled? Who knows what information she might be carrying to the enemy now? Given the risk her defection represents, I recommend we delay the military operation until we can retrieve the Apollo Stone and apprehend her."

Harken looked at Castell. "Is this true?"

Castell's face grew red. "No! It's not true. And even if it were, she doesn't know anything."

The Grand Guardian stared at Castell for a few moments, then looked at Bishop. "You're certain about this, Bishop?"

"Quite certain, sir," Bishop replied with the hint of a smile on his lips.

Harken closed his eyes and rubbed his forehead with his fingertips. He looked at Information and Public Affairs Guardian Hyatt.

"Are your people prepared for the launch?"

"Yes sir," she replied. "The information campaign has been underway for weeks and will soon rise in urgency. By the time our soldiers are ready to cross the Mississippi, the people will be screaming for war."

Harken looked at Commerce and Industry Guardian Hoffman. "How long can we keep the troops supplied before the Capitol District, New York, and Boston residents see food shortages on the shelves?"

Hoffman tapped the end of his pencil on the table and said, "We project that people will begin feeling the pinch by mid-summer. I'd say six weeks from now."

Harken shook his head. Looking around the table at the other Guardians he said, "Six weeks. Six damn weeks. If we haven't secured victory by then, we'll have to implement austerity measures. Extreme austerity measures. There will be unrest in the countryside by week ten and chaos everywhere by week fifteen."

Defense Guardian Castell opened his mouth to say something but Harken cut him off.

"Do not speak!" said the Grand Guardian in an angry tone. He looked around the table at each Guardian and said, "This war is not just about securing a quick victory over our enemies or keeping the people focused and dedicated. This is about the survival of this nation! Look around the world. The old powers and ancient rivalries are reemerging. British warships once again dominate the Atlantic. The Japanese are extending their influence around the Pacific Rim. The Indians, Chinese, and Russians are fighting over old territories in Central Asia. The Germans and French are vying for dominance in Europe. The Turks, Iranians, and Egyptians are expanding their spheres of control throughout the Middle East."

He sat back in his chair and raised his hands in frustration. "Yet, here we are, the former United States of America, still broken into weak rump states, even minuscule city states. We squabble over borders, access to waterways, and tariff levels. And in the PRA, our industrial capacity is crippled by chronic shortages in raw materials, leading to missed production quotas and few goods for consumers to buy, though the black market continues to thrive despite our best efforts to shut it down."

Harken leaned forward and smashed his fist on the table. "This must change! Or one day soon another country will look at North America and realize just how weak we really are. Then we'll be consumed one by one!"

He clenched his jaw muscles and looked intently at each of the other Guardians. Then he leaned back into his chair and continued in a calmer tone. "The attack will occur on schedule, but Defense and Justice must cooperate with each other to retrieve the Apollo Stone and the girl. Use every resource at your disposal not needed for the war. Failure will lead to a speedy trial and public hanging for both of you."

Castell and Bishop quickly said, "Yes sir," but Harken was already out of his seat and walking to the door.

Chapter 34

As the sun sank in the west and shadows began to stretch over the meadow, Ravenwood woke the others. None of them had slept well on the cave's hard cold ground, but at least they'd strung together a few hours of rest. They slipped by the waterfall and back into the open air. As they passed by the little pond, Logan looked up to see the early-evening sun touching the peaks of the Blue Mountain in the distance ahead. It did not look blue to him in the yellow and red evening light.

"Why do they call it the Blue Mountain?" asked Logan.

As he found the narrow trail leading west, Ravenwood replied over his shoulder, "It is named for the events that took place there long ago. As you know, after the Impact there was the Long Winter, caused by the massive amount of debris the collisions threw into the atmosphere. Those lucky enough to have survived the Impact were now in danger of starving. People grew desperate and civil order broke down. That was when the Nine Oligarchs, or Tyrants as they are sometimes called, seized power and directed the military to secure all remaining critical resources and collect them in certain locations. The southern and western states refused to obey the order and the Tyrants ordered the military to enforce it."

"Which sparked a war," added Logan.

"Yes, it was the spark, but the kindling was already quite dry," said Ravenwood.

"Ironic that the Tyrants chose to expend dwindling resources on a civil war," said Lena.

"Those were terrible times," said Ravenwood. "Resources were scarce, but compassion and understanding were scarcer. The fighting soon stopped when it became clear to the Tyrants that they would not achieve a swift victory. They pursued their collection plan here in the east where they had much greater control."

"What about the Midwest?" asked Logan. "We were taught that the population there died from the impacts and the fires that followed, but I always thought there must have been a lot more survivors than we were told."

"There were some, but not many," said Ravenwood. "The direct hits to the Midwest had the destructive power of many atomic bombs. The shockwaves and fires destroyed the land and the people, but some escaped. Almost all of the survivors had been living just west of the Mississippi River. They fled across the water, which acted as a firebreak and prevented the conflagration from spreading."

"What happened to them? Where did they go?" asked Cap.

"Wherever they could," answered Ravenwood. "Unfortunately, these refugees from west of the river were soon viewed as a burden and their presence was no longer welcome. And it was this ill feeling which allowed the Nine to implement harsh policies toward them without fear of opposition. The effects of those policies are still quite visible."

"Such as what?" asked Lena.

"Such as your 'developments'," replied Ravenwood. "Many refugees were gathered into camps, ostensibly to facilitate efficient distribution of food and to shelter them, but they were soon put to work growing food. It wasn't long before more developments were established to produce other necessary materials. You will not be surprised to know that the descendants of those early refugees continue to do much the same work."

Logan looked back at Lena and saw that she was deeply disturbed by what Ravenwood had said. But it also seemed Ravenwood's words confirmed something she already suspected. In school and in the media, developments were described as places where people worked hard but were happy and well cared for. The Guardians and other leaders often publicly praised the development workers for growing the food and building the things society needed to continue its advance. But Logan knew that most people at least suspected that the developments were nothing more than labor camps.

His thoughts were interrupted when Cap said, "Not to condone their methods, but you have to admit the Tyrants' plan to concentrate resources made a certain amount of sense at the time."

"One can see the appeal of their logic. Gathering scarce resources to prevent hording, promote fair distribution, and so on," admitted Ravenwood. "But by the time the order was put into effect, some communities had already made great strides in adapting to the new circumstances. But all of that stopped with the collection."

"Tell us what happened at Blue Mountain," said Lena. "You said this was one of the collection areas."

Ravenwood was silent for a moment, then he said, "Food, fuel, and anything else of value was seized by troops and brought there. But many people resisted the collection and followed the convoy of supply trucks to Blue Mountain. They gathered outside the base's fence and protested the government's actions. But they had nothing to eat and no shelter. As time passed, they grew increasingly desperate. Finally, they rushed the fence in a crudely coordinated attack. Four or five groups attacked simultaneously at different places, hoping to break down the barrier. Leaders in each group flew a blue flag on a long pole to inspire and guide those behind them, hence the name Blue Mountain."

"Did they succeed? Did they break down the barrier?" asked Logan.

"No," replied Ravenwood. "The guards responded with tear gas and water cannons at first, but soon they resorted to live ammunition."

They walked on in silence, each person considering the troubling implications of what Ravenwood had said, until shortly before dawn when they reached an old barn surrounded by trees. The building's gray stone walls still stood strong, but the wooden roof had collapsed long ago. Ravenwood led them to a spot in the woods a few meters away, where they could secretly observe anyone approaching the barn. They placed their packs on the ground and sat down to rest their feet.

"You made good time, Ravenwood," said a voice from the shadows.

Kane stepped out from behind a cluster of trees and approached the group, his silhouette barely visible in the faint morning light.

"As did you," said Ravenwood with a smile. He stood and embraced Kane.

Kane looked at the three friends and said, "Get your packs. There's good cover this way."

They walked about ten minutes until they came to the bottom of a rocky cliff wall. It was surrounded by tall pine trees that blocked out the sky. "We should be safe here," said Kane as he put down his pack. He winced slightly when he did so. Logan noticed his coat was torn near the right shoulder.

Ravenwood noticed too and said, "You're injured."

Kane shook his head and said, "It's not serious."

"How'd you get it?" asked Lena.

"I dodged left when I should have dodged right," he said.

"I mean, what happened?" she asked, irritated.

Kane paused and looked at her. Then he said, "I went back toward Williamsport and found a number of Red Legs and SPD officers were following your trail to Deep Pool. With the help of a dozen Travelers, we were able to lead them away. In fact, one of the Travelers said she knew the three of you."

The image of Claire's kindly face flashed across Logan's mind.

"I'm glad you got away," said Logan.

"Yes. I got away, but unfortunately Red Legs captured one Traveler. Shot him in the head and threw the body in the river."

"Did you know his name?" asked Logan, stunned and saddened by what Kane had told them.

"No," answered Kane.

"Savages," said Lena as she punched her fist into her open palm. "They're not soldiers. They're nothing more than murderers. I'd like to run a blade through all of them, every damn one."

Ravenwood put his hand on her shoulder and said, "We can't do anything to stop the Red Legs from terrorizing the Traveler community. Our task is to defeat Guardian Harken's invasion plan so other people won't come under his power. That is why we have to get the Apollo Stone across the river."

"I am concerned with taking the Cumberland Gap," said Kane. "We could swing south. It will take longer, but the people are friendlier, more predictable."

"Normally I would agree," said Ravenwood. "But we don't have time. The Guardians will soon launch their offensive and we are needed across the river. What about the High View Road?"

"Snow will still be blocking it. Using that route would take even longer than going south."

Ravenwood took a deep breath. "Well that settles it. We will take the most direct route through the Gap and hope the queen is in a generous mood." Ravenwood walked off and found a good spot under a pine tree. He laid out his blanket and prepared to sleep.

Logan looked at Kane. "What do you think will happen? Will this Queen Tamara person help us?"

"Hard to say," he said as he removed his coat, revealing a bloody bandage on his upper right arm.

Lena saw the wound and said, "Let's change that bandage." She opened her pack and pulled out a roll of cloth.

"Don't concern yourself," said Kane. "It'll be all right."

Lena tore a strip of cloth and said, "It's important to keep the wound clean." She looked at Cap and said, "Go and fill this canteen with fresh water from the stream down the hill."

While Cap jogged off to get water, Lena crouched next to Kane and carefully tugged at the bloody bandage. "So you don't trust Queen Tamara."

Kane shook his head, "I don't know what she'll do. She's a calculating old crow. She's held the Greenspurs together for over thirty years by playing one group off another, making and breaking alliances, even killing when necessary."

"Sounds like a Guardian," said Lena as she examined the wound. "You'll need a few stitches." She reached into her pack and pulled out a small kit of first-aid materials. "We should thank whoever packed this bag. They did a good job."

Kane smiled, "You're welcome."

Cap returned with the water and gave it to Lena, who washed the wound and applied an antiseptic solution from the first-aid kit.

Holding a needle in her right hand, she looked at Kane and said, "Here we go."

She pushed the curved needle through his skin above the wound and pulled it out below it. She pulled the thin line tight. Kane clenched his teeth but said nothing.

When she was finished, Kane examined the wound and the six sutures Lena had sewn. "Good job," he said. "I appoint you team surgeon."

Lena smiled. "Hopefully we won't need my services in the future," she said as she repacked the first-aid materials.

Chapter 35

They rested during the day under their reflective camo sheets, but once again Logan could not sleep more than a few minutes at a time. Twice he heard helicopters flying nearby, but neither time did they appear to notice the little company. When evening came, they put on their packs and marched up a trail that soon became quite steep. Although it seemed to Logan that Ravenwood and Kane could have marched all night without a stop, Kane called for short breaks every forty-five minutes or so in order to rest. A little before midnight, they approached a place on the trail that narrowed into a thin crevice between high rock walls.

Kane pointed ahead at two tall rocks on each side of the trail and whispered, "That is the Cumberland East Gate. It's the beginning of Greenspur territory."

They had walked for a few more minutes when they heard a voice from the rocks above their heads.

"Hold it right there," said the voice.

"State your purpose."

Ravenwood stopped and looked up into the darkness. "We need to pass through the Cumberland Gap."

"The Gap is closed. We're locked down. Nobody goes through without special permission," said the voice. "And you ain't got permission. Now drop yer valuables, turn around and head back the way you come."

"We can't do that," said Ravenwood. "Let us talk to Queen Tamara. Tell her Ravenwood is at the East Gate."

"I don't need to tell Tamara spit," said the voice. "Now do as I said."

"I am an old friend of hers," said Ravenwood. "When she learns that you failed to inform her of my presence, she'll cut your whiskey ration in half for a month."

There was no response to this and everything was perfectly silent for several heartbeats. Then they heard the soft chirping sound of a two-way radio as the guard relayed the message. After a few moments the voice said, "Well, you must be someone special. Step forward and drop yer weapons."

They walked forward and soon the trail opened up again. Kane unslung his bow and rifle from his shoulder and put his sword on the ground. He also placed his pack on the ground. The others followed his example. Several men and a few women emerged from the darkness, guns leveled at them.

The voice said, "Get their swords and guns. If they've got swords, they probably have guards and shields. Check 'em good for anything hidden."

They removed their bracers and handed them to the Greenspur guards. A tall man with a thin scraggly beard emerged from the darkness. He held a short-barreled shotgun in his hands. "Make sure they ain't got nothin' hidden in their pockets."

One of the guards removed a knife from Kane's belt and one from his boot. Ravenwood also handed over his knife. One of the guards found Logan's medallion and the sphere.

"Well, that is pretty," said scraggly beard as he slipped the medallion into his vest pocket. "And I don't quite know what to make of this," he said, holding the sphere level with his eye. "But we'll take it along."

He walked up to the five of them and assessed each one. "Yer a strange crew, that's for certain," he said. "All right, let's go see the queen."

He turned and spoke to two of the guards. "You two tie their hands and come with me. The rest of you, get back up in them rocks and keep a look out. Remember, we're in lockdown."

When they finished tying their hands, scraggly beard started up the trail. One of the guards gave Kane a shove in the back to send him along. The others fell in behind Kane and the two guards took up the rear.

After about twenty minutes, scraggly beard started whistling a lively tune as he walked. Logan had never heard the style of music before, but it reminded him of some of the old blues music Cap was fond of. The man stopped whistling after a few minutes and sang a verse.

> *So pick away on the old banjo.*
> *Keep that guitar strummin'.*
> *Put some more water in the soup.*
> *There's better times a-comin'!"*

"Don't 'spose you all know that tune," said the man. "Maybe you can sing us a song 'bout what yer up to?" When no one responded, he said, "Nothin'? Well, you'd best be ready to sing for Tamara. Sing her a song 'bout what yer doin' sneakin' 'round our gate in the middle of the night."

"Make 'em sing, Evret," said one of the guards in the back.

"Shut up, Ned," said the man named Evret.

Evret continued to whistle and occasionally sing as they continued along the trail until they saw firelight in the distance. After another fifteen minutes of walking, they came to the bottom of a stone cliff about ten meters high. Evret stepped aside and indicated for them to go up a staircase cut into the rock. First Kane and then Ravenwood started up. As Logan approached the steps, he saw each one was only about one-meter wide, and frequently uneven.

"Don't be scared, lowlander," said Evret when he saw the look of concern on Logan's face. He grinned and indicated with a nod of his head for Logan to continue. "If you slip, the rocks below will kill you quick. You won't suffer much."

"Not much, not much," snickered Ned.

"Shut up, Ned," said Evret.

Logan ascended several steps. He was followed by Lena, then Cap. He carefully placed his foot onto each rough-hewn step as he climbed. He ran his bound hands along the wall and leaned toward it as much as possible.

Logan reached the little landing cut into the rock where the stairs switched back and continued up in the opposite direction. He stopped and looked up to see Kane and Ravenwood were nearly at the top. He was about to follow them when he heard Lena suddenly gasp.

He turned and saw the toe of her right boot had caught on the edge of a step, causing her to stumble. Lena's left foot searched for a step but found only open air. She fell forward, landing awkwardly on her chest. Her right elbow was on a step but the other was over the edge, and because her hands were tied, she couldn't grab hold of anything. Her left leg swung off the side of the stairs, causing her to slowly roll off the ledge. Her eyes locked onto Logan's and he could see terror seize her as she realized she was going to fall to the rocks below.

Just then, Cap lunged forward and fell on top of Lena, preventing her from falling off the ledge. The two of them lay on the steps, barely able to maintain their balance. Logan got down on his knees and reached his bound hands toward his friends. He grabbed a handful of clothing from each of them and pulled with all his strength. Soon all three were lying on the little switchback landing gasping for air, hearts pounding.

"That was close," said Logan.

Lena sat up and looked at Cap. "I thought I was dead. I owe you one."

Cap pulled himself up until he was resting on one elbow. "No sweat," he said with a smile. "At least now I can tell people I got to jump on you."

Lena smiled and shook her head. "You never let up, do you."

Evret and the two guards came up the steps behind them. "Break's over," he said to the three. "On yer feet and up them steps."

They stood and continued to the top of the stone wall where Kane and Ravenwood were waiting. They'd heard the commotion, and Logan could see that Ravenwood was visibly relieved to see they were all right. Kane's stony expression was impossible to read, but Logan sensed he too was relieved.

"What'd you find, Evret?" asked a guard at the top of the stairs.

"Some lowlanders came knockin' at the East Gate," replied Evret. "Tamara says she wants a little parlay with 'em."

Evret led the way toward a low stone structure built against the side of the mountain. Logan looked to his left and right and saw a number of campfires burning with figures of men and women standing around them. Some had weapons slung over their shoulders. Others were cooking food over the fires or drinking from canteens and bottles. As they got closer to the building, Logan saw it was constructed from large stones of various shapes and sizes with generous amounts of mortar added to hold them together. Two guards were stationed on the roof.

Evret raised a hand to the guards as he approached. "Visitors for Tamara."

A guard nodded and spoke into a radio. After a moment, he said, "She's in the Great Hall."

Someone inside the building opened one of the two large wooden doors. They went through into an antechamber lit by a single lightbulb at the end of a wire hanging from the ceiling. They passed through a second set of doors and entered a large open room with long wooden tables and benches. There were groups of people sitting at some of the benches eating and drinking from wooden mugs. Some of them were talking loudly and laughing. One group started singing a song, slapping the table and banging their mugs in time. Lightbulbs dangling from the ceiling provided modest illumination for the room, but most of the light came from a blazing fire at the far end of the Great Hall. Evret led them toward the fire.

As they approached, a tall, lean woman stood up. "Ah, who's this, Evret?" she asked in a reedy but strong voice. "An old friend come to visit?"

"Found 'em at the East Gate, Tamara," answered Evret. "They had these."

He motioned for Ned and the other guard to come forward. They opened two large sacks containing the guns, swords, and bracers they'd confiscated and placed them on the table in front of the woman. Then Evret plopped the sphere down on the table with a thud.

Tamara leaned forward to examine what they had brought, squinting her eyes and smiling. Logan could see in the dancing light of the fire that her long hair was mostly gray and her thin weather-beaten face was creased with fine lines.

"Mmm. Swords and bracers," she said mostly to herself as she picked up one of the swords and held it up to the light. "Lowlanders with Red Leg weapons. Mighty suspicious, wouldn't you say?"

"Mighty suspicious, Tamara" echoed Evret.

Ravenwood looked at Evret and said, "We'd like the medallion back, if you don't mind. Family heirloom, you see."

Evret scowled at him. Then he looked at Tamara, who was tapping the table with her index finger. He reached into his vest pocket and retrieved the medallion. Placing it on the table, he said, "A man should be compensated for sittin' out there in the cold all night long."

"Two hots and a cot is more than most get, so count yerself lucky," replied Tamara.

A few men and women stood up from nearby tables and gathered around the strangers. One of the women reached for the medallion, but Tamara grabbed her wrist and pushed it away.

"Perhaps I should explain the purpose of our visit to the Gap," said Ravenwood as he stepped forward. Evret immediately put his arm in front of Ravenwood to prevent him from approaching Tamara.

"No need for that, Evret," said the Tamara. "This is Ravenwood. You've heard me talkin' about Ravenwood. He's always been a good friend to the Greenspurs. Hasn't been here in a long while, but he used to bring supplies and news about the great big world below the mountains."

She walked toward Ravenwood and stood in front of him for a moment, studying his face. Then she reached down and untied his hands. She indicated for Evret to untie the others' hands as well. "Sit down and eat something," she said. "You look like you haven't had a hot meal in while."

Ravenwood sat at the bench near the end of the table. "A hot meal would be very welcome," he said. The others sat next to him on the bench.

Tamara indicated for Evret to take the weapons away. "No offense, but my people get a little nervous when they see those things," she said as she sat down across from them. "It's been five years since Red Legs tried to come up here, and we wupped 'em good, but they're damn hard to kill when they got them shields on."

"Don't protect 'em from rollin' boulders," observed Evret.

"No it don't," echoed Ned.

"Evret, Ned, don't you have jobs to do?" asked Tamara. "Git back out to the East Gate."

Evret scowled, but he turned around and smacked the other two guards in the chest. "C'mon. Shift ain't over yet."

Tamara watched them leave, then she looked at the faces of the others who had gathered around. "You all can move along. I'm gonna have a private conversation with these folks."

As she spoke, two women brought bowls of steaming meat stew to Logan and the others. Logan smelled the food and suddenly realized he was famished. He wanted to grab a spoon and dig in, but he hesitated and watched Ravenwood and Kane instead. Cap and Lena did the same. Sensing their eyes on him, Ravenwood looked around the table and smiled. He picked up his spoon, nodded in gratitude toward Tamara, and ate a bite of the stew.

"This is outstanding venison stew," he remarked. "And you are right, it has been a while since we've eaten anything other than stale bread and dried meat."

The others started eating. To Logan, the stew was the best thing he'd ever eaten.

"Now what brings you to Cumberland?" asked Tamara as she watched Ravenwood take a bite. "I can tell you it's been at least twelve years since you last passed through. I remember because that's when the new Grand Guardian Harken thought he'd starve us out of the mountains by cuttin' off trade with the lowlanders. Damned fool."

She looked at Lena and said, "The old bastard didn't understand the mountains give us everything we need. And Ravenwood here brought us a mule train full of supplies. Came up the Old Furnace Trail. Unnecessary, 'cause we were gettin' along just fine, but much appreciated."

Looking at Ravenwood, she said, "Before that, I'd say I was about fifteen years old when I last saw you come through. I remember comin' into the cabin after huntin' and found you chattin' with my daddy, God rest his soul."

Ravenwood nodded his head and smiled as he ate his stew. For the first time, Logan had the impression Ravenwood was not his normal cheerful, confident self. He seemed to be careful not to make eye contact with Tamara.

Tamara leaned toward Ravenwood. "You haven't changed a lick," she said as she studied his face. "I mean, you look exactly the same as when I saw you last. Not much different than when I was a girl either."

Ravenwood put down his spoon and looked at Tamara. "Believe me, I've aged. It may not look like it, but there are a lot of miles on this old cart, as the saying goes." He smiled pleasantly.

Tamara shook her head, "Well, whatever yer doin' keep doin' it." She looked at the faces of Ravenwood's companions, stopping when she saw Kane. "Now, you look like a mean one. Full of piss and vinegar. Don't you ever smile?"

Kane looked at her and gave her a slight smile, but he didn't speak. Tamara shrugged.

"So what brings you and your young delicate friends to the Gap?" she asked, giving Logan, Cap, and Lena a brown toothed smile.

Ravenwood placed his spoon on the table and cleared his throat. "As you no doubt know, the Guardians are preparing an assault on the League of Cities. The spring rains are passed and the ground is drying up so they'll attack soon. They've been moving troops and heavy equipment west, and I'm told they finally have the factories of Detroit up and running, churning out tanks and guns. The League will need all the help they can get to hold the line so we are on our way across the Mississippi to assist in any way we can."

"And you want to pass through the Gap to get to the Big River," said Tamara. "Well, as you might have guessed, the Guardians have tightened everything up. You can get to the other side of the Gap, but there'll be regular Flat Foot soldiers plus Red Legs waitin' for you on the other side. With all them troops swarmin' around, I'm not sure how you even made it to the East Gate without gettin' caught."

"We kept to the old trails," said Ravenwood. He scratched his head then asked, "Have you seen any Flat Foots or Red Legs in the Gap? Are they probing your borders?"

Tamara leaned back and said, "Not yet, but they'll being comin' soon, that's for sure. I don't think they'll launch a full-scale attack, but they'll want to box us in here to make sure we don't cause trouble while they attack across the river."

"And if the invasion is successful, you can be sure they'll turn their full attention to you next," said Ravenwood. "You've been a thorn in the Grand Guardian's side for too long. Your private trade with the lowlands is diverting food and supplies from their intended destinations. He can't let that go on forever."

"Nah," said Tamara with a wave of her hand. "You've got it all wrong. The Grand Guardian needs us. We produce more coal than any of their so-called mining developments. And like you said, Detroit is back on line so they need fuel, lots of it. They don't want to mess with their main coal supplier, so I think our arrangement will continue for a long time to come."

Ravenwood shook his head. "No, Tamara," he said. "The economy of the People's Republic of America can only function if it has complete control of all the inputs and outputs. The Guardians cannot allow you to live as you do without risking the eventual collapse of the order they've constructed."

Tamara looked at the others. "What do you all think of this?" she asked, grinning. "Are you goin' off with Ravenwood to save the free cities? You gonna' cut them Detroit tanks in half with yer little swords? Do yerselves a favor. Stay clear of that fight. You can stay up here with us Greenspurs. Look around you, we've got good lives up here. Hell of a lot better than anything below the mountains."

Logan smiled but he did not respond. The others also remained silent.

"Well, you think about it," she said. She waved at a woman to come to her. "When they're done eatin', take these folks to the bunkhouse. Give 'em blankets and show 'em to the showers. They've been on the trails for a while and could use a little freshnin' up."

She looked at her guests. "We'll get you fixed up and send you on yer way tomorra, but like I said, yer gonna run into Flat Foots and Red Legs as soon as you get through the Gap. Might want to reconsider. Yer welcome to stay here as long as you like."

"Thank you, Tamara," said Ravenwood. "We greatly appreciate your hospitality and your offer. But we will take our chances."

Tamara smiled and stood up. As she walked away, Kane said, "Since we're all best friends, can we have our weapons back?"

Tamara stopped and turned to face him. "You'd better let me hold on to 'em for a little longer," she said, giving Kane a wink. "Don't want folks to see strangers walkin' around with all that hardware. Might make 'em nervous."

Tamara left them to finish their meals, which they ate in silence. Logan tried to ask Ravenwood a question, but he shook his head in warning, nodding slightly toward the nearby red-haired woman Tamara had assigned to attend to them.

When they finished eating, the red-haired woman led them through a large door in the back of the Great Hall. They entered a long stone hallway. There were a few heavy wooden doors on either side. After walking about twenty-five meters they saw a large open room to the right. There were rows of beds and tables, and footlockers were tucked under the beds.

"Pick an unused bed. I'll be back with blankets in a minute," said the red-haired woman, disappearing before anyone could ask her anything.

They found a group of beds near the door that they found suitable. The woman reappeared and tossed blankets at each one of them. "Washroom's down the hall to on the right." Then she held out a single lump of soap and asked, "Who's the lucky one who gits to go first?"

An hour later, they were washed and reasonably clean. They did not have fresh clothes to change into because Evret had left their packs at the gate, but it was an improvement. Logan assumed the guards would pick through the packs and claim any valuables, but he didn't mind. He'd been fed and bathed, and now he had a real bed and a blanket. Life was pretty good.

Logan lay down on the narrow bed and smiled, the bed's leather straps creaking under his weight. He looked up at the others and said, "Good night. Wake me when we're across the Mississippi." He closed his eyes and fell asleep almost immediately.

Chapter 36

The black armored vehicle swiftly rolled into place just passed the three-story building. Security guards dressed in dark uniforms and holding urban assault M-35s exited the vehicle and quickly fanned out in a semicircle about twenty-five meters across. Moments later, a black limousine appeared and stopped in front of the building. It was followed by a second armored vehicle.

Grand Guardian Harken stepped out of the limousine and briskly walked toward the door to the building, two guards trailing in his wake. One of the guards ran ahead and pulled the door open for him. Harken went through and the two guards tried to follow him inside, but he stopped them.

"You won't be needed," he said. "Wait here."

Harken ascended two flights of stairs and walked down a narrow dimly lit passage past several closed doors until he reached a large open room with windows lining the two exterior walls. A tall, lean figure with pale skin and straight white hair reaching past his shoulders stood up from a leather sofa located in the middle of the room.

"Grand Guardian Harken," he said. "What a pleasure, please come in. Sit."

"Mr. Kurak," said Harken as he walked toward the bar to his right. "Glad I caught you at home."

"You know I'm always at home," replied Kurak. "Or at the lab." He smiled to reveal straight white teeth, so perfectly aligned they appeared to be fused together.

Harken poured himself a whiskey out of a heavy crystal decanter. He took two gulps and refilled his glass. He grabbed the decanter and an extra glass and walked toward Kurak. He sat in the leather chair opposite the sofa. He placed the glasses and the decanter on the table next to the chair and motioned for Kurak to sit.

"What troubles you?" asked Kurak.

"You know damn well what troubles me," said Harken, as he picked up the empty glass and the whiskey decanter. He held them out toward his host.

"None for me," said Kurak.

Harken shrugged and put them back down. "I don't trust a man who doesn't drink."

"Then you must be disappointed on several counts," said Kurak with a smile.

Harken took a sip of whiskey and exhaled slowly. He set his glass down and looked at Kurak, whose pale blue eyes calmly returned the gaze.

"Tell me we don't need the Apollo Stone," said Harken. "Tell me the other wonder machines and weapons we will soon deploy will be enough."

"You know I can't tell you that," replied Kurak. "The Apollo Stone is far more significant than all of the other advances combined. You will need it to gain total victory and to maintain order once the battles have been won."

"Our troops are well trained and ready," replied Harken. "We can win without the stone."

Kurak leaned forward. His smile had disappeared. "You know the League's true strength of arms. You outnumber them, of course, but they are well prepared for this fight. Even if we successfully cross the river, they will fall back to Deep Six and continue to fight until our supplies are exhausted. We need a fully functional *Blackhawk* to disrupt their plans, break their spirit, and quickly end the war."

Harken shook his head. "Damn it," he whispered as he took another sip.

"Let me help with the search," said Kurak. "I can locate its space-time signature better than anyone."

"No thank you," said Harken. "Your physical appearance is, how shall I put it, a little unsettling to the troops."

"You don't think they would believe what we tell the lab staff? That I'm an albino with a skin mutation?" asked Kurak with a light chuckle.

"No," said Harken with a mirthless smile. "They would not."

"I wonder why that is?" Kurak mused. "Your people swallow every other story you and the Guardians tell them. Why not this one?"

"Because you're a stone-cold killer, and they can sense that," said Harken without hesitation. "But that's okay. We're all killers. The times call for it. But with you it's different. They can tell there's something unusually dangerous about you, and they fear it."

"I don't think I've given anyone cause to think I am anything other than a devoted servant to the cause of protecting this great nation," said Kurak.

"You can save the bullshit for people like Castell and Chambers," said Harken. "I know the whole story. Who you are. Why you're here."

Kurak leaned back into the sofa but didn't respond.

After a moment, Harken asked, "Why do you think he took it? Why'd Chambers steal the Apollo Stone?"

"I don't know," said Kurak. "He never shared any misgivings with me."

"It's strange how you think you've thoroughly vetted a person only to find out they've been hiding something terrible from you deep down inside. Then one day they do something monumentally stupid like this."

"It might have always been there, as you suggest, but he might not have been aware of it," said Kurak. "Maybe something happened that suddenly brought it forward into the light. Maybe he discovered he wasn't up to the demands of the task."

"So we're all a potential time bomb of conscientious misgivings? Is that what you're saying?" asked Harken, incredulously. "Are you or I going to have a change of heart? Suddenly throw away a lifetime of work and run across the river?"

Kurak smiled. "No. Not your or I. Like you said, we're killers. We exchanged our hearts for power long ago."

Harken gave a light chuckle. Then he raised his glass in a toast and said, "To killers."

Chapter 37

Guardian Castell threw the military intelligence assessment report onto his desk and stood up. He walked to his office window. The Capitol District, illuminated by the early morning light, sprawled out before him. He looked down, past the Defense Ministry's sentry post to the pedestrians and cars on the street below. The sounds of honking horns occasionally drifted up to his spacious tenth-floor office. Looking up, he saw a pair of helicopters fly along the perimeter of the Capitol barrier. The Grand Guardian had asked him to increase the number of patrols following the discovery of the Apollo Stone's theft several days prior. Grand Guardian Harken had also ordered him and Justice Guardian Bishop to cooperate to retrieve it, so Castell ordered more Red Legs to take part in the search, and Bishop cancelled all non-essential travel and ordered a nationwide 8 p.m. curfew.

Guardian Castell looked at the view screen hanging on the wall. He picked up a remote control device and turned it off. For hours, the news headlines repeated the same few pieces of information. A wave of clan attacks had been carried out against developments and towns all along the frontier region while a group of League spies sought to simultaneously sabotage PRA infrastructure targets throughout the country. The worst of these plots, the news anchor repeated every fifteen minutes, was a plan to poison the water supply in the Capitol District, New York, and Boston. Fortunately, Grand Guardian Harken disrupted the plot. People in the major cities and towns were instructed to remain in their homes at night and to conduct only essential business during the day. Intercity travel was restricted to priority-one visas only and all civilian travel to and from the frontier region was prohibited.

Castell heard the sound of a light chime.

He turned and pressed a button on his PDD which lay on his desk. "Yes."

"General Grier is here, sir," said a woman's voice.

"Send him in, please."

A stout man in a green uniform entered through the office door. He approached the Defense Guardian's desk and gave a quick nod of his head.

"Good morning, Guardian Castell. I have the latest readiness reports," he said as he placed a folder on the Guardian's desk.

Castell sat down and opened the folder. He read for a few seconds and then said, "Please sit, general."

General Grier sat in one of the two chairs in front of the Guardian's desk, pulling his uniform jacket down over his round torso.

"I think you'll see things are proceeding nicely, sir," he said in a voice made gravely by thirty years of smoking cigars. "The last of the troop trains are arriving in the staging areas, Special Forces Units are in a full state of readiness, and the additional armored units will be in place by tomorrow evening. If everything goes to plan, we'll be ready to attack within forty-eight hours."

"Supply depots, lines of communication, alternative routes all in order?" asked Castell, as he leafed through the report's pages.

"Yes sir," said Grier, as he once again pulled the waistband of his coat down.

"I detect a note of concern in your voice, general," said Castell. "What's on your mind?"

"No concerns, Guardian Castell," responded Grier.

Castell put the report down on the desk and stared at the general. After a moment, Grier raised his palms slightly and said, "I have an unofficial report from my Special Forces chief, General Pollard." Grier hesitated.

"Judging from your discomfort, I assume this is about my daughter," said Castell, slightly irritated. "Out with it."

"There is an unconfirmed report she was spotted in a small town west of here with the other two cadets. And a known foreign agent."

Castell narrowed his eyes. "What foreign agent?"

"A man called Ravenwood," said Grier.

Castell scoffed. "Ravenwood. He's a mosquito, a nuisance, not a foreign agent. Where are they now?"

"We assume they're on foot. We're focusing our search on all routes leading from the town, sir."

"What about the reported sightings to the south?"

"We are checking those out too, sir, but they seem less likely to be correct."

Castell looked away from the general and drummed his fingers on his desk. "General, you understand the urgency here, right?" he asked, returning his gaze to the red-faced Grier. "I need every available Special Forces unit in the country looking for my daughter. I can still convince the Grand Guardian that this as a case of misguided youthful energy. But the longer she is missing, the more difficult it will become."

"I understand, sir."

"That's good. Because if the SPD finds her first, or if they firmly connect her to the missing item, my days as a Guardian are over. That means a new Defense Guardian will be appointed. And new Guardians get rid of the prior Guardian's staff and install people they know and trust."

"Understood sir," said Grier.

"To be honest," continued Castell, "You and I are lucky to be alive because Harken doesn't want to risk a leadership shakeup so close to the invasion. That has bought us some time, so make good use of it."

"Yes sir," said General Grier.

"Find the girl and the Apollo Stone," said Castell. "Guardian Bishop fucked up when he lost the stone. That would have placed me in a very strong position to succeed Harken as Grand Guardian. But then my daughter had to screw it up for me. If he recovers the stone and my daughter first, he will have redeemed himself, and I'll be on the next train to a textiles development with you at my side. If we get them first, he's on that train. Have I painted the picture clearly enough for you, general?"

"Yes sir," said Grier, nodding his round head repeatedly. "I'll put everyone on it."

"Do that," replied Castell. "Now get out of my office."

Placing both hands on the chair's arms, the general pushed himself to his feet and walked toward the door with short quick steps.

"And Grier," said Castell as the general reached for the door handle.

Grier stopped and turned to face the Guardian. "Sir?"

"If my daughter dies while recovering the Apollo Stone, it would be a tragic but not unexpected outcome."

General Grier paused a moment then said, "Yes sir."

Chapter 38

Logan was in a boat silently moving over calm blue waters. A gentle breeze filled the boat's sails and pushed him toward a distant tropical island. Looking up, he saw large white cumulus clouds drifting along with him like companions on a shared journey. As Logan approached the island, he could see tall palm trees covered the gently rising slope of an ancient volcano in the center of the island.

But before Logan reached his destination, the sky grew dark and swirling gray and black storm clouds filled the horizons as far as the eye could see. Flashes of lightning illuminated the heart of the storm, occasionally leaping down to the sea below. The waters had become dark and rough. Waves splashed over the walls of his little boat, pushing it from side to side. Logan reached behind him and took hold of the tiller, but a violent wind shredded the sail, making it impossible to guide the small craft. He looked toward the island to see if he could swim to it, but towering black waves had pushed him far from the safety of its shores. A great wave crashed into the side of the boat, knocking Logan down to the floor.

"Get up," said a voice from the dark turbulent skies above.

Logan tried to rise up, but his limbs refused to obey.

"Get up!" said the voice again and again.

Logan opened his eyes, only to be blinded by a gas lamp held near his face. "Get up," said the voice. A boot kicked the edge of his bed. The lamp was pulled away from his face, allowing him to see his surroundings.

"Let's go, boy," said a man with a thick black beard. "Queen wants to see you."

A minute later, Logan was stumbling down the hall, still half asleep. With every third or fourth step, the man shoved him in the back. "Let's go," he said. "Queen's awaitin'. And the Queen don't like waitin'."

After they had walked twenty steps, the man shoved Logan to the side through an open door. The room was barely lit, but he could see Ravenwood and the others were already there standing in a line in front of a table. Tamara was sitting in a chair on the other side of the table. Logan could make out the shapes of men standing in the shadows behind Tamara.

"Ah, our final guest has arrived," said Tamara. "Stand here next to your friends." She pointed at a spot next to Cap. Logan complied.

"As you all know, we Greenspurs are the leadin' clan here in the Gap," said Tamara. "We've been the leadin' clan for a long time, and that ain't easy. There's always someone tryin' to knock us off the high perch. Now, a big part of stayin' in charge is doin' what's right for the Greenspurs and all of the Mountaineer clans."

She looked at each of their faces before continuing. Then she said, "Now you all came up on us pretty sudden last night. Ravenwood and Kane here are wanderers of sorts. You know that just from lookin' at 'em. We're used to their kind passin' through."

"But you three," she said, pointing at Logan, Lena, and Cap. "You three are quite rare in these parts. You ain't Travelers. You ain't runaways from some development. You ain't SPD visa dogs. You ain't Flat Foots. You ain't Red Legs. That makes me wonder what the hell you are."

No one spoke.

"Now when in a perplexing situation like this, a good leader seeks advice," she continued. "But you've seen what I've got to work with here. My people are good folk, but they don't understand much of what goes on beyond these mountains. That's why I contacted an old friend down in the lowlands who helped me understand just what I'm dealin' with here"

She looked Logan in the eye, and then she said, "You and your two friends are wanted worse than whiskey, and they were comin' for ya anyway. I had to make a trade. I'm sure you understand. My people come first."

She stood and stepped back toward the wall. As she did so, a man in a blue uniform emerged from the shadows.

"Mr. Brandt and Mr. Caparelli," said Colonel Linsky. "You failed to keep our earlier appointment. I'm so glad I could catch up. And I see we have a new friend. Ms. Castell," he said with a slight bow. "Your father will be so relieved when he learns we've found you."

Several Red Legs armed with M-35s emerged from the shadows. Others entered the room through the door behind Logan.

Logan swore under his breath. He couldn't believe this was happening. He and his friends had traveled hundreds of kilometers, most of it on foot. They'd crossed rivers and climbed mountains to get away. Yet, despite all of their efforts, here was Colonel Linsky standing right in front of him.

Linsky took a few steps toward Ravenwood. "You must be the Ravenwood person I've heard so many rumors about. I had expected something more…regal," he said as he looked with disgust at the man's filthy tattered green coat. "I was told you were some kind of wise man, but you look more like a wild-eyed prophet who wanders in from the wilderness to warn everyone they are going to die a fiery death." Linsky gave Ravenwood a mocking wild-eyed look and waved his hands around as he spoke. Then he lowered his hands and smiled pleasantly.

Ravenwood returned the smile and said, "As a matter of fact, unless we change the course of events, we *are* all going to die a fiery death. You think you know what you have. You think it will give you superiority on the battlefield. Perhaps it will for a time. But what you fail to understand is that the person with whom you have struck your bargain will exact a terrible price from all of us. The Sahiradin don't make deals with humans. The Sahiradin kill humans."

Logan noticed a fleeting shadow of doubt cross Linsky's face, but he quickly recovered his composure.

"Mr. Ravenwood," said Linsky. "I don't know what you are talking about, but we'll have plenty of time together to explore this theme in depth." He looked at Kane, whose face was an impassive mask. He smiled and asked, "And who are you?"

"I'm the man who's going to cut you to pieces," replied Kane in a serious but matter-of-fact tone.

Linsky raised an eyebrow but did not appear to be intimidated. Logan realized the SPD officer had probably heard a thousand similar threats throughout his career. Linsky looked at his Red Leg companions and pointed to Kane. "I don't think we'll need this one. You expressed interest in killing him. Be my guest. I'll take the others with me back to the Capitol District."

Special Forces Colonel Dornicz stepped forward and said, "No. We're taking all of them to HQ. You're forgetting you hitched a ride on our chopper to get here. You can ride back with us to HQ or stay here. Your choice."

Linsky seemed perturbed for a moment, but then he smiled and said, "Fine. We will fly back to your HQ."

Colonel Dornicz walked past the table and stood face to face with Kane. "You and I are going to get to know each other real well."

"Lookin' forward to it," said Kane.

The Red Leg soldiers began tying the prisoners' hands behind their backs with plastic cords. As the soldiers worked, Linsky leaned close to Logan and opened his coat slightly, revealing the bulge of the sphere in his coat's inner pocket.

"This stays with me," he said softly and winked.

Logan looked around the dimly lit room but could find no evidence of the medallion. "You'll need the medallion if you want to be sure it's in there," he said. "The old woman probably has it."

Linsky looked at Tamara. "You took a medallion from these prisoners. Hand it over."

Tamara looked at Logan with contempt in her eyes. She pulled the medallion out of her pocket and gave it to Linsky, who looked closely at it in the dim light.

"Some sort of key, I would assume," he said as he placed it in his breast pocket. "Dr. Chambers' ingenuity continues to astound me even after his death."

Tamara looked at Colonel Dornicz and said, "Okay, okay. Now that our business is complete you boys can be on yer way."

"Why?" answered the Red Leg. "You in some kind of hurry to get rid of us? Maybe we should stay for a while."

Tamara smiled and said, "You can stay as long as you like, Colonel Red Leg. Take yer boots off. Have a snooze. We'll make it so nice you'll *never* leave." The smile disappeared from her face.

Dornicz chuckled and said, "You're a tough old bird, aren't you. Thanks for the invitation, but we're expected back at HQ. We'll stay longer next time. I promise."

Looking at one of the Red Leg soldiers, he said, "Take this trash to the helicopter."

The soldiers led the prisoners into the hallway and turned toward the Great Hall. Colonel Dornicz and Linsky led the group. Two Red Leg soldiers walked on each side of the prisoners. Four more walked behind. Logan pulled at his bindings, turning and twisting them, but he couldn't free his hands. He looked right and left, desperately searching for some opportunity for escape, but there was nothing. As they passed a small room, he looked through the open door to see their swords and bracers on a table. Tamara broke away from the group and went into the room where a fellow Greenspur was guarding the weapons.

Suddenly, a lightbulb hanging above them burst in a shower of sparks. Then the next one burst. And the next one and the next one until the hallway was completely dark. The guards began to yell and fumble to get ahold of the prisoners. Dornicz shouted for Logan and the others to be taken to the helicopter. Someone grabbed Logan's arm and pulled him through the pitch black and slammed him against one of the walls.

"Don't move," Ravenwood whispered into Logan's ear.

The plastic cord fell from Logan's wrists. He tried to make out what was happening around him, but except for the faint light filtering past the edges of the door to the Great Hall, everything was completely black. He heard a man's voice to his right. He slid along the wall in that direction and found the doorway to the little room where he had seen their weapons. He slipped inside and groped for the table in the darkness. He bumped into someone. A hand grabbed his arm and swung him around. He pushed back and heard a man grunt. He felt someone's arms go around his shoulders, then try to push him to the ground, but Logan pivoted and broke free of the man's grasp.

Logan turned toward where he heard someone breathing. He held his hands out in front of him, keeping his elbows close to his hips and legs about shoulder-width apart, one foot slightly forward. He heard the sounds of fighting coming from the hallway but focused on his opponent in the room. He heard a foot scraping against the stone floor. Logan quickly swung his open hand in that direction and felt an arm slip through his grasping hand. He immediately swung with the left hand and caught his opponent by the neck. Logan placed his left heel behind the man's leg and took him down with a thud. The man grunted and swore, but Logan was on him before he could get up. Logan placed a knee on the man's chest, held his neck with his left hand and began smashing his face with his right fist. The fourth punch knocked the Greenspur unconscious.

Logan stood up and found the table. He began feeling for the swords and bracers when there was a sudden intensely bright flash of light in the hallway, but he had been looking away so his eyes were unaffected by the flash. Then someone opened the door to the Great Hall, briefly illuminating the passageway with sunlight before it was suddenly closed, but it was enough for Logan to momentarily see the swords and bracers. He quickly gathered them together, and as he turned he heard Ravenwood's voice from the doorway.

"This way, boy," the old man urged. "No time to lose."

He felt Ravenwood's hand on his elbow, guiding him toward the Great Hall. Men were stumbling around shouting or lying on the ground moaning.

"What about Cap and Lena?" asked Logan. "Where are they?"

"We're here," said Cap from behind Ravenwood.

Ravenwood let go of Logan's elbow and moved ahead a few steps. He heard Ravenwood push on the heavy doors leading to the Great Hall, but they wouldn't open. He saw Ravenwood's silhouette bend low as he seemed to be pressing his open palms against the wooden doors. There was a loud cracking sound then the doors flew open, flooding the hallway with light.

"Quickly!" said Ravenwood to Logan and the others. "They have the sphere and are headed toward the helicopter. They must not escape!"

Kane ran by Logan, grabbing his sword, dagger, and bracer as he passed. He slipped the bracer over his forearm and initiated the antiballistic shield, causing a light to momentarily shimmer around his body. Cap and Lena did the same and followed Kane out the Great Hall's main door and into the morning sun.

Logan slipped on his bracer and gripped his sword. He turned to see if he could assist Ravenwood, but the big man was already gliding past him with the ease of a ten-point buck in an open field. Logan turned and followed, but not before he saw three Red Leg guards and several Greenspurs, including Tamara, emerging from the hallway. They stumbled and squinted their eyes in the light. They all started to run toward him, but Tamara signaled for her Greenspurs to hold back. One of the Red Legs fired a burst from his M-35 at Logan's chest, but the bullets deflected off his shield.

Logan turned and raced after his companions. Once outside in the morning sun, he could see Dornicz, three Red Legs, and Linsky running up a trail, presumably toward a helicopter landing pad somewhere above. He ran with all his strength and soon overtook Lena and Cap, but he could not catch Ravenwood, who bounded up the hill and disappeared behind a cluster of trees and bushes.

He heard shots ringing out. When he reached the cluster of trees, he saw Ravenwood hiding behind a large oak tree. Another shot bounced off the tree's bark, causing Ravenwood to cling closer to the trunk. Logan continued up the path, ignoring the bullets that whistled all around him. He found the source of the bullets, two Red Legs with M-35s. When they realized Logan had a shield, they engaged theirs and pulled out their swords.

Logan immediately attacked, swinging at one and blocking the other's blade with his arm guard. He kicked one of them in the gut and slashed hard at the other but missed. Then Cap and Lena arrived. Cap side-stepped one Red Leg's slashing blade and responded by cutting him across his stomach. Lena parried a flurry of attacks from the other Red Leg, who had the higher ground, but she drove him up the hill with her own attacks until she was able to slice into his right leg. The man collapsed in anguish, screaming and holding his leg.

Ravenwood caught up to them. "The Apollo Stone!" he yelled. "Get the Apollo Stone!"

Logan looked down the hill past Ravenwood and saw three Red Leg soldiers had emerged from the Great Hall and were running toward them. He and the others turned and raced to join Kane.

As he ran, Logan heard the sound of a turbine engine starting. He looked ahead to see a helicopter, its rotors beginning to turn. About fifty meters in front of him Kane was battling Colonel Dornicz and another Red Leg. Logan watched as Kane deflected Dornicz's attack with his sword and countered with a thrust of his dagger, but Dornicz blocked it with his arm guard. The other Red Leg attacked from Kane's right side but lost his footing, leaving him exposed. Kane plunged his sword into the man's side. Dornicz saw Logan and the others approaching and swung at Kane, then retreated toward the helicopter. Kane immediately gave chase. Ahead of everyone was Colonel Linsky, who had nearly reached the helicopter.

Logan stopped running and picked up the M-35 from the Red Leg Kane had killed. He handed it to Cap, who had just arrived with Lena.

"Don't let that helicopter take off," he said. "Lena and I will protect your back."

Cap took the gun and dropped to one knee. "No sweat," he said. "Just shoot the one place the Berring T-85 transport helicopter doesn't have armored plating, the tail rotor axle." He squeezed off a shot but missed his target.

The three Red Legs coming up the hill were nearly upon them. Logan looked at Lena. She was standing with her sword and guard at the ready. Her face was expressionless, but her eyes were intently focused on the approaching men.

Cap fired at the rotor again. "Damn it!" he said.

"Do you want me to take the shot?" Lena asked Cap.

"I got this," replied Cap, irritated.

"Why did you give him the gun?" Lena asked Logan without looking at him.

"I thought he'd know best where to shoot the thing," he responded, a bit defensively.

Another missed shot. Another expletive from Cap.

Logan took a quick look over his shoulder and saw Ravenwood had nearly caught up with Kane, who was once again fighting Dornicz at a spot just twenty meters away from the helicopter. Linsky was already at the helicopter yelling at the pilot to get it into the air. Then Linsky turned and fired his pistol several times at the onrushing Ravenwood, who ducked and swerved, sometimes holding his hands out as if he were pushing the air in front of him.

Logan returned his attention to the three charging Red Legs. Lena took three quick steps and met two of them. Her sword whistled through the air and sliced a Red Leg's throat. Logan charged as well, fooling one of the Red Legs with a feint to the right. He drove his sword forward and pierced the middle soldier's leg, causing him to drop to the ground screaming.

Another shot rang out, and Cap shouted in victory. He picked up his sword and joined Logan and Lena. The remaining Red Leg retreated down the slope several meters and assumed a defensive posture. Logan looked over his shoulder and saw the helicopter's tail rotor was no longer spinning properly.

"Good job, Cap," said Logan. "Now let's go get the stone."

Ignoring the remaining Red Leg, they turned and ran toward the helicopter. Logan saw Kane drive his sword into Dornicz's shoulder then he cut the Red Leg officer's thigh. Dornicz dropped to the ground.

Seeing Dornicz go down, Linsky engaged his arm guard and attacked Kane with a long thin rapier. To Linsky's right, the helicopter pilot was swinging his sword at Ravenwood, who defended himself with a blade he had picked up from the ground, though he was clearly no swordsman.

Logan pointed at Ravenwood with his sword and yelled, "Help Ravenwood!"

Lena and Cap veered toward Ravenwood to assist. Logan stole a look over his shoulder and saw the remaining Red Leg they had left behind was pursuing, but was clearly disinclined to catch up to them.

As Logan approached the helicopter, Linsky was attacking Kane with combinations of feints and strikes, slashes and jabs. Kane retreated several steps, trying to adjust to Linsky's graceful but deadly style of fighting. He raised his dagger to block Linsky's sword but was caught off guard when Linsky shifted the angle of his attack with a slight wrist movement. Kane managed to block the attack, but was unable to block Linsky's vicious kick to his ribs, sending him sprawling against the side of the helicopter.

Logan arrived and immediately slashed at Linsky's exposed right flank, but the SPD officer easily sidestepped the assault. Logan blocked a counterattack from the grinning Linsky, but slipped in some loose gravel, nearly falling to the ground. He regained his balance and barely fended off Linsky's attempt to slit his throat. Then Kane swung for Linsky's neck, but Linsky rolled into the helicopter's open bay door and jumped out the opposite side.

Logan ran around the front of the helicopter in pursuit of Linsky while Kane ran around the back. Linsky was dashing for the tree line, but he stopped when he saw that a deep ravine separated him from his escape route. Logan looked to his right and saw that Lena had wounded the pilot, who sat with his back against the side of the helicopter with one hand holding his bleeding shoulder. Looking down the hill, he saw the remaining Red Leg had stopped and was tending to the wounded Colonel Dornicz.

Hopelessly outnumbered, Linsky dropped his sword and gun, and raised his hands above his head. "I surrender," he said in a strangely amused tone. "Please do not hurt me. I am completely under your control."

As they encircled Linsky, Ravenwood said, "The stone, please." Breathing heavily from his exertions, he held out his hand.

Linsky reached into his inner coat pocket and retrieved the sphere. But instead of placing it in Ravenwood's hand, he dropped it on the ground by Logan's feet.

"And the medallion," said Logan, gripping his sword tightly and pointing it toward the SPD colonel's stomach.

Linsky looked at the blade and smiled. "Come now, Mr. Brandt. You're not the type."

"There's a man in Williamsport who'd differ with you on that," replied Logan.

"Ah. So now you are a killer. You've sipped the wine of ultimate power," said Linsky as he reached his left hand into his breast pocket to retrieve the medallion.

As Linsky brought his hand out of his pocket, Logan heard a clicking sound and a blade shot out from the SPD officer's right sleeve. Linsky quickly swung the blade toward Logan's throat. Logan realized what was happening and tried to move, but he knew he was moving too slowly to avoid the weapon. Just as the knife was about strike home Lena's blade flashed by and sliced off Linsky's right hand at the wrist. Hand and knife fell to the ground.

Linsky screamed and fell to his knees. He dropped the medallion from his left hand and grabbed his right wrist, desperately trying to stop the blood from gushing forth. Then he pulled a handkerchief from his coat pocket and tried to tie it around his wrist using his remaining hand and his teeth.

Kane leaned down and picked up the medallion off the ground. He wiped some blood off of it and handed it to Logan. Ravenwood retrieved the sphere and also handed it to Logan, who put the items in separate pockets.

"What are we going to do with this guy?" asked Kane as he looked at Linsky. "Not the kind of man you want to leave hanging around."

"We could let the Greenspurs hold on to him for a while until we can get away," suggested Cap.

"They won't hold him," said Logan. "They hate the Guardians, but now they have a bunch of dead Red Legs, a wounded SPD officer, and a disabled Berring T-85 to account for. That won't be good for relations, even if the PRA needs their coal."

Logan knelt down and tightened the knot around the now semi-conscious Linsky.

"You all might want to have a look at this," said Kane, who was looking down the hill.

Everyone but Logan stood next to Kane to see a large group of Greenspurs coming up the hill with Tamara in the front. In addition to guns, the Greenspurs were armed with spears, swords, knives, and axes.

Logan joined them a few moments later and they walked toward the Greenspurs.

"I underestimated you lowlanders," said Tamara when the two groups were within ten meters of each other. "I thought them Red Legs would chew you up like hogs in a corn bin. Now look at the mess you made. How am I gonna explain all this?"

Ravenwood raised his hands, "Tamara. *Queen* Tamara. You can lay all the blame at our feet. Just let us pass through the Gap. We will be forever grateful."

"Grateful?" she said. "Grateful! I don't give a gatt damn how *grateful* you are! You put me in a bind here, Ravenwood. You know we need the trade with the lowlanders and we need the Guardians to stay out of our business. That means I gotta make up for this mess somehow."

Ravenwood began to speak, but she held up a hand. "Time for talkin' is past. Now drop yer swords. Turn off yer little shields and come with me peaceably. And hand over that ball. The way that SPD bastard grinned when he saw it tells me it's gotta be of some kind of value."

"Why not just ask him why he wants it?" asked Logan. "He's right back there behind the helicopter."

"Shit, he's still alive?" she asked, craning her neck to get a better look at Linsky. "That is disappointin'!" she yelled. "Very disappointin'!"

"Disappointin'," echoed a voice from the crowd of Greenspurs.

"Shut up, Evret!" she yelled. Returning her attention to Ravenwood, she repeated her earlier demand. "Drop yer weapons and drop the ball."

No one moved. She looked at the sky as if to say *why me?*

"All right," she said after a moment. She turned and addressed the Greenspurs gathered behind her. "Boys, shoot Ravenwood. Them others got shields, so you can knife 'em now or shoot 'em when their shields' charges run out."

Just as she spoke, Lena's shield flickered a few times and disengaged. The Greenspurs started to walk toward them. Kane held his sword and dagger at the ready.

"Wait!" said Logan. "I'll give you the sphere, but you have to let us go. We just want to live."

The Greenspurs halted their advance and looked at Tamara, who replied, "Before I say yes or no, you gotta tell me what that ball is."

"It's a navigation orb for a big ship they built," said Logan. "They can't fly it without this thing, and that's why they're after us. We stole it and we were trying to get it to the free cites, but it's not worth dying for."

Tamara narrowed her eyes at Logan and said, "All right. It's a deal."

Ravenwood tried to stop Logan, but the young man had already tossed the sphere down the hill to Tamara. She picked it up and rolled it around in her hands. Then she looked up and smiled at Logan.

"Boys," she said to her men. "Kill them sunsabitches. And bring me that pretty medallion." She turned and walked down the hill toward the Great Hall, sphere in hand.

"We made a deal!" yelled Logan as the Greenspurs started walking toward them.

Tamara turned and said in a matter of fact tone, "But we didn't spit and shake. Deal ain't sealed 'til ya spit and shake." Then she continued down the hill. Logan heard a whistling sound as one of the Greenspurs fired his riffle at Ravenwood.

Ravenwood suddenly pushed the others toward the west side of the hill and yelled, "Run!"

They all dashed down the western slope toward the main trail with the Greenspurs close on their heels. Those with functioning shields ran in the rear in order to protect the group from bullets.

They were all quick runners, but the Greenspurs were quicker, having lived their entire lives climbing up and down mountain trails. They approached a narrow portion of the trail with a sharp bend. Kane, who was in the rear, suddenly turned and sliced at two of the Greenspurs who'd gotten ahead of the pack. They collapsed to the ground howling and clutching their wounds. Kane turned and resumed running. Other Greenspurs came upon their fallen kinsmen but simply leapt over them and continued the chase.

Kane yelled from behind the group, "Take the trail to the right."

Ravenwood turned right when he reached a fork and found himself struggling through some tree branches and scrub brush that grew nearly sideways out of the mountainside.

"Down into the ravine," said Kane.

Ravenwood and the others did as instructed and jumped down into a shallow dry ravine. Kane leapt over them and took the lead.

"In here," he said after he'd run a few meters.

He slid through a narrow crevice in the mountain, barely wide enough to enter sideways. The others followed. Logan was last in line and slipped through just as the Greenspurs passed by on the trail.

No one moved or said anything for a few moments as they listened to their pursuers run down the trail past the ravine. Then Kane slid along the wall and indicated for the others to follow. Soon the narrow passage opened up into a rather large open cave. It was dimly light by the light filtering in through the narrow entrance.

"This cave is no secret to the Greenspurs," said Kane once everyone was inside. "And I assume they'll retrace their steps and come in here as soon as they realize we're not on the trail."

"Then why the hell are we in here?" asked Cap. "We'll be trapped."

"They know about this cave, but I'm hoping they don't know everything about it," replied Kane.

Lena grabbed Logan by the arm and spun him around to face her. "What the hell was that about back there?" she said angrily. "You gave the sphere to that crazy hillbilly? You know she's going to hand it right over to the SPD. They'll have that gunship fully operational in no time."

Ravenwood stepped between them and put his hand on Logan's shoulder. "You did exactly the right thing," he said with a wink and a smile, patting Logan on his jacket's breast pocket.

Logan reached into the pocket and retrieved the Apollo Stone. Lena and Cap stared wide-eyed at the little black orb resting in Logan's palm. "I took it out of the case when we were at the helicopter, hoping the Greenspurs would let us go if they had the sphere."

"It was a chance worth taking. But now we are exposed to a new danger," said Ravenwood. "The sphere was protecting the Apollo Stone from harm, but I suspect it was also masking its signature. Without the sphere we may be considerably easier to find."

"I thought you said it doesn't emit any radiation?" asked Lena, concerned.

"And it doesn't," answered Ravenwood in a reassuring tone. "But recall what the Apollo Stone is. It is a mechanism for bending space-time, and even when it is not in use it affects the area around it in a very minute way. This minor effect is its signature, for lack of a better term."

"We can talk about that later. Let's focus now on escaping," said Kane. "This is an old smugglers' cave. They used it as a place to hide food, whiskey, and weapons during the Long Winter."

Lena scoffed. "How did they get anything through that narrow crevice?"

Kane ran his fingers along a section of the rock wall. He pointed at a narrow fissure in the wall. "Since you're so curious, I want you to reach in there and tell me what you find."

Lena reluctantly did as Kane asked. She reached into the fissure and felt around until her fingers touched something metal.

"Find something interesting?" asked Kane with a slight grin.

"I think so, yes." she answered. "Feels like a lever."

Loud voices filtered into the cave from the outside. Kane motioned for the others to come to him.

"Pull it," he said to Lena.

Lena pulled but the lever did not move. She heard the voices getting louder and pulled as hard as she could. Finally, there was a slight popping sound as the lever rotated toward her. Kane leaned against the stone wall and it moved slightly. Logan, Cap, and Ravenwood added their weight and a portion of the wall about the size of a door swung slowly open. They entered as quickly as possible. When all were on the other side, Kane and Cap pushed the door shut until they heard a clicking sound.

Chapter 39

Everyone stood still in the perfect blackness of the tunnel. They hardly dared to breathe as they listened to the muffled sounds of people bickering on the other side of the rock door.

After a few minutes, the voices were gone. Kane whispered, "Everyone hold hands. Form a chain and we'll make our way down the tunnel as best we can. There are side tunnels that branch off, but keep going straight. Ravenwood, you lead."

"Certainly," said Ravenwood as he squeezed pass Logan and Kane to get in front of the group. "Is everyone ready?" he asked.

Logan reached forward and took Kane's hand with his right and reached back to Lena with his left. Cap was last in line and took Lena's outstretched hand. When everyone was ready, Ravenwood began inching forward through the darkness, alerting everyone to loose rocks, dips in the floor, and low sections of the ceiling.

As they walked hand in hand, Logan said, "Ravenwood. Who are the Sahiradin?"

"The Sahiradin?" replied the Ravenwood. "You remembered my warning to the SPD officer."

"Yes," said Logan. "You said Sahiradin don't make deals with humans, they kill humans. What did you mean?"

Ravenwood didn't respond right away. Logan wished he could see the older man's face and try to read his thoughts. Finally, Ravenwood said, "The Sahiradin are an ancient people from a place quite distant from here. Twelve thousand light years away from here, to be more precise."

"I assume the survivor that the Apollo astronaut found in the escape pod on the moon was a Sahiradin," said Lena.

"Indeed," said Ravenwood. "In fact, he is the captain of the ship which had exploded."

Cap interjected, "You just said he *is* the captain of the ship. So you think he's still alive?"

"As I told you in Deep Pool, who's to say how long an alien lives," said Ravenwood. "But I'm convinced this particular one is still alive."

"Alive and helping to build up the PRA's war machine," said Kane.

"Is that war machine crippled now?" asked Cap. "Do you think the Guardians will call off the attack now that they don't have the Apollo Stone?"

"Not likely," said Ravenwood. "But I like your optimism."

A moment later Ravenwood said, "Aha. We may be in luck."

A sudden flash of light blinded Logan and the others. Logan let go of Kane's hand and shielded his eyes with his hand. Looking between his fingers, he could see Ravenwood holding an old kerosene lamp. Logan looked around and saw what his feet and hands had already told him. They were in a narrow, rough-hewn tunnel with a dirt and rock floor and low ceiling.

Kane took the lantern from Ravenwood and said, "Let's move. We should soon come to a large natural cave with an underground stream. The water will lead us out of the mountain."

"What else do you know about the Sahiradin?" asked Lena as they continued down the tunnel. "Who are they?"

"The information I have is a little bit out of date," said Ravenwood. "But it is my understanding that they are an extremely aggressive people, and they have conquered many worlds."

"So what were they doing when their ship exploded?" asked Lena.

"I cannot say for sure," said Ravenwood.

"If they're as aggressive as you say," said Cap, "I'll bet they were scouting Earth's defenses, and something went wrong with their ship."

"Possibly," said Ravenwood. "I don't know the details of their mission."

"How do you know *any* of this stuff?" asked Cap, voicing a concern Logan shared. "I mean, how are we supposed to know if you're telling the truth? How are we supposed to know you're not just plain crazy?"

"Valid concerns," said Ravenwood. "All I can say is that I have certain unusual knowledge about these matters."

"Here's the cave," said Kane. He held the lantern in front of him for others to see that the tunnel gave way to a large open space. The light was too weak to illuminate the entire cave, but Logan could see the tips of stalactite hanging from above. He heard the gentle trickling of water nearby as well.

"As for how Ravenwood knows these things, I might be able to help," said Kane as he looked from face to face. "My great grandfather was a woodsman who scraped out a living after the Impact near the old Canadian border. One cold morning he was out checking his traps near a lake called Crow Wing. He saw a figure lying under a tree near a large flat piece of granite called Raven's Rock. He walked closer and there was Ravenwood lying naked and unconscious in the snow."

"The old man didn't know where Ravenwood had come from, but he knew he couldn't leave him naked in the cold. So he took him in and kept him safe. Ravenwood had no memory of who he was or where he came from. He couldn't even speak English. My great grandmother named him Ravenwood, after the place where he was found, and my family's been keeping him safe ever since then."

Cap shook his head. "This is getting too damn weird. Ravenwood magically appeared in the woods?"

"It wasn't magic," said Ravenwood. "It was science. I was sent here."

"Sent here?" asked Cap. "Who sent you?"

"It's all a bit confusing," he said with a smile. "And I don't pretend to know all of the answers, but suffice it to say that I am here to help."

A thought suddenly popped into Logan's head. "It was you who caused the lights to burst back at the Greenspurs' stronghold. And you somehow shattered the doors of the Great Hall."

Ravenwood smiled and winked in reply.

"How is that possible?" asked Logan.

Logan looked from Ravenwood's face to Kane's. Then Kane held up the lamp for all to see. There was no wick and no kerosene in the lamp, but there was a tiny spot of dancing light flickering where the wick should have been.

Cap ran his fingers through his short blond hair and said, "Groovy."

Ravenwood smiled at him, raised an eyebrow, and said, "Right on."

Chapter 40

Kane was the first to break the surface of the pond. The others appeared nearby. They all swam toward the bank as best they could with swords and bracers in their hands.

As he swam, Logan looked around the pond to see it was surrounded by a mixture of hardwood trees. Big oak, maple and chestnut threes encircled the water's edge, like ancient spectators waiting for them to arrive. After they had all climbed onto the shore, they sat for a few minutes to catch their breath and warm themselves in the noonday sun.

"Kane," said Lena. "Why do you know more about that cave and the tunnel than the Greenspurs who've been living in these mountains for generations?"

Ravenwood laughed. "Kane knows every rabbit trail, watering hole, and secret shelter east of the Mississippi."

Kane looked at the treetops and gave an almost wistful smile. "I've spent a lot of time traveling on the east side of the river. I guess it's gotten so I can feel where a trail or cave is."

"You feel them?" asked Lena with a light laugh.

Kane looked at her and said, "If you spend enough time in the wilderness you develop a sense for its language, its hidden rhythms."

"Did you *sense* the cave had a hidden door?" she asked, smiling.

He returned her smile. "No. But I've been through the Gap a number of times, and I've discovered a few of her secrets."

"And we're fortunate you have," said Ravenwood. "Now, we must decide which way to go. We're on the northern slopes of the Allegany Mountains, so we could take our chances and go due west, but I think we'd be picked up in a matter of hours."

"No thanks," said Cap.

"But our other option would take us very far out of our way," continued Ravenwood.

"How far out of our way?" asked Logan.

"We'd have to head east for a day and then south for ten days. Then west for at least a week."

Everyone was silent as they considered these options. Then Cap said, "Why not hitch a ride?"

"How would we do that?" asked Logan.

Cap sat up straight and said, "By now the Guardians have ordered everyone from mailmen to field marshals to beat the bushes and find us. No offense to Kane's knowledge of mountain trails, but we've got a snowball's chance in hell of getting to the Mississippi on foot. It doesn't matter if we go south or west. We can't evade an all-hands-on-deck search for very long."

"So what's your plan?" asked Lena.

"If the Guardians are shipping every piece of equipment they can spare west to fight the League, we should sneak onto one of those shipments," he said. "Get on a supply train, or something."

Ravenwood shook his head. "I'm sure they've considered that possibility. Those trains are very well protected."

"I agree the supply trains are heavily guarded," said Kane after a moment's consideration. "But we still might be able to do it."

Ravenwood looked puzzled. "How?"

"I know a transportation officer in Fairhope where the PRA built a major food and supply depot," said Kane. "I've worked with him a few times to smuggle things in and out of the PRA. Maybe he can get us out."

"Will he help us or turn us in?" asked Lena.

"He might refuse to help, but I don't think he'll turn us in," said Kane. "Can't rule it out, though."

Logan watched Ravenwood's face as he weighed their options. The old man raised his eyes toward the sky as the faint sound of approaching helicopters drifted over the mountain peaks and down to the bank of the mountain stream where they sat. He took a deep breath and looked at Logan. Then he clapped his hands and said with a broad grin, "Let's do it. As Kane said, it's not without risk, but it offers a better chance of success than trudging through the Allegheny foothills with no food or supplies."

Ravenwood stood and offered Cap his hand. He pulled the young man to his feet and said, "Hitch a ride," he said with a warm smile. "Good thinking, my boy!"

It was ten o'clock that evening when they reached Fairhope, a tiny town of about 1,000 inhabitants. They saw the supply depot complex, which consisted of several large warehouses and a network of train tracks and roads connecting it to food and manufacturing developments and the cities they supplied.

From their position in a cluster of trees about five hundred meters from the depot, Logan could see a supply train slowly roll in and position itself under three large chutes. Grain poured into the railcar below each chute. A few minutes later, the train inched forward and the next group of railcars was filled.

They had been waiting in the shadows for over an hour when they heard a door slam. A flickering light appeared in the window of a nearby house. Kane stood and quickly crossed the open ground separating them from the house, motioning for the others to follow. When they had all reached the house, Kane lightly rapped his knuckles on the back door.

The door slowly opened to reveal a middle-aged man with a scraggly graying beard and tangled brown hair. Seeing Kane and the others, he shot a nervous glance around the outside of the house, then signaled for them to enter. When the last person went by, he gave the area one final look and closed the door.

The man signaled for them to remain silent and quickly walked toward a door, grabbing the lit kerosene lamp off a table along the way. He led them through a door and down a staircase into a cellar with rough stone walls and a dirt floor. Once everyone was down the steps, he looked at Kane and asked in an exasperated voice, "Damn it! What are you doing here? What did I do to deserve this?"

Kane held up his hands to calm the man down. "Now, now, Bernie," he said. "Settle down. We just came to do a little business."

"Everyone is looking for you and your friends, and I mean *everyone*," said Bernie as he eyed the group suspiciously. "I've had SPD officers inspecting my trains all day long. Army regulars have been marching up and down the rail yard. Helicopters been buzzing over my head."

Pointing his finger, Bernie said, "Pictures of these three are in everybody's hands. And they've got pretty good descriptions of you and the old man, too."

"Well, then you know why we're here," said Kane. "You need to get us out of the PRA and across the Mississippi."

Bernie laughed and shook his head. "Get you across the river? I deal in merchandise. I don't smuggle people. And even if I did, tell me why I should risk my life? Good way to get myself hung."

"Settle down, Bernie. You're all worked up. This isn't the Bernie I know," said Kane in an easy tone. "The Bernie I know would factor the level of risk into the price and find a way to get it done."

"You're not listening to me," said Bernie, leaning forward. "This isn't just trading food or booze. What you're talking about is treason. They will kill me if they find out, and believe me, with the way they're looking for you guys, they *will* find out."

"C'mon, Bernie," said Kane. "There must be a price inside that calculating head of yours. How much do you want?"

Bernie didn't say anything. He just looked at the group of people in his cellar and nervously scratched his stubbly beard.

Kane turned Bernie's shoulder to face him. He looked in his eyes and said, "If you get us across the river, I'll get you fifty cases of Iowa rye whiskey. Best stuff you've ever had."

"Kane, I'm telling you it ain't about the whiskey. It's about me in an unmarked grave."

"Seventy-five cases," said Kane.

Bernie didn't answer, but something in his eyes changed. Logan could see he was thinking about the offer. After a couple heartbeats Bernie said, "Two hundred cases. That's what it'll cost me to get a visa and smuggle my fat ass out of this shithole and across the river."

"Why do you want to leave?" asked Kane, surprised. "You've got a good thing going here. You must have enough money stashed away to buy a false identity and live well in one of the coastal cities. Nice car, good food, pretty girls."

Bernie dismissed that with a wave of his hand. "A couple years ago, yeah, that was the plan," he said. "But things have changed."

"What's changed," asked Kane.

Bernie leaned toward them and whispered, "The blight."

Kane's eyes narrowed. "What do you mean?"

"The crops are failing," said Bernie, looking at the stairs as if SPD officers were about to rush down and arrest them all.

He looked back at Kane. "It started five years ago. First, it hit the northeast. Government had to burn millions of bushels of spoiled corn, potatoes, and wheat. Then it spread south and west. Rumor is over fifty percent of this year's yield will be affected."

Ravenwood stepped forward. "Are you sure about this? Are you absolutely sure?" he asked.

Bernie nodded his head. "Yeah, I'm sure. I've been working at this depot for twenty-two years. The depot chief's been cooking the numbers, but he can't fool me. I see what comes in and what goes out. I know the blight is real and it's getting worse."

"What's causing it?" asked Logan.

"Do I look like a fucking farmer?" replied Bernie angrily. "How the fuck should I know?"

Lena looked at Ravenwood. "Have crops across the river been affected?"

Ravenwood shook his head. "No. I don't believe so."

"It would explain why the Guardians are throwing everything they've got into this attack," said Kane. "It would also explain what the Travelers have been seeing for a while now. It's getting harder for them to find crops to scavenge. They've been relying more and more on what they can gather or kill in the forests."

"But why do the Guardians think gaining territory on the west side of the river will change anything? The blight will probably hit there soon, too," said Cap.

"Unless the blight only affects crops grown in the People's Republic of America," offered Ravenwood. "None of you would recall this, but in the years after the Long Winter, the PRA experienced the biggest population boom on the continent. That population growth was fueled by modifications to their crops combined with soil treatments, which greatly boosted yields in the new environmental conditions."

"So you think there's something about those modifications that's making the plants here susceptible to the blight?" asked Logan.

"It's a hypothesis," said Ravenwood. "But as Kane suggested, it would explain why the Guardians are anxious to acquire new untreated land."

"And if the food runs out the Guardians won't stay in power for very long," said Kane.

Lena nodded, "A steady food supply and maintaining public order are at the heart of the Guardian's claim to legitimacy. If there's a serious food shortage, people will become angry and desperate. Harken won't hesitate to unleash the SPD and Red Legs to stay in power, but he'd prefer not to. His dream is to bring the entire continent under his control, not spend his days putting down food riots."

"I don't mean to interrupt your fascinating chat about crop yields," said Cap. "But let's get back to the part about how we're going to get out of here."

Bernie looked at Kane. "I'm gonna help you, but you had better help me when I get to the other side of the river. I had better not get stopped at the border or chucked into some shithole prison."

Kane nodded, "I promise."

"And you're going to give me two hundred cases of Iowa rye whiskey," added Bernie.

"I will, but that's a lot of whiskey to move," said Kane. "We'll have to break up the shipments or they'll be confiscated."

"Don't send it over the Heartland Road. For big shipments, I've got another way," said the supply officer, a broad grin on his face.

Chapter 41

The abundance inspector uniform and coat Bernie had acquired fit Logan reasonably well, so he was chosen to be the lookout for the group as they traveled. Bernie explained the role of the inspector to Logan, which was basically to check the food containers' locks and monitor the inventory on departure, on arrival, and at any depots they stop at in between. Bernie's other inspectors on the train were part of the smuggling operation, but they wouldn't know that part of this train's illicit cargo included people.

Bernie led the group to the depot just before dawn and led them to a railcar in the middle of a long string of cars. He explained that the cars' load of potatoes was loaded through holes in the top by a large chute and unloaded by opening the bottom of the railcar into special receptacles at the destination. This particular railcar had been fitted with a false wall, which created a space about a meter wide, where the others would have to sit single file. All railcars were outfitted with a narrow gangplank running along the outside, which inspectors used to move up and down the train. There would be a railcar in the middle where inspectors could sleep and eat, but Bernie did not recommend Logan go in there. His inspectors were used to seeing the occasional stranger on the train, but the less they knew the better.

"If I can't go into the inspector's railcar, where am I supposed to be while the train is moving?" asked Logan.

"There's a little place for you to stand between this railcar and the one in front of it," explained Bernie.

Logan wasn't too happy with that answer but nodded his head.

"Don't complain," said Cap. "At least you'll be in the open air."

"The train is bound for Erie," explained Bernie. "It'll go directly to the shipyard, but you'll have to be careful getting out. Look for a cargo ship called the *Chippewa*. The captain is named Larson. He'll get you to Lake Michigan where he's already planning to meet a few of my business partners to exchange a little extra cargo. That's when you all get onto a ship called the *North Witch*. Captain's name is Carrington. He'll get you to shore. You're on your own after that."

"Are Larson and Carrington aware we'll be coming?" asked Ravenwood.

"They will be," said Bernie. "Leave it to me."

Bernie looked at Logan. "To get your friends out of the compartment, pull this bolt." He demonstrated and they heard a click. Bernie pulled on the bottom of the false wall to reveal a door about two meters high and a little over one meter wide.

"Any questions?" asked Bernie.

Kane shook his hand and said, "Thank you. We'll make arrangements with Captain Larson for your whiskey."

"And for my new home in Kansas City," added Bernie.

"Sure thing, but why Kansas City?" asked Kane.

Bernie shrugged. "I like the sound of it. Now get in there, Flat Foots will be here at dawn to do a sweep of the rail yard."

He nodded to the others, hopped off the train, and headed toward the rail yard's control tower. The others slipped into the hidden compartment and Logan closed it behind them.

Logan buttoned his coat and raised his collar to keep out the morning chill and hide his face. A few minutes later, a line of about twenty regular army troops appeared at the end of the rail yard. As they slowly walked along, they looked under and between railcars. A separate group was inspecting the various small buildings along the yard's perimeter. As the line of Flat Foots approached Logan's railcar, he pulled his collar close to his face.

Suddenly, Logan heard a metal clank above his head. He looked up to see a soldier on the top of the car looking down at him. Just then, the line of Flat Foots reached his car as well. The soldier above him pulled his M-35 from his shoulder.

"See anything?" asked the soldier.

"All's quiet," said Logan, trying not give the soldier a very good look at his face.

The soldier stared at Logan for a few moments and then stepped onto the top of the next railcar. The soldiers on the ground moved on as well.

A few minutes later, the train lurched into motion, causing Logan to stumble. He regained his balance and cursed his clumsiness. He told himself a seasoned abundance inspector would have anticipated the train's movement. He did his best to remain alert but appear bored as the train slowly gained speed and left the rail yard. After a few kilometers, the train split away from the westbound track and headed due north.

Logan watched from his post as the landscape passed by. He saw many abandoned farmhouses and rotted barns along the train's path. Contrasting with these scenes of abandonment, there were large areas of land enclosed by concertina wire. SPD officers occupied towers outside the wire. Inside these farm developments, he occasionally saw tractors traversing the length of the fields. Spring plantings were starting to emerge from the soil. The tractors were spraying the small plants with chemicals from large containers of liquid mounted on trailers they pulled. Dozens of people walked behind the tractors, stooping down from time to time to dig in the dirt with little hand trowels, not bothering to look up from their work as the train passed by.

He passed by four or five similar farm developments before they arrived at a small depot. As the train eased ahead to fill cars with grain, a group of kids in dirty coveralls came to the fence of the adjoining farm development. They stared at the train as it was being loaded. A girl in the group waved at Logan. He fought the impulse to wave back.

An SPD guard in a nearby tower noticed the children. Using an amplifier, the female guard said, "Return to your development team. Return to your development team."

The children gazed at the tower. Then they turned around and ran back toward a group of people swinging hoes on the crest of a hill.

The train left the depot about ten minutes later. It passed by more farm developments and old ruins, not just of farmhouses and barns, but also of little towns. Logan could tell that most of them had not been occupied since the Impact, but a few showed signs of life. Sometimes he saw little lines of smoke rising from a chimney or the occasional person staring at the train from the doorway of a rundown building.

Late in the afternoon, Logan caught a glimpse of a wide expanse of blue water. He knocked on the metal wall and said, "We'll be in Erie in a few minutes. Get ready."

Erie's boundary was fenced off from the surrounding countryside by concertina wire. There were SPD guard posts located at the few entrances Logan could see. Erie did not appear to be a wealthy city, but its inhabitants were clearly better off than their neighbors in the countryside Logan had just passed through. There was another SPD inspection station at the shipyard entrance where SPD officers boarded the train and walked up and down its length, occasionally asking for a compartment to be opened for them to see inside. One of them asked to see Logan's inventory list, which he handed over without speaking. The officer reviewed it and handed it back.

After the inspection, the train rumbled forward half a kilometer, finally stopping near the ships. Logan saw the first few railcars open their bottoms and dump their contents into large receptacles. Leaning out the right side of the train, he saw several ships moored along the docks, including the *Chippewa*.

"Okay, get ready," he said to the others inside the secret compartment.

He pulled on the bolt to open the hidden door, and they all exited, blinking in the sunlight. With Logan leading them, they quickly hurried across a number of tracks toward the ships, hiding behind parked railcars as they went. They were about to dash to the next group of cars when Logan held up his hand. They instantly froze as a large truck drove up to their hiding spot. It suddenly stopped. Kane drew his sword and the others did the same.

They heard a door slam shut and a man came into view from the other side of the truck. He looked at Logan and said, "You lookin' for the *Chippewa?*"

Logan nodded.

"Okay, let's go."

The man waved his hand and opened the doors to the cargo space in the back of the truck. Seeing that Logan and the others hesitated, he said, "It's now or never, let's go."

Logan took several quick steps and jumped into the truck. The others followed him. The man closed the doors, and soon they felt the truck move forward. It turned sharply left and headed back in the direction it had come from. After a minute or two, the truck stopped and the man opened the doors.

"Out!" he ordered.

As they got out of the truck, he handed each one of them a heavy sack of grain. "Up the walkway. Captain's waitin' for you at the top."

Logan pulled at his coat's lapel and asked, "What about the uniform?"

"No time. Just put the sack on your shoulder and go."

They did as instructed as the man got back into the truck and drove away. Kane led the way, hefting a large sack on his bent back. When he reached the top, a man took the sack from him and stacked in on top of some others. He did the same for each of them as they reached the top.

"I'm Larson," said the man. "Follow me."

He quickly ducked into a door in the side of the ship and turned immediately to his left. He led them down a few flights of metal stairs until they reached the bottom of the ship's hold. He walked toward some large boxes stacked on top of each other along the wall. He pushed some boxes aside to reveal a door.

"Get inside," he said. "I'll come for you when we're out of the harbor."

As Cap walked by him, he said, "I need to piss."

"Hold it for another hour," said Larson.

"I'll try," said Cap, "But my eyes are turning yellow."

Larson turned on a light in the storage room before he left, closing the door behind him. Logan heard him push the crates in front of the door and rush back up the steps.

"Well, it's been an interesting day so far," said Ravenwood as he sat down against the wall of the dimly lit room.

"We covered a lot of distance," said Kane. "Let's hope the boat ride is a smooth one."

"I'm sure we're safe as kittens," said Cap ironically as he sat down on a crate.

Just then they heard the deep rumbling of the engines coming on line. A few minutes after that, they felt the ship starting to move. Thirty minutes later, Larson returned and pushed the boxes aside.

"Here are some bottles of water. I will take you to a bathroom on the deck above us, but you have to be very careful not to draw attention to yourself. Every cargo ship has an SPD officer on board to keep an eye on things. They know about the trading arrangements we have, and we pay them to stay in their cabins when the exchanges occur. But smuggling people is different. Stay down here in the room unless I come for you. It's a two-day trip to the rendezvous point with the *North Witch*. If you stay out of sight, everything will be fine."

Late that night, Larson returned with some food and more water. "There's a general alert out for all of you. I don't know what you're wanted for, but I've never seen anything like it. About two hours ago, the SPD officer questioned us all in the galley. Nobody said anything. The only other person who knows you're on board is Watts, the man who met you with the truck. But be alert. The SPD officer is doing a lot more walking around on this trip and might come down here."

They tried to get some sleep that night, fashioning makeshift beds out of the boxes and canvas coverings they found in the room. They slept in shifts, leaving at least one person awake to listen for any unusual sounds outside their compartment.

Chapter 42

Attika followed the nurse's movements through bloodshot eyes as she walked around the table checking each wrist and ankle fastening. The walls of the small room were painted white. One wall contained a large tinted window. Above Attika's head was a large bright circular lamp. The nurse tightened the strap holding her forehead and chin in place, preventing her from turning her head in either direction.

The nurse stepped out of the room but soon returned with a metal cart. She pushed it to a spot next to Attika's left side. On the cart were a number of surgical instruments spread out on a sterile white cloth. Knitting her brow, the nurse mumbled something to herself and rearranged the order of the instruments, occasionally looking at Attika and smiling warmly as she worked. When they were organized to her satisfaction, she turned and left the room.

Colonel Linsky looked through the tinted glass at Attika. His eyes drifted down to where his missing right hand should have been. In its place he saw a black bandage over the stump where his arm ended. When he looked up, he noticed SPD Chief Special Investigator Kosta's eyes had also come to rest on his bandages.

"You're lucky to have survived," said the Chief Special Investigator. "You could have easily bled out on that mountain, and that would have been that." He snapped his fingers.

"Yes," replied Linsky. "I was very fortunate."

The rescue helicopter had flown him and the wounded Special Forces soldiers to a nearby military hospital. The doctors there had moved quickly and efficiently to attend to his wound. They firmly secured the arteries to prevent further blood loss, pared back the nerve endings to reduce the chances of neuroma-related phantom pain, and closed the wound with the latest version of synthetic skin.

"The pain must be immense," said Kosta.

"It's manageable," said Linsky with a faint smile.

Kosta turned his attention to Attika and said, "But instead of recovering in a hospital bed like a reasonable patient, you came to see our prisoner. The item she helped steal must be very important."

"It is," replied Linsky. "Thank you for extracting what she knew. It may prove to be critical."

"Happy we were able to help," replied the Chief Special Investigator. "And it gave us an opportunity to test some of our new cocktails. Standard interrogation techniques didn't really seem to be having much of an effect on her. Sleep deprivation, physical persuasion, psych interrogations, all that stuff was failing. They actually seemed to make her stronger."

"Our interrogation methods are no secret to our enemies," observed Linsky. "She'd prepared herself. She may have actually enjoyed the interrogation on some level. Studies have shown that fanatics like her get an endorphin rush when they are punished for their beliefs."

"These people are nuts," said Kosta as he folded his arms in front of him. "At any rate, she also failed to respond to the standard drug therapy. Apparently, she'd injected herself with something prior to her arrest, which reduced the treatment's efficacy."

Linsky nodded as he stared at Attika. "Yes, so I was told. We will have to dig deeper into that. It concerns me that terrorists like her have access to this new drug. It blunts our ability to gather information and prevent future attacks."

He looked back at Kosta and said, "Thankfully your new therapy produced results. And the residual migraines should provide us with assurances of future cooperation as well."

"Agreed," said Kosta. He took a deep breath and said, "Shall we proceed?"

"Yes," said Linsky.

Kosta nodded toward a guard standing near the door. He saluted and exited the little room.

The door to Attika's room opened and a man in surgical attire entered along with the nurse, who now wore green scrubs, a surgical mask, and latex gloves. The man walked to Attika's side and leaned close to her face, examining her forehead. He removed a pen light from his pocket and shined it in her eyes, causing her to moan with pain. The doctor pulled his mask up to his mouth and walked behind Attika's head.

The nurse moved a cart carrying a small metal tank next to Attika's head. Attached to the tank was a hose and plastic mask. A computer of some kind rested on top of the cart. She handed the man a black marker.

He examined Attika's head where the hair had been shaved off. Then he drew several dashes on the patch of skin on her head just above the forehead.

"Call in the anesthesiologist," said the man. "We're ready to begin." She heard the whirring sound of a drill and closed her eyes.

"Please don't do this," she whispered. "Please don't do this."

"Just relax," said the man in a soft tone. "We'll have you all fixed up in just a bit. You won't feel a thing. And when you wake up, the headaches will be gone."

Attika whispered again and again as tears flowed out of the corners of her eyes, "Please don't do this."

The door opened and a woman in surgical gear entered. She stood over Attika and tightened her head restraint. Then she turned to the cart the nurse had just wheeled in. She activated the computer and adjusted the mask to fit Attika's face.

"I think we're ready to begin, Dr. Wilson," said the anesthesiologist.

"Very good. Please proceed with anesthetizing the patient, Dr. Van. Nurse, please apply the preoperative antiseptic to the patient's forehead."

Attika clenched her teeth and tried to free her hands. She thrashed against her head restraint, but it wouldn't yield. She screamed, "No! No! No!"

The nurse put her hands on Attika's temples and tried to calm her. Dr. Wilson leaned over the table and held both her arms firmly against the bed as Dr. Van placed the mask over Attika's face. Dr. Van pressed a few buttons on the computer. Attika tried to free herself of the mask, but it was firmly strapped onto her face. After a few moments, her struggling became less pronounced and her eyes started to close.

Suddenly, the door swung open and Linsky entered the room. Pushing aside the nurse, he ordered the anesthesiologist to turn her computer off. He quickly removed the mask from Attika's face and leaned over her.

"Attika," said Linsky, gently shaking her. "Wake up, Attika."

She slowly blinked her eyes. After a few moments, she was able to keep them open, focusing them on Linsky's smiling face.

"There you are," said Linsky. He gently caressed her cheek with his left hand. Straining her eyes to the side, she saw the black bandages around his right wrist where his hand should have been.

Linsky watched her eyes then raised his right arm for her to see. "You and I have both been wounded by this senseless struggle," he said in a soft voice. "My wound is here for all to see, but yours are hidden deep in your mind. My name is Linsky. I heard about your adverse reaction to the therapy and came as quickly as I could. I know you're suffering terribly, and I'm deeply sorry. But happily, this surgical procedure won't be necessary."

Attika looked at Linsky, tears welling in her eyes.

"I think you've provided us with everything you know, haven't you?"

She nodded her head as much as her restraints would permit and gently sobbed.

"Of course you have," he said softly. "And although this medical procedure would cure you of your migraine headaches, it would leave you…diminished. And we don't want that, do we?"

Attika mouthed the word "no" as a tear fell down the side of her face.

"No, of course not," said Linsky.

He looked at the nurse. "Please unfasten the restraints."

The nurse quickly moved to comply. When Attika was free, Linsky gently slipped his left hand behind her head. He slowly lifted her into a sitting position. Her face contorted in pain as she sat up, but she said nothing.

When she was sitting upright with her feet hanging off the edge of the operating table, Linsky sat down next to her and smiled. He reached into his pocket and removed a bottle of pills and held them in front of Attika.

"The doctors tell me the migraines will never go away," he said. "But they can be managed with medication. You will need to take two pills every day or the migraines will return, perhaps with even greater severity. You will need to report to your assigned clinic once per month for evaluation and to refill your prescription. Is that understood?"

She narrowed her eyelids and stared at the bottle.

"The alternative is to undergo the procedure," he said as his eyes darted toward the tray full of surgical tools. "The choice is yours."

Attika looked into Linsky's gray eyes. She slowly reached for the bottle. Linsky popped open the top with his thumb and shook two little blue pills into the palm of her hand. He signaled for the nurse to give him a cup of water, which was sitting on the cart. Attika put the pills in her mouth and accepted the cup from the nurse. She drank a sip, wincing as she swallowed.

"Good," said Linsky.

He looked at the nurse and said, "Please bring us a wheelchair. I believe our patient would like to return to her room."

He gently patted Attika's left hand with his. The nurse returned with the wheelchair and they helped her move from the operating table to the chair. The nurse started to spin her around toward the door when Linsky crouched down, his eyes level with Attika's.

"I hope you don't mind if we chat from time to time," he said. "Although you've provided us with essential information about the item of interest and where it is being taken, I think we still have much to discuss. Agreed?"

Attika remained silent.

"I need to hear you say that you agree," said Linsky, a hint of steel in his voice.

"Yes," whispered Attika as she looked away.

Linsky looked at the side of Attika's face for a few moments. Then he nodded to the nurse. She rotated the wheelchair and pushed Attika out of the room.

Chapter 43

"Tell me about your father," said Ravenwood to Logan.

It was their second day on board the *Chippewa* and conversation had dried up.

"I suspect you already know about my father," said Logan.

"I know something about him, but I want to hear your perspective," said Ravenwood. "You don't want to speak about him. I understand and respect that. But your mind dwells on memories of him. You should give voice to your thoughts. Do not let reflection turn to rotting rumination."

Logan took a deep breath and said. "Fine. He was an army captain. During the Rededication, he and a dozen other officers in his battalion signed a letter to protest a series of unlawful orders they'd been given. They were immediately charged with treason and executed by firing squad."

Ravenwood nodded. "I'm told he was a good man. I'm sorry he was taken from you."

Logan shrugged. "It happened to a lot of officers," he said. "It's okay."

"I'm surprised they admitted you into the Weller Academy if his name was on the purge list when Harken took over," said Kane. "You must have been under a cloud of suspicion while you were there."

Logan nodded. "Yes. I had to be very careful not to give them any reason to think I was undedicated."

Cap got up from the floor where he had been sitting and said, "But then all that bottled-up emotion exploded when he got a note from his grandfather and decided to steal the biggest military secret the world has ever known."

"Your academy admissions officer must be very proud of you right now," said Lena with a grin.

"What about your mother?" Ravenwood asked. "May I ask if you know what has happened to her since you became the PRA's most wanted fugitive?"

Logan shrugged. "She's probably doing just fine. She's always been a dedicated PRA citizen, but when my father was reported dead, it intensified. She was constantly praising the Guardians' wisdom, condemning whatever country we were at war with. She even reported colleagues to the SPD from time to time."

Ravenwood rubbed his short gray hair and said, "Sounds like you had to hide your thoughts from a very early age," said Kane. "Probably came in handy at the Weller Academy."

Logan nodded. "Everyone needs to pretend if they want to succeed in the PRA, but I probably did it better than most."

"Sorry friend," said Cap, "but that honor goes to Lena. Think about it. Her father is the damn Defense Guardian and no one had a clue. She's hardcore."

"Thanks for the compliment," said Lena in an ironic tone.

"And what about you, Cap?" asked Ravenwood. "What's your story?"

"Not much to tell," said Cap. "Both my parents died when I was baby. I have no idea who they were. Like thousands of other kids, I grew up in various government institutions and foster homes, causing as much trouble as I could along the way. Finally, I landed in the home of a really nice old lady down the street from Logan's place. Logan and I got to be good friends. When I found out he was going to Weller Academy, I applied and got in. The rest you know."

He sat down on a makeshift chair of canvas and storage crates and laced his fingers behind his head.

"You must be pretty smart," said Kane.

"I am," said Cap, smiling.

"Weller Academy isn't interested in troublemakers unless they're smart, right?" continued Kane, his eyes glinting.

Cap shifted somewhat in his chair. "Yes. Well, I have a variety of talents which qualified me."

Logan chuckled.

"What are you laughing at?" asked Cap, defensively.

"You want to tell them or should I?" asked Logan, a wide grin on his face.

Cap narrowed his eyes at Logan. Then he said, "I may have gotten some advance notice of what would be on the entrance exam."

"You *cheated?!*" Lena jumped to her feet. "I *knew* you couldn't have gotten in without help."

"Hey now!" said Cap. "I did all right once I got in. And I'm the best damn pilot they ever saw. Best scores in the history of the academy's pilot program!"

Ravenwood laughed loudly and clapped his hands. "Bravo, Cap. Your resourcefulness never ceases to amaze me. I wish the PRA produced more people like you."

Lena wasn't so quick to find the humor in Cap's entrance-exam story, but she eventually smiled at him and sat back down.

"I guess every team needs at least one person with a questionable character," she said.

Conversation died down again. Logan yawned repeatedly. He was exhausted, but he could not sleep except for a few minutes at a time. He was finally dozing off when he felt a tingle in his left hand.

Here we go, he thought to himself, resigned to what was about to happen. After a moment, he lost all sense of where he was. His thoughts went blank. He started clenching and unclenching his jaw muscles.

Suddenly he saw a million lights appear all around him, and he felt as though he were floating among them. He saw a small orange and red light. He moved toward it with amazing swiftness. Soon he was surrounded by yellow, green, orange, and red gases in what he could only describe as a nebula. He saw two lights circling each other. He moved toward them and was suddenly facing massive stars in orbit around each other. He looked into the distance and saw a bright circle of colored lights with a great pillar of white light piercing the middle like a great lance. He approached the lights and peered into the circle to see a black void. Bright gases were disappearing over its black rim.

Then Logan was back on the *Chippewa*. He blinked a few times and saw the others were standing in a circle around him.

"What happened?" he asked as he looked from face to face.

"You tell us," said Cap. "I'd say you were having one of your seizures, but this time your eyes were wide open and darting back and forth. Normally, you just have a blank look. And you were talking to yourself. You've never done that before."

Logan ran the fingers of his left hand through his hair and exhaled a long breath. "It was different this time. I felt like I was in space, shooting from star to star."

Ravenwood crouched down next to him. "Are you sure that's what you saw? You were moving among the stars?"

Logan nodded his head. "It was like I was flying from place to place looking at nebulae, black holes, binary stars."

"Do you have the Apollo Stone?" asked Ravenwood.

Logan looked down at his right hand. He opened it to reveal the small black orb. A red and yellow ribbon of light rolled into view inside the little sphere, followed by a streak of bright white, then it faded to black.

Ravenwood suddenly stood and stepped back from Logan, an expression of wonder on his face. "This is extraordinary," he said mostly to himself. "Absolutely extraordinary. Highly unlikely, but why not? It must be possible, however remote the chances."

Realizing the others were watching him, Ravenwood stopped his muttering. He looked from face to face, finally resting his eyes on Logan.

He cleared his throat and said, "As I previously explained, your grandfather and his Sahiradin helper had been working to create a navigation device for the *Blackhawk* to shift space. The Sahiradin ships have been able to shift space for a very long time, but only with the assistance of a navigation device, an interface between what we call the Apollo Stone and the ship. But you must understand the Sahiradin stole the Apollo Stone, and a dozen others like it, from another race, called the Alamani. Among the Alamani there were a few who could shift space using just their minds to connect with the small orbs. It's been centuries since the last of the Alamani were slaughtered, but it is possible you have this ability to connect directly with the stone. *You* may be a navigator."

"A navigator? I don't understand. How is that possible?" said Logan.

Ravenwood raised his hand to his head and vigorously rubbed his short hair. "It was an extremely rare talent among the Alamani, and the odds against you also having this gift are incalculable, but I don't know how else to explain what you just experienced."

"I don't know what happened," replied Logan, "but it doesn't mean I'm one of these navigators."

Ravenwood was about to respond, but before he could speak, Lena said, "And what did you mean when you said the Alamani were slaughtered?"

"The Sahiradin hunted them down on world after world and killed them," said Ravenwood, his voice tinged with sadness. "They are a species entirely devoid of mercy."

"Why?" asked Lena. "Why did the Sahiradin exterminate another species?"

"It's a very long story," said Ravenwood.

"We're stuck in the hold of a ship. We've got time to kill," said Cap.

Ravenwood looked at his companions' faces and took a deep breath. "Very well. What I'm going to tell you is going to sound extremely farfetched, but I assure you, it is the truth as I understand it."

"We past farfetched when Kane told us how you appeared naked in the snow over a hundred years ago," said Cap.

"I see your point," said Ravenwood. "Well then, as I said, the Apollo Stone, and twelve other orbs like it, belonged to a species called the Alamani. They were a technologically advanced species living in an area of the galaxy many light years from Earth, and they successfully colonized many distant worlds using the Apollo Stone orbs, what they called Kaiytáva."

"The Alamani would use the Kaiytávae to leap across vast distances of space to habitable worlds and establish colonies. Once they had reached the new solar system one of the first things they would do is build a *khâl* in nearby space. The *khâl* could generate a single, point-to-point, stabilized wormhole gate. These gates allowed other ships to follow and integrate the colony into the vast Alamani trade network."

"So that's how they were able to overcome classic limitations on exceeding the speed of light," said Lena. "Their ships didn't need to go faster than the speed of light in order to go from colony to colony. They were taking shortcuts through space."

"That's a good way of explaining it," said Ravenwood.

"Okay, so what happened?" asked Cap. "One day they start a colony and find the planet is already occupied by these Sahiradin guys?"

"Not quite," said Ravenwood. He rubbed his head again before continuing. "The relationship between Sahiradin and Alamani was complex. At one time, the Alamani helped the Sahiradin considerably, and in return the Sahiradin protected the Alamani."

"Protected them from what?" asked Lena.

Ravenwood did not respond.

"I get the feeling you're holding something back," said Cap. "What's going on?"

Ravenwood paused before replying. "Please understand that I do not have a perfect understanding of how I came here or how I know what I know." He looked from face to face. "Many people believe I am a lunatic, and at first I doubted myself as well. But even though I do not know why I have certain knowledge, I have learned over time to trust my instincts."

"Okay, we get it. Your knowledge is patchy and there's a chance you might be crazy." said Cap. "So what are you holding back?"

Ravenwood folded his arms across his chest and continued. "There were species other than the Alamani who participated in the Alamani trade network. And, as with any trading relationship, there were rules which needed to be enforced. The Sahiradin enforced these rules, and I believe the other species came to resent the sometimes heavy-handed Sahiradin methods, which they felt worked in favor of the Alamani. These other species conspired to split the Sahiradin away from the Alamani, and they succeeded. The Sahiradin turned on the Alamani, but they went too far and they exterminated them. The Alamani trading partners formed what they call the Lycian Alliance and sought to intervene, to stop what they had started, but the Sahiradin were too strong and too determined. What had begun as a plot to win more advantageous trade terms escalated into a war for survival. And not just for the Alamani, but for each species because the Sahiradin do not make peace. Now, with the arrival of the Sahiradin and the Apollo Stone, the war has come to Earth."

"But what brought the Sahiradin here in the first place?" asked Cap. "It sounds like we're thousands of light years from the fight."

"That is exactly why the Sahiradin came here," said Ravenwood. "The Alamani had explored Earth long ago but plans to colonize it were abandoned."

"They probably found it was already occupied," said Logan.

"Possibly. At any rate, the records of that ancient exploration were forgotten until the Sahiradin rediscovered them. Earth is a perfect place for them to establish a base and launch strikes using the Apollo Stone without fear of reprisal due to Earth's immense distance from the area of conflict."

For a few moments they thought about what Ravenwood had told them. Logan listened to the *Chippewa* creak as it rolled over waves.

"Maybe the war is over," said Logan, breaking the silence. "It's been over a hundred years since the Sahiradin ship exploded."

Ravenwood frowned and shook his head. "It is tempting to believe the war is over, but I'm afraid it will continue as long as there is one Sahiradin left to fight."

"Given the present state of things here on Earth, the longer we can stay out of an interplanetary war the better," said Cap. "Maybe if those asteroids hadn't clobbered us we'd have advanced enough to be able to handle the Sahiradin. But not now."

Lena suddenly looked at Cap and then at Ravenwood. "It isn't a coincidence that the Sahiradin ship appeared in our solar system and fifty-five years later Earth was struck by asteroids, is it Ravenwood."

Ravenwood leaned against the wall near the door and glanced at Kane, who raised his eyebrows and said, "You've told them this much, you might as well complete the picture."

Ravenwood nodded his head. "I suppose you're right." He looked at Lena and said, "I strongly suspect the wounded Sahiradin ship which arrived in our solar system in the early 1970s did indeed use its remaining time to launch an attack against Earth. The Sahiradin have demonstrated they are capable of waging a campaign of extinction against a sentient species, and I see no reason why they would not have looked at Earth's inhabitants from the same perspective. Murdering billions of people on this planet would be a mere footnote in their long history of atrocities."

"Not just people," said Lena, fixing her gaze on Ravenwood. "Descendants of the Alamani."

Ravenwood returned her gaze. "Yes, descendants of the Alamani." He looked at Logan. "Perhaps even the rarest of them."

"And the asteroid impacts were a way of killing as many of us as possible in order to pave the way for a Sahiradin colony," added Kane.

"Son of a bitch," said Cap, sitting up and looking at Kane.

"So my grandfather worked side by side with a Sahiradin to adapt Sahiradin technology to human uses, and it was the same bastard who'd launched the asteroid attack on Earth," said Logan in disbelief. "What is the Sahiradin getting out of helping the PRA? What's his goal?"

"The mission has not changed for the Sahiradin," said Ravenwood. "His goal is to prepare the way for the rest of the Sahiradin forces, and in order to do that he needs a ship with the ability to shift space."

"And the Apollo Stone," said Lena. She looked at Logan and Cap. "The Guardians think they're getting a ship to fight their enemies here on Earth, but they're actually playing right into the Sahiradin's plan to wipe us all out."

"The Sahiradin has misled your leaders," said Ravenwood. "That is clear."

"They're not my leaders," interjected Cap. "I resign my commission."

Kane looked at Cap and said, "The Guardians know the Sahiradin wants the Apollo Stone, but they have fooled themselves into believing he simply wants to return home. They may have promised to help him in order to gain his assistance with building their war machine, but they would never actually let him go."

"Why not?" asked Cap. "They might help him get back home in the belief the Sahiradin will help them with their plan to reunite the United States."

"I doubt they're that stupid," said Kane.

"What if they think it's a forgone conclusion that the Sahiradin will eventually get here and they are positioning themselves as their future allies?" said Lena.

"You think they'd rather be top dog on a conquered planet than resist the Sahiradin?" asked Logan.

Kane shook his head. "If they think that, then they are fools."

"I would not dismiss it as a possibility," said Ravenwood. "They may suffer under the delusion that the Sahiradin only mean to rule Earth, not annihilate us all."

"Hell," said Cap. "I don't know about you guys, but I'm pretty damn pissed right now. We've been at war for over a hundred years and didn't even know it."

"Assuming it's all true," added Lena. "No offense, Ravenwood, but this is all just talk so far."

Ravenwood nodded. "No offense. I understand it's a lot to take in. But allow me to add one more wrinkle to this story. As already stated, Earth was an Alamani colony that the Sahiradin believed was abandoned long ago. Recall that for every colony, the Alamani built a gate, a *khâl*, which could generate a stabilized wormhole to another *khâl*. We must assume the ancient Alamani settlers followed their standard practice and created a *khâl* somewhere in our solar system. If this is correct, it does not function or the Sahiradin would have overrun us long ago. Therefore, I suspect the Sahiradin crash survivor does not intend to use the *Blackhawk* to immediately return to his kind. I think he may first try to repair the *khâl* to permit the Sahiradin to send as many ships through as they wish. Once through, they can shut it down and prevent their enemies from following because there are no other stones. The Lycians have captured the other twelve at various times in this conflict, and upon discovering they could not destroy them, propelled them one by one into a black hole."

Logan was about to say something, but he went silent at the sound of a metallic clanking sound outside their compartment. The boxes were pulled to the side, but instead of Captain Larson two men entered the room.

"Come with us," said one of them. "We've reached the meeting spot. The captain sent us to get you."

Chapter 44

Logan looked at the two men who had come to retrieve them. One had a thick beard and short brown hair. The other was taller and had long blond hair.

"Captain Larson told us only he and Watts know we're here," said Logan. "Who are you two?"

"The captain sent us to get you," said the bearded man. "He and Watts are being watched so he sent us. There's no time to waste. The SPD officer will be down here in a few minutes."

Logan looked at the others as he felt the ship begin to slow. "I don't like it, but we can't take the chance of being discovered by the SPD. Let's go."

They quickly gathered their weapons and followed the men up to the deck above. The blond-haired man cautioned for them to wait while he crept up to the next level. He looked down the ladder and waved them to follow. This was repeated several times until they were on the main deck. Logan looked out a window they passed by and saw it was a dark moonless night.

The two men led them down a long passage to a cabin door. They opened the door and motioned for Cap, who was in front of the group, to go in. Cap looked in and saw it was empty. He looked back, an expression of uncertainty on his face.

"Go in," said the bearded man. "The captain will be here in a minute."

Kane looked at the bearded man. "I don't like it. And I don't like you."

Logan saw doubt flash across the sailors' faces.

"Why are you so eager to get us into that room?" asked Kane.

Cap looked at the door handle and said, "I'll bet it's because the door to this room has a lock. The storage room we were in doesn't."

The sailors' expressions quickly changed from doubt to anger. The blond one smashed Cap in the face with his elbow, knocking him to the floor. Then he pulled out a pistol. Ravenwood grabbed the pistol and struggled with the sailor to point the weapon away from the others.

The bearded sailor pulled out a long knife and lunged for Kane, who sidestepped the attack. He grabbed the man's knife hand with his right and dislocated his elbow. The sailor cried out, but Kane slammed his head against the bulkhead, rendering him unconscious.

The blond sailor freed his pistol hand from Ravenwood's grip and pointed it at him. Cap quickly got up from the floor and gave him three quick punches to the kidneys, knocking the wind out of him. The sailor collapsed to the ground, gasping for air. Kane smashed him in the face with the pummel of his dagger, stunning him.

They dragged the two men into the room. Cap located a key on the bearded sailor that fit the door and locked them inside.

"Let's move," said Kane as he picked the pistol up off the floor.

They trotted down the passage until they came to a door with a small window. Kane peered through it. Then he slowly opened the door and stepped into the chilly night air. They ran along a balcony until he came to a ladder. Logan looked toward the water and saw the soft red glow of the bridges of three nearby smaller ships. They descended a ladder and found themselves near Captain Larson. Logan looked up and saw a crane with a bulging cargo net ready to transfer goods from the *Chippewa* to one of the three dark ships, which was quietly gliding toward them.

Captain Larson turned and saw them. He looked around to see if anyone was watching and quickly walked toward them. Kane drew his dagger, but the captain opened his hands to show he was unarmed.

"What are you doing here? It's too soon," said Larson, agitated. "I was not going to get you until all other business was complete."

"I'll tell you what we're doing here," said Kane through clenched teeth. "We're getting off this damn boat right now. Your men tried to lock us up and when we declined their invitation, they tried to kill us."

Larson looked surprised and frightened. "Something is wrong," he whispered. He looked around and then up. He swore under his breath. Logan followed his gaze and saw a female SPD officer smiling down at them from two decks above.

Just then a white spotlight lanced through the darkness and they heard the sounds of engines revving. A voice boomed over the water. "All ships prepare to be boarded! Stop your engines! All ships prepare to be boarded!"

"Damn! A patrol cutter," said Larson. He yelled at two nearby men. "Decker! Get up to the bridge and get us out of here. Vick, get behind that 50-caliber in case we need it."

The two men ran to follow the captain's orders but were soon fired on by the SPD officer from above. Kane fired two shots at her, forcing her to seek cover. Upon hearing the shots, the patrol cutter shined its light on the *Chippewa*. Logan heard a popping sound, which was immediately followed by a huge splash of water next to the freighter. The cutter's explosive shell had fallen just short of the *Chippewa's* port side.

The loudspeaker blared out another message as the cutter raced toward the group of ships. "That was the only warning shot you will receive! All ships stand down and prepare to be boarded!"

One of the smuggler ships engaged its engines and quickly shot forward. The cutter fired two explosive rounds, one of which hit its mark. A red and yellow ball of fire erupted in the middle of the hull where the ship was hit. Then Logan heard the *tac-tac-tac* of a heavy-caliber weapon coming from the damaged ship returning fire. The other two ships engaged their engines and began racing away.

Captain Larson looked at one of his crew and yelled, "Vick. Get on the 50-caliber and fire on those smugglers, but don't hit anybody."

He looked at Kane and the others. "Follow me."

He raced toward the stern. As he ran, he yelled over his shoulder, "Do you know how to drive a boat?"

"Not really," yelled Kane.

"I'm going to put you on a very fast boat. She can outrun the cutter, but those things can move too, so you'd better be a fast learner."

When they reached the stern, Larson opened a small metal box attached to a wall. He pressed a button inside the box with his thumb. Then he ran toward the stern of the ship and looked over the guardrail at the water below. The others followed. A bottom-hinged door was opening just below them. When it had completely opened, two booms holding a ten-meter-long speedboat emerged from inside the ship.

"Nice GoFast boat," said Cap.

Larson looked at Kane and said, "We're sixty kilometers east of the Wisconsin shore, forty-three degrees latitude. Get out of here and don't look back." He handed him the boat key.

Kane hesitated, looking at the key with a furrowed brow.

Cap took the key from Kane's hand. "I'll drive."

"Why aren't you using this boat to escape?" asked Lena, looking at Larson. "Why are you giving it to us?"

"As a smuggler, I'm in trouble," replied Larson. "As a traitor, I'm a dead man walking. I can explain away how you got on board, but only if I'm here to do it."

Just then they heard a slug whistle through the air above their heads. The SPD officer was standing at the railing of the deck above them. Kane returned fire, causing her to duck inside an open door.

"But there's one thing I need to take care of before we're boarded," said Larson. "Give me the gun."

Kane handed him the weapon. "Thank you, and good luck."

"Go," said Larson. He started to run toward the door the SPD officer had disappeared into, but Kane caught his arm. He whispered something into the captain's ear. He looked at Kane and nodded. Then he dashed away.

They climbed down a short ladder and jumped into the speedboat. When they were all in, Logan pressed a button on the front supporting arm, causing cables attached to the bow and stern to swiftly lower the boat down to the water, then Logan hit the release button and Cap started the engine. He took a few seconds to study the boat's controls, then he pushed a lever to his right slightly forward and the GoFast slipped away from the *Chippewa*.

Logan felt nervous about their chances of getting away. How fast was this boat? Larson had said the cutter was fast. Would they be able to outrun it? More importantly, would they be able to outrun its guns? Logan felt the floor of the boat tremble as Cap revved the engines. He looked at Cap, who wore a wide grin on his face.

Cap looked around and said, "Sit your butts down, everyone." He pushed the throttle forward and the speedboat surged ahead. The others gripped their seats and nearby gunwales as the speedboat shot over the big rolling waves of Lake Michigan.

Cap yelled to Kane over the screaming engine, "I'm headed due west, but tell me where we should be going."

Kane carefully walked to Cap, holding onto anything solid his hands could find as the boat bounced over the waves. Cap pointed at the navigation screen. "Based on the location Larson gave us, I think we're about here."

Kane peered at the map screen. "There," he said. "Windy Point. It's in hostile territory, but we don't dare land farther south. Chicago and the surrounding area are firmly in the grip of the PRA."

"Why is Windy Point hostile territory if it's not in the PRA?" yelled Cap.

"All of Wisconsin is Dellian territory, and they're friendly to the PRA. The Guardians give them guns and food in exchange for the Dellians keeping the northern border secure. They'll turn us over to the Guardians if they catch us. Or eat us."

Cap gave Kane a wide-eyed look. "Eat us? Seriously?"

"Protein's protein," answered Kane with a grin.

A shell hit the water just in front of them, sending spray into their faces. Cap stayed on course. A second shell fell just to their starboard.

"Aren't you going to swerve to dodge the shells?" asked Kane, a hint of concern in his voice.

"No," said Cap. "Lake cutters can go forty-five knots, maximum. We're going fifty-five."

"Yeah, but their shells are going a hell of a lot faster than that," yelled

Lena after another shell sent spray into the air in front of them.

"They can't lock on," yelled Cap. "Our profile is too low for their radar. They're shooting by line of sight."

"Well they're getting pretty damn close," replied Kane.

"We just need to outrun their spotlight," yelled Cap. "If they can't see us they can't hit us."

After a couple more near misses, Cap looked back over his shoulder at the pursuing cutter. The spotlight was throwing much less light on them, so he swerved to port. The spotlight followed them and a shell landed ahead and to the side. He swerved to starboard ten seconds later and nothing happened. He looked back and saw the cutter had widened the beam of light in an attempt to locate them.

"They've lost us," he said. "But I'm sure they've got a few helicopters coming up from Chicago to assist."

Fifteen minutes later, they approached Windy Point, which formed a small bump in the Wisconsin shoreline. He guided the boat toward a group of trees that hung over the water in order to hide the boat under the branches. As soon as the hull touched the shore, everyone jumped out.

"I wish we could hide the boat better," said Logan as he tied the stern line to a tree trunk.

"No time," said Kane. "Remember, Wisconsin is enemy territory. Keep your heads down and don't make any unnecessary sound."

"How long can we last on foot?" asked Lena. "The Mississippi is at least two hundred kilometers from here. We have no food, no water, and they'll be scouring the area for us."

"And don't forget the cannibals," said Cap.

Lena raised her eyebrow, "Cannibals? What cannibals?"

"When we were on the *Chippewa* I asked Captain Larson to send a coded signal," said Kane. "We should have help waiting for us, but the rendezvous spot is a few hours' march from here. We have to move quickly."

"And what about the PRA helicopters with infrared scanners?" asked Lena.

"These woods are full of game," said Kane. "Pretend to be a deer." He slipped through the trees and the others followed.

It wasn't long before they heard the sound of the cutter approaching the shoreline, but it traveled south. Soon after, they heard the sound of helicopters. "They'll concentrate on locating the boat," said Cap.

"That's good," said Logan.

"Not really. We were running at full speed for about thirty minutes, so that engine is damn warm. They'll find it fast."

"Shut up and keep moving," whispered Kane. He had found a trail leading west and was following it at a trot. They reached a small clearing and Kane dropped to one knee. He looked up at the stars and then got back to his feet, slightly adjusting his course and going off the trail.

They traveled through the trees and brush for an hour before Kane stopped again. They all gathered around him, panting heavily. "Okay. Catch your breath."

One minute later, Kane stood up. "Let's go."

"How much farther?" asked Cap as he got to his feet.

"Not sure. We're headed the right way, but I'm not so familiar with these woods..." Kane stopped talking and signaled for the others to be quiet. He listened for a moment. The woods were perfectly silent. A bird chirped once and flew away.

Kane whispered, "Follow me as fast as you can. Stop for nothing."

He turned and bolted through brush. The others did the same. Logan heard a blood-curdling scream. *Ayeeaaa!* Bullets whistled by, striking tree trunks and tearing through leaves. More screams followed, but now they came from both sides. Another burst of bullets. Logan ran as fast as his legs could carry him. Behind him, he could hear Cap puffing and swearing. Ahead of him, Ravenwood glided through the underbrush with amazing ease, and Lena nimbly hurtled over a log.

Soon the terrain angled upward. At times it was so steep Logan used his hands to help pull himself up, running on all fours. The screams grew louder. *Ayeeaaa! Ayeeaaa!* More and more voices joined the terrifying chorus.

They burst out of the trees and into a large clearing, now dimly lit by the early morning sun. Kane didn't slow down. He sprinted across the open ground. When he reached the center of the clearing, he suddenly stopped. Logan looked ahead and saw dark silhouettes emerging from the far side of the clearing, echoing the *Ayeeaaa* call of those pursuing them. They were completely surrounded, driven like animals to the slaughterhouse.

The dark figures slowly walked toward them, tightening the circle. Kane drew his sword. Cap, Logan and Lena followed his example. Laughing, taunting voices replaced the war cries. The Dellian ring grew tighter. Then Logan heard the sound of helicopters approaching. He was almost relieved at the sound.

"Well," he said to Kane. "At least the Red Legs don't eat people."

Cap turned his head to the side and listened to the approaching aircraft. "Guys?" he said. "I'm not sure what's coming, but it's not a PRA bird."

Kane looked at Cap and grinned. "Everyone lie down! Here comes Puff."

Just then the ground exploded as a thousand rounds ripped through the clearing. The dark figures screamed and turned to run, but the automatic gunfire shredded them to pieces before they could take two steps. Burst after burst cut down clusters of retreating dark figures. A few of them managed to reach the relative protection of the tree line, but even there many met their fates.

Ten seconds later, it was all over. Kane stood and raised his hands in the air as a helicopter quickly descended. Automatic gunfire erupted from the tree line as it approached. The helicopter returned fire using the rotary cannon mounted under its nose, then it landed.

A blonde-haired young woman in a green and brown uniform opened the side door of the helicopter. Next to her was a man behind a 50-caliber machine gun hooked into a sling hanging from the ceiling. She waved and yelled, "Get in! Let's go! Let's go!"

They leapt to their feet and ran for the aircraft. One by one, she pulled them aboard and directed them to a spot on a bench. As he boarded, Logan saw the woman had a thin scar running the length of her right jaw; the scar arced up toward the corner of her mouth.

There was a burst of automatic gunfire from the forest.

"Keep 'em honest," she said to the man behind the 50-cal.

"Keepin' 'em honest, lieutenant," said the man as he fired several bursts into the trees.

The helicopter lifted back into the air as the woman pulled the sliding door shut. They were joined by three other helicopters, which had been flying in a wide circle above the clearing and periodically firing on pockets of Dellians on the ground.

The pilot looked over his shoulder and said, "We've got company, lieutenant. PRA choppers."

Logan looked through the sliding door's window and saw four distant dots in the early morning sun.

"Take care of them," she said.

"Fox one, two and three. Engage the bogies," the pilot said into his radio.

Cap looked at the distant pursuing aircraft. "Those are probably Rammer 450s. They're faster and more heavily armed than what we're in."

The lieutenant said, "Really? What are we in?"

Cap shrugged and replied, "Some kind of modified old Lockheed design."

She smiled and said, "I see."

Cap looked away from her and watched through the side window as the three other helicopters broke away from them and turned toward their pursuers. "I guess the plan is to buy us time with their lives," he said grimly.

The woman said nothing as Cap continued to watch. Then he leaned forward and placed a hand on the window, staring intently. Logan looked out the window and was amazed by what he saw. Wings emerged from the three helicopters' undercarriages. As the wings locked into place, a rear-mounted jet engine came to life and provided forward propulsion. The main and tail rotors quickly folded into the fuselage, and the three aircraft suddenly shot forward toward the four PRA helicopters.

The Rammers tried to bank away, but they were too slow. Each one was hit by two guided missiles apiece, causing them to explode and plummet toward the Earth. The fighters continued south and engaged against additional distant PRA helicopters with the same results. Then the fighters turned and headed back.

The woman said, "Take us to fixed wing. Let's get out of here."

"Going to fixed wing configuration," said the pilot. Logan felt the floor vibrate as the wings slid into place. Then they also shot forward, quickly gaining speed and altitude. They joined the three other aircraft as they flew southwest.

"Impressive," Logan said to the woman, but she did not respond.

Logan looked at Cap. "You didn't know they had these things, did you." he said.

Cap shook his head. "Nope."

"I guess they wait until you're on active duty before they tell you how dangerous the enemy really is," said Lena. "Surprise! Here's a missile up your tailpipe!"

The lieutenant smiled as she listened to the exchange. Then she said, "All right, you three," pointing the muzzle of a pistol at Logan, Cap, and Lena. "Drop the swords and keep your hands where I can see them."

Logan looked at Kane, who nodded. "Do what she says," he said. "It'll be okay."

They followed her instructions and placed their swords on the floor of the aircraft. The other soldier gathered the swords and tucked them under the bench he was sitting on.

As they flew toward the southwest Logan noted that the airplane was flying level and straight. He asked the lieutenant if they were concerned about surface-to-air missiles.

"Not since we silenced them last night," she answered.

Soon the plane rapidly descended and banked left, affording Logan a view of the ground. He saw the wide Mississippi River winding its way south along its ancient course. On the main channel was a line of five long barges traveling downstream. Each barge had guns mounted at the front, middle, and rear.

"What are those?" he asked Kane.

"Northrunner trade barges headed south to the Gulf of Mexico," replied Kane.

"They look like they're well prepared for a fight."

"They are," he said. "The guns are mostly intended to ward off river pirates."

"What do they trade?"

"A lot of things. Manufactured goods, grain, timber. They're most valuable good is iron ore. They've got access to the highest-grade ore in the hemisphere, maybe the world."

"Are they part of the League of Free Cities?"

"No."

"Why not?"

Kane smiled. "They're friendly toward the League, but they'd rather trade with everyone than pick a side, although they've recently stopped trading with the PRA. They object to the PRA's practice of arming the Dellians, who are the Northrunners' only real enemy."

Logan looked out the window again and saw some fields on the west side of the river had been tilled. Between the fields were dozens of ten meter tall vase-shaped structures.

"What are those?" he asked Ravenwood.

"Water collectors. They extract water out of the morning dew and fog."

"Really?" asked Lena, leaning forward to see the objects. "How much can a collector gather?"

"About a hundred gallons per day," he replied.

She looked at him in disbelief. "Impossible."

Ravenwood smiled. "Really?" he said. "We must inform the farmers."

After a moment, Ravenwood continued. "The water collectors and other arid farming techniques are becoming less essential, though. The pre-Impact weather patterns are returning. The Waste is turning green again."

"Why not just use the river to irrigate the land?" asked Lena.

"The river water is needed to replenish nearly exhausted continental aquifers, so farmers rely on the collectors instead."

Logan heard the aircraft's landing gear opening. In a few moments they were on the ground at an air base. As they taxied along, Logan saw other aircraft parked in small groups around what he assumed were air defense batteries. When they came to a stop, the lieutenant slid the side door open. They stepped on the wing and hopped down to the ground, where they were greeted by three soldiers with automatic weapons.

Chapter 45

"Welcome to Jasper Air Force Base," said Kane.

The lieutenant pointed at the swords under the bench and one of the guards collected them. Kane handed over his sword, dagger, and knives, and Ravenwood gave them his knife. Another soldier gave them all a pat-down. They found the Apollo Stone and medallion and handed them to the lieutenant. Logan was about to protest, but Ravenwood shot him a look that silenced him.

Satisfied they were unarmed, the lieutenant led them toward a long two-story building at the edge of the airstrip. The guards fell into line behind them. They reached the building, and a guard at the door stood to attention as they entered. The lieutenant led them down a flight of stairs and opened the door to a room with a large conference table in the middle. Two women dressed in civilian clothing were seated at the table. One was rather stocky and wore her red hair in a braided ponytail. The other had a thin athletic build. She had black hair, although there were strands of gray running through it. Next to the black-haired woman sat a man in his early fifties with a pockmarked, face. He wore a League uniform with a general's star on each epaulette.

The red-haired women at the table smiled and said, "Ravenwood. Glad you made it."

She nodded at Kane. "You never cease to amaze, Kane. It was a difficult mission, but somehow you managed to rescue these three on your own. It's nothing short of a miracle."

"Thank you, Consul Sawyer. Ravenwood was there too, and the Pacific Federation's satellites jammed their drone signals which helped us slip through their net." he replied. He looked at Logan, Cap, and Lena. "And these three pulled their weight."

Consul Sawyer turned her attention to the three young people. "Welcome to Jasper Air Force Base, Free City of Davenport. You look exhausted."

No one spoke for a moment. The three friends looked at each other, hesitating. Then Logan said, "We've had a long journey, much of it on foot."

"We could use a shower and a hot meal," said Lena.

"And a week of sleep," added Cap.

"Of course," said Consul Sawyer. "Let me first introduce myself. I am Consul Sawyer and this is Consul Young. I represent the cities of Iowa. Consul Young represents the cities of Missouri." The dark-haired woman nodded without smiling.

"And to my right is the Jasper Base commander, General Espinoza."

"What are your names," asked Consul Sawyer.

"I suspect you already know our names," said Logan.

Sawyer smiled at him. "Yes, but I'd like to hear you say them."

"I'm Logan Brandt. These are my friends Lena Castell and Michael Caparelli."

Consul Young directed her dark eyes toward Lena and said in a raspy voice, "We understand you're Guardian Castell's daughter. Is that right?"

Lena nodded. "Yes, that's right."

"That would explain why the PRA's comms traffic has tripled in the past week," said General Espinoza.

"This must be very embarrassing for your father," said Consul Young. "How's he going to succeed as Grand Guardian with you defecting to the enemy?"

"Who says I'm defecting?" asked Lena, returning Consul Young's gaze.

"You're on the wrong side of the river, my dear," said Consul Young after a pause. "What would you call that?"

General Espinoza leaned forward and said, "And if you're not a defector, you'd sure as hell better not be a spy."

Lena did not respond, but Logan could see she was fighting to suppress her anger.

Ravenwood cleared his throat. He laced his fingers together in front of his waist and gave a slight bow. "Consuls Sawyer and Young. General Espinoza. We have new information that will help explain why the PRA is preparing its all-out offensive."

Espinoza nodded and said to the lieutenant. "Lieutenant Styles, please show these three where they can get cleaned up and eat some hot chow. Then get them each a bunk. They are to be under observation at all times, lieutenant. I don't care if they're sittin' on the head sweatin' one out. I want eyes on them."

"Yes sir," said Lieutenant Styles.

"Lieutenant Styles," said Ravenwood. "Before you go, can you please hand over the small round object and medallion the guards took from Mr. Brandt?"

Lieutenant Styles looked at General Espinoza. He nodded. Styles handed the items to Ravenwood.

As they were leaving, Logan heard Consul Young say, "Okay,

Ravenwood. What's on your mind this time?"

Chapter 46

Thirty minutes after they had left the conference room, Logan, Cap, and Lena were showered and sitting at a table in the mess hall. Their guards stood behind them a few meters away.

"This stuff isn't bad," said Cap around a mouthful of food.

"Speak for yourself," said Lena as she wrinkled her nose at something she had speared with her fork.

"After this, I'm taking a twelve-hour nap," continued Cap. "My bones are tired."

"And what's with these ridiculous beige jumpers?" Lena continued, pulling on the material.

"At least they're clean," said Cap.

"Lena," said Logan. "You should eat. The way things have been going for us lately, I'm not sure where our next meal is coming from."

"Or when," added Cap.

Lena folded her arms and frowned at her plate. "What are we supposed to do now?" she asked. "We were so focused on getting out of the PRA that we never stopped to think about what we'd do when we got here."

Logan nodded. "True. They're going to debrief us. The question is, how much do they think we know."

"They'll be disappointed with me," said Cap. "I know Jack Shit, and Jack just left town. But they're going to want to have a long talk with you, Lena."

"And right away," said Logan. "I hate to say it, but word that we crossed the river has probably gotten back to the Capitol District. Your father's under suspicion by now if he wasn't already."

"I'm aware of the situation," she answered tersely.

"What made you start working with Attika and her people anyway?" asked Cap as he bit into an apple.

"Why should I tell you?" she snapped.

Cap shrugged as he ate. "Suit yourself."

Lena looked at her food and tapped her fork in the tray a couple times. Then she said, "It started when my father was chief of National Infrastructure Security. I used to hear him talk on the phone about the mining developments a lot. It was a tough job. He was constantly under

224

pressure to maintain coal production. Ninety percent of the energy required to power the PRA's electric grid is pulled out of holes in the ground. But the mines were always under-producing. To keep the Capitol District and major cities lit at night, he had to cut power to the regions at seven or eight p.m. And sometimes the regions suffered rolling brownouts during the hours of peak energy demand. They still do, I'm sure."

"So your dad wasn't in the military?" asked Cap. "I would have thought the Defense Guardian would have to be an army guy."

"No," answered Lena. "He was made Defense Guardian because of his support for Harken during the Rededication. The power struggle could have gone a couple different ways. His support helped Harken isolate his main rival, so when he became Grand Guardian, Harken put him in charge of Defense."

"Loyalty over competency," said Cap. "It's the PRA way."

"My father is extremely competent," said Lena, coolly.

Cap held up his hands in apology. Then he picked up the apple from Lena's plate and took a bite. She glared at him but continued.

"Three years ago, I found records of a massive mining cave-in that had happened while he was still in charge of infrastructure. Hundreds, maybe even thousands of people died, but his main concern was to get production back on line. To meet his quota, he ordered heavy equipment in to dig out the rubble. He didn't care about searching for survivors or returning bodies to families. That's when I realized our government has made people into monsters."

She looked at Logan and then Cap. "My father's not a bad man. He made perfectly rational decisions to keep production up, to keep the PRA progressing forward, but the effects of those decisions on people were horrible. I decided then that things had to change, fast."

"So what did you do?" asked Cap.

"I hacked his computer and stole production figures, military-installation plans, troop-movement schedules. Whatever I could get my hands on." she said. "Then I let Professor Garrison know that I was not the enthusiastic lover of the Guardians I pretended to be."

"Garrison?" asked Cap.

"Makes sense," said Logan. "He's the one who tipped me off to the Apollo space program, and I met Attika through him."

Lena nodded. "That's how it worked for me too," she said. "It started out as a few innocent conversations. He was very careful about what he said, but after a couple weeks he felt satisfied that I was sincere and he put me in touch with Attika. I started feeding her information."

"And then a week ago she called you and said she needed you to rescue yours truly out of the back of an SPD patrol car," said Cap. "I was just about to spring my trap on those SPD guys when you came along, you know." He held out his hand, then made a fist. "I had 'em right where I wanted 'em."

"Don't flatter yourself," she said, suppressing a smile. "Attika had received the message to get Logan out of there, and we needed to know where he was."

"A likely excuse," said Cap with a grin.

"Why'd you do it, Lena?" asked Logan.

"I just told you," she answered.

"No. Why'd you help me?" asked Logan. "It was a big step up from what you'd been doing. You got directly involved in a dangerous operation. One with a low chance for success."

Lena shrugged. "I guess I was ready to do more."

"Well, I'm glad you did it," said Logan. "If you hadn't, I'd be slaving away in one of those coal mines by now."

"And they'd have the Apollo Stone," added Cap.

"Do you think it's true?" asked Lena. "All that stuff Ravenwood told us?"

"Sounds pretty crazy to me," said Cap. "It's convincing when he's saying it, but when I think about it later I just shake my head. Can't be true."

"Yeah," said Logan. "We know the Apollo Stone is important because my grandfather risked his life getting it out of the lab. But what is it really? And all of that stuff about an alien helping the PRA with advanced technology? Pretty hard to believe."

"I don't know," said Lena. "Colonel Linsky really wants the Apollo Stone back. And what about that strange seizure Logan had?"

Logan took a deep breath. "Maybe it was just a wild, sleep-deprived, stress-induced hallucination."

"I don't think so," said Lena. "I think you saw something different, something remarkable."

"It sure was different," Logan admitted. "I know it's hard to understand. I think it started as a seizure but it became something else. When I have a seizure, I blank out and I don't remember a thing afterward. This time my mind was racing. It was more vivid than any dream I've ever experienced, and I still remember every little detail like it just happened."

They were silent as each person considered the situation. Then Lena spoke up. "I have to admit Ravenwood's story kind of makes sense to me. I've seen enough manufacturing and production data to know how inefficient our government is at doing things. The tank assembly line we opened in Detroit is using one hundred-year old-designs. And look at the technology used to power our shields. Those design concepts are a thousand years ahead of our other energy-production methods. We can't even keep the lights on for more than a week without experiencing a couple blackouts. Something is giving us a massive development boost in some areas but not others."

"You believe the Sahiradin is real?" asked Cap.

"Maybe," said Lena.

"Well," said Logan. "Ravenwood and Kane went to a lot of trouble to get us out of the PRA, and they believe it's true. Maybe we should give them the benefit of the doubt."

"Can't hurt, might help," said Cap. He cast his eyes upon Logan's plate and said, "You gonna eat your pasta?"

Logan looked at his plate for a moment, then slid it toward Cap.

Chapter 47

KB923 came back on line when the lights along the *khâl* pillars started glowing blue. The droid checked the gate's major systems to ensure they were functioning properly. The ten-meter gap that spanned the pillars shimmered slightly. Fifty thousand kilometers away from the *khâl*, the starlight passing through a small spot in the vacuum of space began to bend. The area of distorted light grew and soon it was a bright sphere of swirling distorted light one kilometer in diameter. The blue lights of the *khâl* pillars pulsed ever faster until they were a solid blue. Suddenly, four small spacecraft emerged from the sphere, which then burst in a great flash of light, leaving behind no trace of its existence.

One of the craft shot out a dozen small discs in various directions. A disc flew past KB923 and attempted but failed to retrieve the ancient droid's data logs going back as far as when the droid's mothership exploded in the asteroid belt. The disc continued on toward Jupiter and her other moons to take readings and relay the data to the ships. Other discs raced toward the other planets, their moons, and the asteroid belt with the same mission to collect and transmit data.

A few minutes later, the pillars began to pulse with blue light again. A bright sphere of distorted light formed, but this time it was much closer to the *khâl* than the first one had been, just two thousand kilometers away. When the pillars turned a solid blue, the prow of a large ship pushed its way through the sphere. KB923 scanned the emerging ship and compared it to records of known ships. It conformed with basic Sahiradin design principles, but KB923 had no record of anything this massive or so heavily armed. When the ship had passed through it, the sphere burst in a brilliant flash just as the prior one had done.

The newly arrived ship signaled KB923 to come to one of its landing bays, but the repair droid had difficulty complying with the command because of differences in communications protocols. After a few moments, the ship's systems identified the correct protocols from its historical files and successfully transmitted the recall code to KB923, which immediately started to traverse the distance to the ship.

As it made its way to the beckoning ship, KB923 reviewed the data the ship had transmitted to it as well as the data the droid had gathered from its own scans. The Devastator Class Battleship, *Dominion,* was twice as large as the battleships in KB923 records. It was black with heavy borelium-plated armor running the length of its upper and lower sides, and it bristled with a variety of weapons, including ten massive particle-beam blasters, hundreds of ballistic guns, and an array of smaller energy weapons. Dozens of small portals on each side were capable of launching deadly guided missiles, and there were two massive ion cannons, ship killers, mounted on rotating turrets in the middle of the ship, one above and one below.

KB923 headed toward one of the four landing bays. As it approached, a sortie of V-shaped Codex all-purpose fighter craft flew out of the landing bay and took up positions under the *khâl*.

The droid's propulsion mechanism was not sufficiently strong to catch up with the accelerating *Dominion*, so a small utility craft launched from the nearest landing bay and retrieved it. Just as the utility craft locked KB923 into a small external droid portal, KB923 recorded the *khâl* begin to generate another wormhole gate roughly ten thousand kilometers away. The Sahiradin fighters raced toward the growing sphere of light. Five oval single-pilot ships burst through the sphere, followed by a ship about one-fifth the size of *Dominion*. KB923 recognized the ship as Lycian; most likely a patrol frigate. The Sahiradin fighters blasted two of the small Lycian ships into a thousand pieces, but the others evaded the Sahiradin trap and returned fire. *Dominion* issued an encrypted order to the fighters. KB923 then observed them turn toward the Lycian frigate.

KB923 plugged into *Dominion's* interface and began downloading its entire data set into the ship's main systems, but it continued to observe the battle against the Lycian frigate, which KB923 learned was called *Challenger*.

The Codex fighters were joined by a dozen more, plus several fighter-bombers, and they immediately engaged *Challenger* and her fighter support. *Challenger* returned fire from a hundred automated ballistic and energy batteries. More oval shaped fighters shot out from her only landing bay to defend their mothership. Two Sahiradin torpedo fighter-bombers attempted to lock and fire their missiles, but oval fighters destroyed them before they could launch their ordnance.

After surviving the threat of the fighter-bombers, *Challenger* and her support fighters quickly cleared the nearby space of Codex fighters and began to turn in the direction of *Dominion*. But before they could launch their assault, *Dominion* fired one of its ion cannons. The bright red ball of energy struck the *Challenger's* starboard side and caused a series of critical systems failures on the Lycian frigate, leaving her dangerously exposed.

Severely wounded, *Challenger* altered course to retreat toward

Ganymede, firing its ion defense pods as it banked away. A second ion blast was somewhat dissipated as it passed through the defense pod screen, but it succeeded in striking the stern of the fleeing frigate, causing further systems failures. A third blast, though dissipated by the distance it traveled to its target, hit its mark and left *Challenger* all but dead in space, her shields down and engines offline. She drifted toward Jupiter's gravity well as a new wave of Codex fighters raced toward her.

At the last moment, one of her engines came alive again and she continued her retreat, though at one-third her maximum speed. As it fled the engagement, the Lycian frigate dropped mines and launched missiles from its aft weapons array while pushing its one functioning engine to the limit. Fortunately for *Challenger,* the Sahiradin battleship did not give chase. Instead, *Dominion* recalled her Codex fighters and continued to accelerate toward the center of the system.

As *Dominion's* engines rapidly increased their thrust, a general utility droid retrieved KB923 from its exterior docking station and brought it into one of *Dominion's* four massive landing bays. The utility droid placed it on a hovering engineering platform and brought it into the main diagnostic and repair facility, where engineers uploaded all remaining data from the droid's systems.

A tall being with white hair reaching to his shoulders and tiny scales covering his pale skin entered the repair facility. He wore a captain's silver and red insignia on the left breast of his black uniform. He approached the group of engineers surrounding the hovering workstation, and in the concise language of his species he asked, "Any information about the Kaiytáva?"

The engineers snapped to attention. "Captain Vilna," said one of them, "we are reviewing the data now." He indicated a three-dimensional schematic of the droid at the head of the workstation. "We have not discovered anything about the orb thus far, but much of the data appears to be corrupted. It will take time to finish our analysis. In fact, given the droid's poor condition and ancient design, we may need to manufacture replacement parts and repair it before we can retrieve everything from its systems."

"Do whatever is necessary, but do it quickly," said the captain. "The Kaiytáva aside, have you learned anything of use?"

"Sir, our preliminary analysis indicates that, as we had long suspected, *Vanquisher* was attacked and severely damaged before shifting to this solar system. Upon arrival, the captain determined *Vanquisher* was beyond repair, so he ordered four repair droids, including this one, KB923, and a manufacturing module to undertake repairing the *khâl* for others to follow."

"Just four droids? That would explain why it took so long for the *khâl* to open. Still, it is remarkable the repairs were completed at all. Why did the *Vanquisher* captain assign so few droids to the task?" asked Vilna.

"It appears *Vanquisher's* engineering bay was badly damaged in the attack and only a few could be dispatched. KB923's logs were periodically updated by *Vanquisher* for later transmission to any Sahiradin ships arriving through the *khâl* after it was repaired. These logs indicate *Vanquisher* made its way at best possible speed to S10122-P3. However, it soon discovered that, contrary to expectations, the colony was not abandoned. In fact, P3 had an estimated population of three billion inhabitants."

"Interesting," said the captain. "What else?"

"We've loaded *Vanquisher's* transmissions into *Dominion's* systems for further analysis. Much of it is corrupted, but the droid did record *Vanquisher's* destruction."

"Where did that occur?" asked Captain Vilna.

"A ring of asteroids between S10122-P4 and P5."

Captain Vilna walked around KB923. "With *Vanquisher's* destruction, the Kaiytáva could have been blown in any direction, perhaps even into this system's sun."

"Possibly," said the engineer. "However, KB923 may have recorded something important after explosion."

"What is that?"

"An escape pod beacon," said the engineer. "We're still working to confirm that, but it came from the region near P3."

Vilna looked up from KB923 and said, "I want you to learn as much as you can about that beacon. Map its trajectory and send me your best estimate of its current location."

"Understood, sir."

"And keep looking for any information regarding the Kaiytáva," said the captain as he started walking toward the exit. "It's your top priority."

Captain Vilna entered the corridor outside of the engineering department. Other Sahiradin he encountered in the passage stood at attention as he passed. They all had a similar tall lean build and pale skin of fine scales. Most of them had shoulder-length white hair and pale blue eyes, but a few had black hair and dark eyes. He stepped into an elevator encased in a transparent material, which quickly ascended to the bridge level.

"Captain on the bridge," said the duty watch officer from his station near the entrance

Dominion's bridge was large but dimly lit. The blue and red light from view screens and three dimensional projections illuminated the faces of the Sahiradin attending to various stations around the room. Vilna walked across the bridge to the chair located toward the back on a two-step high platform. He stood at the bottom of the steps at attention until the Sahiradin sitting in the high-backed chair acknowledged him.

"Commodore Lansu," he said. "I've spoken with the lead engineering technician and he informed me *Vanquisher* exploded in the solar system's asteroid ring. Also, as suspected, it had been damaged prior to shifting to this system."

"So it made it as far as the asteroid belt before exploding," said Lansu. "Anything about the Kaiytáva?"

"No sir, but we are still scanning for its signature and the repair droid's data has not been fully assessed," answered Vilna. "Furthermore, there is a possibility that an escape pod survived the explosion. We are continuing to investigate that."

"What else?" asked Lansu.

"The droid had another piece of interesting information. The estimated population of P3 is far less now than when *Vanquisher* arrived. Something happened to dramatically reduce it."

"What do you think caused that?" asked Lansu. "Disease? War?"

"Perhaps. It is also possible that *Vanquisher,* though heavily damaged, was able to initiate an assault using asteroids from the ring beyond P4."

"Hmm," said Lansu, nodding his head. "An extinction event like that may have made the world uninhabitable for us as well, but only for a short time if done properly. Given his options, a dying ship and a heavily populated target world, it could have been the most reasonable course to take."

"Yes sir."

Commodore Lansu thought for a moment. "And what about the current inhabitants of P3? Are they a threat to us?"

"Uncertain at this point sir," replied Captain Vilna. "*Vanquisher* transmitted data to the repair droid we recovered which may help answer that question. We have uploaded the information but the droid is in very poor condition due to its unusually long deployment. It will take time to repair it and complete our analysis."

"Very well," said Lansu. "And what about the Lycian frigate? What is its status?"

"Our ion cannon damaged it but we were unable to finish it off," replied the captain, placing subtle emphasis on the word *unable*.

Lansu fixed his pale blue eyes on the captain's. "Your tone suggests disagreement with my order to proceed with all haste to P3."

"No, sir," said Vilna. "I do not question your orders."

Commodore Lansu looked over his first officer's shoulder at the bridge's main view screen. Then he said, "We could have destroyed the frigate like we have so many others, but we would have lost valuable time chasing it down. Other Lycian ships will soon follow. Had we followed the frigate we could easily have become embroiled in a full-scale battle. That is not our goal. We must find the Kaiytáva. Everything else is of secondary importance."

He looked into Vilna's eyes and shook his head, disappointed at what he saw. "It is easy to always attack, but if you wish to be a Commodore when your generation becomes eligible and command a major war vessel such as *Dominion*, you must learn restraint when it is in the interests of complete victory."

Vilna nodded his head. "Yes, Commodore Lansu. Thank you for your guidance."

"Captain," said a Sahiradin standing next to one of the bridge stations. "We have discovered something you should see."

Vilna walked to the waiting officer. "It's an old hailing code, but it's unmistakably one of our own."

"Am I reading this correctly? Is it coming from P3?"

"Yes sir."

"Lock onto it and monitor," said Vilna. "Send an acknowledgement, but nothing more. Inform me if anything changes."

He turned and looked at the Commodore, who had heard the report and nodded his head.

Chapter 48

"Let's go," said one of the two guards standing outside their room. "All of you."

"What now?" asked Logan, annoyed. He'd just spent yet another three-hour session with two military intelligence officers and couldn't possibly think of anything else he hadn't already told them, twice.

Cap had been dozing when the guards entered. He stretched and yawned. "I hope there's coffee and food wherever we're going," he said.

"You've been stuffing your face for the last thirty-six hours," said Lena. "I'm surprised there's any room left in your stomach."

The guards directed the three of them down a corridor to a locked door. One of them ran a card through an electronic reader and entered a code. The light above the reader flashed green and he opened the door into a short hallway. They walked a few meters down the hall and stopped in front of a clear partition with an opening large enough for one person to pass through.

A guard on the other side of the partition waved for Lena to walk through the opening. As she did, red beams of light shot out from the edges of the partition and quickly passed over her body. A light above the opening flashed green. Logan and Cap followed Lena. They were led to another locked door where the guard from the partition pressed a button on the wall to the side of the door.

A voice from a speaker said, "ID."

The guard held his ID up to a small camera above the door. A moment later, there was a click, followed by a buzzing sound. The guard opened the door for the group to enter and then returned to his station at the partition. The room they entered was dimly lit. Soldiers sat in front of a dozen view screens showing a variety of data or images. Their two guards led them through the darkened space to a conference room on the other side. When they entered, they saw Ravenwood, Kane, Consul Sawyer, General Espinoza, and two other army officers.

"Take a seat," said Consul Sawyer, indicating three empty chairs.

"What's going on?" asked Logan.

Consul Sawyer smiled and cleared her throat. "We've heard Ravenwood's explanation of what you call the Apollo Stone and its purpose. Needless to say, we found it highly implausible. In fact, many of us still feel that way." She looked at General Espinoza.

"However, something extraordinary has happened which lends credence to the story," continued Sawyer. "Last night, at eleven twenty-two, we picked up what are undoubtedly coded signals emanating from an area near Jupiter. Then, at twelve twenty-seven this morning, we detected another very strange signal similar to what we had heard from near Ganymede. But this second signal originated from somewhere in the PRA."

Cap looked at Ravenwood. "Sounds like you were right, Ravenwood. The Sahiradin is calling his friends to come pick him up."

"I'd prefer to have been wrong," said Ravenwood gravely.

Consul Sawyer continued. "We believe there are two or perhaps three distinct sets of codes in play here. We have identified at least ten sources of one of the signals. The most active of these is headed straight for Earth."

"A mothership and probes," said Lena.

"Excuse me?" said Espinoza.

"If I were the captain of a ship that just arrived in a new solar system, I'd want to know as much about it as possible. I'd send probes in all directions."

Sawyer nodded her head and said, "Yes. That's a possibility."

"I agree with your assessment," Ravenwood said to Lena. "The probes are looking for the Stone. We have to assume the signals we are detecting are also being beamed back to a mothership, as you say. Or perhaps multiple ships."

"So the Sahiradin are coming, and they want the Apollo Stone back," said Logan. "What do you want from us?"

"Two things," said Espinoza. He looked at Lena. "First, do you remember seeing or hearing anything indicating the PRA was expecting these transmissions? Is there any reason to believe they have some kind of relationship with these Sahiradin, beyond the alleged crash survivor?"

Lena shook her head. "No. I don't think so."

"Okay," said Espinoza. He looked at Logan. "Second, Ravenwood tells us you had some kind of mental episode when your brain hooked up with the Apollo Stone. Personally, I think that's a bunch of horseshit. But I gotta ask, have you had any other of these mental fits since you arrived here at Jasper Air Force base?"

"No," said Logan coolly. "I haven't."

Consul Sawyer looked at Ravenwood and then at Espinoza. "So what now?" she asked. "There's a League Council meeting in thirty minutes to discuss these signals from space as well as the apparent response transmitted from the PRA. What am I supposed to tell them?"

"Tell them the truth," said Ravenwood. "We're about to have direct contact with one or more alien species, and there's a very good chance that soon we'll be fighting for the survival of humanity."

"We've got our hands full with the PRA," said General Espinoza. "The last thing we need is a dustup with a bunch of bug-eyed little aliens."

"It will be more than a 'dustup', General," said Ravenwood. "I believe the two types of signals you've detected belong to the Sahiradin and the Lycians; the latter is a group of allied species fighting the Sahiradin. I hope the Lycians arrive first, but we should prepare ourselves if it is the Sahiradin."

"Prepare for what? How in the hell would you know any of this?" asked General Espinoza. "I'm not doing one damn thing until I know how you get your information. We've got a huge PRA army massing across the river from St. Louis, and we'll need every gun we've got to keep them from crossing. I'm not taking one soldier off the line to fight these boogiemen until I can confirm what you're saying is correct!"

"I can't point you to any convincing evidence," admitted Ravenwood. "But what I'm saying is true, and by the time you've seen enough to be convinced, it will be too late!"

Angered by Ravenwood's tone of voice, General Espinoza rose to his feet and was about to respond, but Consul Sawyer raised her hand and said in a loud voice, "Your point is well taken, General Espinoza. But something alien is coming toward Earth, and fast. That much is beyond dispute. I honestly don't know what we can do to respond to this potential new threat and still maintain our forces on the river. For better or for worse, we'll know their intentions in a matter of days."

Chapter 49

Kurak entered his identity card into the slot in the wall. He placed his palm on a nearby pad until the light turned green and then punched in his code. The door opened and he walked into the hangar bay. The guard on the other side of the door noticed him, but quickly directed his eyes straight ahead.

Kurak knew his long white hair, pale blue eyes and pale scaly skin made people uncomfortable. They had all been told the same story about him. He had been born not only an albino but also with a rare form of leprosy. An absurd lie, of course, but he discovered long ago that humans often prefer an absurd lie over a disturbing truth.

He climbed up the ladder to the scaffolding that ran along all four walls. Below him, technicians were completing the *Blackhawk's* pre-flight preparations. The human leadership had been extremely upset with the loss of the Apollo Stone, the *Kaiytáva*. Even he had been interrogated for hours after they discovered it was missing. They tore apart the laboratory and Chambers' office, and they launched their massive search operation to locate the three fugitives who had taken it. But they had failed. The *Kaiytáva* was now in the hands of the League, though not for much longer.

Kurak looked down at the *Blackhawk* from his perch on the scaffolding. One of the technicians glanced up but quickly looked away when he saw Kurak ghostlike visage staring down at him. The technician tapped his companion on the shoulder and they moved to another section of the large craft. The thirty-seven-meter-long *Blackhawk* was equal parts gunship, troop transport, and spacecraft. It was powered by a highly advanced fusion reactor engine, and her remarkably nimble flight abilities were enhanced by a gravity dampener equal to nearly seventy-five percent of its mass, making it extremely light and maneuverable. The gravity dampeners also allowed engineers to heavily arm the ship without compromising speed or agility. Humans had never built anything like it. Never would have built anything like it for centuries or longer without his help.

Well, perhaps not centuries, admitted Kurak to himself. There were a few shining lights, the late Dr. Chambers having been perhaps the brightest among them. Chambers had overcome a number of seemingly impossible challenges with remarkable ease. Kurak had admired his ability to adapt advanced Sahiradin technological concepts to the PRA's engineering and manufacturing capabilities. But now the traitor was dead, just as his greatest achievements were to be put to the test.

Kurak walked along the length of the scaffolding, looking at the sleek dark gray ship and the graceful sweep of its wings. They were short, but could afford to be shorter than any typical aircraft of this size due to the *Blackhawk's* gravity dampeners. Under the wings were a number of missile launchers and small gun turrets. The fuselage was long enough to carry two hundred soldiers, two hundred and fifty if the seats were retracted and everyone stood. Round nodes housing the energy pulse guns were located at various places along the length of the ship. Capable of firing bursts of high energy photons coupled with focused sonic waves, the pulse guns could disrupt enemy electrical systems or destroy human targets with extreme and deadly accuracy. The ship was covered in heat-resistant tiles and protective stealth shielding to make it both space worthy and invisible to any known detection system. And an advanced long duration antiballistic shield made it practically impervious to conventional projectile weapons.

Kurak saw Red Leg soldiers lining up behind the *Blackhawk.* Their shoulders, torsos, thighs, and shins were covered in dark gray Provex armor. The Provex could deflect most sword strikes and even bullets if your shield was down and you had a little luck. The Red Leg captain leading the assault gave the soldiers a few last-minute instructions. The men and women, armed with M-35s, bracers, and swords shouted *Yes sir!* They marched up the short ramp and into the rear of the *Blackhawk's* fuselage.

Kurak checked his more advanced bracer to ensure it was fully powered. Then he pulled his sword out of its scabbard to examine the blade. It was made of inferior metal when compared with his Sahiradin blade, but that had been lost long ago when his ship, *Vanquisher,* exploded. He reached over his left shoulder and slid the blade into the scabbard of his battle pack and took a deep breath. He descended from the scaffolding on a ladder nearest to the cockpit and walked toward the gunship.

The men were all on board now and the pilot and co-pilot were just completing their systems check. The pilot exchanged a few words with the control tower. Kurak sat in the vacant navigator's seat and strapped himself in. The pilot acknowledged his presence with a nod but did not speak to him. A moment later Kurak heard a soft humming sound as the fusion reactor sent power to the gravity dampeners and thrusters. The *Blackhawk* rolled through the hangar door and taxied to the head of a nearby runway.

"Roger that, control," said the pilot. "All systems are go. Awaiting flight clearance."

"Clearance granted, *Blackhawk*," said the voice from the control tower. "Good hunting."

"Prepare for takeoff," said the pilot through the intercom to the troops in the back.

A heartbeat later, the *Blackhawk* raced down the runway and quickly leapt into the air. Kurak saw the pilot smile as he guided the agile ship into the sky and bank left. The pilot turned west and gunned the engines, flying just above the treetops toward the Mississippi River half a continent away.

Chapter 50

When the alarms at Jasper Air Base sounded, *Blackhawk* was already firing on the defensive batteries. The base's automated defense systems had failed to detect the ship's approach, and the manned guns were unable to penetrate the ship's antiballistic shield. Men and women poured out of their barracks in response to the sirens in varying states of readiness. Those without shields were cut down by *Blackhawk's* automated gun turrets. Others found cover and began firing at the low hovering ship.

Red Legs quickly deployed out of the gunship's rear, jumping the short distance to the ground and dashing toward previously determined goals. As soon as the troops were off, the gunship rose into the air and fired its ballistic weapons to clear the way for the charging Republican Special Forces. It also continued to target the base's defensive systems using its pulse guns, silencing all of them in under a minute.

Logan, Cap and Lena woke to the sound of blaring alarms. They looked at each other, momentarily confused, but then they heard shouting through their closed door as a group of armed troopers ran by. The lights flickered and then the power went out. A backup generator kicked in and dim red lights came on.

"The base is under attack!" Logan shouted to the others above the sound of a nearby explosion.

He stood and pulled on the locked door, banging on it and shouting for someone to open it. After a few frustrating moments, he heard Ravenwood's voice shout, "Stand back!"

The door burst open and they immediately ran through it. Ravenwood was already running down the hallway but not toward the exit. They followed him into the heart of the building.

"We have to get the Apollo Stone," he shouted over his shoulder.

Troopers ran past them toward the exits and the PRA attackers, but they continued toward the building's interior. The hallway ended in a T intersection. A heavy metal door stood in front of them. Ravenwood looked down each hall, then back at the metal door.

Rubbing his head in agitation, he said, "I'm not sure which way to go."

"It's this way," said Logan, pointing down the right hand corridor.

Ravenwood ran in the direction Logan had pointed. There was an explosion just in front of them and plaster and concrete fell from the ceiling. They closed their eyes and covered their faces as dust filled the air around them. A few moments later, Logan opened his eyes to see Ravenwood pulling stones from the pile, revealing a gap to the other side. He squeezed through. Logan, Cap, and Lena followed him through and found three dead League troopers on the other side. The sound of shouting voices came toward them from farther down the corridor.

Ravenwood squinted to see through the smoke and dust. Then he turned and said, "Red Legs!"

"Get their bracers and weapons," yelled Lena as she knelt down by the dead League troopers. In moments the three of them had strapped on the bracers and engaged the League version of the arm guard and shield.

Ravenwood cautiously led them down the corridor. Logan saw a group of League troopers firing into the shadows. Suddenly a number of Red Legs rushed forward, swords drawn. The troopers drew their blades and a vicious close-quarters battle ensued. More Red Legs joined the fight, overrunning the League's position and killing the defenders. Then they saw Logan and the others and attacked.

Lena stepped forward. Logan's heart skipped a beat as he watched the lead Red Leg race toward her. Lena was not in a proper defensive stance, but rather stood flatfooted with her sword at her side. Suddenly, just as the Red Leg was upon her, she spun low and sliced her assailant at the knee just above his shin guard, sending him to the ground.

More Red Legs attacked. Logan fended off an assault from two of them. Cap faced three and rapidly gave up ground while using sword and guard to deflect their attacks. Lena dropped back to be level with Cap, trying to offer a unified front in the narrow hallway.

"It's on the other side," yelled Logan as he took a step forward and slashed at one of his opponents with the League sword he'd picked up. "We have to get through!"

More Red Legs arrived. The four of them were now outnumbered three to one and were forced to give up more and more ground, though they tried to mount counterattacks. Lena used a quick parry and lunge to drive her sword through the shoulder of a Red Leg. As she did so, another swung at her exposed flank, but Logan stepped in to block the attack.

Then Logan heard the sound of metal striking metal from behind the Red Legs. Through the dim light he saw Kane attacking the enemy from the rear. Some of them turned to attack him, but they were met by League troopers, including Lieutenant Styles. Logan saw her drive a dagger through a Red Leg's thigh and then cut him down with her sword. More League troopers joined her and Kane. Sensing they were surrounded, the Red Legs changed their formation into a phalanx and charged toward Kane and the troopers, hoping to get out. Though they killed five defenders, they couldn't break through, and in a few moments the Red Legs were dead.

Logan looked at Kane and Lieutenant Styles. "Just in time," he said with a smile.

The sounds of shouting voices and gunfire erupted from behind Kane and Styles. A group of Red Legs was trying to break through from behind. Styles turned and ordered her troopers to advance and form a defensive line.

"We need to get the stone!" yelled Ravenwood.

"We'll hold them off!" yelled Styles. "Get to the command center. That's where it is."

Ravenwood looked at Logan and said, "Which way?"

Logan pointed with his sword. "Through there."

Logan ran forward and the others followed. They wound their way around several smoke-filled halls until they entered the base's central command center through a hole that had been blown in the wall. Logan peered through the hole and saw several dead League troopers on the floor. On the far side of the room were half a dozen Red Legs and a tall white-haired figure dressed in black Provex armor. He was holding the Apollo Stone up to the room's dim red emergency lighting, his thin pale lips pulled into a grin. The enemy soldiers turned to face Logan and the others as they entered the room.

Ravenwood whispered to the others, "At last, we meet our Sahiradin castaway."

Kurak tucked the Apollo Stone into an inner pocket behind his breastplate and drew his sword. The other Red Legs drew their swords and slowly advanced, spreading out as they approached. The sound of distant explosions and firing weapons filtered into the room as Kane walked forward with arms slightly outstretched, inviting the Red Legs to attack. Two of them accepted the invitation. Lena moved quickly to support Kane's right side and Cap followed. Logan moved up to Kane's left side. Ravenwood stood next to Logan, a sword in his large hands.

Kane quickly dropped one of his opponents and the other slid over to face him. He lunged at Kane, but it was a ruse and he joined the attack on Cap. Surprised, Cap blocked the new opponent's sword but could not stop the first Red Leg from slicing his shoulder. Cursing, Cap grabbed his wound and dropped back. Lena moved over to fill the gap, but her opponent cut her thigh as she moved, which sent her to the ground. Kane spun toward Lena and thrust a sword at a Red Leg's ribs. His blade slid off the Red Leg's Provex armor, but his dagger found the gap between the man's shoulder plate and neck, giving him a vicious gash.

There was a momentary break in the fighting as the two sides considered their next move. Ravenwood took the opportunity to assist Lena, who could not stand, and pulled her out of the fray.

Kurak walked forward toward Kane and stood with his sword pointing down and to his side. He flashed Kane a predator's grin.

"You are skilled with a blade," said the Sahiradin. "But you have not been truly tested."

Kurak glided two steps forward and swung his sword with remarkable precision and grace, as though it were an extension of his body. Kane fended off the attack and the flood of others that followed, but he was clearly hard put to keep from being cut. Kurak turned and spun, thrusting and slicing at Kane in a deadly display of sword mastery. Cap attempted to assist Kane, but the Sahiradin blocked the young man's attacks with ease. While Kurak and Kane were locked in battle, the Red Legs set upon Logan and Cap, forcing them to retreat toward the blast hole through which they had entered.

Kane countered Kurak's attacks with a thrust of his sword and then his dagger, but the Sahiradin struck the dagger so hard it flew from Kane's hand. Now Kurak attacked in earnest, launching one deadly attack after another. Kane defended well, even without his dagger, but was nicked and cut again and again.

As Kane fought the Sahiradin, Logan was doing his best to defend himself against two attacking Red Legs. Little by little, he gave ground until he could feel the wall against his back. One of the Red Legs feigned an attack but pulled back while the other thrust with his sword, wounding Logan's right shoulder.

As Logan rolled to the right to avoid another Red Leg blade, he looked at Kane and saw him desperately fending off his black-armored opponent. Next to Kane, Cap parried attack after attack from his two Red Leg attackers.

The wound to his right shoulder throbbed with intense pain. Logan lifted the sword with both hands and grimaced as his two opponents prepared to finish him off. He could see their eyes glinting in anticipation of the kill, and there was little he could do to disappoint them.

Then he saw Ravenwood enter through the blast hole in the wall, having pulled Lena through the hole and into the relative safety of the hallway. His face was set in stony determination. Tightly gripping a sword in both hands, he closed his eyes and focused his thoughts. Then he looked at the Sahiradin and like an enraged bear, charged forward.

Ravenwood's attack, though swift and determined, was rather clumsy. Nevertheless, Kurak was surprised by the ferocity of the assault and was forced to give up ground, although Logan could tell by the grin on the alien's face that he was enjoying the turn the fight had taken.

Kane and Cap took advantage of the momentary shift in momentum that Ravenwood's attack had provided and went on the offensive. Logan also stepped forward and swung his blade, keeping his two opponents occupied long enough for Kane to drive his sword into the side of a Red Leg's thigh, ripping through his hamstring muscles. As the Red Leg collapsed, Kane turned to assist Ravenwood but a Red Leg peeled off of his fight with Cap to block him.

Logan glanced at Ravenwood and saw the momentary advantage his flurry of swings had provided was spent. The Sahiradin was now easily avoiding or blocking his attacks, but surprisingly, his counterattacks were not finding their mark. His sword was repeatedly and inexplicably turned to the side at the last moment whenever he tried to deal Ravenwood a deathblow. The grin on his face was gone, replaced by an expression of angry frustration.

Ravenwood deflected several strikes and raised his sword for a great downward swing. Just then, the Sahiradin stunned him with a quick punch to the face. The blow caused Ravenwood to stumble backward just as Kurak glided forward and drove his sword into Ravenwood's stomach. The Sahiradin paused and flashed a serpent's grin as he looked menacingly into Ravenwood's surprised eyes.

Ravenwood gasped and dropped his sword, but remained focused on Kurak's face. Then he wrapped both of his hands around the hilt of the Sahiradin's sword and with a great heave pulled himself closer. He grabbed hold of the black armor and reached behind the breastplate. Kurak realized what Ravenwood was attempting to do and tried to break free, but could not escape the big man's powerful grip. Kurak covered the breast pocket containing the Apollo Stone with his free hand as Ravenwood pulled at the clothing under the armor, desperately trying to extract the stone. Finally, Ravenwood's strength failed him and his blood-stained hands slipped from the black Provex armor. Kurak pulled his sword from Ravenwood's stomach and watched him drop to his knees.

Kane screamed and slit the throat of his Red Leg opponent. He lunged at Kurak, but he was met by yet another Red Leg. Kane dropped him with a slice to the man's exposed knee and turned to attack the Sahiradin, but he had already disappeared through a door in the far side of the room. The two remaining Red Legs guarded his escape, frustrating Kane's attempts to pursue. After parrying several attacks, the Red Legs heard approaching voices through the blast hole in the wall. Lieutenant Styles and several troopers entered the room, prompting the Red Legs to quickly follow the Sahiradin through the door. Kane picked up his dagger from the floor and raced after them.

Logan ran to Ravenwood, who lay on the floor clutching his stomach. He was breathing in quick shallow puffs.

"Failed. I didn't get it," he said, gasping for air and holding his trembling hands over his stomach as blood flowed from the wound. He looked into Logan's eyes and whispered, "Don't let him have the stone."

Logan nodded and said, "We'll get it. I promise."

Logan looked over his shoulder at Lieutenant Styles as she entered the room and said, "He's badly wounded and needs a doctor right away."

Ravenwood tried to sit up. "Forget me. *Get the stone!*" he said in the loudest voice he could muster. He pushed Logan toward the door through which Kurak had retreated.

Logan looked at Ravenwood and then at Cap, who had just finished checking on Lena.

"Let's go," he said to Cap.

They ran through the door after the Sahiradin. As they raced down the red-lit corridor, Logan could hear shouting voices and ringing swords. They turned a corner and saw Kane fighting a Red Leg near a door that opened to the airfield. Five meters closer to them was the body of a Red Leg. Kane kneed his opponent in the groin and smashed the pummel of his sword into the back of his head, causing the man to fall to the floor. Then he turned and ran onto the airfield.

When Logan and Cap reached the door, the Red Leg Kane had struck was struggling to his feet. Cap bowled him over and punched him in the jaw, knocking him unconscious. They ran into the morning light and saw Kane fighting the Sahiradin thirty meters away. The two were spinning and thrusting with lightning speed, each one eager to cut the flesh of the other.

Cap was the first to join Kane. He swung his sword at the Sahiradin's skull, but Kurak leaned back and raised his foot to Cap's chest, kicking him back several steps. Logan arrived and stood to Kane's left. Kane attacked, but Kurak sidestepped him and swung low at Logan, who struggled to bring his sword around in time to block the attack. The Sahiradin then blocked Kane's dagger with his sword and smashed his fist into Kane's jaw, causing him to stumble backward and fall.

Kurak turned to attack Logan, but just then he saw League troopers pouring onto the airfield and running toward him. He swung at Logan's head, causing the young man to duck low, then he fled toward the awaiting *Blackhawk*.

As Kurak ran, the *Blackhawk* trained its weapons on the fast-approaching troopers, spraying the area with high-caliber bullets. Two of the *Blackhawk's* pulse guns also fired at an air defense battery that was just coming back on line, causing it to explode.

Logan and Cap pulled the semi-conscious Kane behind a pallet of supplies while League troopers fired on the ship, but their weapons were useless against its shields. Logan looked to his right and saw about fifty Red Legs running from the base's headquarters building toward the *Blackhawk*. They fired on League troopers as they dashed across the open tarmac. Suddenly, they stopped running and took cover behind some destroyed vehicles. Logan looked at the *Blackhawk* and saw it was lifting off just as Kurak boarded the rear ramp. A handful of Red Legs on the ramp provided him with covering fire as he went inside.

Helpless to stop the Sahiradin from escaping, Kane, Logan, and Cap watched as the *Blackhawk* lifted into the air. But as it gained altitude, a red beam of light struck the gunship. Logan looked behind him and saw that some troopers had brought one of the mounted pulse guns back on line and were manually targeting the *Blackhawk*. Another beam flashed toward *Blackhawk* but like the first, it failed to pierce the gunship's shield. They fired again and a spot on the gunship momentarily glowed red as the gunship turned northeast. A final beam from the pulse gun hummed through the air. Black smoke erupted from the fleeing *Blackhawk* and it shimmered momentarily with silver light.

"Shit," said Cap. "I think that final shot took her shields out, but now they're gone."

"And so is the Apollo Stone," added Logan as he watched the gunship fly away.

Something suddenly roared over their heads. Logan looked toward the source of the sound and saw a group of missiles racing through the air in the direction of the *Blackhawk*. After a few seconds, the *Blackhawk's* anti-missile defenses fired something at the onrushing missiles, which destroyed several of them, but a few continued toward the gunship. One more was intercepted by *Blackhawk* defenses, but two reached their target and exploded in bright red and orange light.

Logan looked behind him toward the main building to see a handful of troopers with handheld missile launchers. Among them was Lena. She was leaning against the side of the building holding a spent launcher in her hands. He turned toward the north and saw the retreating gunship trailing black smoke.

Hearing gunfire, Logan looked at the remaining Red Legs as they continued to fire on any League troopers that appeared on the tarmac. But their position behind the wrecked vehicles did not afford much protection. Troopers began firing on them from on top of nearby buildings. Several RPG rounds landed in their midst, throwing bodies into the air. Their still-active shields protected them from the explosives' shrapnel but not the concussions and broken bones the blast waves caused. Yet, despite the fact that they had no hope of escape or victory, they continued to fight for several minutes until there were fewer than ten left who finally surrendered.

Logan and Cap ran back to Lena. Kane followed them, turning from time to time to gaze at the still-visible trail of smoke in the northern sky.

"I can't believe you two left me behind," said Lena angrily.

"I can't believe you walked all the way here with this wound," said Cap, looking at the bloody bandage on her leg. He took the missile launcher from her hand and put it on the ground.

"How's Ravenwood?" asked Kane when he arrived seconds later.

Lena shook her head. "It doesn't look good. They've taken him to the infirmary."

Kane nodded and dashed into the building.

"What are you doing?" she asked Cap as he tried to lead her toward a nearby mobile medical crew.

"I'm taking you to see the medic," he said, confused.

"Why?" she asked, pulling her arm out of his hand.

"Because you're wounded," replied Cap, angrily.

"I saw an undamaged fighter in the back of the hangar," said Lena. "Get in it and go shoot down the *Blackhawk.*"

Cap stared at her for a moment, mouth slightly open. Then he said, "So you're telling me to waltz into a League hangar, steal one of their planes, and go after the most advanced aircraft the PRA has ever put in the air."

"Yes," she replied without hesitation.

"It takes a half dozen people to get a plane ready for flight," he protested. "How am I supposed to get it off the ground with no fuel? How am I supposed to shoot down the *Blackhawk* with no ordnance? And how am I supposed to avoid being shot to hell by League missiles as soon as they see me taxi out of the hangar?"

Lena leaned forward and cupped his face in her hands. "Improvise. I've already wounded the thing for you. Just go finish it off."

She gently patted his cheek and removed her hands.

Cap was about to respond, but reconsidered and looked at Logan. "You want to help me steal an airplane?"

Chapter 51

Kane found Ravenwood on a stretcher in the makeshift hospital ward outside the infirmary amid dozens of wounded troopers. A doctor was looking at the dressing on his wound.

"How's he doing, doc?" asked Kane as he looked at Ravenwood's unconscious face.

"Not good," said the doctor without looking up. "He took a sword in the stomach and it passed through his back." She stood and faced Kane. "I did some very quick surgery, which stopped the worst of the bleeding, but it's a mess in there and I didn't have much time."

"Well, get back in there and finish the job," said Kane through clenched teeth.

She looked around the room. "There are a lot of wounded soldiers whose lives can be saved but only if I move quickly to help them. I did my best with your friend, but now it's out of my hands. I'm sorry."

She walked over to the triage nurse. "Okay. Who's next?" she asked.

"Doc," said Kane. "I don't think you understand, I..."

But the doctor cut him off. "I understand perfectly well," she said in a firm but professional tone. "Now let me do my job." She returned her attention to the triage nurse.

Kane stared at the doctor's back but said nothing more. Then he crouched next to Ravenwood and saw the normally energetic man was pale from blood loss. He was still breathing but his breaths were shallow and irregular.

"Ravenwood," Kane whispered. There was no response.

Kane waited a few more minutes, holding Ravenwood's hand and watching his face until his chest ceased to rise. Then he placed the man's hand on his chest and stood to walk away.

Suddenly, Ravenwood reached out and caught his hand. "Did you get it?" he asked in a hoarse whisper.

Kane took Ravenwood's hand again and looked into his eyes. He shook his head. "No."

"We must not let them have it," said Ravenwood. He shut his eyes, but he gripped Kane's hand tightly. "It will be the end. The true end of the Alamani."

"The Alamani," said Kane bitterly. "Look at us. We're not Alamani.

We're little more than a bunch of bickering savages. Maybe it's not such a bad thing if this is the end."

Ravenwood smiled. He let go of Kane's hand and patted his arm. "Resigned to defeat so soon? That's the easy road."

"If extinction is the easy road, what's the hard one?" asked Kane in a grim tone.

"Redemption," answered Ravenwood weakly. "The Alamani have much to answer for and much still to offer."

"We aren't the Alamani," said Kane.

Ravenwood slowly turned his head back and forth. "Isolation on this world has made you different. Tougher, crueler," he said in a whisper. "But there are others like you, Kane. Other sparks able to ignite the flame. Others like our young friends. Help them."

Then Ravenwood's eyes went blank and he slowly exhaled.

Chapter 52

Cap slipped into a flight suit and climbed into the cockpit of the X-1 prototype. "It looks a lot like the Phantom 2," he said in disbelief.

"Then you should know where everything is," said Logan as he climbed into the rear-facing gunner's seat.

Cap was checking the plane's ordnance readings, hoping by some miracle there were a few rounds in it, when a man in a dirty blue jumpsuit approached from an open door. "What the fuck do you think you're doing with my plane?" he yelled.

"I'm going after that gunship," said Cap as he hastily ran through a mental pre-flight systems check. "Why do you guys always take out the bullets after a flight? Unloading the missiles makes sense. I get that. But why the bullets?"

"So stupid fuckers don't sneak in and shoot the hell out the place. Now, who the fuck are you?" repeated the man. A few men and women, also in blue jumpsuits, gathered around.

Cap looked at the man. "I've flown the Phantom 2 and I know how to fly this bird. I'm going after that gunship. Unless you've got someone better to do the job, get the fuck out of the way."

"I'll piss on a live wire before I let some stranger just take one of my birds," said the man. "Someone call security!"

No one moved. "Didn't you hear me?" yelled the man, but everyone was looking at the doorway.

Consul Sawyer was standing there, her tan blouse covered in other people's blood. "What are you doing, Cap?" she asked in a strangely calm voice.

"I'm going after the *Blackhawk*."

"I see. And you're taking our most advanced aircraft to do it?"

"You mean this modified PRA Phantom 2?" asked Cap. "Yeah, that's right."

Sawyer thought for a moment. "Well, you're the only pilot around here able to walk, so I guess you get the job."

The man in the blue jumpsuit objected. "Consul, I think we'd better get General Espinoza's okay on this."

"He's dead," she said. "His throat was cut and he bled out on the floor in front of me. As Iowa's Consul, I say we go after them."

The man clenched his right hand into a tight fist, then he nodded his head. He looked at the others standing around him. "Well, you heard the woman. Let's get the X-1 ready for flight. You've got two minutes."

No one moved.

"Now, you wrench monkeys!" he yelled.

"Yes, Crew Chief McKinney!" responded one of them. They scrambled to comply with the crew chief's order.

"Keep it simple," yelled the crew chief. "She's already fueled so load her with weapons package 1, that's weapons 1, people."

A technician climbed up the pilot's ladder and leaned in. Pointing to a few displays, he quickly explained what they meant, what to look out for, and how to make necessary adjustments in the event certain things happened.

"I get it. I get it," said Cap dismissively as he continued his pre-flight check. "Just tell me when she's armed."

After two minutes of hectic but efficient activity, and more than a little colorful encouragement from Crew Chief McKinney, the X-1 was ready. McKinney rolled the ladder away from the cockpit. "If you put one scratch on this aircraft, I will cut your balls off and shove them down your throat."

"Understood chief," said Cap. "Is she ready?"

"She's ready. I called the tower. They know you're taking her out fast."

"Good. At least they won't shoot at me."

"I can't promise you that," responded McKinney. "Now get the fuck out of here and shoot those bastards down."

Cap fired up the engines and quickly taxied to the end of a nearby runway. The ground crew had removed debris in order to clear a path for takeoff.

"You ready?" Cap asked Logan through their helmets' integrated communications system, or ICS.

"I guess so. What do you want me to do?" he asked as he checked his restraints for the tenth time.

"Nothing. You're here as ballast. She handles better with a full crew."

They saw Lena waving to them from the hangar door. She blew them a kiss.

"I'll be back to collect that," said Cap more to himself than Logan.

"How do you know she meant it for you?" asked Logan with a chuckle.

"Because you have a face only a monkey could love," said Cap as he lowered his helmet visor.

Cap sent power flowing to the engines and the X-1 shot forward along the runway. Seconds later, Cap pulled back on the stick and the aircraft lifted nimbly into the air. He banked right and followed the *Blackhawk's* trail of smoke.

Logan heard a woman's voice in his helmet's ICS. "X-1, this is control. Bogey is heading northeast, bearing fifteen degrees."

"Looks like they're heading north to avoid the League's missile defenses on the river," said Logan.

"Control," said Cap a few moments later, "I have a visual. Any chance there are friendly birds nearby?"

"Negative, X-1," said the voice from Control.

"Logan," said Cap.

"Ballast reporting, sir," said Logan.

"Engage the weapons heads-up display and let me know if you see any incoming bogeys. We're not going to get any League help, so anything you see is going to be PRA aircraft."

"HUD engaged," said Logan. "According to this thing, at our current speed we'll have the *Blackhawk* in range in two minutes."

"She's barely moving," said Cap. "Lena's missile must have hit her real bad. We'll be crossing the Mississippi in about ten minutes, and we should expect the PRA to send help as soon as possible. The anti-aircraft defenses along the river will probably keep them out of League airspace, but they'll shoot at us from the east side of the river if they can."

"Understood. Let me know when to shoot," said Logan.

"I've transferred weapons control to myself," said Cap, "but do you see that stick on your right side?"

"Yes."

"That'll fire the wing cannons," said Cap. "When we're close enough, you can shoot that. You can adjust fire about fifteen degrees by moving the stick."

"Got it."

Logan looked at the weapons HUD. "Just about in range of the *Blackhawk*. How are you going to bring it down?"

"I'm going to put a missile up its tailpipe," replied Cap.

"We can't blow it up," said Logan. "We need the Apollo Stone."

"That's asking for a lot of precision," said Cap. "These weapons are designed to obliterate a target, not gently bring it down."

"Do your best," said Logan. He looked at his HUD. "Almost in range of the *Blackhawk*." He paused a moment as he looked at his screen. "And I'm seeing bogeys to the east. A lot of them."

"Yup," said Cap. "I see them. Readying wasp missiles."

Using his thumb, Cap lifted a trigger guard. "Firing."

Two wasp missiles ignited and flew out from their perch under each wing, leaving a stream of white smoke behind them. After they had closed about half of the distance between the two aircraft, *Blackhawk* fired her pulse guns at the oncoming missiles. One missile began to turn and twist, then it shot off to the right and downward. The other stayed on course. The *Blackhawk* fired a series of small countermeasure missiles. They quickly closed on the remaining wasp and exploded when they were within twenty meters, sending thousands of metal balls in in every direction. The wasp was hit multiple times and could not maintain its flight path. It flew to the left and then exploded far from its target.

Cap fired two more wasps and two hammerheads, but they also succumbed to *Blackhawk's* countermeasures. He was preparing to fire his final two missiles, but he had to suddenly roll the X-1 to the left as two enemy missiles shot past him. Then *Blackhawk* fired six more air-to-air missiles.

"Do you see what's coming our way?" asked Logan, staring at his HUD.

"I do," replied Cap. He quickly scrolled through his countermeasure screens and made several adjustments. "Let me know when you see two concentric circles with a blinking red line through them."

After three heartbeats, which felt like an eternity, Logan said, "I see it!"

Cap immediately engaged the X-1's afterburner, sending them hurtling toward the oncoming missiles. The g-forces threatened to cause Logan to black out, but his flight suit filled automatically with air pressure to force blood into his brain and keep him conscious.

"What are you doing, Cap?" asked Logan, trying his best to hide his rising panic.

"I'm either a genius or suicidal. We'll know in about three seconds."

Logan watched on the HUD as the oncoming missiles closed the gap. He shut his eyes, but nothing happened. He opened them and saw that the missiles had all raced past the X-1.

"Hey, they missed us," Logan said, smiling.

"Yeah. Those are K-150s. They have an on-board targeting radar. I recorded their signals and repeated them back. It momentarily confuses them."

"It's a good thing you know about PRA air-to-air missile vulnerabilities," said Logan.

"Yeah. They built a fancy new gunship but kept the same old ordnance. But check your HUD."

Logan looked at the screen and saw that two of the missiles were turning toward them.

"They must have locked onto us just before they passed," said Cap.

"I thought this thing was stealthy," said Logan.

"It is," said Cap as he readied his final two hammerheads. "Only two out of six locked on."

"That's two too many."

"There's just no pleasing some people," said Cap. "Get ready with your wing cannons. You're on deck."

"Control, this is X-1" said Cap. "How much time before the bogeys across the river get involved?"

"X-1, Control. You've got about twenty seconds before you're within their range. Don't forget those bluebirds are on their way up your tailpipe."

"Roger that," said Cap. He checked the progress of the two missiles rapidly approaching from behind.

"We're gaining fast on the *Blackhawk*, but still too far for your cannons," said Cap.

"Those missiles are about ten seconds away from vaporizing us," said Logan. Cap remained silent.

"Five seconds."

Logan cleared his throat. "Now's a good time to do something, Cap."

"Fire your guns," said Cap.

Logan pressed the button on the stick and a few hundred rounds of bullets spat out from both wings toward the *Blackhawk*. Then Cap took a breath and gently pressed the thumb trigger, sending his final two missiles after the gunship. He immediately fired the X-1's missile countermeasures and pulled hard left. The stress on the wings was well beyond tolerances, and Cap struggled to maintain velocity in the high G turn. The G forces caused Logan to pass out, despite the flight suit's added air pressure and extra oxygen from his mask.

One of the missiles lost contact with the X-1, but the other reached its proximity boundary and detonated, sending shrapnel in all directions. A few pieces connected with the X-1's right tail wing, causing the plane to shake violently in its high G turn. After a few moments, Cap regained control and turned away from the river and the prowling PRA fighters on the eastern side. He checked his radar to see the hammerheads closing the gap with the *Blackhawk*. He grinned when the gunship's countermeasures failed to destroy or distract the missiles. Suddenly, one of them exploded and then the other.

"Yeah!" he shouted. "Logan, we got it! We got it!"

Logan was just regaining consciousness. "We got it?" he asked, groggily.

"Control. X-1," said Cap. "We got it!"

There was a long pause. "X-1, this is control. We're not sure how to say this, but you didn't get it. The hammerheads did their job, but the bogey is gone."

"You mean it blew up?" asked Cap.

"No, it's just not there."

Logan cursed. "The Apollo Stone. *Blackhawk* shifted space just before the missiles detonated."

"Shit!" cursed Cap. He shook his head a few times, then asked, "What do we do now? Where did it go?"

"I don't know," answered Logan. "Anywhere, I guess."

"No. Not anywhere," said Cap. "Not with the hole Lena and her friends put in it. It might have taken a hit from the hammerheads, too. It must be nearby."

"Control. X-1. Any sign of the target yet?"

"No, X-1," said the voice. "Return to base."

Chapter 53

Commodore Lansu looked up from his report to see *Dominion* was approaching P4, a small red planet. The Sahiradin scrolled through the report. It stated that, although P4 was devoid of life, there was evidence that liquid water had once flowed on its surface and still existed in frozen form at the poles. The report also indicated there was no evidence of any Alamani occupation.

He accessed the report from the Sahiradin on P3. According to the crash survivor, a Captain Kurak, P3's population was split into numerous tribes, but there were also large areas where there was no recognized central political authority. The report was dismissive of P3 military strength, although the inhabitants could be aggressive and did wage war against each other from time to time.

"Incoming signal from P3, sir," said a communications officer.

Lansu stood and walked to the communications station. His pale blue eyes lit up when he read the decoded information.

"High command is hailing us, sir," said another officer.

"Put it through to the secure room," said Lansu.

"Yes sir."

The commodore walked across the bridge toward a nearby door. Bridge officers of varying ranks stood at attention when he passed by and then resumed their duties. He walked through an open door and into a rectangular room equipped with a tactical command and control station and a secure communications portal. The door slid shut behind him. Six high-backed chairs occupied each side of the room's longer walls, with a very grand one occupying the space between the two rows. Lansu touched a few keys on the communications array and holographic images of five Sahiradin flickered into sight, each occupying one of the chairs.

"What is your status, Commodore Lansu?" asked a holographic Sahiradin dressed in red robes over a black tunic.

"Master Tel, we will soon be within striking distance of P3," replied Lansu. "We have reviewed the reports from the Sahiradin, who has been living among the Alamani there. We do not anticipate significant resistance."

"How do we know these reports are accurate and not some trick?" asked the Sahiradin to Tel's left.

"Master Travant, our advance probes are already in orbit around P3 and have confirmed much of what is in the survivor's reports. However, we won't have a complete understanding of the situation until *Dominion* arrives and we can assess for ourselves."

"What information do you have about the Kaiytáva?" asked Master Tel.

"I'm happy to report that the survivor on P3 has just informed us that he has secured the Kaiytáva, but his ship was damaged. He was able to land the craft in a remote area, and he and a few loyal Alamani soldiers are now taking up a defensive position on some nearby high ground. He anticipates opposing Alamani tribes will be racing to either capture or rescue him, depending on who arrives first."

"Warring *tribes* of Alamani?" asked Master Tel. "Your descriptions of this savage litter of Alamani continue to amaze me."

"How will you assist our Sahiradin survivor?" asked Master Travant. "We must secure the Kaiytáva."

"As you know, we have a greatly diminished crew on board," replied Lansu, "but a small expedition force is already underway to rescue him. *Dominion* will arrive shortly after they do. We are moving with all haste to find him and retrieve the Kaiytáva."

"Very good," said Master Tel. "Do whatever is needed to accomplish your mission. You have absolute authority. Report back as soon as you have the Kaiytáva."

The holographic images flickered and disappeared. The commodore returned to the bridge and called for his first officer to join him. "Captain Vilna, prepare *Dominion* for surface bombardment and order the Codex fighters to destroy all P3 communications satellites. They are then to reconnoiter the area around the extraction area and provide support to the ground forces when they arrive."

"Yes sir!"

"Get me General Urkona!" he said to his communications officer.

"Urkona, here," said a voice.

"General," said Lansu. "The Sahiradin survivor on P3 reports he has the Kaiytáva. Your lead elements must land and retrieve him immediately. Do you understand? Immediately!"

"We'll do our duty," said Urkona. "Send me the coordinates."

"Transmitting them now," said the commodore as he nodded to one of his officers.

Lansu turned to his navigation officer. "When we reach P3, bring us into orbit above the extraction point."

Chapter 54

Kane was inside an old training helicopter adjusting the straps around Ravenwood's stretcher when the others caught up with him. Logan looked at the old man's pale face, now devoid of the intelligence and passion which had once animated it. He placed his hand on Ravenwood's forehead. It was cold. He looked at Kane, who was busily making final preparations before taking off.

"Where are you taking his body?" asked Lena.

"To Raven's Rock, where my great grandfather found him."

"That sounds like a good place to bury him," said Cap.

"I'm not going to bury him," said Kane as he loaded a pack and his weapons into the helicopter. "He's not dead. But he will be soon if I don't get him to the lake."

Logan looked at Lena and Cap. Each face wore a concerned look. He knew what they were thinking. Ravenwood's body was cold, and the doctor had declared him dead an hour earlier.

"Kane," said Logan, gently pulling Kane's shoulder in an attempt to interrupt his preparations. "He's gone."

Kane turned to face the three of them, ignoring what Logan had said. "I've talked to Consul Sawyer. She's pulled some strings and got you three into the League army. You're troopers now. Do your best to help them. They don't understand what's about to happen and will need guidance."

Kane turned and looked at Ravenwood's limp body inside the old helicopter. "I have to go now."

He shook Logan and Cap's hands. He tried to take Lena's hand, but she shook her head and hugged him.

"Take care of Ravenwood," she said. "Come back when you're ready."

"We will," said Kane with a rare smile. He boarded the helicopter and instructed the pilot to start the engine. The three friends stepped back and watched as the helicopter took off and flew north toward the hundreds of lakes and rivers of the Boundary Waters.

Chapter 55

"Lieutenant Styles. I think you should have a look at this."

Styles walked past the command and control center's destroyed main computer stations to a terminal against the wall. The bodies of General Espinoza and Captains Grey and Omar had been removed just a few hours earlier. She was in charge of operations while Colonel Anderson briefed Joint Army Chief McIntyre and his staff and Colonel Longmire toured the base to assess the damage the PRA raiders had done.

"What have you got, corporal?" she asked.

"I was able to check the Texas Satcom feed before it went down and searched the area north of us."

"Why north of us?" asked Styles.

The corporal looked up at Styles. "The *Blackhawk* pilot knew the missiles were about to hit, so I assumed they would program the simplest coordinates possible when they pulled their disappearing trick. I looked in a straight line along their last recorded trajectory, which was north."

"Okay. What did you find?"

"The resolution is poor, but that looks like the wounded gunship," he said as he pointed at a black dot.

Styles leaned close to the monitor. The corporal increased the magnification for her. She grinned. "That's some damn fine work, corporal."

She picked up a phone and dialed a three-digit number. "Sorry to interrupt the briefing, Colonel Anderson. I think we found the PRA gunship. It crashed near the river, north of us." She listened for a moment and said, "Right away, sir."

She hung up and dialed another number. "Tell Crew Chief McKinney he has ten minutes to get any serviceable Talon copters prepped for flight. And get me those three PRA defectors, double quick time."

Two minutes later, a soldier escorted Logan and Cap into the control room.

"How's your friend doing?" asked Styles.

"She's getting her stitches looked at, but she'll be fine," said Cap.

"Good," said Styles. "Do you want a second chance at getting your magic rock back?"

"Hell yes," they said in unison.

"Great. I'm told you're now privates in the League Army. Get to hangar one. They're prepping the Talons for flight. Be ready to brief the team on whatever you know."

Cap left the room, but Logan stayed behind. Cap turned to look at him, but Logan waived him on. Then he turned to face Lieutenant Styles and said, "You don't believe us about the Apollo Stone, do you."

"I'm not sure what to believe," she said, facing Logan. "But I know that gunship and those Red Legs demolished this airbase in less than fifteen minutes. Then the gunship disappeared and reappeared two hundred fifty kilometers to the north. I don't know how it did that, but you three seem to be the foremost experts on it."

"We know a little. Ravenwood knew more," said Logan.

"Well, he's dead now and Kane's gone. It's up to you to get that stone away from the PRA."

"We'll try," said Logan.

Lieutenant Styles took a few steps toward Logan. "I didn't know what to make of you and your friends. But seeing the way you fought today, and the fact that you almost shot down the gunship, convinced me you're here to help, so I'm going to lay it out for you. You know that hundreds of thousands of PRA troops are massing near St. Louis. They'll pour across the river within days, and we can't stop them. The League has a quarter as many troops as the PRA. We have a unified command structure, but some cities refused to commit everything they have and insisted on keeping troops and weapons close to home in order to defend themselves if the war comes to their door."

"Understandable," said Logan. "They've got their own people to protect."

"Understandable but regrettable," said Styles. "We need every single soldier, tank, and plane we can get our hands on. The PRA's forces will be most vulnerable when they're crossing the river at St. Louis. We need to hit them there hard, weaken them as much as possible, so when we fall back to the fortress at Deep Six we'll be able to hold out."

"What if they starve you out?"

"We've been preparing for this for years," said Styles. "Deep Six is well supplied and heavily fortified, but it'll be our tomb if we can't cut the PRA troop numbers at least in half at St. Louis."

"You'll need to do better than that," said Logan. "The PRA won't leave any troops behind to secure the territory they've gained as they chase you to Deep Six. Behind the advancing army will be thousands of SPD officers. And the SPD is very good at keeping civilians under control. That means every Flat Foot and Red Leg that crosses the river will be on your heels."

"All the more reason to get that magic rock and disable the gunship," replied Styles.

"Agreed," said Logan.

Chapter 56

Logan caught up with Cap and together they entered the hangar. Ground crews were rushing to finish preparing four Talon helicopters for flight. A lieutenant was briefing a group of fifty League troopers about the upcoming mission. Logan and Cap trotted over to the group. They were surprised to see Lena there, already in League-issued green and brown Provex field armor.

"What are you doing here?" asked Cap. "You're supposed to be in the infirmary recovering."

Lena smiled. "You didn't think I was going to let you go on the mission of a lifetime and leave me behind, did you?"

"Your leg wound is going to slow you down," said Cap. He folded his arms. "You're not ready for combat."

"Hey!" shouted the lieutenant. "You mind?"

"Sorry L.T.," said Cap.

"That's Lieutenant Pierce to you, Private New Guy."

Cap was about to respond, but shut his mouth when he caught a warning look from Lena.

"As I was saying," continued Pierce. "We have recent intel putting the *Blackhawk* gunship in the Mississippi river valley two hundred fifty klicks due north. She's wounded and apparently had to make an emergency landing. We're going to go and pay the Red Legs back for what they did today. Crew Chief McKinney's worked his magic and got four of the damaged Talons in serviceable condition."

Pierce walked over to a view screen and pulled up the satellite image of the downed *Blackhawk*. "It's in an abandoned river town. There might be a few Travelers in the area, but no permanent population. There are hostile Dellians just across the river, but with the nearest bridge out of commission, they can only cross by boat. No sign of them in the area yet, but keep an eye on the river. Also, be aware that the pasty albino we saw today and about five Red Legs made it on board before they took off. We believe they have abandoned the gunship and moved to the high ground just west of the crash site."

"Sir," said a soldier. "We hear the *Blackhawk* somehow disappeared and reappeared at the crash site. Any word on how they did that?"

Pierce took a deep breath. "No idea. But now's our chance to get it and find out."

"And why did they hit this base?" asked another trooper. "There are other bases closer to St. Louis that would have made more sense if they're prepping for the main offensive."

Cap leaned toward Logan and whispered, "What's with all the questions?"

Logan nodded his head slightly and whispered, "Sergeant Major Mojeski would have quashed this in a heartbeat."

"I know there are a lot of rumors flying around," said Pierce. "So I'm going to hand it over to an expert on the *Blackhawk* who will be joining us."

He looked at Logan and said, "Private Brandt, please enlighten the team on everything you know about the *Blackhawk* that might help."

Logan looked at the soldiers who had turned to face him. He shot a glance toward Cap and saw he was wearing an amused grin but offered no help. Logan cleared his throat. "Well, you know about the *Blackhawk's* firepower, but the thing that makes it so dangerous is its navigation system, which allows it to instantaneously move from one place to another. That's how it disappeared and reappeared so far north. But for the navigation system to work it needs something called the Apollo Stone. It's a little round black ball, about the size of a marble. My friends and I stole the stone from the PRA and brought it here. That's why they hit this base. They took it from us and we need to get it back."

"Okay," said Pierce. "We're splitting Charlie and Dog Platoons into four Talons. Twenty troopers per bird. Charlie 1 will deploy in the high ground to the enemy's right. Charlie 2 will be on the enemy's left. Dog 1 will deploy on top of the hill to prevent them from moving west, although there's wide-open terrain in that direction, so we don't expect them to go that way. We expect more troopers will join as soon after landing. We'll flush them out then.

Dog 2 and Crew Chief McKinney's team will deploy near the *Blackhawk*. Your mission is to secure the area while the techs work to get the gunship operational. Lieutenant Styles tells me we'll be getting fighter support, which will help keep the PRA's air force off our backs."

Logan looked to his left and saw Lieutenant Styles had entered the hanger. She was wearing green and brown battle armor.

Pierce continued his briefing. "Now these bastards aren't going to let us just take their gunship, so expect company. Like I said, we'll be getting additional trooper support, probably from Dubuque and Rockford Forward Station, but we'll be first on site. When the *Blackhawk* is operational, we pull out."

"What if we can't get it to fly?" asked a soldier.

"Then we blow it to hell."

"The task force will be under the command of Colonel Longmire." Pierce looked at an officer standing off to the side. "Anything to add, sir?"

Colonel Longmire, a broad shouldered, squared jawed man of about forty, took a step forward. "You all know how to do your jobs, so I'm not going to waste my breath on that. But I want you to understand that what happened here this morning wasn't a one-off raid. It was the first battle in a war with the PRA. There's a hell of a lot more fighting ahead of us. We can win it if you remember your training. Just keep your chin up, your head down, and one round in the chamber."

He paused a moment, scanning the young faces of the soldiers he was about to lead on the mission. "Saddle up, let's go."

The troopers boarded the four waiting Talons. Logan looked across the aircraft's small cabin at Lieutenant Styles, who had her hand pressed against her ear in order to hear something she was receiving through her integrated communications system. Her blue eyes were focused on the floor. She nodded her head as she listened to the ICS, then she said something about watching for hostiles trying to cross from the east side of the river. Logan looked at the long thin scar along her jawline and wondered how she'd gotten it. She looked up at Logan and he turned away.

"You ready?" she shouted above the engine noise as they lifted off.

Logan looked at her again and said, "Yes I am."

"How's your shoulder wound?"

"Better," he replied. "The doc injected it with super HGH – that stuff's amazing."

"They're good at patching us up to fight again," she said with a nod. She turned to her left to talk to some of the other soldiers, asking them if they were prepared or had questions. After a few minutes, she turned to Logan again and said, "Who was that albino I saw you fighting back at the base?"

"He's an old secret the PRA's been keeping. You heard about the signals we've been hearing coming from space? There's a good chance there's a bunch more like him on the way here. They're bad news for Earth. If you see him, watch out."

"He should watch out for me," she answered, her blue eyes cold as ice.

"He's very good with a sword," said Logan. "My advice is don't fight him alone."

She said nothing and turned her attention to the soldier next to her, offering some guidance on what to do when they landed.

They had been flying for forty minutes when Logan heard a voice in his ICS. "Approaching the LZ. One minute to touch."

Logan reached over his shoulder and felt the handle of his sword in the battle pack. The League version of field armor felt a little strange, but it was lighter, less bulky. He hoped it was as strong. Then he reached behind his waist and felt the stock of his K-45 assault gun sticking out the bottom of his battle pack. They were shorter guns than the PRA's M-35, and they slipped more smoothly into the battle pack, making it easier to switch between gun and blade.

He looked at Cap, who nodded to him and gave a thumbs up. Lena was lost in thought, but she felt Logan's eyes on her. She looked at him and smiled.

"Okay, troopers," yelled Lieutenant Styles. "Put on your war faces. It's go time."

The Talon quickly descended toward the smoking *Blackhawk*. Logan saw the other Talons slip past them and hover over their assigned places in the hills above the town. Troopers quickly rappelled from the helicopters down multiple lines to the ground. As soon as the last trooper touched earth, each Talon flew off to await the call to retrieve them.

Dog 2's Talon landed in the town near what was once a levee, but was now a series of overgrown ledges and crumbling concrete walls. Nevertheless, it managed to keep the high spring waters out of the town's center. Logan, Lena, Cap and the twelve other troopers stormed out of the Talon and took up defensive positions around the *Blackhawk*. Several troopers entered the craft and quickly checked it for Red Legs. When they gave the all clear, Crew Chief McKinney and three technicians entered the gunship and got to work trying to make her flight ready. Lieutenant Styles gave a few troopers some orders and they started offloading some equipment from the Talon.

Colonel Longmire approached the troopers around the gunship. He pulled a well-chewed unlit cigar out of his mouth. "Lieutenant Styles, make sure we get those auto Air Defense Arrays set up on each side of the LZ; two ADAs on each side, one hundred meters out from our position."

"Already on it, Colonel," she said. "We're also stationing the scramblers about twenty meters west of the ADAs."

"Good thinking," replied Longmire.

Colonel Longmire surveyed the area. Then he jammed his cigar between his teeth and walked parallel to the little river town's main street, eyeing the long-abandoned shops. He toggled a switch on the ICS attached to his hip. Through his helmet's ICS, Logan heard the colonel say, "Dog 2 troopers identify secondary and tertiary fall-back positions in case the shit hits the fan."

He walked toward the *Blackhawk* with an eye on the river and said,

"Lt. Gutierrez, what's your status?"

"All three patrols are in position. No sign of the enemy."

"Understood. The more I think about it, the more I think we need to get that albino bastard. I want you to very slowly and carefully sweep the hillside."

"Roger wilco," said Lt. Gutierrez.

Colonel Longmire toggled his ICS. "Central, this is Madhat."

"Go ahead, Madhat."

"We're deployed and pursuing our primary objective. What's the ETA of additional ground support?"

"Madhat, ETA of your ground support is fifteen minutes. High top-cover is already in place but maintaining high altitude."

"Understood."

"What is the status of your primary objective?"

"Checking," said Colonel Longmire. He adjusted his ICS and said, "Lieutenant Styles, how is McKinney's team doing?"

"They think they can get her flying. It'll be ready in an hour, maybe two."

"Copy that." Colonel Longmire. "Central, this is Madhat. We should be able to get her flying inside of two hours."

"Roger that, Madhat. Your estimate for repair time is longer than expected. Keep at it but rig her for detonation."

"Roger that," said Longmire. He relayed the order to Lieutenant Styles, who put a couple of soldiers to work setting explosive charges at different locations on the *Blackhawk*.

Thirty meters away, Logan could hear Crew Chief McKinney cursing at the demolition team and warning them "they had better not fucking blow me up!"

Longmire chewed on his cigar as he walked the perimeter of the landing zone checking on the status of his soldiers' efforts, occasionally looking at the hills above the town. The four anti-aircraft and two signal scrambling systems were well positioned. Then he walked to the crumbled remains of the town levee and pulled out his field sensors. He held it to his eyes and looked across the swiftly flowing Mississippi River, scanning the far side.

Logan was standing at his assigned position on the landing zone perimeter when Lieutenant Styles walked by. "How's it looking, Private Brandt?" she asked.

"Good, Lieutenant," he answered. He looked at Colonel Longmire, who was standing at the river's edge. "What's he doing?"

"He's looking for signs of Dellian activity. They're not well equipped, but highly motivated," answered Styles.

"We were told they were friendly independent people fighting the evil League and their clan surrogates."

"I guess that's how the Guardians would see it," she said.

"Who are the Dellians, in your opinion?" he asked.

Lieutenant Styles looked out across the river. "The people on that side of the river have resisted reintegration with their neighbors. They fight the PRA, the League, Canada. They hate everybody. The story is after the Impact they followed the teachings of a nut-job prophet, Raymond Dell. And his successors have kept his teachings going."

"What kind of teachings?" asked Logan.

"The usual end-of-the-world stuff that so many people bought into after the Impact," she answered. "Can't blame them, I guess. It *was* the end of the world for four-fifths of the people on the planet."

"Kane told me they're cannibals."

Lieutenant Styles smiled. "They've been known to engage in a little ritual human sacrifice from time to time. They think the Impact was punishment for breaking our covenant with the Creator, who has a dual personality from which all good and evil flow. Restoring the covenant, and the balance between good and evil, requires blood payment as evidence of our commitment."

"How much blood?" asked Logan.

"They haven't quite decided on that yet," replied Styles.

And what about people on this side of the river?" asked Logan, looking at the hills above the abandoned river town. "Kane called them Northrunners. He described them as neutral traders."

Styles shrugged. "Sounds about right. This used to be the Minnesota side of the river. After the Impact, the people here broke up into competing clans like so many other places, but that didn't last too long here. They keep to themselves now. And they strongly discourage visitors from entering their territory. Kane's description of them as traders is a good one. They move a lot of goods up and down the river. Rumor is their trading has made them very wealthy."

"Are they peaceful?" asked Logan.

"Yes and no," she said. "We're in their territory without permission, so we'll have to watch out for angry locals. But the only people they really hate are the Dellians. The Northrunners rely on the river for trade, and the Dellians sometimes interfere with that trade or try to expand their territory across the river. That's when fighting breaks out."

Logan nodded and looked out over the wide channel to the distant eastern bank. Swirling brown water flowed swiftly past carrying with it large pieces of wood and broken branches flushed out of the backwaters by the spring rains and snowmelt. A flock of ducks flew over their heads from the west and glide across the channel to calmer waters sheltered by a large sandbar on the far side. Just as the flock arrived, a dozen or so birds took off from behind the sandbar, then a hundred more. Soon thousands of birds were lifting themselves into the air in a cacophony of slapping water and birdcalls. As they gained altitude, they quickly organized themselves into several flocks and turned north, toward their summer breading grounds.

"Amazing, isn't it?" said Styles.

"I've never seen anything like it," said Logan as he watched the sky fill with thousands and thousands of birds.

"It's a good sign," continued Styles. "The old migration patterns are back."

Logan didn't respond, but seeing all of those birds take flight brought a smile to his face.

Chapter 57

An hour passed while the soldiers waited for Crew Chief McKinney and his team to get the *Blackhawk* flight ready. The tension Logan felt when they first landed was replaced by mild boredom. Lieutenant Styles introduced him to a couple of troopers who had escaped the PRA when they were in their early teens. They talked for a while, but it was soon clear that their experiences growing up on farming and manufacturing developments were very different from his life in the Capitol District, and they considered him to be from a privileged class, which he had trouble denying after what he'd seen while on the train to Erie.

A little later, Logan was watching the water for signs of the Dellians when he heard a distant popping sound. He spun around to see if it was coming from the hills, but saw nothing. He saw Colonel Longmire quickly walking toward town, speaking into his ICS and surveying the hills above. After a moment, Logan heard the colonel's voice in his ICS.

"Lt. Gutierrez , report. What's going on up there?"

"Nothing up here, sir," answered Gutierrez. "No sign of the enemy, either. We're expanding our sweep."

"Sir, this is Private Zinder. Look up."

Everyone looked to the sky and saw a fiery ball falling to Earth, a trail of black smoke in its wake. A second later, each of the two ADAs fired two missiles into the air. As Logan watched the missiles' flight paths, he saw two League aircraft out of the corner of his eye. They were chasing a large black dot as it raced across the sky, but it was much too fast for them to overtake.

Logan heard Colonel Longmire's voice in his helmet's ICS. "Hostile aircraft. Take cover. McKinney, what's your status?"

"I need ten, maybe fifteen more minutes, sir."

"You've got five," replied Longmire, shouting over the sound of the ADAs as they launched one more missile each. "Talon support, prepare for extraction."

The ground next to Logan suddenly exploded, throwing him two-meters high in the air. He landed on his back with a thud. Lieutenant Styles, who had been standing next to him, was thrown against the side of a nearby building. Cap and Lena were on the ground to his right. Another explosion ripped apart Dog 2's Talon helicopter, which was sitting near the levee.

Fire and black smoke filled the air to Logan's right as another Talon suddenly burst into flames as it tried to swoop in for a quick landing. A third Talon aborted its landing procedure about twenty meters off the ground and spat 50-caliber shells as it sought to gain altitude. It launched two hellcat missiles into the air.

Logan watched the hellcats' exhaust trail as they streaked into the sky. They simultaneously exploded in a ball of fire and white smoke. Then a black V-shaped ship shot through the fire and smoke and fired on the remaining Talon, which exploded and crashed to the ground in the middle of the town's main street.

Logan scrambled to his feet. The troopers of Dog 2 fired their weapons at the V-shaped craft as it approached to land. The craft hovered just above the ground as twenty or thirty white-haired soldiers in black armor dropped to the ground through openings on either side of the ship.

Sahiradin! thought Logan.

The ADA shifted ordnance and pumped two dozen heavy caliber slugs at the craft as it lifted into the air. The ADA appeared to damage the Sahiradin ship somewhat, but not enough to slow it down. The V-wing returned fire and silenced the ADA with one shot. It did the same to the other air defenses in rapid succession.

A second V-shaped craft swooped low and another twenty to thirty soldiers leapt to the ground. The two groups of Sahiradin soldiers quickly grouped together and dashed for cover behind the river levee's half-crumbled wall, firing their weapons as they ran. League soldiers returned fire, but Logan could see their bullets were ineffective against the attackers' shields. He slipped his K-45 into his battle pack and drew his sword. He activated his shield and snapped his guard into place.

Through his helmet's ICS, Logan heard Lieutenant Styles order everyone to activate shields and move forward to support Chief McKinney and his team, who were still in the *Blackhawk*. But as he stood up to comply, Logan could see it was already too late. The Sahiradin were storming toward the PRA gunship. Logan saw McKinney step out. His shield was on and he was firing his pistol at the fast-approaching Sahiradin, shouting curses at them with each shot. His crew joined him with swords drawn, but they were all swiftly cut down by six Sahiradin with black blades.

"Fall back! Fall back!" ordered Colonel Longmire.

The troopers retreated to their designated secondary positions. Another black V-shaped craft unloaded its cargo of soldiers, bringing the total to about seventy-five, and lifted off to join the first two as they raced into the sky.

Moments later, Logan and Cap made it to their fall-back position. "Good. You're still alive." said Logan. He nodded to Lieutenant Styles, who ran to their position.

"Where's Lena?" asked Cap.

"I don't know."

They heard automatic weapons firing in the hills behind them. Colonel Longmire ran to their location. He knelt on one knee and talked to Lt. Gutierrez though his ICS.

"Pull the patrols together, lieutenant," he said. "We've got between fifty to seventy-five of those albino bastards at the LZ. They'll be coming your way soon. Be aware they have swords and shields, so be ready to go old school on them."

Just then, a dark gray oval ship descended and quickly landed near the *Blackhawk*. A mixture of strange-looking figures ran down the craft's open ramp, some of them firing long-barreled weapons as they advanced. Like the Sahiradin, they were humanoid, but most of them were small, light-framed beings except for five massive creatures that were twice Logan's height and built like bulldozers. The newly arrived beings attacked the Sahiradin flank as it moved in a phalanx formation toward the hills.

Colonel Longmire was speechless as he watched the scene unfold before him. After a few seconds, he looked at Lieutenant Styles, pulled the cigar out of his mouth and barked, "Lieutenant, who are those bastards? What the hell is happening on my LZ?"

Lieutenant Styles replied, "Not sure, sir."

"The white-haired ones are Sahiradin, sir," said Logan.

Longmire looked at Logan. "What the hell's a Sahiradin?"

"Hard to explain sir, but they're here for the Apollo Stone and to rescue their friend, the albino who was part of this morning's raid on Jasper Air Base," replied Logan.

"They're bad guys from another planet, sir," said Cap in a matter-of-fact tone.

"You don't say, private," said Longmire to Cap in a mocking tone. "And how do you two know all this?"

"They're associates of Ravenwood and Kane," said Styles.

Longmire raised his eyebrows. "Ravenwood? Maybe that crazy SOB wasn't so crazy," he said as he watched the fighting between the Sahiradin rearguard and the advancing group of other alien beings.

"Sir," said Cap. "If it helps put things in perspective, the Sahiradin are the ones who caused the Impact. They're the reason seven billion people died."

Longmire processed this information for a moment. "Then who the hell are those other…individuals?"

"I don't know for sure," said Logan. "But I think they're allied species who've been fighting the Sahiradin for centuries. Ravenwood called them Lycians."

Longmire put his cigar back in his mouth and stood watching, hands on his hips. A group of Sahiradin detached from the phalanx and attacked the left flank of the League's line. Logan could hear the sound of ringing swords as the League soldiers sought to repel the Sahiradin.

"Dog 2 units disengage from fighting and fall back," said Longmire into his ICS. "Repeat, disengage."

"This is highly irregular," Colonel Longmire said as he watched the troopers withdraw and the Sahiradin detachment return to the fight against the Lycians. "Highly damned irregular."

He held his field sensors to his eyes to get a close look at the Sahiradin and the Lycians. The lead element of the Sahiradin soldiers was dashing toward the hills while the remainder battled to slow their enemy's advance. Longmire toggled through the field sensors' display to see body temperature and estimated height, mass, and distance.

He focused on one of the big gray-skinned Lycians and took some readings. It was over four and a half meters tall, well over twice his height. "Those are some big sons-of-bitches," he said half to himself. He saved a dozen images of the fight and other sensor readings.

He engaged his ICS. "Central, this is Madhat."

"Go ahead, Madhat."

"I'm not sure how to explain this, but we've got an estimated seventy-five hostiles of unknown origin on the ground. Also be advised there are also hostile black V-wing craft in the airspace over our position. They fragged three Talons."

"We're tracking those craft, Madhat. We're also seeing unknown oval craft."

"We've seen them, too. They've deployed an estimated fifty soldiers at our location. It's a damn carnival here. The two sides are going at it tooth and nail. And be advised the V-wing soldiers have engaged against us. We pulled back, and I recommend you consider them hostile."

"Understood, Madhat. They've downed several League aircraft."

"I just uploaded images, video, and sensor readings of what we're seeing here on the ground. You better be sitting down when you review," said Longmire. "To avoid getting tangled up in whatever's going on here, I'm pulling my troops back."

"Roger that, Madhat. We're receiving your upload now and will review. Be aware that we've lost satellite support. We put several Ajax command birds in the air, but if we're forced to land them and ground towers are hit, communications will be interrupted. Central out."

Longmire adjusted his ICS. "Lt. Gutierrez," he said.

"Gutierrez here."

"Be advised the Sahiradin are moving up the hill, fast. Move your troops south two hundred meters."

"Sahiradin, sir?"

"More of those albino SOBs."

"Roger, wilco, falling back."

"Colonel," said Logan. "They're trying to locate the Sahiradin with the Apollo Stone. We can't let them have it."

"Private," said Longmire, "In case you hadn't noticed I don't have the troops to keep them from going anywhere. I'm staying the hell out of this alley fight."

He looked through his field sensors again and swore under his breath as one of the large creatures gave a loud deep howl and smashed a long club-like weapon into the midst of a group of Sahiradin. There was a bright green flash of light at the point of impact, which sent four Sahiradin flying through the air. The battling aliens moved into the trees toward the high ground where the *Blackhawk* crash survivors had taken refuge.

"I'm going to find Lena," Cap whispered to Logan. He was about to run off, but Logan caught his arm and pointed toward the *Blackhawk*. Five Sahiradin stepped out from behind the gunship and began easing their way toward the troopers' position, blades in their hands.

Logan quietly alerted Styles and Longmire. Longmire reached for his ICS to issue an order just as Lena and six other troopers charged the Sahiradin from behind some nearby rubble. The white-haired aliens saw the troopers and advanced toward them. The Sahiradin were extremely fast and moved with deadly grace. One of the troopers fell immediately and another was wounded in the arm. A Sahiradin attacked Lena, but she fell back and deftly countered her opponent's slashing attack. Then, with blinding speed, she spun on her right foot and crouched low, slicing the Sahiradin's leg between his thigh and shin armor, sending him to the ground. She immediately drove her blade into his throat above his breast protection.

Three more League troopers ran out to join the fight. The remaining four Sahiradin began to work in pairs, moving and fighting in close coordination. As one attacked, the one next to him defended his exposed back or flank. In this manner, they kept the troopers at bay and stayed on the offensive.

A trooper dropped to the ground with a deep gash to his right leg, but as he fell another trooper slipped through the Sahiradin defense and drove his sword into a Sahiradin's unprotected back. The Sahiradin fell, but was not dead. He deflected several sword strikes, and quickly got to his feet.

Lena stumbled, which drew a Sahiradin a few steps out from their formation. He lunged for the kill, but it was a trap. Lena deflected the blade and countered with a flurry of counter strikes. The surprised Sahiradin deflected several, but Lena's blade finally struck home and the Sahiradin collapsed to the ground clasping a deep wound to his throat. Another trooper finished him off.

The remaining three Sahiradin formed a triangle with their backs to each other, slashing and lunging at any trooper who got too close. They withstood a remarkable number of wounds before finally succumbing to the troopers' repeated attacks. One by one, they dropped to the ground, dead.

Longmire and Styles ran forward to where the troopers had killed the Sahiradin. Logan and Cap were right behind them. The circle of troopers around the dead Sahiradin parted to allow Colonel Longmire to pass. He knelt close to one of the dead aliens.

"Their skin looks like it's made out of tiny scales," he said.

"It's hard to cut through," said Lena. Pointing at one of them, she said, "I know I scored a couple of good hits against this one, but my sword barely broke the skin."

"Aside from the hair and the skin, they look a lot like us," said Logan.

"And they seem comfortable with our atmosphere," said Lena. "No need for an environment suit."

"Same story with the Lycians," said Logan.

"Lieutenant, order the troops to pull back," said Longmire as he stared at the strange bodies at his feet. He took some additional sensor readings and uploaded the data to Central Command. Then he said, "Let's not go looking for a fight with these guys until we know what we're getting into."

"Yes sir," said Styles.

Longmire looked at Lena and then at the other troopers who'd been in the fight. "Good job taking these guys out," he said. "But you're not John Wayne and this ain't Texas. Don't attacked unless ordered, got it?"

"Yes sir," said Lena.

As they moved toward their new positions farther from the landing zone, a trooper's voice sounded in Logan's earpiece. "Lieutenant Styles, this is Private Rieger. We're at the levee. We've got something you should see."

Lieutenant Styles started running toward the river. As she ran by them, she said, "Brandt and Castell, you're with me."

When they arrived at the levee, a trooper pointed north to a bend in the river. A convoy of small boats was crossing the water from the east side.

Lieutenant Styles looked through her field sensors and scowled. "Colonel," she said into her ICS. "We've got an estimated two or three hundred individuals in boats crossing the river north of us about two klicks. Looks like the Dellians are getting into the fight."

"Copy that, Lieutenant," said Longmire.

"What are the chances we can get air support to take them out?" asked Styles.

"No chance, lieutenant," replied Longmire. "Our fighters are still fully engaged with V-wing hostiles. The Lycians seem to be assisting us, but I just got a report that PRA fixed-wing aircraft are about five minutes away from our location and may try to hit us. Order your troops to dig in. Engage the Dellians only if you have to, but fall back if you can."

"Understood, sir," she replied.

"I'm on my way up the hill to assess the situation with Gutierrez. You're in command of the LZ. And there's no extraction option at the moment. We're going to be here until the skies are clear."

"Yes sir," said Styles. She looked at Logan. "Looks like we're it against those Dellians. Fortunately, they don't usually have shields."

"That should even the odds," said Lena with a wry grin.

"Speak for yourself," said Logan. "My shield is only two-thirds charged."

"Conserve it as much as possible," said Styles. "You'll need it before long."

Chapter 58

"Commodore Lansu, we've located the Lycian ships," said his first officer from the far side of the bridge. Another Sahiradin was sitting at the duty station, quickly adjusting the controls of a holographic image of the Earth. Small dots near the Earth represented the geosynchronous orbit of *Dominion* over North America.

"Where are the scum?" asked the Commodore, agitated with the unexpected turn in events. He walked to the sensor station.

"In orbit over the northern polar icecap," answered Vilna as the image scrolled north to show the Lycian position.

"How did they get there undetected? We have probes all around P3 and throughout the system."

"We believe that when they entered through the *khâl* they masked the newly arrived ships' signature by detonating a number of missiles in succession. We interpreted the noise to be explosions on their damaged frigate, *Challenger*, and perhaps even its complete destruction. But closer analysis has revealed the sound of accelerating engines hidden within the explosions. Once the newly arrived ships had reached a high velocity, they cut their engines and ran silent until reaching P3. We heard their rapid deceleration, but by then they were in position."

Lansu smashed his fist against the sensor station's console. It was not the first time the Lycian fleet's greater maneuverability had frustrated the Commodore. "Typical conniving separatist trick," he said between clenched teeth. "What ships do they have in orbit?"

"Two light destroyers, *Resolve* and *Glory*, and a heavy cruiser, *Defiant*."

Lansu smiled. "Two light destroyers and a heavy cruiser. No match for *Dominion*. What about *Challenger?*"

"She's limping toward P3 at quarter speed, sir."

Lansu nodded. "Even healthy, she's hardly more than a nuisance. Signal High Command about the situation. They assured us they had gained control of this *khâl's* access gates in Lycian space. They were clearly mistaken. They must rectify this immediately to prevent any further ships from coming through."

"And should we request additional support, sir?" asked Vilna.

Commodore Lansu fixed his blue eyes on the captain. "This is a devastator-class battleship. We do not need additional support if access to this system can be blocked."

"But given the sensitivity of our mission, perhaps…"

"You have my orders, captain!" shouted Lansu.

"Yes sir," said Vilna with a slight deferential nod. "What are your orders regarding the Lycian ships in orbit?"

"Prepare torpedo ships and fighter support," he said. "Alter *Dominion's* orbit to engage the enemy. And deploy remaining ground troops. We must gain control of the Kaiytáva. Order the ground forces to find it and take up a defensive position as recommended by Kurak."

Vilna was unable to hide his displeasure with this order. "Am I to understand that we are going to follow his recommendation and ally ourselves with one of the Alamani factions?" he asked.

Lansu looked at the holographic image of the Earth. "If we are to regain the glory of the past and finally put down the Lycian separatists, we will need to replenish our ranks. Supplementing our forces with Alamani soldiers is one way to do that. If Kurak's plan can help us gain a complete victory, we must consider it, although I find it just as distasteful as you."

He looked at Captain Vilna. "But our first order of business is to smash the Lycian ships. Now carry out my orders."

"Yes sir."

Chapter 59

Kurak and the five Red Leg survivors from the attack on Jasper Air Base had been slowly creeping up a muddy ravine toward the top of a hill overlooking the Mississippi River. They could hear the League troops searching for them on both flanks and knew it was simply a matter of time before they were discovered.

They could also hear the fighting down in the abandoned town below. The Red Legs had initially thought it was a PRA extraction force, but then they saw the strange V-shaped craft and grew uncertain.

"Help is on its way," said Kurak. "Those are advanced PRA fighters coming for us. We have to get back down the hill."

He led his men down the ravine toward the abandoned town. The sounds of fighting grew louder. Kurak crept over the ravine's edge to see what was happening on the slope below. The lead element of the Sahiradin phalanx was advancing up the hill toward him. The remaining Sahiradin were fighting what he recognized as Lycian soldiers. The Sahiradin had cut down about half of the Lycians and the rest were beginning to waver. A few more Lycians fell and the remaining soldiers retreated back down the slope.

Kurak's Red Leg companions also crept up and peered over the edge of the ravine to see the battle below. As they watched, Kurak slipped back a few steps and silently drew his blade. Then, with deadly efficiency, he slaughtered three of his Red Leg companions. Two of them were able to draw their swords and block a few of Kurak's attacks, but the Sahiradin made quick work of them as well.

With a broad grin on his face, Kurak climbed out of the ravine and quickly scampered down the hill. When the lead Sahiradin saw him, Kurak stopped and made several hand signals. One of the Sahiradin responded with a hand signal. Kurak then continued down the hill.

"I am Captain Kurak. Lone survivor of the *Vanquisher*. I have long awaited this moment. Where is the extraction site?"

One of the Sahiradin answered, "There is a force of natives near the crashed ship below. They are receiving aid from the Lycian. We'll need to find a different place for our ships to retrieve us."

Kurak nodded, "This way."

He started running north along the hillside. Moments later, they heard a humming sound and looked down to the town. An oval-shaped craft landed near the *Blackhawk*.

One of the Sahiradin said, "A Lycian frigate followed us through the *khâl*. They must be sending additional ground forces."

They continued running north and at an uphill angle until they reached the tree line of a large open field on top of the hill. The lead Sahiradin pressed a button on his belt. "They will be here in a moment."

Kurak nodded. "What is your name?"

"Bre Veru, sir."

"Bre Veru, welcome to the lost Alamani colony."

Bre Veru looked over the river valley. After a moment he asked, "How did you survive living among them for so long, sir?"

Kurak spat. "By living a lie. I have long endured their foul company, but now that will change."

Bre Veru nodded. "They are different than their Alamani ancestors. The ones we saw by the river are fierce fighters."

"The result of having to survive on this planet for so long without the comforts of their precious technology," answered Kurak.

Bre Veru placed his hand over his ear as he received a transmission into a small communications implant. After a moment he said, "A small task force of Lycian ships is in orbit around this planet. *Dominion* is moving against them. They cannot retrieve us now, but we are to go to the landing site you had recommended. When *Dominion* has destroyed the enemy, she will return for us."

Kurak's thin lips turned into a thin smile. "Good."

"Sir, may I ask why we are landing our ground forces here?"

Kurak turned and looked at the dozens of Sahiradin who stood at attention behind Bre Veru and smiled. "The Alamani in this region are about to engage in a civil war. One side in the conflict might be of use to us. If we support them in their war and they win, we will have gained a strong advantage over the others. They will help us master this planet."

Veru looked puzzled. "Ally ourselves with Alamani?"

"For now," replied Kurak.

Veru was clearly uncomfortable with the thought but said nothing. Instead, he pointed at a hilltop just to the north. "There they are, sir."

Kurak looked across the valley to the nearby hill and saw a dozen large transport craft landing. Moments later, Sahiradin soldiers began streaming out of the ships.

Quickly," said Kurak, his heart swelling with pride at the sight of so many of his warrior brethren. "We must join the army."

Chapter 60

Logan looked down at the town from his position on the hill. Colonel Longmire had ordered everyone to the top after the Lycians had boarded their oval ship that had come to retrieve them. They carried many wounded compatriots with them but no Sahiradin captives. Logan looked to the north at the hill across from theirs. His heart sank as he watched thousands of Sahiradin busily working to erect small buildings and what appeared to be defensive batteries of some kind.

He looked to his right along the line of troopers and saw Cap, Lena, and a few PRA defectors talking. Cap told a joke that made the others chuckle, but their laughter was mingled with fear. One of them shot a quick look at the Sahiradin camp, then looked back at Cap, who was regaling them with the story of how he had pursued the *Blackhawk* in the X-1 earlier that day.

Additional League troops had arrived about two hours earlier from Rockford Forward Station, as well as from Davenport and Dubuque. More troops from other League cities had just arrived and were being deployed along the hill. They all wore the same uniform, but they had different patches on their right shoulders to indicate which city they represented. Kansas City, Omaha, Lincoln, and Tulsa had all sent troops, but they were lightly armed and poorly provisioned. Lieutenant Styles told Logan that Longmire's data and image uploads had sent shockwaves through the League's command structure, prompting them to send whatever troops they could spare to their hill on the Mississippi River.

After the new troops had settled in, Lieutenant Styles briefed everyone about the current situation. The PRA had set its war machine into motion. As anticipated, a large force was marching on St. Louis, which the PRA would have to take if it hoped to carve out territory west of the river. But in an unanticipated move, the PRA was also sending thousands of troops, artillery, and tanks north through Dellian territory on rail lines the League had believed to be unusable. It was clear that the Dellians were permitting the PRA to pass through their land in order to launch an attack across the river well north of the League's strongest defensive positions.

This level of cooperation between the extremely hostile and isolated Dellians and PRA surprised everyone, and some still doubted it. But there was no debating that the Dellians had crossed the river earlier that day in wave after wave of small boats. Surprisingly, they did not march south against the League troops or north against the Northrunners. Instead, they began repairing a nearby ancient rail bridge. And they were not alone. PRA engineers and about five hundred regular PRA soldiers were among the Dellians repair crews.

To further complicate matters, the Dellian incursion west of the river and the sudden appearance of Sahiradin troops had drawn Northrunner defenders south. They were now about ten klicks north of the Sahiradin camp, but they were apparently content to simply observe things for the time being.

After the briefing, Lena and Cap walked over to Logan and sat down. Cap handed a small container of food to Logan. Lena opened her food packet, sniffed at the food, and made a face.

"Either of you get a good look at those Sahiradin encamped on the hill north of us?" she asked.

"Looks like about five thousand of the pasty bastards," said Cap as he poked at his dinner with the tip of his fork.

"I'd say more like ten," said Lena.

Cap shrugged and took a bite of something that looked like green beans. He swallowed and nodded approvingly. "Not bad." He took another bite and then he asked, "I still don't understand why the Sahiradin and those other aliens don't have to wear spacesuits. They're on an alien planet, but they don't seem to be affected at all."

Lena took a small bite of something resembling mashed potatoes. "Good question. It suggests they share a common origin, maybe even with the Alamani."

"Okay, but why does Earth have the right atmosphere and temperature for them?" asked Cap.

"Earth is a former Alamani colony," said Logan. "Maybe they reshaped its environment to support them. Who knows? Maybe these trees around us aren't indigenous to Earth. Maybe they were brought here as part of a terraforming effort when the Alamani colonized the place."

"Makes sense," said Lena. "After thousands and thousands of years of being transplanted, I don't think we will ever know for sure what plants or animals on Earth are truly indigenous and which are invasive. Aside from us, that is."

"Well," said Cap as he chased some peas around his plate with a spoon, "it's our planet now and they can all fuck off."

Logan took a drink from his canteen. He wiped his mouth and said, "You can tell them that, but they aren't going anywhere without a fight. They exterminated the Alamani in their corner of the galaxy, and now they've found a planet full of Alamani descendants that they tried to wipe out with a meteor attack."

Lena handed Cap a package of something purporting to be dessert, which he happily accepted. "And don't forget about the troops on the hill over there and the fact that they have at least one ship in orbit above our heads."

"And the PRA is about to invade," said Cap. "So we'll be fighting each other while the Sahiradin plot our extinction. It's a great situation all around. And who knows what the Germans, Egyptians, Thai, Chinese, and everyone else are going to do. They must know an alien species has arrived in orbit. Hell, if you look closely you can see their orbiting ship with the naked eye."

He pointed up where the Sahiradin ship had been in orbit in the southern sky, but now the bright dot was racing north until it was directly over their heads.

"Guys," he said. "That Sahiradin ship is moving north. And fast."

Logan and Lena looked up into the sky.

"And look!" said Lena pointing north. "There are three more dots heading south."

Little red puffs of light began erupting high over their heads as the ships' paths converged.

"Looks like they're going at it," said Logan.

"Who should we root for?" asked Cap.

Chapter 61

"Sir, Lycian fighters inbound," said an officer at a duty station on *Dominion's* bridge.

"Number and composition?" asked Captain Vilna.

"Fifty fighters escorting ten fighter-bombers."

"Order squadrons 1 and 2 to engage against the fighters. Destroy those bombers. Squadrons three and four are to remain with *Dominion*."

"Yes sir."

Two squadrons of Codex fighters pulled out of the group of ships circling *Dominion* and moved toward the onrushing Lycian ships.

"They are badly outnumbered. What are they hoping to achieve?" asked Commodore Lansu.

"I don't know, sir," said Captain Vilna. "They are committing the few fighters they have to a hopeless attack."

"Pointless sacrifice is not their way," said the Commodore. "They have two light destroyers, a heavy cruiser, and a handful of fighters." He put his hand to his chin as he watched the screen. His Codex fighters were nearly in range of the enemy ships and would begin their attack in moments.

"What is the position of their frigate, *Challenger*?" asked Commodore Lansu.

"Just reaching P4 now, sir," said an officer. "The battle at the *khâl* badly damaged her. She's limping along at just one-eighth speed."

"Even with *Challenger*, they cannot hope to destroy us," said Lansu. After a moment he said, "Pull us back, quarter speed. Release mines." *Dominion* began moving away from the quickly approaching enemy fighters and warships, releasing small black pods as it did so.

As *Dominion* retreated, Codex fighters were quickly gaining the upper hand against the significantly outnumbered Lycian fighters and some of them were moving toward the heavy cruiser, *Defiant*, which was leading the Lycian warships. Green lights began to erupt from *Defiant* as its automated defense systems targeted the approaching Codex fighters. The fighters changed course to remain out of range and flew parallel with *Defiant*.

"Sir," said Vilna. "Codex squadron 1 is requesting additional fighter support and torpedo bombers. They're asking for permission to attack

Defiant."

"Request denied. They are to maintain position," said Lansu. "Launch three vector missiles at *Defiant.*"

"Sir," said Vilna. "We're out of effective range. *Defiant* will destroy or evade them without difficulty."

"You have my order," said Lansu. "They are up to something, Vilna. Lycians do not take these kinds of risks without a carefully considered plan. It's not in their nature."

Three vector missiles sprang out from launchers positioned along the sides of *Dominion*. The vectors raced toward *Defiant,* which fired a dozen small missiles to intercept the vectors.

"Are the ion cannons ready?" asked Lansu?

"Yes sir," answered Vilna.

"Fire on *Defiant* when she's within range," ordered Lansu.

After a few moments, Lansu said, "On my mark, detonate one of the vector missiles. Coverage one hundred eighty degrees."

"Yes sir," said one of his officers.

Defiant and the two light destroyers were rapidly approaching *Dominion*. The vectors missiles and countermeasure missiles came within five hundred meters of each other.

"Now!" said Lansu.

The warhead on the first vector missile exploded, but the blast directed the metal piercing load forward and to the sides. Half of *Defiant's* defensive missiles were shredded by the blast, but the remainder was unaffected or received only minor damage. Two of them connected with one of the two remaining vector missiles and disabled it. The third vector missile made its way through and locked onto *Defiant*.

Defiant turned her nose directly into the path of the vector missile. Automated defensive fire scored several hits but could not disable the oncoming Sahiradin missile. Suddenly a powerful red beam of light shot out from the front of *Defiant* and cut the vector in half, causing the warhead to spin wildly into the void.

"*Defiant* has fired her main battery!" said Vilna.

"Quickly, full stop and reverse course before she recharges. Neutralize the mines," said the Lansu. "Aim both ion cannons at *Defiant* and fire on my mark."

Dominion fully engaged her massive main engines and quickly came to a stop. She began moving forward toward the still-accelerating *Defiant* and her support ships. *Defiant* fired her forward ballistic and energy guns but they had a minimal effect on Dominion, whose shields held firm against the barrage.

"Ion cannons ready?" asked Lansu.

"Yes sir," said Vilna.

Lansu leaned forward, staring at the tactical display before him and the data scrolling in the upper right corner. He waited a few moments.

"Sir," said Vilna, his voice slightly urgent.

Lansu didn't respond.

"Sir?"

"Fire both cannons!" yelled the Commodore.

"Firing cannons," said an officer.

Lansu rapidly issued a series of orders. "Full reverse, starboard thirty degrees, z minus five thousand. Drop mines."

Two bright balls of red light shot out from *Dominion's* ion cannon nodes. They raced toward *Defiant,* which continued forward, quickly closing the distance to *Dominion.* The tip of her bow began to glow red as her main gun recharged and came back on line. Suddenly both ion energy charges burst in brilliant red light.

Lansu and the others on board *Dominion* squinted their pale blue eyes as the ion charges disbursed against the enemy ship. But when the light subsided, they saw *Defiant's* red glowing prow rushing toward them.

Lansu's eyes grew wide. "Order all Codex fighters to attack *Defiant!* Fire all weapons!"

As he spoke, the *Defiant's* main battery fired on *Dominion* at a distance of five thousand meters. The Sahiradin battleship's shields briefly held, but the beam soon overloaded them and reached the hull. It tore a long gash in the *Dominion's* port side near the prow.

Moments later, *Dominion* fired all her weapons on *Defiant.* The Lycian ship's forward shield absorbed most of the missile and energy attacks, but it finally collapsed, allowing two missiles through. They struck her and tore deep holes in her prow, demolishing her main battery in the process. Also, because of *Dominion's* maneuvering, *Defiant's* port side of her stern was exposed to a number of the vector missiles. Her main engines took direct hits, rendering them useless.

"Sir," shouted Vilna. "The other Lycian ships are firing on us!"

Resolve and *Glory* fired their full array of missile and energy weapons at the Sahiradin battleship. Many of the missiles were destroyed by anti-missile projectiles and other counter measures, but four torpedoes made it through *Dominion's* defensive gauntlet and struck their target, tearing holes in the now shieldless hull.

Lansu ordered the ion cannons to fire on the two remaining ships as soon as they were recharged. Fighters were ordered to maintain distance or be affected by the ion energy surge.

"Sir!" said one of his bridge officers.

"What is it?" asked Commodore Lansu, trying to keep his anger in check.

"It's *Challenger,* sir. She's approaching from P4 at full speed. She's almost within targeting range."

"Not so wounded as we were meant to believe," said Lansu grimly. After a moment's consideration he said, "Withdraw from orbit. Make for the P3 moon and take up a defensive position there. Deploy defense drones when we establish orbit. Inform General Urkona we will return for him after making repairs. Until then, he and his ground forces will be on their own."

"But sir," objected Vilna. "Even wounded as we are, we can destroy these ships. And without us, General Urkona's men will be exposed to attack, both on the ground and by orbital bombardment."

Lansu said, "They have their base shield and several thousand Sahiradin soldiers. They are protected from orbital bombardment and can repel any ground attack. Risk to them is minimal."

Captain Vilna began to speak, but Lansu cut him off. "You have my orders. Withdraw to the P3 moon."

Chapter 62

On Earth, millions of faces continued to stare up at the skies as the small dot moved rapidly away from the other three. The people of the North American continent had seen similar dots in the sky in the form of the handful of satellites that had begun to orbit Earth in the past few years. But these were different. They were much larger, and they frequently changed speed and direction. And, of course, they had never before seen the bright red, orange, and yellow flashes that burst like distant fireworks. The flashes of light ended after a few minutes, but the impression they made on the millions of witnesses lasted much longer.

On the hilltop overlooking the Mississippi River, Lieutenant Styles put down her field sensors and turned her attention to Colonel Longmire. He wasn't looking at the sky anymore. He was looking at the lights of the Sahiradin camp on the hilltop three kilometers across the valley.

"Sir," said his communications officer.

"Yes, Lieutenant," answered Longmire.

"Control is on the secure line. They want you right away."

"I'm not surprised," he said. "I'll be right there."

He looked at Lieutenant Styles. "Go get those new troopers from the PRA. They're the only ones around here who might have a clue about what the hell just happened."

When Logan, Lena and Cap arrived in the command tent, Colonel Longmire was standing in front of a table with a variety of communications equipment on it. Standing to his side was Consul Sawyer, who had just arrived by helicopter, against the advice of military leadership. On a view screen in front of Longmire was the image of a conference room with several high-ranking military officers and a few civilians sitting at a long table.

"Here they are now," he said.

Longmire directed the three friends to stand next to him and said, "You've all seen the video and sensor data we uploaded earlier. And we can all make a few safe assumptions about what we and about twenty million other people just witnessed in Earth's orbit. But none of us know why it's happening or what might happen next. Hopefully these three recent PRA defectors can enlighten us."

Logan didn't like hearing him and his friends described as "defectors," but he let it go. He cleared his throat and said, "Yes sir. How can we help?"

A woman in a light blue uniform said, "Let's start with a few basics like who are we dealing with, how many are there, and what do they want?"

"Based on what Ravenwood told us, we're seeing two warring factions from another area of the galaxy."

"Ravenwood?" interrupted an older dark-haired woman in civilian clothing. "Are we going to accept anything that crazy old man had to say?"

Consul Sawyer stepped forward and stood next to Logan. "I consider Ravenwood to have been a valuable adviser. Now he's dead. Killed by one of these white-haired alien invaders during the attack on Jasper Air Base."

"I thought that was a PRA Special Forces raid," replied the female officer in the blue uniform. "Are you suggesting the PRA is working with these invaders?"

"We're not sure what to think right now," replied Sawyer. "But we know there was at least one Sahiradin among the Red Legs."

"Sahiradin?"

"That's what Ravenwood called them," said Logan, picking up the thread of conversation. "The Sahiradin have been at war with a collection of other alien species for hundreds of years. As a group, these allied species are called the Lycians. It's a war of total annihilation. At one time, the Sahiradin had a significant tactical advantage because of something we call the Apollo Stone and they call a Kaiytáva. The Kaiytáva allowed the Sahiradin to basically connect two points anywhere in the universe and travel there instantaneously. It's my understanding that interstellar travel is possible even without the Kaiytáva, but ships must pass through a specially constructed gate. These gates create a momentarily stable wormhole connecting one gate to another."

"Okay," said one of the uniformed men in a deep gravelly voice. He had a fleshy round face and receding red hair. "So there are two sides at war. One uses the Apollo Stone, or whatever they call it, to jump around and launch surprise attacks against the other."

"That's exactly right," said Logan. "The Sahiradin used the Kaiytáva to surprise their Lycian enemies. But over time, the Lycians managed to destroy the Sahiradin ships carrying Kaiytáva until there was only one left."

Logan waited a moment to let his words sink in. He could see several of his listeners had already decided he was a crackpot, but not all of them.

He continued. "The Sahiradin used their last Kaiytáva to send a ship from their area of the galaxy to a faraway planet in order to set up a safe haven to regroup, expand their population, and rebuild their military. They chose Earth because it was a former colony, abandoned hundreds of thousands of years ago, maybe longer. But their ship was damaged when it arrived in our solar system, and they found that Earth was not in fact abandoned."

"So you're saying we're living on an old abandoned alien colony?" asked the red-haired soldier, incredulously.

"General, I suggest we hear everything the PRA defector has to say before passing judgment," said Consul Sawyer.

Logan grit his teeth at hearing the word "defector" applied to him again.

Consul Sawyer turned her attention to Logan and said, "So that's why they're here? They're here to reclaim the planet for themselves?"

"I think their primary goal is to retrieve the Kaiytáva, which has been on Earth for almost two hundred years."

"Okay. So how did this thing come to Earth?" asked one of the civilians, clearly growing impatient with a story that seemed increasingly absurd.

"The Sahiradin ship arrived in our solar system in 1972, but it was badly damaged, and it could not launch an effective attack on Earth by itself," said Logan.

"I think we would have noticed that," said the red-haired general, his voice laced with sarcasm.

"So they didn't attack us directly," continued Logan. "They sent asteroids into Earth's path instead. Those asteroids impacted fifty years later and wiped out eighty percent of the population."

No one spoke for a moment except for the red-haired general, who mumbled, "I'll be damned."

"The Sahiradin ship exploded soon after they launched the asteroid attack, but an escape pod landed on the moon," said Logan. "The United States retrieved the escape pod during an Apollo moon landing. Inside the pod was the Kaiytáva and a survivor."

"I think I've heard enough," said one of the civilians. "This is becoming too ridiculous to bear."

"Wait a second," said Consul Sawyer. "So the United States had this thing that allowed a ship to leap across the universe, an alien escape pod, and an alien survivor? What happened to these things after the Impact?"

"I'm not sure," said Logan. "But the People's Republic of America gained control over them at some point."

"And used them to help build advanced weapons systems," said Consul Sawyer as she connected the dots. "Antiballistic shields, hyper accurate targeting systems, gravity-dampening flight technology. It would explain how the People's Republic of America, which can't build a decent car, can leap from one stunning military innovation to the next. Innovations which we later acquire with great difficulty and adapt for our own use."

"You mean to say they've been getting help from a two-hundred-year-old space alien?" asked the red-headed general, grinning and shaking his head in disbelief. He looked around the table at the others. "How long are we going to sit here and listen to this fairytale?"

"The alien's alive, General Myer" said Consul Sawyer. "And we saw him during the raid on the air base. And now there are over five thousand of them on a hill a few kilometers from where I'm standing. Explain that!"

"You say these aliens are here for this Apollo Stone or whatever you call it, which can connect them to any spot in the universe. Where is it now?" asked a woman in a blue uniform.

Logan took a deep breath. "We had it until they raided Jasper Air Base and took it."

"And now the Sahiradin have it," said Lena, impatiently. "We have to get it back."

"But where is it exactly?" asked General Myer. "Is it in a spaceship?"

"I don't know," replied Logan. "They might have retrieved it already, but if they haven't it's somewhere in that camp guarded by over five thousand soldiers."

"Colonel Longmire, you're on the ground there. What's your assessment of all of this?" asked a uniformed man with tightly cut graying hair.

Longmire picked up a PDD and looked at a report. "General McIntyre, our latest estimates put the Sahiradin numbers at between six and eight thousand. But there are about fifteen hundred Dellians that crossed the river by boat earlier today. They secured the west side of a nearby ancient rail bridge. They're in the process of repairing the bridge, aided by a few PRA troops and engineers. Add to that an unknown number of Dellians in the forest on the east side."

Longmire put the PDD down and continued. "Despite the army of Sahiradin camped a few klicks north of us, my greatest concern is the repair activity on the bridge. They've brought in heavy equipment, and I'm sorry to say they're making good progress."

"Which explains the intelligence reports we've received and forwarded to you indicating there are multiple trains full of troops and equipment heading north to that bridge," added General McIntyre.

"And let's not forget we are in Northrunner territory," added

Longmire. "They've been steadily gathering their forces just north of the Sahiradin camp."

"And true to their nature, they've refused to discuss their intentions with us," said Consul Sawyer, permitting herself to reveal a little of her frustration.

"Why haven't we bombed the rail lines or the bridge?" asked Lena.

"With what?" asked General McIntyre. "Our air force took heavy losses during today's fighting. Those Sahiradin V-wings cut through us like piss through snow. And the PRA just introduced us to their new Phantom 2 fighters, which outperform anything we have."

"What about the X-1 fighter I flew?" asked Cap. "That's based on the Phantom 2 and should be a good match."

"Who the hell put you in the cockpit of our X-1?" demanded the woman in the blue uniform.

"Air Marshal West. I approved the use of the X-1," said Consul Sawyer in a slightly raised tone. "It was the only thing ready to go after the PRA's new gunship that attacked Jasper Air Base. And it was this young man's skill with the X-1 which ultimately brought the *Blackhawk* down."

The air marshal stared at Consul Sawyer through the view screen, her teeth clenched as she sought to control her anger. "Consul Sawyer," she said after a moment. "With all due respect, you are a politician. You represent the Iowan cities in the League. I am chief of the entire League Air Force. You do not have authority to allow *anyone* access to military equipment, especially something as sophisticated as the X-1."

Logan could see Consul Sawyer was beginning to lose her composure. She responded in an icy but measured tone. "The military is ultimately under civilian control, Air Marshal West. As you may recall, my colleagues and I approved your appointment to your position."

"All right, all right," said General McIntyre, raising a cautionary hand to Air Marshal West, who was about to respond. "Consul Sawyer, we understand you exercised emergency powers as a representative of the League Council when you approved the use of the X-1. However, in my capacity as League Forces Chief, I must state that such actions should be taken only in the rarest of circumstances. You and the League Council determine war goals, the League Forces Joint Command develops and executes the plan to achieve those goals. That's how it works. Agreed?"

"Well said," answered Consul Sawyer with a smile. "Agreed."

Seeking to change the focus of the conversation, General McIntyre said, "Now let's get back to the challenge we're facing. We have a handful of fighter aircraft left, but they're busy fending off PRA air attacks all along the frontier, especially near St. Louis. The great majority of PRA ground forces are preparing to attack at any moment, also near St. Louis. If PRA forces cross the river at St. Louis, and they get help from an army swinging south, they'll have enough troops to both lay siege to our fortress at Deep Six and drive on to Denver. They'll split the League in two."

"And don't look for help from the Southern Union or the Pacific Federation," said Consul Sawyer. "The SU still hasn't recovered from their fight last year with the PRA and the Pacific Federation just doesn't have that much to send."

"Okay," said the red-haired general. "What about the Northrunners? Can we get any help from them?"

"Colonel Longmire, you're up there in the middle of it all," said General McIntyre. "What are your impressions about the Northrunners' intentions?"

"Sir, one of our Talon pilots was able to do some recon before being chased out by their anti-aircraft fire. She reported they appear to be checking their ammo and sharpening their bayonets. I'd say their plan is to dig in and block any northward movement."

General McIntyre nodded his head and said, "And what is your assessment on whether the Dellians and the PRA are working together with these Sahiradin?"

"I don't know sir," replied Longmire. "We've got scouts trying to gather intelligence on the ground, but they're encountering some Sahiradin pickets. I've lost two troopers already, sir. But, if it's true that a Sahiradin crash survivor has been helping the PRA build high-tech weapons, I think we should assume they are working together."

"I think that's a wise approach," said Consul Sawyer.

"Anything else to report, colonel?" asked General McIntyre.

"Not at this time, sir."

"Okay. You're heavily outnumbered, so if the Dellians or Sahiradin make any moves toward you, your orders are to pull stakes and hightail it south. Join up with the main League army."

"Understood, sir," said Longmire.

Chapter 63

Colonel Linsky stood in Grand Guardian Harken's spacious office, which had an expansive view of the Capitol and the Potomac River. The last light of the day fell on low gray buildings sprawling along each side of the Potomac River. The only visible vertical break in the cityscape was the massive statue of The People in Victory, erected shortly after the death of Malcom Weller. Linsky could see the occasional white flash in the distance as the safety towers along the Capitol barrier washed the quickly darkening streets and buildings in the light of their powerful lamps.

"Colonel Linsky," said Harken in a sharp tone. "You have failed the People's Republic on multiple occasions with disastrous results. You allowed the Apollo Stone to be removed from the laboratory and you failed to recover it even when you literally had it in your hand."

Harken looked at Linsky's right arm, noting the absent appendage.

"And you failed to anticipate the Sahiradin alien's true intention to take the stone for himself. Now we not only have enemies on all our borders, but also in our skies."

"Grand Guardian Harken," stammered Colonel Linsky. "I can explain; I..."

"I'm not finished!" yelled Harken, slamming his open hand on his desk. "Your failures have placed this nation in a desperate situation. You forced us to make premature use of the *Blackhawk* in order to recover the stone, and now that gunship, the result of fifteen years of hard work, is a smoldering hulk on the bank of the Mississippi River. The *west* bank of the Mississippi River."

Harken stood up from behind his desk and approached Linsky's side. Linsky kept looking straight ahead at the darkening skies outside the Grand Guardian's window, not daring to return Harken's gaze.

"Six months ago, we had the Apollo Stone, the *Blackhawk*, and a large highly trained army," said Harken in a voice laced with venom. "We were poised to reunite this land under one flag, to bring the people together into one great nation. But that's all changed. What was once a foregone conclusion has become a desperate gamble."

He stepped in front of Linsky and shouted in his face. "I could have you executed for treason! There would be no trial, no tribunal. Just a firing squad and a corpse in the river."

Linsky swallowed. His upper lip glistened with sweat.

Harken stared for a moment at the SPD colonel as though daring him to make eye contact. Harken then walked toward the window and looked out over the Capitol. "But, I must admit, you had an outstanding career until this series of debacles, so I'm giving you one last opportunity to redeem yourself."

"Thank you," said Colonel Linsky.

"Our world is changed forever," said Harken as he watched a helicopter fly along the Capitol barrier. "The other Guardians have not yet come to terms with it. They are in a state of panic, worrying how people will react when they learn that we are not alone in the universe. But you are a different kind of animal. You understand what our new future holds."

Harken walked toward his desk and rested his hands on the back of the leather chair. "You've worked with the Sahiradin. You understand how much more advanced his species is."

"Yes sir," answered Linsky, relieved that Harken was no longer talking about his execution.

"We always knew there was a chance that more of his kind would come one day, but without the Apollo Stone we assured ourselves that the risk was minimal. We were wrong. Now we not only have Sahiradin in our skies, but we must also contend with their enemies."

"Yes sir," said Linsky.

Harken took a deep breath. "The time has come to strike a bargain. As I said, the other Guardians haven't come to grips with what is happening, but you and I know we cannot survive as an independent nation in this new environment. Therefore, we must ally ourselves with the Sahiradin. As evidence of our usefulness and willingness to cooperate, we can point to our years of successful collaboration with Kurak. I believe our good treatment of him will also work to our advantage."

"I would assume so, sir"

"As you may be aware, we have struck a bargain with the Dellians, and so far they have done what we have asked. They are guarding a rail bridge and assisting our engineers to repair it. Soon, we will deploy the northern wing of our army on the west side of the river. That army will march south and unite with the main force when it crosses the river near St. Louis, smashing the League forces in a pincer move."

"An excellent plan, sir."

Harken ignored Linsky's compliment and opened his desk drawer. He removed a sealed envelope and laid it on the desk in front of him. "The

Sahiradin leaders have deployed a small army on a hill just above the Dellian position. We have convinced the Dellians that the Sahiradin are an elite PRA force, but if they come into close contact our assertion will be difficult to maintain. That is why I want you to travel to the Sahiradin camp and talk to our former associate. He has already secretly indicated to me that the Sahiradin are interested in a dialogue."

Linsky raised an eyebrow at the mention of secret communications but said nothing.

"You are to offer the following terms, which are contained in this letter." Harken touched the envelope with his fingertips. "First, in exchange for Sahiradin assistance reclaiming our lost states, we will assist in their fight against their alien enemies. Second, if the Sahiradin support the continued growth of the PRA, we will act as the Sahiradin representatives on Earth. Our administration of the planet will ensure Sahiradin interests are protected without requiring their direct involvement."

"Yes sir," said Linsky.

"If they are receptive to these general terms, we will meet with them to discuss the details." Harken folded his arms across his chest and said, "You know the Sahiradin better than anyone else. You must do your best to set the proper tone with them in order to ensure successful negotiations."

"Yes sir," said Linsky. He was silent after that, but Harken could see he was struggling with something.

"What is it Linsky? Out with it."

"Sir, the citizens will need to be told something to ease their concerns. And I wonder how the other Guardians will accept the new arrangement."

"As for the people, they've witnessed a battle in orbit above our heads. They've seen the Sahiradin spacecraft in our skies, even over the Capitol District. We cannot protect them from this startling new situation. But they will follow our guidance, just as they always have. As for the Guardians, leave them to me."

Linsky nodded. "Yes sir."

"And Linsky, if you succeed, there may be a place for you in the new arrangement. If you fail, I will have to make a difficult choice: firing squad or the hangman's noose. Now go to the Sahiradin camp and deliver the letter."

Harken handed Linsky the letter. The SPD officer carefully slid it under his coat and tucked it into an inner pocket. Then he saluted with his left hand, turned and exited the Grand Guardian's office.

Chapter 64

Kurak stood before General Urkona in his command hut. The general was a rare black-eyed, black-haired Sahiradin. There were a number of other Sahiradin in the hut, but they stood at a respectful distance, ready to respond to orders if called upon.

"Captain Kurak, as you know, *Dominion* was forced to withdraw for the time being," said Urkona. "That gives us time to get to know each other a little." He offered Kurak a drink of dark liquid, which Kurak accepted with a slight nod of the head.

"Veresch from the slopes of the Sacred Mountain," said Urkona.

Kurak tasted it and smiled. "You can imagine how long it has been since I have tasted its bitter bite."

General Urkona smiled, but his dark eyes lacked emotion.

"I have read your report regarding the Alamani and your experiences with them," said the general. "As you know, we have several thousand Alamani savages near the bridge below our camp. A different group is on the ridgeline just to the south. A third group is massing farther to the north. Although I do not consider any of these tribes to be a serious threat, I am concerned that we are penned in against the river with no room to maneuver. What do you know of these Alamani tribes and what are their intentions?"

Kurak took another sip from his cup and set it down on the table. He approached the holographic map of the region and pointed at the railroad bridge. "This Alamani tribe is called the Dellians. A savage group of fanatics that have temporarily allied themselves with the Alamani of the east, called the PRA. You will recall that I lived in the PRA for many years. These Alamani on the hill to the south are the enemies of the PRA. They belong to a loose collection of Alamani city states called the League of Free Cities. They call themselves a league, but in truth they're little more than a trade union with a loose mutual-defense agreement."

Kurak scrolled the holographic map north. "This third group of Alamani is called the Northrunners. They are extremely reclusive and few in numbers. This hill we find ourselves on is inside territory that both the Northrunners and the Dellians claim, which is why the Northrunner defenders have come south. They will want to observe our actions but are unlikely to attack unless provoked.

General Urkona nodded, his black eyes focused on the map. He motioned the other Sahiradin to gather around. "As I said, I do not like being penned in against the river. To create breathing room, my staff recommends we slaughter the Alamani on the hill. You are familiar with the politics and military capabilities of these tribes, Captain Kurak. Should we attack or wait for their assault?"

"I agree the Alamani on the hill are the greatest threat. At least to the extent that *any* Alamani are a threat to us," said Kurak with a grin. "The Dellians present no danger."

"And what about these Northrunners?" asked the general, pointing farther north.

"As I said, I think they will be satisfied to watch and wait, but they will fight if we move north," said Kurak. "As is the case with the Dellians, they are no real threat to us. Unlike the Alamani of the east and the League, they do not have shields and they rely on projectile weapons."

Urkona rotated the map to study the terrain and enemy positions from different angles. After a few moments, he asked, "How certain are you the Alamani from the east, the PRA, will execute their war plans as you described?"

"Very certain," said Kurak. "They have been planning this war for years, and have put so much effort into precisely timing the various elements of their plan that I do not think they would dare deviate from it."

"And why are they at war with this other tribe, the League?" asked General Urkona.

"It is simple," said Kurak. "They are starving. Their crops are dying. And although they've been planning the war for years, this is the year they must attack if they want to avoid the social unrest that will certainly occur this winter when the last scraps of food have been consumed."

"And their enemy, the League, has food?" asked Urkona.

"They do. And more importantly, their crops are not affected by the blight."

General Urkona raised his hand to his chin and studied the map a few moments longer. Then he said, "Very well. The troops are eager to engage against our ancient enemy, our greatest enemy. We will attack the Alamani on the hill."

Chapter 65

The *khâl* turned blue as the fast attack frigate passed through the nearby wormhole. The Lycians had been fortunate. The gate had created this particular wormhole much closer to P3 than the gate through which the Sahiradin fleet had arrived. The Lycian frigate quickly located the Sahiradin fleet on the far side of P6 and signaled for the other ships to follow. Soon the Lycian flagship, a battleship called *Intrepid,* and an array of frigates, cruisers and patrol vessels came through the wormhole, followed by several warrior transports. The ships assumed a standard protective formation around *Intrepid* and launched hundreds of small craft and drones to search for hidden enemy vessels and gather intelligence about the system they had just entered.

On board *Intrepid,* Admiral Var-Imar, a slender female with olive-colored skin and short black hair, ordered her communications officer to contact the Lycian heavy cruiser, *Defiant.*

"Your report please, captain," said Var-Imar.

"Admiral, Commander Dor-Ingaroth reporting," said the blond-haired officer with almond-shaped eyes. Captain Sul-Turov died during the recent battle." He waited a moment before continuing. "We failed to destroy the Sahiradin battleship, called *Dominion,* but it was sufficiently damaged that it was forced to retreat to the moon orbiting P3. Our enhanced ion shield proved its value, but *Defiant* was badly damaged in the battle. Our engines are disabled and our orbit around P3 is decaying. Unless we can quickly repair our engines, *Defiant* will crash to the planet surface."

Var-Imar nodded her head and said, "You did well to force them to retreat. The Sahiradin devastator-class battleship is a formidable opponent."

"In all honesty, I think we were lucky," said Commander Dor-Ingaroth. "We don't think *Dominion* was so heavily damaged that she couldn't fight on, especially against an enemy with no engine power. We're continuing to investigate why they chose to retreat to the nearby moon."

"Interesting. Please let me know if you learn anything new," said Var-Imar. She laced her fingers and tapped her thumbs together as she considered what the commander had told her. Then she said, "What is the status of your repair efforts?"

"Assuming no further complications, we should be able to restore at least partial power to the engines before we enter the planet's atmosphere," said Dor-Ingaroth.

"What about your support ships? What condition are they in?"

"Light destroyers *Glory* and *Resolve* suffered minor damage and are combat ready," replied the commander. "The frigate *Challenger* was badly damaged by the Sahiradin ion cannon, but they have repaired or replaced most of their affected systems and will soon be battle ready."

"And what about the newly arrived Sahiradin fleet?" asked Admiral Var-Imar. "What is its composition?"

"Admiral, the Sahiradin have sent an additional battleship, four heavy cruisers, a fighter hive, and seven frigates. They also have three large troop transports."

"With *Dominion*, that makes two battleships," observed Var-Imar. "They are truly committed to exterminating the Alamani descendants you've encountered on P3. And what is the situation on the planet surface?"

"Confused. As reported, the Alamani on P3 consist of many rival factions living in different areas of the planet, and their technical capabilities are...rudimentary."

"I see. So we should not look for help from them," said Var-Imar.

"Not in the way we would expect, but unlike their ancestors, the Alamani of P3 are warriors. In fact, we are observing the beginnings of what appears to be a large-scale war between two rival Alamani factions."

Var-Imar scoffed. "You say they are warriors, but they are fighting each other. What use is that to us?"

"They fight each other, but also the Sahiradin, sir," replied Dor-Ingaroth. "We observed a group of Alamani engage against a small detachment of Sahiradin and defeat them using swords and antiballistic shields."

"Interesting," replied Var-Imar. "I consider it an unlikely coincidence that both this forgotten colony of Alamani and the Sahiradin use sword and shield. Thank you for this report. We will join you at P3 as quickly as possible. Continue to watch *Dominion,* and if the Sahiradin fleet arrives before we do, fall back."

"And if they come before we can repair *Defiant's* engines?" asked Dor-Ingaroth.

"Destroy her," said Var-Imar, grimly.

"Yes Admiral."

Chapter 66

General McIntyre, Chief of League Forces, leaned toward the view screen camera and said, "Colonel Longmire, we're shifting our strategy."

Colonel Longmire raised his eyebrows. "Yes sir. What's the plan?"

"We're going to hit those Dellian troops defending the bridgehead and sweep them from this side of the river. Then we're going to blow the bridge."

"Yes sir," said Longmire with a grin, "but I can't accomplish that mission without additional troops, sir."

"Understood," said the general. "That's why I'm shipping you an additional five thousand troops and giving you a field promotion to brigadier general. We're pulling four heavy battalions out of the 2nd Army Corp and sending them to you instead of St. Louis."

"Yes sir," said Longmire.

"And I should mention the Northrunners have officially protested your presence in their territory. They've given us twenty-four hours to withdraw," said General McIntyre, "so they won't like the additional soldiers we're sending you. But that can't be helped. Those battalions will be at your location within six hours."

"Sir, I read the recent reports indicating the Northrunner defenders are inching south. What should I do if they fire on us?" asked Longmire.

"Do *not* engage against them under any circumstances," said McIntyre. "The politocos are still trying to get them to pitch in, at least against the Dellians."

"Understood, sir," said Longmire.

"Now you'll have overall command of what we're calling Operation Torchlight. Each battalion's commanding officer will report to you, and you will retain direct command over the troops you've got now."

"Yes sir," said Longmire.

"Those four battalions are lugging some artillery with them, but because we've been able to reestablish air superiority west of the river, I'm also sending an additional three thousand troops and equipment by air," said McIntyre. "Keep an eye out for Titan IVs with a fighter escort. They'll be airdropping field guns and a dozen tanks within a couple hours."

Longmire was surprised by this last piece of information. "Sounds like overkill, if you don't mind my saying. Is there more to this?"

"Yes, there is," said McIntyre. "Two more things, actually. The PRA has upped the number of troop trains going in your direction. It's slow going on those old tracks, but they'll arrive by tomorrow noon. You'll need to get the field pieces I'm sending you unpacked and pointed at that bridge double quick."

"Estimated numbers of PRA troops?"

"At this point, it looks like a division, at least. Maybe it's their entire 1st Corp."

Longmire swallowed. "That's fifty thousand soldiers, sir. With the reinforcements you're sending, I'll have a maximum of twelve thousand soldiers. We can't hold out against an entire corps for very long, even with the bridge blown. They'll just get the Dellians to ferry them across somewhere upriver."

"But that would cause a substantial delay, which they can't afford," replied McIntyre. "The rail line on the eastern side goes as far north as your spot, so I think the fight is going to take place right there."

Longmire nodded and said, "Yes sir."

"I didn't say it would be easy," said McIntyre, his voice softening a bit. "But you're the shield that will blunt their northern spear. Our troops in St. Louis are going to inflict as many casualties as possible when the PRA crosses the river, when they're most vulnerable. Then the troopers will disengage and hightail it to Deep Six. When that happens, we can't allow the PRA's northern army to swing south unopposed and smash into our right flank. Someone's got to stop them or at least slow them down."

"Understood, sir," said Longmire. Then he asked, "What are my orders about the Sahiradin? They've been quiet so far, but what if they decide to support the Dellians?"

General McIntyre nodded. "And that's the second thing I planned to tell you. We have new intel that their big ship left our orbit and retreated to the moon. That battle we witnessed gave them a bloody nose and they pulled out."

"And we're willing to trust the Lycians won't attack us?" asked Longmire.

"Well, your defectors seemed pretty convinced they're here to help."

Longmire nodded. "How certain can we be the Sahiradin ship is really gone? Maybe it's just below the horizon, and we're blind without the satellites they destroyed."

General McIntyre said, "That's true, but they didn't think about the moon."

"We have satellites in the moon's orbit?"

"No, but the Chinese have had a spy telescope up there for the past five years. They shared images of the battle and the retreating Sahiradin."

"A spy telescope on the moon?" said Longmire, surprised. "That's damned clever, sir."

"And there's more," said McIntyre. "Radio telescopes in the Mojave Desert have picked up more signal traffic. We believe the Sahiradin and the Lycians have more ships on the way."

"Any idea when they'll arrive, sir?"

"Not sure, but since we can't do anything about it, our main concern right now is the PRA invasion," said General McIntyre. "And before you can move against their Dellian cronies on the bridge, you'll need to convince those Sahiradin camped north of you to stay out of the fight. You orders are to engage against them and either push them off that hill or pin them down. Keep them out of the main fight against the Dellians. Just remember, your main objective is to blow that bridge to hell and gone."

"Yes sir."

"That's all I've got for now," said General McIntyre. "Now swap those birds on your collar for stars and get to work, General."

Chapter 67

Logan looked over the edge of the shallow trench they had dug and watched the Dellians reinforcing their position on the west side of the river near the bridgehead. They had worked through the night, and Logan was disheartened to see how much progress they had made. He watched as Dellians and PRA soldiers busily laid new track on the bridge and replaced rotted wood with metal supports. In the water below the bridge, they had divers working on the bridge's footings as well.

"Whatever they're sending across that bridge will be bad news for us. Hope they pull us back soon," said Cap as he and Lena sat down next to Logan. Lena handed Logan a cup of coffee, steam rising from the cup in the chilly morning air.

"The word is we're being reinforced," said Lena, looking up and down the trench at the little groups of soldiers.

Cap was not happy with this news and swore under his breath. "I did not sign up for this sitting in the dirt shit. I belong in the climate-controlled cabin of a fighter."

Logan clapped him on the back. "Don't worry, Cap. We troopers will take care of you and your delicate flyboy hands."

Lieutenant Styles walked to their position and called for Dog Platoon to gather round.

"We've got orders," she said to the troopers. "A column of troopers arrived last night. We've been reinforced up to heavy brigade level. They're parachuting in troops and equipment, too. Our job will be to destroy that bridge before PRA troop trains arrive from the south."

The troopers of Dog Patrol looked at each other, their faces clearly showing they were not happy with this change in circumstances. Then one of them raised a hand and asked, "Lieutenant Styles, what about those guys on the hill?"

"We and some of the troops that arrived last night are going to maneuver around the hill to the north and attack those pasty Sahiradin bastards. At least keep them pinned down so they can't cause trouble for the main assault on the bridge. And before you ask, there is limited air and artillery support, so they'll hit the Sahiradin for a few minutes, but it's up to us to get the job done."

She paused and looked at each of their faces before continuing. "As you know, the Sahiradin use swords and we believe they have shields, so sharpen your blades and check your charges."

"What about the Northrunners?" another soldier asked. "Whose side are they on?"

"Unknown," replied Styles. "But we are under orders not to engage against them if you see any."

She looked around and saw there were no more questions. "Okay, everyone double check your gear. And don't forget to check your armor for damage or defects. Now's the time to replace anything. Be ready when the order comes down to move out."

As the troopers dispersed, Lieutenant Styles looked at Logan. "General wants to see you and your friends."

"What general?" asked Cap.

"General Longmire," she replied. "He's a one-star now and in charge of Operation Torchlight."

A few minutes later, they were standing at attention in front of General Longmire.

"Privates, things have changed," he said. "No doubt Lieutenant Styles has informed you of your objective. Apparently, the Sahiradin and the Lycians have decided to make Earth ground zero for the next battle in their war. We have reports that both sides have sent fleets, and we expect them to arrive here within the next couple of days. And you can bet the Sahiradin are going to focus on us because we've got their friends sitting on that hill to the north."

"Getting the Apollo Stone is their primary objective," said Logan. "If they get it, they'll cut the Lycians to pieces."

"Maybe, but we also need to assume that the Lycians would rather blow us all to hell rather than let the Sahiradin have the stone. That means we need to get it back and either destroy it so no one can have it or give it over to the Lycians so they can deal with the Sahiradin, hopefully someplace very far away. We don't want that thing here on Earth or we'll never get rid of these bastards."

"It can't be destroyed, sir," said Logan. "Ravenwood said the Lycians tried to destroy the other stones they'd acquired during the war but couldn't. They ended up throwing them into a black hole."

"Why didn't they just use them against the Sahiradin?" asked Longmire.

"I don't know," said Logan. "I guess that's a question for the Lycians."

"All right," said Longmire as he folded his arms across his chest. "We need to focus on getting that Apollo Stone away from the Sahiradin." Looking at Logan, he asked, "How confident are you that you can find it if we can get into the Sahiradin camp?"

"Very confident," answered Logan. "I know exactly where it is. Right now it's in their command tent."

"How do you know?" asked Lieutenant Styles.

"Because I hear it," said Logan.

"You hear it? How do we know you're not schizoid?" asked Longmire.

"That's a fair question. What if I told you that right now the Sahiradin battleship is in orbit around the moon and the three Lycian ships are in Earth orbit? One of them is badly damaged and might crash to Earth."

"How the hell do you know that?" asked Longmire, shocked.

"I can't explain it sir, but I just know it. I have to assume the Apollo Stone is the source."

Longmire looked at him in the eye for a moment. Then he said, "What you said is correct. I just learned about it last night." He looked at all three of them. "We can't do anything about those ships in orbit, so let's focus on what we can do here on Earth. Your mission is to dislodge the Sahiradin from their hill or at least pin them down during the main attack against the Dellians on the bridge. But if during the fighting you can get the Apollo Stone, do it."

"Sir," said a communications soldier sitting in front of an array of computer screens. "The Titans are delivering their payload now."

"Good. Any sign of PRA or V-wing aircraft?"

"No sir. X-1s from Denver are escorting the Titans. A few PRA fighters approached but were driven away."

"So Denver finally decided to get in the game," said Longmire with a smile. "Things are looking up."

Later that evening, Lieutenant Styles inspected her troops' position after they had been shifted to the far left end of the line. An additional two thousand troops had parachuted in with the Titan super transports and were being used to fill the line to their right. The three recently arrived battalions had spent the afternoon positioning themselves along the northern edge of the little river town. Soldiers were moving the newly arrived artillery pieces onto the ridgeline, where they had a commanding view of the Dellians at the bridgehead, the Sahiradin camp, and the eastern bank of the river.

"Get some sleep tonight," Styles told her troopers. "Tomorrow's going to be a busy day."

Chapter 68

Kurak entered the command tent and found General Urkona standing near a table consulting with several members of his staff. When the general saw Kurak, he stepped away from the table and ushered him to the corner of the hut where there was an ornately carved desk made of a material resembling bone. Urkona sat down in a high-backed black chair behind the desk but did not offer Kurak a seat at one of the several nearby tripod chairs.

"And what did the your crippled Alamani friend have to say?" asked General Urkona.

Kurak smiled and took a deep breath. "The People's Republic of America has offered to support us in our fight against the Lycians in exchange for helping them win their war against the other Alamani."

Urkona scoffed. "What possible use can these Alamani be in our fight?" he asked. "They are technologically backward and low minded. And, according to you, they cannot even feed themselves."

"All true," replied Kurak. "But we could still use them in the coming fight. We know the Alamani across the valley are preparing to launch an attack. They have been gathering troops and artillery over the past several days."

"Yes. And we will slaughter them like animals," said Urkona. "And when *Dominion* and the rest of our fleet come for us, the Alamani can have their little war."

"But what if the Separatist fleet arrives first? If they land troops, we could use the help of the PRA to defeat them."

"The Separatists and their fighting machines are no match for us. We have demonstrated that time and again."

"True," said Kurak. "But always at the cost of Sahiradin lives. We enjoy long lives, but we can only reproduce during the queen's cycle."

Kurak looked around the command tent at the Sahiradin performing various tasks. "Why are there no younger brothers?" he asked. "I have walked the length and breadth of this camp and I have not seen a single young soldier. They're all in their fourth cycle or later."

"There are no twentieth-generation Sahiradin in the camp either, except for you," said Urkona disdainfully. "They all died in battle long before they reached your venerable age."

A light smile touched Kurak's lips. "What happened? Did the queen die without producing a new queen?"

General Urkona shot Kurak a warning look with his dark eyes. "The queen lives!" he shouted emphatically as he smashed his open palm on the desk. "How dare you even suggest such a thing?"

"Then what's happening?" asked Kurak. "When did the queen last produce a warrior class? How many cycles have gone by without replenishing our ranks?"

Urkona took a deep breath and slowly exhaled. He looked around the hut and leaned forward. "It's been three cycles," he said quietly.

"Why is there no new queen?" asked Kurak, placing his hands on the desk and leaning toward the general. "Each queen must produce a fertile female to replace her before she dies."

Urkona was growing angry with Kurak's questions. He whispered in a low growl, "The queen lives, and she is not infertile."

Kurak stood straight and scratched his chin. "Saying she is not infertile is not the same as saying she is fertile. You're a poor deceiver."

"I take that as a compliment," said Urkona.

"Whatever is happening, the fact remains," said Kurak. "Our warrior population dwindles. We need the Alamani to help us win this war. You know Commodore Lansu is in favor of this arrangement. And I believe he outranks you."

General Urkona scoffed. "Lansu," he said dismissively. "He's desperate to be chosen as the next consort. Believe me, the Sahiradin of that cycle would be sadly deficient."

Kurak eyed the general for a moment. "Tell me, General Urkona," he said. "Why do you oppose this alliance?"

Urkona narrowed his eyes. "Have you forgotten how the Alamani sought to subjugate us?"

"Of course not, but these are not the same Alamani," replied Kurak. "They have no memory of their ancient ancestors. What's more, they are bigger, stronger, more warlike. I've seen them in battle. They lack sophistication and skill, but they are aggressive and not without valor. We can equip them to fight against the Lycians and help us to conquer this planet."

"But they are *still* Alamani," hissed Urkona.

"So let them die for us and our just cause," said Kurak with a shrug. "I think the Council would appreciate the irony."

"I am finished discussing this," said the general. "We do not need help from these backward Alamani, and I will oppose any arrangement with them."

Chapter 69

It was two hours before dawn and the troopers were already in their battle gear. Cap and Lena watched Logan's face as he slowly regained awareness of his surroundings. His left hand stopped its repetitive twitching and his eyes no longer darted back and forth.

"How many times has it happened this week?" asked Cap.

Logan rubbed his face and took a deep breath. He tried to stand up, but was still too dazed to rise to his feet.

"Two times," he answered, avoiding Cap's eyes.

"Okay. Four," he admitted after a few moments.

"We need to get you back on your medication," said Cap as he placed a hand on Logan's shoulder.

"No. I don't want to. They can't know about my condition," said Logan. "And besides, it's not just seizures. I'm seeing things. And if I take the meds, the visions will stop, too."

Cap shook his head. "But four seizures in a week? You've never had four in a week. This Apollo Stone is messing with your mind. It's dangerous."

"It doesn't feel dangerous," replied Logan as he looked toward the Sahiradin hill. "It's calming. And he tells me things."

"So you're hearing a voice in your head when you have your seizures?" asked Cap.

"Not really," replied Logan. He looked back at the hill and stared for a few moments before continuing. "It's more like impressions and thoughts that come to me. There's intelligence in the stone, but it doesn't scare me. It's…welcoming."

"Visions? The stone is telling you things? What is going on, Logan?" asked Cap, raising his voice slightly. "And how do you know what you're seeing or feeling is real? Maybe you're imagining all this."

"It's not my imagination," said Logan. "General Longmire confirmed what I said about the outcome of the battle in orbit and the withdrawal of the Sahiradin ship to the moon."

Lena crouched down and looked into Logan's eyes. "Cap's right. This is dangerous. What if you have a seizure when we're in battle? You could be killed. Or get someone else killed."

"It won't happen," said Logan. "The Apollo Stone wants me to find it. It wouldn't call to me if it would put me in danger."

"It calls to you?" asked Cap. "This is getting weirder and weirder."

"How does it call to you?" asked Lena.

"It starts with a rushing sound, like wind blowing through the trees," said Logan. "When I hear it, my hand starts to shake and I sit down. A few seconds later I'm in the universe, stars all around me."

"And that's when you get these messages?" asked Cap.

"Yes."

Lena asked, "Do you see anyone or anything during your seizures?"

"No. But there's definitely someone there. I feel him watching me, but I can't see who he is."

"Him?" asked Lena.

"I feel like it's a man. Someone ancient," answered Logan.

"I'd freak out if this happened to me," said Cap. "And you should be freaking out, too."

Logan was about to respond, but then he saw Lieutenant Styles and another trooper approaching. They were both wearing Provex armor.

"Check your armor and your weapons. Be ready to move," said Styles as the three quickly got to their feet. "And meet Lance Corporal Heath." She pointed to a young man standing next to her. "You'll be on his fire team."

Styles nodded and continued walking to the next group of soldiers down the line.

"Privates Castell, Brandt, and Caparelli," said Lance Corporal Heath. "I hear you defected from the PRA. I don't have a problem with that, but you have not trained with us. You're just as likely to get yourselves killed as kill the enemy. Even worse, you might get me killed. Therefore, your job will be to stick close to me. Do what I say and copy what I do. Execute every order I give you when I give it to you. Understood?"

"They all nodded their heads and said in unison, "Yes, Lance Corporal Heath."

"You can call me L.C. Heath. Now follow me."

L.C. Heath quickly walked in the direction Lieutenant Styles had gone. Logan, Lena and Cap double checked their K-45s and swords that were in in their battle packs. They checked their bracers and fell in behind L.C. Heath. They soon joined a line of marching troops heading west down the slope of the hill.

As they marched, L.C. Heath introduced them to the other members of his fire team. Bedford, Franks, Thompson, Lee, Flores, and Garcia. Franks, a big man with a deep baritone voice, and Flores, a broad-chested muscular man with tattoos on his neck and as far up his forearms as his rolled-up sleeves would reveal, were from Indianapolis. They had fled across the river when the SPD sought to arrest them for dealing in false buy cards.

"Were you guilty?" asked Cap.

"Hell yes," laughed Franks.

"Of that and more," added Flores with a grin.

"Then we should get along great," said Cap with a grin.

"Pipe down," said L.C. Heath.

Moments later, Logan heard the sound of artillery firing from their base on top of the hill in the direction of the bridge. Momentary flashes illuminated the still-darkened sky as the shells exploded in and around the Dellian camp. The troopers then broke into a trot for the next fifteen minutes.

As the edge of the eastern horizon began to glow with the rising sun, Dog Patrol and the other five hundred marching troops joined the five thousand already in place on the northwest side of the hill on which the Sahiradin had established their camp.

As the stars disappeared from the morning sky, Logan heard the high whistle of artillery being fired on the Sahiradin position. He looked up expecting to see explosions on the hill above, but was disappointed to see the shells were detonating high in the air. They were apparently striking a dome shield that protected the camp. Shell after shell exploded two hundred meters above the ground without touching the target below. Logan looked at the faces of the troopers at the foot of the hill. They were all watching the bombardment, waiting for the order to advance. Some wore fearful expressions, others were angry, but none of them were happy with what they were seeing.

"Damn it," whispered Flores. "Come on, boys, soften 'em up a little for us."

The bombardment ceased and the seconds ticked by. Logan assumed the order to attack was about to come, but then he heard a whistle in the air. It was a lower-pitched sound than the other shells, more of a hum. The surface of the hilltop flashed with an explosion. Then another and another shell found its target. Logan suppressed a cheer as his feet felt the rumbling of the explosions in the Sahiradin camp above.

"We must have switched from high-velocity shells to mortars," said Lena.

"Chew 'em up, boys," said Franks.

Thirty seconds later, even the mortar shells couldn't penetrate the Sahiradin shield.

"Looks like they tightened up the shield," said Lena.

"Tighten it enough and they'll suffocate," said Cap. "I'd dig that."

"Always the optimist," said Logan.

Seeing the artillery was no longer having any effect, the order came down to engage shields and advance. Logan had been told that League shields could hold their charge longer than PRA standard-issue shields, but L.C. Heath warned his team not to count on them for more than one hour.

"Listen for my order to disengage shields to save your charge," he said. "And you all know that the Sahiradin have shields too, so be ready to switch out your K-45s for swords."

Logan looked at Cap and Lena as the line quietly advanced toward the base of the Sahiradin hill. They were carrying their short K-45 assault rifles but were prepared to draw swords if necessary. As they began ascending the hill, Logan could sense his fellow soldiers were growing increasingly tense. They had not seen any movement from the camp and everything was eerily quiet now that the bombardment had ceased. Logan knew the others must be thinking the same thing as he was. With each step forward, the likelihood of a close-quarters engagement with the Sahiradin grew greater and greater.

To his left, Cap stumbled and fell to the ground. Franks reached down to help him to his feet. As Franks bent down, Logan noticed dirt crumbling into a crack in the ground. Cap got back on his feet, and he and Franks quickly caught up with the rest of the fire team. Fifteen meters behind Logan, the next line of League soldiers was approaching where he stood.

Logan slowly drew his sword, making as little noise as possible. Using the sword tip, he touched the edge of the crack in the ground. More Earth tumbled into the darkness. He slid his K-45 into the slot in his battle pack. Placing both hands on the hilt of his sword, he moved the tip back and forth. He found the edge of something solid. As he lifted with his sword, the object began to move. Then it suddenly burst open, and five white-haired Sahiradin leapt out of a shallow hole in the ground.

Startled by the sudden appearance of the Sahiradin, Logan stumbled backward but managed to block the swinging sword of a screaming Sahiradin. The other four dashed toward the approaching second line of League soldiers, who fired on them but to no effect due to the Sahiradin shields.

Logan heard the sound of gunfire erupting along the League line as hundreds of Sahiradin sprang from hidden positions on the hillside. Soldiers yelled in a mixture of anger, fear, and pain as many were cut down by Sahiradin blades. Those who survived the first few moments of the surprise attack drew their swords and charged the enemy.

Logan regained his balance and deflected two quick strikes from his opponent. The Sahiradin moved with lightning speed, but the surrounding tree trunks and branches limited his range of motion. Logan used these obstructions to his advantage, ducking and gliding behind trees or low-hanging branches. Fortunately, several League troopers rushed forward to assist him. As the Sahiradin blocked the attacks of two soldiers, Logan drove the tip of his sword into the Sahiradin between his shoulder and breast protection. Although Logan pushed hard, the alien's tough, scaly skin prevented the blade from reaching deep into the Sahiradin's flesh.

The Sahiradin turned to his left, pulling his wounded shoulder away from Logan's barely embedded blade. Then he quickly struck down two League soldiers. Suddenly, Flores came from behind and cut a long gash along the alien's back parallel to the edge of his armor. Screaming in pain and anger, the Sahiradin turned and swung twice at Flores, who blocked the first attack with his guard and the second with his blade. Then another trooper cut the unprotected back of the alien's right leg, causing him to stumble. The Sahiradin recovered his footing and stabbed the trooper in the throat with a short blade that popped out from the pummel of his sword.

Logan looked at the Sahiradin withdraw the blade from the trooper and felt a rage surge through him like he'd never felt before. He roared and swung for the Sahiradin's wounded leg, but he blocked Logan's blade with his own. Logan then lunged forward and thrust his sword up through the Sahiradin's jaw and into his skull. The alien's pale blue eyes opened wide, but the light quickly left them. Logan withdrew his blade and the Sahiradin's body collapsed to the ground.

Logan looked at the three dead troopers and then at Flores. Flores was breathing heavily, his eyes fixed on the Sahiradin body. Then he held up his sword for Logan to see. The Sahiradin's blow had cut the trooper's blade in two. He dropped his broken blade and picked up the Sahiradin's black sword. He swung it a few times, admiring its weight and balance.

Logan nodded and said, "Let's go."

The two of them dashed up the hill, but couldn't find anyone from L.C. Heath's fire team in the confused melee that surrounded them. Before the fighting began, Logan had expected a swift, pitched battle against the Sahiradin with his comrades fighting next to him shoulder to shoulder. Instead, the battle consisted of hundreds of isolated but vicious sword fights. The hillside echoed with the sounds of screaming combatants and ringing swords. He and Flores ran through the trees, engaging in fight after fight, assisting fellow troopers to overcome Sahiradin. And with each fight the same story playing out - two, three or even four dead troopers for every one dead Sahiradin. Yet, the momentum of the battle was shifting, despite the confusion the surprise attack had caused and the Sahiradin soldiers' remarkable skill with the sword. The troopers were gaining the upper hand and slowly advancing up the hill.

Logan finally spotted L.C. Heath and Lena fighting a Sahiradin near the top of the hill. Cap was on the ground, motionless. The rest of the fire team was still alive by some miracle and fully engaged in a fight with two other Sahiradin to the left of Heath and Lena. Heath ducked under his opponent's black blade and Lena drove her sword into the Sahiradin's right side, but it was not enough to bring him down. The Sahiradin spun around to face her. She blocked two of his attacks, but had to backpedal to avoid a third. Heath attacked the Sahiradin's exposed leg, cutting his calf muscle, but it was also not enough to drop him.

Logan and Flores screamed and charged forward. Together, they launched a flurry of attacks, but the Sahiradin managed to deflect them. Lena and Heath attacked from the Sahiradin's flanks, slashing and piercing his body in multiple places. He finally fell to the ground with a dozen wounds. He tried to rise, swinging his sword at anyone within reach, but his body wouldn't comply. Finally, Heath stepped on the alien's sword hand while Flores drove his black Sahiradin blade through the alien's breast protection. He kept pushing until it went all the way through his hard scaly back.

Lena ran a few steps toward Cap, who lay on the ground with a head wound. A knot formed in Logan's stomach as he watched her examine the injury. Then she looked at Logan and nodded.

"He's okay," she said. "Saved my life with a stupid screaming attack when this pasty bastard popped up from the ground."

She reached into Cap's battle pack and removed a small packet containing antiseptic powder and a bandage and applied it to Cap's still-bleeding wound.

While Lena attended to Cap, Logan ran to join L.C. Heath and the others at the edge of a large clearing on top of the hill. What he saw when he emerged from the trees made his heart sink. Standing thirty meters in front of them were thousands of armored Sahiradin in a four-line-deep formation.

Logan looked to his left and right along the tree line. Scattered groups of troopers were appearing out of the forest and stepping onto the field. They were all breathing heavily, and each one held a bloody sword in his or her hand. Logan returned his attention to the silent and perfectly still Sahiradin formation. In the distance, he heard the sounds of battle as the main League force attacked the Dellian position near the bridge.

After a few moments, a Sahiradin standing just to the left of their front line drew his sword. He held it high in the air and barked out a command. The other Sahiradin shouted a reply, reached over their shoulders, and drew their swords in perfect unison. The sound of all those voices shouting as one sent a chill down Logan's spine. Then the Sahiradin officer shouted again, and the formation started its advance.

Chapter 70

"Sir, you'd better have a look at this."

"What is it, lieutenant?" said General Longmire as he looked at a view screen depicting the current Dellian position near the bridgehead. The Dellians were deeply entrenched, more deeply than anticipated, and they had received heavy guns from their PRA allies; the new artillery was proving difficult to silence. The handful of PRA soldiers who had come to work on the bridge were also fighting with considerable tenacity.

"We're getting reports on the attack on the Sahiradin camp," replied the lieutenant.

"Finally," said Longmire. "What have you got?"

"We've reached the camp, but suffered heavy casualties in the process."

Longmire took the PDD out of the lieutenant's hands. "How heavy?"

He read for a few seconds and said, "Damn it. Send the order to withdraw. Immediately!"

Longmire quickly walked across the command center to a soldier sitting in front of an array of communications devices. "Corporal, get me Lt. Colonel Brinks."

He toggled his ICS attached to his belt and said, "Captain Martins, we'll need mortar shells on the northwest side of the Sahiradin camp, just past their shield dome. Start there and move north into the tree line. The Sahiradin are advancing and we need to provide our troops cover as they pull out."

"I've got Lieutenant Colonel Brinks, sir," said the corporal as he handed Longmire a headset.

"Lieutenant Colonel Brinks, I'm activating your reserve troops. I want you to hit the Sahiradin camp from the south side. Colonel Ambrose's forces are taking a pounding and we need you to get some of those Sahiradin troops off his back. Do not engage in close quarters if you can avoid it. Withdraw if they push back hard. I'm going to direct artillery fire on the hillside above you and on the tree line to soften up any enemy troops waiting in the woods."

"Yes sir," said a woman's voice. "We're ready."

Longmire ran to the forward observation post about thirty meters away from the command tent. He raised his field sensors to his eyes and surveyed the Sahiradin camp. On the northern edge of the hill, he saw the dark-armored Sahiradin troops quickly marching toward the tree line, where a few League troops could be seen disappearing into the trees. Suddenly the ground erupted in the midst of the Sahiradin line, sending many of them flying in the air. As mortar shells exploded around them, the Sahiradin quickened their advance, running across the field and into the forest in pursuit of the fleeing League soldiers.

The bombardment of the northern side of the hill ceased. Then, after a brief pause, artillery shells began ripping up the ground and shattering trees on the southern slope. Lieutenant Colonel Brinks' five hundred troopers began marching up the hill as the artillery fire advanced ahead of them.

Longmire toggled his ICS. "Captain Park."

"Yes sir," said a voice a moment later.

"We're going to need your birds to disengage against the Dellians and swing around the Sahiradin hill. Hit the enemy units pursuing our troops down the northern slope."

"Yes sir."

Moments later, Longmire looked to his right and saw six Nightwing combat helicopters abort a strafing run against the enemy position near the bridgehead and fly north up the river valley. As they turned toward the hill's northern slope, jagged red beams of energy shot into the air from a long gray object in the Sahiradin camp. One of the helicopters exploded, and the burning hulk hurtled toward the ground. More leaping red fire shot out from the base and damaged a second helicopter, which began smoking and rapidly lost altitude.

"Park, get the hell out of there!" Longmire yelled into his ICS. "Pull back!" The remaining four helicopters turned away from the Sahiradin camp.

Longmire raised his field sensors to his eyes again and looked at the Dellian camp below. The League forces were finally pushing the enemy from their position at the bridgehead. Some Dellians tried to flee across the bridge, but the majority retreated north in a disorderly mob along the river bank toward the boats they had used to cross the river a few days earlier. A number of half-full boats were already crossing the water.

"Captain Park," said Longmire. "Swing wide around the Sahiradin hill and see if you can't come down the river to provide support to our withdrawing troops. If you come under fire from the Sahiradin camp, disengage. Your secondary target is the Dellian boats crossing to the east side of the river."

"Roger wilco," said Park.

Moments later, Captain Park said, "General Longmire, sir. We've got a situation on the north side of the Sahiradin camp."

"What situation?" asked Longmire.

Chapter 71

Logan and Lena supported Cap, who was barely conscious, as they ran down the hill. Mortars exploded on the hilltop behind them. Based on the troopers he'd seen on the hilltop, Logan estimated only two thousand of the five thousand troops who marched up that hill were still alive. They had tried to withdraw in an orderly manner, but discipline quickly broke down and everyone simply fled as quickly as possible down the hill.

Cap pulled his arms from around Lena and Logan's shoulders and began to run under his own power. Lena drew her sword, which Logan noted was a Sahiradin black blade. Three Sahiradin rushed down the hill behind them. She ducked behind a tree to avoid one Sahiradin's attack and thrust her sword through his side. The blade pierced the alien's scaly skin and went deep into his body.

Lena turned and ran just as the other two Sahiradin arrived. Logan blocked an attack from one of them and knocked him over with his shoulder. The Sahiradin fell awkwardly to the ground. Logan drove his sword toward his stomach, but it slid off his armor. He thrust again and sent the tip of his blade through the alien's left eye, killing him instantly.

Cap stopped running when he saw Lena fighting a third Sahiradin. The Sahiradin took hold of her sword arm, preventing her from escaping, and was preparing to run her through. Cap grabbed a log from the ground and smashed the Sahiradin in the back of his head. The unexpected heavy blow knocked him to the ground. Lena pulled her sword hand free and drove her blade into the Sahiradin's throat.

"Let's go!" yelled Logan as more Sahiradin charged down the hill toward them.

They all raced as quickly as they could, dodging around tree trunks and ducking low branches. To their right, some of the Sahiradin had caught up with fleeing troopers and cut them down from behind. And those who turned to fight were quickly overwhelmed and killed.

Logan, Cap and Lena burst through the trees and dashed across the small field at the foot of the hill. Lieutenant Styles stood on the far side. She was facing the retreating troopers with her sword raised high in the air. Logan looked over his shoulder and saw the Sahiradin had slowed their pursuit.

"Re-form the line!" she yelled. "Re-form the line!"

The remnants of the League force quickly responded and started to form a two-person-deep line where Styles stood. Logan, Lena, and Cap fell in next to L.C. Heath, Franks, Lee, and Flores. He didn't see the rest of the fire team. Logan scanned the area but couldn't see Colonel Ambrose or either of the two captains who had led them up the hill that morning.

When the end of the line was anchored, Styles quickly marched along the front of the formation, giving instruction and encouragement to the troopers. When she reached the middle, she ordered the ends to curve slightly back to help avoid being enveloped by the larger Sahiradin force. Then she turned and took several steps toward the hill to face the enemy.

The Sahiradin emerged from the shadows of the trees into the sunny field. One of them barked out a command and they formed their line. It was four-ranks deep and stretching the entire length of the field. The officer took a position next to the left end of the first row. For a few moments, everything was silent except for the breeze in the treetops and the occasional *Caw! Caw!* of a black crow in the blue sky over their heads.

The Sahiradin officer gave another command and the line started walking toward the League troops. After taking five steps, the second line began its advance. The third did likewise. The fourth turned and quickly marched back up the hill.

"They're sending one of their ranks back up the hill," said Lena.

"I guess they don't think they need them to get the job done," said Cap.

"Maybe," said Logan. "But maybe Longmire's activated the reserve units on the south side to draw off their strength."

Logan glanced to his left and saw the faces of his brothers and sisters in arms. Some were clearly frightened, but determined. Others were angry, eager for the fight to begin anew. They'd all had their first taste of battle against a powerful new enemy on the slopes of that hill and they had lost. They'd run like rabbits as soon as the order to retreat had been given. But now they'd settled down. They knew their enemy, they knew the odds, and they were ready.

"League!" yelled Lieutenant Styles. "Swords at the ready!"

As one, the League troopers lifted their swords over their heads and yelled "*Hoo*rah!" Then they turned slightly to the side, placing one foot forward, raised their guards to chest level, and pointed their blades toward the oncoming enemy.

Logan watched the line of Sahiradin marching across the field toward them. The black-armored warriors held their swords in both hands with the back of the blades resting against their shoulders, ready for the first downward swing. The wings of their line stretched much farther than the League's formation, and Logan had no doubt they would quickly close in around its edges to attack their flanks and rear.

Just then, something caught Logan's eye. "Do you see that Sahiradin?" he whispered to Cap.

"Which one? They kind of all look alike to me. Pasty and ugly," replied Cap, tightening his hand around the hilt of his sword.

"I mean the one who attacked the air base. The one who took the stone. He's standing off to the right in the trees."

Cap squinted and saw a Sahiradin standing just inside the tree line on the far side of the field. "Yeah, I see him. What's your point?"

"We have to get the Apollo Stone from him," said Logan.

"Maybe later," said Cap. "First we have to kill a few thousand Sahiradin. Then we'll get the guy."

"Steady," yelled Lieutenant Styles, still standing in front of the line. "Make them pay for it."

Just as she spoke, Logan's antiballistic shield began to flicker. Three seconds later it disappeared.

Cap looked at Logan out of the corner of his eye. "This just keeps getting better and better."

Another League soldier's shield flickered and disappeared. Then another and another. Cap's flickered and disappeared, as did Lena's.

Logan could see the Sahiradin in the shade of the trees step forward. He seemed to be grinning as he watched shield after shield flicker and disappear.

"Why aren't they shooting us?" asked Lena. "Our shields are spent. You can see they have guns locked into the back of their armor. Their shields are still working and we're sitting ducks."

"Maybe they like killing up close," said Logan. "Maybe it gives them a kick to look you in the eye when you die."

"That's fucked up," said Cap. "But possible."

The Sahiradin formation was now about thirty meters away. The Sahiradin officer shouted an order and the front line shouted something in response. They slowly lifted their swords from their shoulders and prepared to charge the League line. When they were just twenty meters away, the Sahiradin officer lifted his face to the sky and shouted a war cry. It was a terrifying howl that reminded Logan of a wild animal closing in on its prey.

Then Logan heard a whistling sound, and the howling stopped. Logan looked at the Sahiradin and saw an arrow had pierced his throat. The Sahiradin stumbled and pulled on the arrow shaft, but he could not remove it. He dropped to his knees, gurgling dark blood, and fell face forward into the Earth.

The other Sahiradin were momentarily confused, but then they let out a war cry and charged forward. More arrows flew into their ranks, striking many but more frequently bouncing off their black armor or failing to penetrate far into the scaly skin. As the Sahiradin closed the gap, Logan turned his head for a split second to look for the source of the arrows. He saw a line of men and women behind him nocking arrows and firing them over the troopers' heads at the charging Sahiradin.

Lieutenant Styles turned and saw the same thing. She called out, "Fall back! Into the trees! Fall back!"

The League soldiers quickly complied. As they ran, Logan could see shadowy shapes in the forest behind the line of archers. The archers formed gaps for the League soldiers to pass by, then fired one more volley into the fast-approaching Sahiradin.

Once inside the forest, Logan saw hundreds of men and women, perhaps thousands, dressed in the green and gray uniforms of the Northrunner army. They motioned for the League soldiers to continue past them. The archers were right behind Logan and the others. As soon as the archers had passed them, the line of soldiers knelt down to the ground, but they did not move. Three heartbeats later, one of them shouted, "Now!"

The troops lifted up long iron-tipped spears that were lying on the ground next to them. They charged out of the trees and into the Sahiradin, driving their pikes into the first and second rows. Many of the pikes slid off of the Sahiradin armor or scales, but many others tore holes in their throats, arms and legs. They fell to the ground enraged and screaming, swinging their swords but with little effect.

Seeing that the newly arrived soldiers lacked shields, the Sahiradin in the third line quickly returned their swords to their scabbards and unlocked the short-barreled guns embedded in the back of their armor. They began firing into the ranks of the charging Northrunners.

Lieutenant Styles ordered her troops to re-form and attack the Sahiradin. Lena and Cap joined the others and charged into the fray, but Logan saw something that made him pause. He looked to his left and there was Kane, dropping his bow and drawing his sword. And next to him was Ravenwood.

"Ravenwood!" Logan yelled. He ran to them.

"Ah. You're still alive, my boy!" exclaimed Ravenwood. "Glad to see you."

Yes, I'm alive, but how are you alive?" asked Logan.

"No time to explain now," said Ravenwood. "Now we must find the Apollo Stone."

"I know where it is," said Logan. "I saw the Sahiradin who took it. He's somewhere on the field."

Logan looked at the battle unfolding on the field. The Sahiradin were cutting down the Northrunner and League troops at an alarming rate, but they were suffering their own heavy losses. He searched the field and saw the Sahiradin who had taken the stone charging across the open space to join the fight.

"There." He pointed at Kurak.

"Here's our chance," said Ravenwood. "He's a Sahiradin and cannot resist the need to join his kind in battle."

The three of them ran forward and joined the other soldiers on the right side of the line. Logan saw Kurak a few meters away and tried to shift to the left to face him. Next to Logan, Kane and Ravenwood slashed and jabbed at their Sahiradin opponents who struggled to get past the Northrunners' spears.

Chapter 72

"It's the Northrunners, sir," said Captain Park as he looked down at the battle unfolding on the field. "They charged the Sahiradin line."

"What kind of support can you provide the troops?" asked General Longmire.

"They're fighting like hell, sir," replied Park. "But there's not much I can do without getting shot down in seconds. If you can neutralize their air defenses, I'll blow the hell out of them."

"I'm working on a solution. Stand by."

Longmire raised his field sensors to his eyes and looked at the southern side of the hill leading up to the Sahiradin camp. Lieutenant Colonel Brinks' troopers were nearly at the top. The mortar fire had taken out a number of hidden Sahiradin and the troopers took care of more. He turned his gaze toward the river and saw the Dellians were in full retreat, fleeing north in a jumbled panic.

Longmire looked at the Sahiradin hill again. Just as Lieutenant Colonel Brinks' force reached the top of the hill, a long line of Sahiradin emerged from the trees on the north side of the camp. They were quickly moving to reinforce the Sahiradin standing under the protection of their shield dome waiting for Brinks' force to arrive. For the moment, Brinks' force outnumbered the Sahiradin defenders in the camp by more than two to one, but she was going to lose that advantage as soon as the Sahiradin from the north side arrived.

"Brinks, attack now," said Longmire into his ICS. "Your main objective is their air defense. Go! Go! Go!"

He watched as the troops stormed over the top of the hill. The two hundred Sahiradin defending the camp's southern perimeter rushed forward. As they charged, the League line suddenly split into two groups. The larger one continued forward to engage the Sahiradin. The other group of about fifty troopers which included a demolition team, veered right toward the air-defense battery. The Sahiradin saw what was happening and adjusted their line of advance, but they were blocked by the first group of troopers. The Sahiradin formed into two tight rectangular formations of one hundred soldiers each and smashed into the League line, which gave ground but did not break.

The second group of League soldiers reached the shield dome but stopped. As Longmire had feared, the troops could not pass through the shield dome because the Sahiradin had adjusted its settings to make it solid. If kept at that level for too long, the Sahiradin inside would likely suffocate, but it could be maintained long enough to repel an attack such as this. On the north side of the camp, the Sahiradin were racing toward the air-defense system.

The demolition team struggled to force its way past the shield dome, but without success. It was as solid as glass and seemingly unbreakable. Longmire looked at the group of soldiers trying to hold back the Sahiradin and saw they were near breaking. He was about to give the order to withdraw when he heard a charge detonate. He looked to the right and saw debris flying up into the air. A second detonation followed right after the first. Then the demolition team leapt into the hole created by the explosions. They dug with shovels and bare hands where the shield met the Earth. As they had hoped, the rigidity of the shield that kept them out also prevented it from adjusting to the new contour of the ground created by their hastily dug trench. Two dozen soldiers quickly slipped through the wide but shallow trench under the dome's edge. Three of them ran for the air-defense battery while the others drew swords and stood guard.

The demolition team placed explosive charges on the air-defense battery and ran back toward the trench. The others quickly followed. A few Sahiradin reached their positions but did not attempt to stop them from escaping. Instead they ran toward the air-defense battery. But just as they arrived, it erupted in a ball of fire and smoke.

"Pull back, Brinks!" yelled Longmire into his ICS. "Artillery, lay down suppression fire and cover Brinks' withdrawal."

He toggled his ICS. "Air defense is down, Captain Park. Hit that north side."

Longmire watched as the Nightwing attack helicopters swooped in from the northwest toward the battle in the field north of the Sahiradin camp. The Nightwings fired air-to-surface missiles at the rear of the Sahiradin lines. The invaders' shields protected them from flying shrapnel and debris but did nothing against the shockwaves. Sahiradin warriors flew in the air or were thrown against each other. Many were killed by the powerful blasts. Others suffered broken bones or were knocked unconscious.

The League troops and Northrunners cheered as the helicopters attacked. After the second run, the Sahiradin began a swift but orderly withdrawal from the field, maintaining their formation and striking out against those who pursued.

The League and Northrunner troops followed the retreating Sahiradin as far as the foot of the hill, but they were not eager to enter the woods. Lieutenant Styles called for a halt, as did the Northrunner commander.

Logan turned and looked back over the field. It was littered with dead human and Sahiradin soldiers. Some lay on top of each other, sword in hand, as though still locked in combat. Above their heads and in the surrounding trees, crows and black vultures were already gathering.

Chapter 73

"The Dellians have failed us," said Grand Guardian Harken to the other Guardians seated at the long table. "I just received word that they are in full retreat."

"It was a mistake to have entrusted such an important mission to them," said Defense Guardian Castell. He looked at all of the Guardians' faces but stopped when he came to Guardian Bishop. He continued. "In exchange for a thousand tons of meat and grain and two major weapons deliveries, we got a handful of undisciplined savages to protect and assist our engineers repair the bridge. I think most would agree that was a bad bargain you negotiated, Mr. Bishop."

Guardian Bishop's face grew red. "Their numbers would have been more than adequate if the League had not sent *four* battalions against them. How did they catch wind of our plans for the bridge? Perhaps your daughter warned them."

Castell ignored Bishop's allegation and looked at Guardian Hyatt. He nodded slightly.

After a moment's hesitation, Hyatt leaned forward and cleared her throat. "I'm concerned about the repercussions this will have on our information campaign," she said, looking at Bishop and then Harken. "As we had planned, we've already announced our successful push across the Mississippi River at the bridge. People will not understand how that victory has become a defeat."

Bishop scoffed. "We just won't tell them about it. This is a momentary setback; we're going to cross the river. And since when does victory or defeat on the frontier or anywhere else affect what we tell the people?"

"Word will leak out," replied Hyatt. "It always seems to."

"Well, that's your problem to handle," retorted Bishop. "Don't try and hang information leaks on me."

"You asked how the plan to use the bridge was leaked," said Castell to Bishop. "I can tell you it wasn't leaked. The League concentrated its forces at the bridge because your creature, your Sahiradin, led them there when he tried to escape in the *Blackhawk*. And he wouldn't have been in the *Blackhawk* if you hadn't lost control of the Apollo Stone."

"Which was stolen by *your* daughter," snapped Bishop. He shot a quick look at Harken, who was sitting back in his chair calmly watching the exchange.

"That's a lie! It was stolen from under your nose by Chambers!" yelled Castell.

"And that's not all she stole," said Bishop, refusing to abandon his line of argument. "My people have linked numerous leaks of highly sensitive information, even military information, to your treasonous daughter!"

"Lies!" yelled Castell. "Damned lies!"

"Enough! Enough bickering!" yelled Harken. He rubbed his hands together and looked at the table. Everyone was silent, waiting for him to speak. Finally, he pressed a button on a PDD resting on the table. "Captain, please come in."

A moment later the door opened and a large man dressed in the uniform of the Capitol Guard entered. Behind him were four armed guards.

"Captain, please remove Guardians Bishop and Castell. Hold them in a secure place until further notice."

Castell looked at Harken and then at the two guards as they approached him. "What the hell is going on? Guardian Harken. Joseph. You know this is a mistake. We're about to launch a major offensive and you're removing the head of your military? Think about the impact arresting me will have on our plans! What will the troops think? Be reasonable!"

Harken did not respond to Castell. He simply stared at him, his face expressionless, as the guards pulled him from his chair. Castell struggled in vain against the strong hands pulling him up.

In contrast to Castell's loud protestations, Bishop said nothing. He simply looked at Harken and smiled. The guards reached for his arms, but he waved them off. Then he stood up, smoothed his tie, and buttoned his suit jacket. He held his hands out to the guards.

"Slap on the cuffs," he said with a grin.

When both men had been escorted out of the room, Harken looked at Guardian Hyatt and said, "Castell and Bishop are guilty of gross incompetence and perhaps even treason. I'll convene a tribunal to investigate further. Please prepare an appropriate statement that won't upset the people. They must feel reassured by this little shakeup in leadership and believe that it will lead to victory and prosperity. We will begin the process of selecting new Guardians after the offensive has come to its successful conclusion. In the meantime, I will assume responsibility for both Justice and Defense. Additionally, authority over the Republican

Guard and Republican Special Forces will now rest exclusively in the office of the Grand Guardian.

"Yes sir," said Hyatt in a slightly unsteady voice. "I'll have something ready for your approval within the hour."

"I look forward to reading it," said Harken. He stood and left the room.

Chapter 74

As they marched back across the little patch of land where so much blood had been spilled, Logan searched the faces of the Sahiradin bodies. Although they had distinct facial features, he was struck by how many similarities they shared. Except for one with black hair, they all had shoulder-length white hair. And each one had a tall, lean body type.

Soldiers from the League and Northrunner armies were assisting the wounded. Talon helicopters were already landing to ferry them to medical aid stations. Others were laying the dead in a row along the tree line. Logan saw a Sahiradin body lying face down on top of a human. Something seemed familiar about the alien. He rolled the Sahiradin over with a push of his boot.

"Ravenwood!" he yelled. "Come here!"

Ravenwood ran to Logan and asked, "What is it?"

Logan pointed at the Sahiradin. "Recognize this guy?"

Ravenwood peered at the face of the Sahiradin. "Ah, yes. Our old friend. And he's still alive. We must get him away from here before the Sahiradin return for their own."

Logan caught Cap's attention, and waved for him to come and assist.

"Ravenwood!" exclaimed Cap when he arrived. "I thought you were dead."

"I wish people would stop saying that," said Ravenwood.

"How'd you recover so fast? What happened?"

"Never mind that now," he replied. "Help us with this Sahiradin."

"Holy shit," said Cap, looking at the Sahiradin's face. "Is this the guy?"

"This is the guy," said Logan. "Grab his legs."

As Talon transport helicopters filled with the seriously wounded lifted off from the field, they carried the Sahiradin to the tree line, where they were able to secure a stretcher that was no longer needed. They bound his hands and feet and placed him on the stretcher. Then they followed the other able-bodied soldiers into the forest. They walked through the trees in a northerly direction for about a kilometer until they came to a newly plowed farm field. The Northrunners then put them on a road that would lead them around the still heavily defended enemy hill and back to the League's base.

As the highest ranking surviving League officer, Lieutenant Styles thanked the Northrunners for their assistance. She ordered the remaining League troops to fall in. When the troopers were in formation, they saluted their Northrunner counterparts, who returned the compliment.

As the Northrunners marched north, Logan and the others returned to the spot where they had set down the stretcher. They were joined by Lieutenant Styles as they pulled off the Sahiradin's light but strong breast armor and searched for the Apollo Stone, but they could not find it. As they searched, he began to move and groan, though he did not regain consciousness.

"And you think this is the Sahiradin who's been helping the PRA all these years?" asked Styles.

"I'm pretty sure," said Logan.

"I'm positive," said Ravenwood.

She looked at Ravenwood and let her eyes rest on his face. "I seem to recall you were reported dead," she said after a moment.

"An exaggeration," he said without elaborating.

"I see," said the lieutenant, not convinced but unwilling to press the matter. She looked at Kurak and continued. "Let's bring him along. We've got about a two-hour march ahead of us. You'll have to keep up, so switch out carriers every fifteen minutes." She assigned several troopers to assist.

They lifted the stretcher, with Logan and Cap taking the back two handles and Ravenwood and Kane taking the front two. They followed the line of troopers marching along the dirt and gravel road, which ran straight west along the field for about three-quarters of a kilometer. Then it bent to the south and disappeared into the forest. Logan looked at the unconscious Sahiradin and then up at the blue sky. It was about 10 a.m. and Logan could tell it was going to be a hot day. He hoped it would be worth the effort to carry their prisoner through the oppressive heat for the next two hours.

As they walked, Logan said to Ravenwood, "So tell us what happened. And don't say the report of your death was an 'exaggeration'. The last we saw of you, Kane was loading your body into an old helicopter. Then he flew you up north to bury you."

Kane interrupted, "Not to bury him. To return him to the place where he came from."

"So what did you do?" Lena asked Kane.

"I placed him on the rock overlooking the waters of Crow Wing where my great grandfather had found him. I started a fire and stood vigil, talking to him, remembering our times together. It was a moonless night and dark as pitch. Then, in the early-morning hours I saw a shimmering light around his body. At first I thought it was a trick of the firelight, but it grew brighter and brighter. Then he woke."

Cap said, "I know they say seeing is believing, but this is impossible. You were dead, Ravenwood. You'd stopped breathing. Your heart stopped beating."

Ravenwood adjusted his grip on the stretcher and replied, "I'm not sure myself. But there are special places in the world. Places of power where the laws of physics don't apply in quite the same way as one would expect. The rock at Crow Wing is one such place."

"There's more to it than that. I've never heard of a special place where the dead come back to life," said Cap. "And what about your stomach wound? You were stabbed all the way through your back. Even if it didn't kill you, it should take weeks to recover enough to even walk."

"I've always been a quick healer," replied Ravenwood.

"Whatever happened at that lake, it's a good thing you came when you did," said Lena. She took his free hand in hers. "I don't think we would have made it out of that fight without your help. And the help of the Northrunners, of course."

"As for the Northrunners, you can thank Kane for that," said Ravenwood. "He's well known and respected among the Northrunners. When he asked them to come to your aid, they didn't hesitate."

An hour and a half later, they reached the League camp, and the troopers Styles had assigned to assist set down the stretcher. General Longmire and two guards came out of the nearby command tent to greet them.

"Glad you made it back," said the general. "That was one hell of a fight, and you all performed admirably."

He looked at the still-unconscious Kurak and said, "So this is the Sahiradin who was helping the PRA."

"Yes sir," said Logan. "Unfortunately, he didn't have the stone on him."

"He may not have the Apollo Stone," said Kane. "But he has useful information. He's been in the center of the PRA's efforts to develop advanced weapons for many years. He could tell us a lot if we can get him to cooperate."

"Agreed," said Longmire. Turning to the two guards he said, "Take him to the medical tent and ask the doctors to do what they can to make sure he recovers." Then he nodded to the group and returned to the command tent.

Before the guards picked up the stretcher, Cap said, "You all realize he's responsible for the deaths of billions of people. Maybe we should torture the hell out of him. Whatever the punishment is for the crimes he's committed, it isn't enough."

"Defeating him and his kind and throwing them back into their corner of the galaxy is the greatest punishment we can inflict," said Ravenwood.

A soldier trotted out of the command tent and asked Kane and Ravenwood to join Longmire and several Northrunner officers who had just arrived. Ravenwood was rather surprised by the invitation, given the level of skepticism the military traditionally held for his opinions.

"I guess the evidence has become too convincing to ignore," he said with a smile.

"Don't volunteer us for anything," yelled Cap as Ravenwood disappeared into the tent.

Logan, Cap, and Lena then walked toward their camp to take off their gear and get some rest. As they walked, there was a massive explosion to their right. They jogged over to the edge of the hill and looked down toward the bridge to see wood and metal flying high into the air. A second and a third explosion followed. The explosions caused the bridge to break in two. The western half completely collapsed into the river. The eastern half still stood, though it leaned to the south at a fifteen-degree angle and much of its superstructure fell into the river.

"Well, the PRA won't be using that bridge to cross the river," said Lena.

"I guess not," agreed Cap.

They watched the debris flow downstream for a few minutes, then joined L.C. Heath and the two surviving fire team members, Flores and Lee, at their campsite. They all took short showers and went to the mess tent for a meal. They toasted their fallen comrades and talked about what the upcoming battle with the PRA would be like. They'd all heard that the PRA's First Corp was on its way north by train. And although they'd destroyed the bridge, they knew that wouldn't keep a determined enemy from crossing, but at least they'd slowed them down. They hoped it was enough to give the defenders in St. Louis a chance.

They talked about that day's battle against the Sahiradin. They all commented on how hard it was to pierce the aliens' skin, but Logan shared that they were vulnerable in the neck and under the jaw. Lena showed them the Sahiradin sword she'd picked up off the battlefield. It was very light. The edge was sharpened to an atom's width but didn't show any nicks or chips.

"And it cuts through their skin like it was paper," she said as she ran her thumb along the side of the blade.

After they finished eating, they heard the assembly bugle. They hurried to the command tent and fell into line in the clearing in front of it.

When the troopers had gathered, General Longmire came out of the tent and stepped onto the top of a wooden table where everyone could see him. Several Northrunner officers and Kane also emerged from the command tent.

"Soldiers of the League, I want to commend you all on an outstanding performance today," he said. "You fought like hell to secure the bridge against an entrenched and heavily armed enemy. Well done. You heard our demolitions team blowing it to hell a little while ago. No PRA tanks will be crossing that bridge any time soon."

They all cheered.

Longmire clapped his hands a couple times and gave the troops a thumbs up, then he continued. "While some of you attacked the bridge others engaged against a new enemy, the Sahiradin, in close combat. For centuries humans have wondered what our first encounter with intelligent alien life would be like. Now we know. Bloody. But with the help of our Northrunner friends, you forced the bastards to abandon the field."

The soldiers cheered and clapped. General Longmire nodded toward the Northrunner military representatives with whom he'd been talking inside the command tent. "I know that, together, we can defeat not only the PRA but whatever the Sahiradin throw at us too."

"*Hoo*rah!" yelled a trooper. The call was echoed by the other troopers, along with applause.

Longmire faced the Northrunners and clapped his hands. "Now, I know there are a lot of questions about the Sahiradin. I'll tell you our current understanding of the situation." He folded his arms across his chest and took a breath before speaking.

"The Sahiradin have been fighting a war against an allied group of species called the Lycians for a very long time. Maybe hundreds of years. Their war has brought them to Earth because of an item they believe is here. It's something the Sahiradin use to travel from star to star. Now, that *might* be why they're here. Might not be. Frankly, I don't give a damn. Whatever the reason, they're not welcome on Earth. And if they don't leave on their own, we'll put a boot up their ass."

"*Hoo*rah!" yelled the soldiers.

"Now as you all know if you had bothered to look up in the sky the other night, the Sahiradin and the Lycians had a battle up there in Earth orbit. The word from central command is the Lycians drove off the Sahiradin ship, at least as far as the moon. I don't need to tell you that we should not assume the Sahiradin are beaten. They might have lost a battle, but they've been fighting the Lycians for a very long time, so one lost battle won't mean much."

He looked at the faces of the young men and women under his command. Then he said, "I'll be honest with you. It's going to get worse before it gets better. We have word that both sides have more ships on the way to Earth, and their fight might continue here on the planet."

He let that news sink in for a few seconds, then he gave them a broad smile. "But we'll deal with that if and when it comes. For now, enjoy your victory. Get some rest tonight, and be ready for whatever tomorrow has in store for us."

A voice shouted, "Dismissed!"

Logan, Lena, and Cap began walking toward their camp when a soldier called them into the command tent. When he entered, Logan saw Ravenwood, Kane and two Northrunner officers talking to General Longmire near the center of the tent. The three privates walked to the group, stood at attention, and saluted.

Longmire looked at them and said, "At ease."

"You heard what I just said about the fleets approaching Earth," he said. He pointed at a piece of paper with something written on it. "Well, we just got word they're already here. At least the Lycian fleet is. The Sahiradin fleet is believed to be gathering near the moon. It won't be long before they lock horns again, and when they do the Sahiradin will come for their troops on the hill."

Longmire paused before continuing, deciding how much more needed to be shared. Then he said, "As you may have guessed, Central Command's initial position was to do our best to stay out of a conflict between two alien species, despite our engagement with the Sahiradin today. But that changed about twenty-four hours ago. We intercepted and deciphered a PRA transmission stating the Sahiradin had accepted the PRA offer. We don't know what the terms are, but it's a safe bet they'll be providing some kind of mutual aid. I would consider them allies at this point."

"That would explain why the Sahiradin parked those troops on the hill," said Cap. "If we hadn't attacked their camp from the north, they would have hit us at the bridgehead."

"Maybe," answered Longmire. "But I think it's bigger than a little help here on the Mississippi. Don't forget that prisoner you caught was not only living in the PRA for many years, he was also assisting their top scientists develop weapons based on Sahiradin technology. If they've struck a bargain, he's probably in the middle of it."

"Where is he now?" asked Lena.

"Still unconscious, but the doc thinks he'll be awake soon," replied Longmire.

"It's too bad he didn't have the Apollo Stone on him," said Cap. "We could have used it to bargain with the Sahiradin. Get them to take their fight with the Lycians somewhere else."

"You can't bargain with them," said Ravenwood. "They won't tolerate our continued existence."

"Which brings me to the reason why I asked you three to come," said Longmire. He nodded to a soldier, who brought him a metal box from a nearby table. Longmire opened the box and pulled out a golden sphere about the size of a tangerine.

"You said the Apollo Stone was about the size of a marble, but I wonder if this might be it," said Longmire.

Logan's heart leapt in his chest when he saw the golden sphere. "Yes. I'm sure this is it. It was in a metal sphere when we got it, too. And it was about this same size."

"How did we get this?" asked Lena, puzzled. "We didn't get inside the Sahiradin camp and our prisoner didn't have it."

Longmire grinned. "We *did* get into the Sahiradin camp. Remember when we blew up their air-defense battery? While our troops were laying charges, an enterprising young private first class slipped into their command tent unnoticed and grabbed as much as he could lay his hands on and stuffed it in a backpack."

Ravenwood held the sphere in his hand and slowly turned it from side to side, gazing at the perfectly smooth surface. "This changes everything. We still need help from the Lycians. But if we can keep this out of Sahiradin hands, we might have a chance. We might win."

"We have the sphere," said Cap. "But it would be nice if we could confirm the Apollo Stone is really in there." He looked at Logan. "Does your medallion work on this?"

Logan retrieved the medallion from his pocket and held it near the sphere, but nothing happened.

"We need the proper key. This medallion probably only works on the sphere we had," said Logan.

Cap scoffed and said, "Okay, who's going back into the Sahiradin camp to get it?"

"Maybe we don't need to," said Lena. "Let's go talk to our Sahiradin friend."

Chapter 75

Kurak's eyes flew open when Logan pulled the medallion from its hiding place in the lining of his tunic. He screamed at Logan in his native Sahiradin language, causing Logan to jump back in surprise. Kurak struggled to rise up from the cot, but his hands and feet were tied securely to its frame so he had to satisfy himself with hurling insults.

"Oh, you tricky bastard!" said Logan, laughing.

"How long have you been pretending to be unconscious, Kurak, former captain of the *Vanquisher*?" asked Ravenwood.

Kurak looked at Ravenwood and cursed at him in Sahiradin, "Vleck dam Aresch!"

Logan held the medallion high the air between his thumb and index finger where Kurak could see it. It was black and smaller than the one Logan's grandfather had sent him. On one side was an etched image of a mountain with a single star above it. On the other was an intricate grooved pattern similar to Logan's medallion. Kurak watched intently as Logan slowly rotated the medallion between his fingers and studied its markings.

"You really don't want us to have this do you," said Logan with a grin as he looked down on Kurak.

"It is a personal item," said Kurak, suddenly showing a warm smile. "Keep it as my gift to you if you wish."

"We've had enough gifts from you," said Lena.

Kurak looked up at her. He shrugged his shoulders with indifference.

"You smug son of a bitch," said Cap. "You tried to wipe us out, but you failed. And now we know who you are. We're going to kick your scaly asses off our planet!"

"I don't know what you're talking about," said Kurak with a surprised look on his face.

"The asteroid attack," said Cap. "We know it was you. And you're going to pay. You and your nasty, pasty friends."

Kurak slowly shook his head, a menacing laugh bubbling up from his throat. "You stupid simpering Alamani," he said, venom dripping from each word. "You have no idea what you're up against."

He stared at Cap for a moment, then he spat at him. "You're a damned infestation," he snarled. "There won't be one of you left on this planet when we're finished. Your kind thought you could keep us under your heel, wipe us out. But now we've got our boot on your throat! This planet will soon be free of your stink!"

"And I supposed the Sahiradin will replace us?" asked Lena.

Kurak laid his head back on the cot and looked at the ceiling. "If we choose," he said without looking at her.

"Come now, Kurak," said Ravenwood. "Let's be honest. It has always been your plan to use Earth as a remote base to build your ships. And with the help of the Kaiytáva, you'll attack the Lycians any place in the galaxy at the time of your choosing."

Kurak looked at Ravenwood, eyeing him up and down, and said, "I remember you from Jasper Air Base. I slit your stinking guts open. You should be dead."

"And your old bones should be in the foulest hole in the Sacred Mountain's catacombs," replied Ravenwood. "Yet, here we are."

Kurak narrowed his eyes and gave Ravenwood a long, appraising look. Then he said, "I don't know what you are or why you *think* you know the truth, but you are misinformed. I wonder how many people have you misled with your ravings? Do you know who the Alamani were? What they did to my people? I…"

"You're not dealing with fools, Kurak!" said Ravenwood, cutting him off. "We are not the useful idiots you've been manipulating in the east. We know that with the Kaiytáva in your possession you will be able to go anywhere in the universe you choose. And you won't need the nearby *khâl* gate any longer. You'll disable it, and then it will be impossible for the Lycians to reach your safe haven on Earth."

"It is the *Lycians* who are the aggressors!" yelled Kurak. "The Sahiradin have always stood for what is just. We have always protected the Five Pillars of the Law against the assaults of the separatist Lycian scum, just as we did against the treacherous Alamani. We will annihilate the Lycians and these ignorant, mongrel Alamani descendants!"

Ravenwood leaned closer to the Sahiradin's face. "There is one more aspect of your plan we have not discussed. If Earth is to be used as a true safe haven, you will need to bring your queen here. She is your single source of reproduction, your sole means of regeneration. Without her the Sahiradin will die out. Tell me, is her new cycle upon us?"

Kurak's already pale face seemed to turn ashen as he listened to Ravenwood speak. He stared into the old man's eyes as though trying to see behind them into his mind. He opened his mouth but no words came out. But the old hatred soon returned to his pale blue eyes and he regained control over himself.

"Who are you?" he asked, angrily. "You're not human. You're not a true Alamani. They're all dead, and you're too oafishly big and hairy to be one. Who are you?!"

Ignoring Kurak's questions, Ravenwood continued asking about the queen. "I wonder if she's on board one of those ships near our moon. I wonder if you'd risk bringing her here before you've secured the planet. Gamble it all with a desperate throw of the dice."

Kurak did not respond. But his eyes briefly betrayed a tumult of anger and fear roiling beneath the surface of his mind. He took a deep breath and clenched his hands into tight fists.

"I suppose it would depend on how desperate the situation is on your home world. Wouldn't it?" said Ravenwood. "If she is safe there, you'll leave her. If she is threatened, you'll move her."

Kurak closed his eyes, as if doing so would make Ravenwood disappear. "Theorize all you wish. Victory will be ours," he said after a long pause. "I will no longer answer your questions."

Chapter 76

After they left the medical tent, Logan asked Ravenwood if everything he'd said about the Sahiradin queen was true.

"It is," said Ravenwood. "Each Sahiradin generation comes from a single female, a queen. And she is fertile only once every ten Earth years. During her fertility period, she produces millions of eggs, which a single male consort fertilizes."

"Sounds exhausting," said Cap.

"I understand it is a rather tumultuous process," said Ravenwood.

"It explains why every Sahiradin looks so similar," said Logan.

"Each generation has its distinguishing characteristics because each is sired by a different male consort," said Ravenwood. "But yes, there is a great deal of similarity within each generation."

"Why is she fertile only every ten years?" asked Cap. "Doesn't seem like Mother Nature made a good evolutionary choice."

Ravenwood shrugged. "Yet each generation, millions of Sahiradin, reaches maturity in just ten years. Perhaps that is the reason."

"They mature that fast?" asked Logan.

"Yes. And they train hard throughout their youth so they are ready to fight when they reach maturity."

They walked in silence for few moments. Then Lena asked, "If there's only one fertile female, does it mean only males are born?"

"Excellent question," replied Ravenwood with a smile. "The answer is no. Although the very large majority of offspring a queen produces is male or gender neutral, some females are born, but they are not fertile. Only when the queen is in the final cycle of her life will she produce a fertile female to replace her."

"What are the gender-neutral Sahiradin like?" asked Cap.

"Surprisingly unaggressive. They are used as servants, builders, administrators, that sort of thing," said Ravenwood. "They are also responsible for rearing the young Sahiradin."

"What about the sterile females?" asked Logan. "I don't think we've seen any female Sahiradin yet. Are they not allowed to be soldiers?"

Ravenwood looked at Logan and his eyes grew dark. "Quite the contrary. Although there are few females born, they are the most formidable warriors the Sahiradin have. And they are totally committed to protecting the queen. They make up her personal guard, the Karazan. You will know a Karazan from her long dark hair and blood-red armor."

"We haven't seen any soldiers in red," said Cap. "They've all been males in black armor."

Ravenwood nodded and said, "Be thankful you haven't. I doubt you will see any Karazan on Earth. The queen periodically sends a certain number of them into battle to keep them sharp and satisfy their bloodlust. But as I say, there are few of them and they are rarely seen."

"But if we do see one," continued Lena, "how should we fight them? What are their vulnerabilities?"

"They have none to my knowledge," said Ravenwood. "And they usually fight in cohorts of twenty, so where there's one, many more are certainly nearby."

Ravenwood stopped and faced Lena. "I've seen you fight. You're extremely talented. No doubt you've been training since you were quite young."

"Yes," she said. "My father insisted on it, so I grew up playing with swords instead of dolls. My trainer was a Baku Sword Master."

Logan raised an eyebrow upon hearing this. The Baku of the northern Himalayas were regarded as the deadliest swordsmen in the world, pre- and post-Impact. Logan had heard stories, perhaps apocryphal yet widely believed, that Baku warriors had defended their homeland against post-Impact Chinese, Indian, and Russian invaders using nothing more than iron blades and deadly cunning. Legends say that foreign soldiers would awaken, horrified by the discovery that every fourth comrade's throat had been slit while they slept. After a few such experiences, terrorized armies would refuse to march any farther into Baku territory, forcing several ambitious despots to abandon their dreams of forging a Central Asian empire. And those armies which nevertheless pressed on into the foothills of Hell's Teeth, as the mountains in that region had come to be known, were soon cut to pieces by Baku warriors.

Yet, despite offers of wealth and power, the Baku rarely revealed their warrior secrets to outsiders because their skills were not simply martial in nature. The way of the blade, as they called it, was deeply rooted in ancient mysticism which few non-Baku truly understood. The fact that Lena trained under a Baku Sword Master spoke both to her father's influence and to her natural talent. The Baku would never waste their time on anyone who was anything less than exceptional.

Ravenwood smiled and said, "The Baku are extraordinary swordsmen." He paused and placed his hands on her shoulders. "Yet, despite your skills, if you see a Karazan, my advice is to run. Run like hell's demons are at your throat. Because they are, my dear. They truly are."

Chapter 77

Once again inside the command tent, Logan held Kurak's medallion near the gold sphere, but the little interface port did not open. He pulled the medallion away and tried again, but nothing happened.

"What are we waiting for?" asked Consul Sawyer, impatiently.

"It's supposed to open up," said Logan. "The stone should be inside."

"Are you sure this is the key to open it?" she asked.

"Pretty sure, yes."

"Perhaps we shouldn't be surprised it doesn't open," said Ravenwood. "This medallion may be just one part of the key. The Sahiradin could easily have encrypted it for voice recognition or a verbal password as well."

"So the medallion is useless," said General Longmire.

"Not useless," said Ravenwood. "Just insufficient by itself."

"Let's go talk to our prisoner again," said Cap. "He knows the password."

Ravenwood shook his head. "He won't tell us."

"What if we beat the hell out of him?" asked Cap. "I'll go first."

"Sahiradin thrive on physical confrontation," said Lena. "He might actually like it. It would be an opportunity to prove his worth."

"I agree," said Ravenwood. "It would allow him to reaffirm his warrior code. He would also enjoy seeing how desperate we've become."

Logan looked at Ravenwood and said, "Do you speak their language?"

Ravenwood gave a slight shrug. "I know something of it, yes," he said. "It is an exceedingly ugly language, and I prefer not to speak it."

"You'll need to get over that," replied Logan. "You might be the only one who can open the sphere."

"It could be any word or phrase," protested Ravenwood. "The chances of my guessing the right thing are very slim. Slim beyond calculation."

"It's worth a shot," said Sawyer, fixing her gaze on Ravenwood.

"Very well," said Ravenwood, reluctantly. "Let me have the medallion and I will try."

Chapter 78

On board the Lycian ship, *Intrepid,* Admiral Var-Imar was giving final instructions for the upcoming battle against the Sahiradin fleet. She had read the report of the recent land battle between the Alamani and the Sahiradin. Though well versed in military history, she struggled to recall any precedents for what the report had said.

"I find it difficult to believe the Alamani are capable of engaging the Sahiradin in battle at all, much less doing so well against them," she said to her first officer. "The histories of the great Sahiradin betrayal and subsequent massacres make no reference to Alamani directly engaging in battle. Never. Not once."

"I agree that it is perplexing, Admiral," said the first officer.

Admiral Var-Imar continued. "Of course the Alamani helped the Lycian allies develop advanced weapons and ships, but they never directly participated in any battles. Even when the Sahiradin put them to the blade by the thousands, they did not fight back, always preferring to run. Physical conflict simply was not in their nature, as impossible for them as sprouting wings and flying away."

"Admiral," said one of the officers near a tactical display station. "The Sahiradin are landing their troops. Our fighter craft are engaging but the enemy transports are protected by a strong contingent of escort fighters. We expect the large majority of their troops will reach P3's surface unharmed."

"Understood," said Var-Imar. She looked at her first officer and said, "Commander, give the order to land troops. And I want an immediate report on how the Alamani respond. We believe they understand our intentions, but there's no guarantee they will welcome our presence."

"Yes admiral."

The commander walked toward one of the duty stations. Moments later, Admiral Var-Imar looked at the large three-dimensional display showing the troop transports and their fighter escorts flowing from the Lycian ships toward the long river on the land mass below them. When the last of the ships was under way, Var-Imar looked around the bridge. Apprehensive faces watched the ships as they descended to the planet's surface, momentarily glowing from the friction of passing through the atmosphere.

"Open a line to all ships," said Var-Imar to her communications officer. A moment later the officer nodded her head.

"Lycian brothers and sisters," said the admiral in a strong voice. "Now that the Sahiradin are landing their main force, they'll send their fleet against us. I don't need to tell you how disastrous it would be if the Sahiradin Scales regain the last Kaiytáva. None of our worlds will be safe from them. And if they expel us from this remote system, we will have no way of retaliating. They will have control of the only *khâl*, and although we are building a second one, it will not be completed soon enough. That means we are it. We are the only members of the Lycian Alliance who can prevent the Sahiradin from destroying cities and indiscriminately killing millions upon millions of us."

Var-Imar gave her listeners a moment to consider her words, then she said, "You're all aware of the roles you play in our battle plan. Some of you will be fighting on the surface of a new world populated by a strange new species. Some of you will face the dangers of ship-to-ship battle. But be strong – understand that with every Scale you kill, that's one less who can murder our families."

"Now, we all know the Scales are determined warriors. We must match that determination and surpass it with an iron will to win this battle. Our plan of attack is a good one, but timing is absolutely critical. If everyone performs his or her duty, we will be victorious. The Ancestors' blessing on you all."

Chapter 79

Colonel Linsky sat in the back seat of the PRA Army staff officer vehicle. A small SPD flag waved over its left headlight, and the PRA national flag waved above the right one. He looked out the left side window and gazed at the ancient train tracks. Just beyond them was the Mississippi River, still swollen from spring rains and snowmelt. To his right was dense forest and high hills, populated by wild tribes and Dellian fanatics.

Linsky's vehicle approached a column of regular army troops marching north. The soldiers shifted to the right in order to allow his vehicle to pass. A few saluted as he drove by. Linsky occasionally returned the salute with a touch to the rim of his hat with his left hand. After about ten minutes his vehicle caught up to the Special Forces troops. Linsky looked at their faces and knew the Red Legs were hardened veterans, every last one of them. They were marching in four straight columns. They moved to the side so he could pass, but they did not salute. Finally, Linsky reached the armored column. Tanks, armored vehicles, and artillery units travelled in two columns, one on each side of the train tracks, forcing Linsky's driver to drive on the railroad ties. Linsky placed his hand on the seat to steady himself as the staff car bumped and slid on the uneven surface.

Linsky knew the soldiers didn't like having to march from the place thirty kilometers to the south where they had disembarked from the trains. If things had gone according to plan, the one hundred thousand troops of the First Corp would have ridden by train across the river and as far south on the west side as the tracks would allow. At that point, they would have marched into the heart of the League and slammed into the northern flank of the enemy.

But those plans had to be modified because the only repairable bridge for five hundred kilometers up or down the river had been demolished by a handful of League troopers. But the loss of the bridge simply delayed the inevitable. The First Corp was adapting to the situation and would still achieve its objective of uniting with the much larger PRA force near St. Louis. The armies were like a hammer and anvil, and together they would crush the much smaller League army.

Linsky looked ahead and saw that the twin columns of armored vehicles were splitting away from the train tracks and following an old road up into the hills overlooking the river valley. Linsky's vehicle had difficulty weaving between tanks to reach the top, but once there Linsky ordered the driver to stop. He got out and surveyed the landscape. He could see the small League force on the western side of the river. To his right he saw PRA soldiers busily positioning artillery pieces that would soon begin pummeling the League camp into dust. In addition to the artillery, a number of tanks had already formed a line on the edge of the hill. Their guns were pointed high, ready for a high-trajectory bombardment.

Linsky saw a few puffs of smoke from the League camp. Their artillery batteries were targeting the PRA camp and the column as it emerged from the protection of the hillside. PRA soldiers in the camp saw the puffs of smoke as well and ran for cover, but as the first shell approached it exploded in the air above the camp. Another did the same, as did the next dozen rounds. The explosions were quite loud, but the shells failed to reach the ground.

Linsky smiled. The bargain he and Grand Guardian Harken had struck with the Sahiradin was already paying off. The shield dome they had given him would protect the PRA troops as they assembled their forces and prepared for the charge across the river. Linsky estimated they could fit ten to fifteen thousand troops plus artillery and tank support under the dome. The rest would remain behind the hill and out of League gun range, waiting for the order to attack. Of course, the PRA artillery could not return fire without lowering the shield, but being able to prepare without the threat of bombardment was enough.

Linsky walked past PRA soldiers as they hurried to erect thousands of tents and establish supply depots, medical stations, chow halls and the myriad of other things necessary to organize a base camp for one hundred thousand soldiers. He carefully stepped around some muddy ground ripped up by tank treads and entered the command tent. General Vessey and his staff were reviewing the latest high-altitude images of League positions, which the Sahiradin had provided.

"General Vessey," said Colonel Linsky as he ignored staff officers and walked straight to the general. "I am Grand Guardian Harken's special advisor, Colonel Alexander Linsky." He saluted with his left hand.

General Vessey, a stocky man in his fifties with a double chin and thick black hair, removed his black-framed reading glasses. "Ah, yes. Colonel Linsky," he said unenthusiastically while casually returning the salute. "We received a communication informing us that you would be coming."

Linsky's eyes wandered to the right and locked on to a number of view screens standing on a large rectangular table in the middle of the command tent. He tried to read the data and examine the images rolling across the screens, but General Vessey moved slightly toward Linsky, forcing him to take a step back away from the table.

"How are things progressing?" asked the SPD officer, taking in the disapproving expressions on the faces of the general's staff.

"Just fine, Colonel," said General Vessey. "But I must say it is unusual for there to be an SPD presence on the front lines. You and your colleagues normally do your work behind the lines after territory has been taken." He smiled for a moment, but it quickly faded.

Linsky stiffened and gave Vessey a thin, mirthless smile of his own. "Yes General. The SPD is responsible for securing newly acquired territory. As you know, just because the enemy's defenses have been overcome does not mean the territory is secure. There are spies, malcontents, and the misinformed which must be dealt with. And because civilian authority has broken down after your troops have done their job, someone has to assume the responsibilities of the mayor, the police chief, the fire chief, and so on."

General Vessey wasn't listening to the colonel, having returned his attention to the information in the view screens.

Undaunted by the general's lack of interest, Linsky spoke loudly and addressed everyone around the table. "The SPD takes on all of these challenges in order to cement your victories and to ensure there is a peaceful transition from violent enemy to ardent supporter."

"You talk a lot," said Vessey, suddenly looking Linsky in the eye. "Grand Guardian Harken may have appointed you as some kind of advisor, but let's be clear. I will not tolerate any interference with my command of the First Corp. We are an army and our mission is to destroy the adversary's army, not round up women, children, or 'the misinformed,' as you put it."

Linsky narrowed his eyes and said, "You say you will not tolerate interference. I wonder what do you mean by that? Does interference include things like securing an antiballistic shield which is protecting this entire camp from enemy artillery?" He pointed his finger into the air, listening as several artillery rounds exploded overhead. "Does it include securing an alliance with the Sahiradin, a highly advanced and powerful species who will help us gain victory?"

General Vessey took a step closer to Linsky until their faces were nearly touching, but this time Linsky did not step back. "This is not a political operation," said the general through clenched teeth. "This is a military action and I have complete authority to prosecute the upcoming battle in the manner I see fit. Stay the hell away from me and my troops! And just for the record, I don't trust this dome or the freak show aliens who gave it to you."

Vessey gave Linsky a slight push with his finger, forcing the SPD officer to step back.

"But you should trust the Sahiradin, General Vessey," responded Linsky with a smile, which he shared with everyone watching the exchange. Then he said in a loud voice, "The Sahiradin have been on Earth for many years, assisting us to develop advanced weapons that have saved soldiers' lives. You're familiar with the antiballistic shield and our high-performance aircraft, yes? We have them to thank for these and many more advances. They have shown their good will toward us time and again. Now it is time for us to show our support for them in their fight against an ancient enemy who seeks to annihilate them. They are honorable warriors. *We* are honorable warriors. We share common values and goals, and together we will secure victory over our enemies, here on Earth and elsewhere."

General Vessey's face turned red with anger. "Colonel Linsky. I will not be lectured by you or any other SPD thug on the topic of honor. I have served in this nation's army for thirty years, and my first duty has always been to protect the Republic. As for the Sahiradin, I will decide whether to cooperate with them."

The two men stared at each other for a moment. Linsky wore an impassive expression, but Vessey's face was still red with anger.

Then Linsky smiled and said, "I understand your position, General. But if you wish to continue to receive valuable battlefield intelligence," Linsky pointed at the high-altitude surveillance images, "you will cooperate with me and the Sahiradin. They are providing substantial support which will save many of your soldiers' lives. And if you cannot bring yourself to honor our bargain with the Sahiradin, I'm sure the Grand Guardian can find a duty for which you are better suited. How would you like to spend your remaining years below ground swinging a pick?"

Linsky leaned close to the general and whispered, "No one is invulnerable. When was the last time you spoke to Guardian Castell?"

Linsky paused to ensure his point was understood, then he looked at the faces of the other soldiers. "I am going now to report to Grand Guardian Harken on our progress, but I will be back in an hour and I expect to receive a thorough update on the status of our preparations and regular briefings thereafter."

He gave the general a casual salute, turned around, and exited the command tent.

Chapter 80

Major General Quince, a fifty-three-year-old bald man with a crooked boxer's nose and ruddy complexion, stepped out of the Talon helicopter. Longmire was waiting for him at the edge of the landing space and saluted him as he approached. Quince returned his salute. They shook hands and walked together toward the command tent.

"Well done, General," said Quince as he scanned the camp and the ongoing preparations to resist the PRA assault. "You pushed the Dellians back across the river, blew the bridge, and I'm told you got a hold of this Apollo Stone I've been hearing about. Hell, you even got the Northrunners to pitch in. No one's accomplished that in over fifty years of trying. Keep this up and you might get another star on your collar like mine."

"I can't take credit for it, sir," replied Longmire. "The troops were outstanding."

General Quince nodded his head. "You and your troops here have saved our bacon, I won't lie. And it's given us an opportunity to inflict further damage on the enemy as they cross the river. That's why we decided to bring up two full divisions of the League's Second Corp. That's twenty thousand troops, plus armor and artillery. That'll put you at about thirty-five thousand troops to their one hundred thousand, but the river and terrain will work to your advantage if you can get everything in place. The PRA is committed to executing a pincer maneuver, and to do that they'll need to get the northern army cross the river ASAP."

"Yes sir," said Longhorn, "but are we sure they'll try to cross here?"

Quince stopped and pulled out his field scanner. He looked at the PRA position on the east side of the river. "Well, it certainly looks like they've decided this is the spot. And that makes sense. If they go farther north the river widens and they'll have to face tenacious Northrunner defenders well versed at repelling Dellian incursions. If they go south, they'll have to contend with marshes and our fixed gun emplacements on the western side. That all adds up to one thing - they'll try to cross right here." He pointed his finger to the ground as he spoke.

"Yes sir," said Longmire. "That was our assessment too."

Quince nodded and said, "Still no sign of boats or bridge-building equipment?"

"Not yet," replied Longmire. "But they haven't unpacked everything."

"Well, assume they've got some kind of plan to get across somewhere nearby. Be ready to move quickly."

"Will do, sir. What about the Sahiradin camp, sir?" asked Longmire. "If we're facing off against the PRA's First Corp, we can't just leave them on that hill."

"Agreed," said Quince. "That communication we intercepted about some kind of agreement between the Sahiradin and the PRA got everyone thinking that we'd better officially treat the Sahiradin as the enemy."

"Yes sir. But that shield over their camp is going to make it hard to take them out, though," said Longmire. "Even if we find a way in, it'll be hand to hand. And if it goes anything like our first engagement, we can expect a three-to-one casualty rate. And that's an unacceptable outcome."

"Agreed," said Quince. "Better find a different way to deal with them. And I can't spare any more soldiers, so don't bother asking."

"Yes sir," said Longmire. "We were thinking of bunker busters. A few deep penetrating guided missiles fired into the steeper eastern side of the hill could cause the whole hill to collapse. In fact…"

Longmire was interrupted by the pop-pop-pop of explosions high above them. Looking up, they saw hundreds of contrails streaming from the edges of large, rapidly descending craft. The ships were protected by V-wing fighters. The V-wings peeled away from the larger craft and headed back up where they engaged against pursuing Lycian fighters, and a dogfight quickly developed. Lycian and Sahiradin fighters fired energy pulse and guided projectile weapons at each other in a tangled confusion of swirling ships.

Moments later, a group of the larger Sahiradin craft landed just west of the Sahiradin camp. They opened their massive payload doors and Sahiradin soldiers and heavy equipment quickly deployed to positions adjacent to the Sahiradin camp on the hill and stretching to the west.

Then Quince and Longmire heard the sound of heavy engines behind them. They turned to see large Lycian troop transport ships landing a few hundred meters away. Their doors opened and various species composing the Lycian Alliance exited the ships. General Quince's eyes widened with surprise as he watched the Lycian soldiers march to their predetermined positions. Behind them came a line of what appeared to be mechanized soldiers. Hundreds and hundreds of them. The machines assembled in a long three-deep line facing the newly arrived Sahiradin forces just a few kilometers to the north.

A small group of Lycian allies walked toward Quince and Longmire.

"Looks like things just got a lot more complicated," said Longmire. "What's the plan, sir?"

Quince looked at him and raised his eyebrows. "I don't think there's anything in the army's playbook for this particular scenario. We're going to have to wing it."

"Sir, we do have Consul Sawyer in our camp," said Longmire.

"Ah yes," replied General Quince. "She pissed everybody off when she came up here against General McIntyre's recommendation. Turns out we could use a politico up here after all."

"I'll send for her," said Longmire.

"Do that," said Quince as he smiled and turned toward the approaching delegation.

Chapter 81

The Lycian representative who spoke to Ravenwood was short, about as tall as Ravenwood's chest, and her straight black hair reached her shoulders. Her diminutive stature and smooth tan skin gave Logan the impression she was very young, but her light brown eyes had something about them that said they had witnessed much. She had two companions. One of them was a slightly taller male with sandy brown hair, light-colored skin, and almond-shaped blue eyes. His face wore a pleasant expression. He periodically looked from face to face and smiled but said nothing.

The other companion was enormous. He was over twice Ravenwood's height with massive shoulders, muscular arms, and short but powerful legs. His skin was bumpy and grayish. His hair was black and his eyes were a bright green. Logan had seen them from a distance during the battle near the *Blackhawk* crash site, but seeing them up close made him uneasy. He knew that one swat of the alien's massive hand would crush him like an insect.

Ravenwood nodded periodically as the female Lycian representative spoke. Her language's cadence reminded Logan of a birdsong mixed with occasional whirs and clicks. Ravenwood responded now and again, somewhat haltingly, but not in the same language as the Lycian. He spoke in a language that had elongated vowels and many *sh*, *th*, and *oth* sounds. Logan found both languages to be beautiful in their own way.

"Well," asked General Quince rather loudly. "What the hell is she saying?"

Consul Sawyer shot Quince a sharp look and cautioned, "General. This is our first contact with an extremely advanced alien species. It is a pivotal moment in our history. Please be patient."

General Quince scoffed. "Our first contact with an advanced alien species happened two days ago when we went blade to blade with those albino bastards on that hill." He pointed toward the north as he spoke.

Sawyer didn't take the bait. Instead, she softly replied, "Nevertheless, please be patient, general. We cannot assume these beings have the same attitude toward us."

General Quince was clearly not happy with her diplomatic, but somewhat condescending tone of voice.

"Consul Sawyer," he said. "I have one objective. That objective is to keep those PRA bastards on the other side of the Mississippi River. If we fail, we'll have one hundred thousand regulars and five thousand Red Legs sweeping down to meet their friends at St. Louis, who I shouldn't need to remind you have just launched a massive assault on that city. The defenders are already outnumbered three to one; they'd collapse under a flank attack."

Sawyer glared at Quince. "General Quince, I'm aware of the situation, but this discussion must be conducted with care," she said in a slightly annoyed tone. Then she leaned close to the general and whispered, "In army speak, don't turn this into a cluster fuck."

Quince was surprised but undeterred by her strong language. "Consul, we don't have time to sit around jabbering. There is a very good chance our defenses at St. Louis will fail and we'll all have to fall back to Deep Six. That withdrawal will be a hell of a lot harder if a hundred thousand PRA troops swoop down from the north and slam into our right flank. And now we've got an army of Sahiradin a few klicks to the north of us to contend with, so I'm sorry if I seem a little impatient to wrap up our little chat."

Sawyer was about to respond when Ravenwood cleared his throat. "I believe I have a good understanding of the situation."

"Finally. Please, enlighten us," said General Quince, not trying to hide his irritation. "You can explain to us how you happen to speak their language later."

Ravenwood ignored the general's challenge and said, "First, a little background. These three represent three of the seven allied species who belong to what they call the Lycian Alliance. The female is a Rahani, the taller male is a Brevian, and the large fellow is a Grensch. As I have previously stated, they have been fighting a centuries long war with the Sahiradin. The fighting has ravaged dozens of worlds, but neither side has been able to deal the other side a decisive blow."

"And why are they here?" asked Quince. "How did their war end up at our doorstep?"

Ravenwood replied, "As suspected, the Sahiradin whom we captured was part of an expedition many years ago to resettle Earth, which the Sahiradin thought was an abandoned and long-forgotten colony."

"How long forgotten?" asked Sawyer.

"I'm not quite sure," answered Ravenwood. "Hundreds of thousands of years. Longer, perhaps. The records had been lost until the Sahiradin rediscovered them."

"Back to the war," said the general. "We need to know what's going on now, today, not thousands of years ago."

"Certainly," said Ravenwood. "The Sahiradin ship that arrived here prior to Impact was damaged; apparently it had been attacked before shifting space. It managed to make the leap to our solar system, but it was crippled beyond repair. I believe they used what time and resources they had remaining to redirect asteroids toward Earth's path, which led to the Impact years later."

"Did she tell you all that?" asked Consul Sawyer.

"No, but I have little doubt of it," replied Ravenwood. "At any rate, when that first Sahiradin ship exploded, Kurak, our Sahiradin prisoner, escaped and landed on the moon. His life-support systems were failing and he would have died, if his escape pod had not been recovered by American Apollo mission astronauts. The astronauts also recovered something called the Kaiytáva, which we call the Apollo Stone. It is the Apollo Stone which both the Sahiradin and the Lycians are after."

"I was briefed on this. The Apollo Stone is the thing that allows their ships to jump from place to place, correct?" asked General Quince.

"Correct," said Ravenwood. "Both species avail themselves of point-to-point interstellar travel using wormhole gates, but the Stone allows a ship to travel anywhere in the galaxy, perhaps the universe, at will.

"Is this the only Apollo Stone?" asked General Quince.

Ravenwood looked at the female Rahani and asked her. As she spoke, Ravenwood translated. "It is the only remaining one."

"Well, I can understand why neither side wants the other to have it," said the general. He looked at Longmire. "Can we have a look at this thing?"

"We believe we have it, but it's locked inside a Sahiradin case and we haven't been able to open it," said Longmire.

General Quince looked at Ravenwood. "You didn't tell them we have this thing, did you?"

"Not yet."

"Good. Let's keep it that way. Until we know what the hell is going on, let's keep it under wraps."

Sawyer shook her head. "If they don't know we have it already, they'll learn soon enough. The Sahiradin know we have it, so we'd be keeping a secret which is known to the enemy from our ally."

General Quince could no longer contain himself. "Ally? Who the hell is talking about allies? For all we know, these Lycians are just as nasty as the Sahiradin, or worse."

"They've offered their help against the Sahiradin," said Ravenwood. "They are offering to fight them here on the ground as well as engage their fleet."

Quince chuckled. "They're going to fight them here on the ground and in space? Well ain't that nice." He looked at Ravenwood and then Sawyer. "Don't you get it? They'd be doing that anyway! What they really want is for is us to help *them* in *their* war, not the other way around."

"Either way, the Sahiradin have demonstrated their hostility toward Earth," said Sawyer. "And you know the old saying, 'the enemy of my enemy is my friend.'"

"Consul Sawyer, do you really think species as advanced as these guys have any interest in treating us as equals?" asked General Quince as he pointed his thumb toward the Lycian delegation. "Believe me, if we agree to work together, humans will be very junior partners in the arrangement. And if we win, how generous do you think they'll be toward us? How do we know they won't finish the job the Sahiradin started?"

"All good points," said Sawyer. "But let's look at the situation we're in. We've got a known enemy, the PRA, working with a new and very advanced enemy, the Sahiradin. The PRA shield dome across the river is evidence of that partnership. Up in space we've got hostile Sahiradin ships that are itching to wipe us out if they can get past the Lycian fleet. We don't know what the Lycian will do in the long run, I admit that, but we know what the Sahiradin will do to us right now if they get the chance. I say we cooperate with the Lycians as much as needed to win this fight."

General Quince opened his mouth to speak, but Consul Sawyer held up her hand to silence him. "General, your mission is to defeat the enemy, and you have a free hand in doing so. But it's the League Council's responsibility to determine overall objectives. As the only representative of the Council here, I'm ordering you to cooperate with the Lycians."

"Are you sure the rest of the Council would agree?" asked Quince. "I'm no lawyer, but I think the League Compact requires a unanimous vote on something this significant."

"Perhaps, but because our communications are being jammed, we can't put it to a vote."

Quince stared at her for a moment. Then he said, "You realize you're not just assuming responsibility for the entire League, but the whole damn planet. I don't see any African, Asian, South American, or European representatives around here."

"Believe me, general, I understand the significance of what I'm asking you to do, but it's the least distasteful choice on a list of bad options."

General Quince took a deep breath and turned toward Logan. "And what do you think, private? Mr. Ravenwood and Consul Sawyer must have had some reason for insisting that you take part in this discussion."

Logan stood at attention and said, "Sir, I've fought against the Sahiradin. They love war, sir. They love fighting, especially up close. Hand to hand. And they're built for war, too. Their skin is made up of tiny scales that work like armor. These other aliens seem to be less aggressive. Except for the Grensch, they're much smaller and frailer than the Sahiradin. Also, I see they offloaded a lot of automated warriors. My guess is they use robots to do much of their fighting since the Sahiradin are so much bigger and deadlier than they are. If I had to pick a side that's the least aggressive, it would be the Lycians, sir."

"Aggression can take many forms both on and off the battlefield," said General Quince. "Where are you from?"

Logan hesitated.

"He's a PRA defector, sir," said General Longmire.

Quince looked at Longmire, then at Logan. "We've got a lot of good soldiers from east of the river in our army. They know how things will go if we lose this war."

He looked at Sawyer and said, "Well, Consul. You're the most senior civilian leader here, so we'll follow your instructions, but I'd hate to be you if you're wrong about these Lycians."

"Thank you," replied Sawyer. "We'll know soon enough if I'm wrong."

Quince looked at Ravenwood, then Longmire.

"Okay," he said. "Let's get to the command tent and hash this out."

Chapter 82

It was evening when Ravenwood left the command tent where the League and the Lycians had agreed on a basic plan to repel the Sahiradin and PRA armies. Logan, Cap, and Lena had just finished their duties helping to reinforce the camp's defenses when they saw him walking toward the mess tent.

"Took you long enough," said Cap when they caught up with him. "What's the plan?"

"Well," said Ravenwood. "Nothing too elaborate. The Lycians are going to take the left side of the line and deal with the Sahiradin. A few of them will be stationed on the right side with us in case the Sahiradin try to storm the hill. The League is responsible for preventing the PRA from crossing the river and for keeping the Sahiradin on the hill from outflanking us."

"Sounds pretty vague," said Lena. "I hope we don't end up shooting each other."

"Where's Kane?" asked Logan. "Is he still in the tent?"

"No," said Ravenwood. "He escorted the Northrunner delegation back to their territory."

"Are they going to provide more help?" asked Logan.

"They have refused to commit troops to this fight," answered Ravenwood with a sigh. "Kane will try to convince them to change their minds, but their military is better suited for defense than offense. Furthermore, they suffered heavy casualties in the battle against the Sahiradin, heavier even than the League. They are understandably reluctant to send their soldiers off to an almost certain death."

As they walked, Logan looked at Ravenwood and said, "When you talked to the Rahani, I could tell you were keeping a lot to yourself. What else did they say?"

Ravenwood smiled and said, "You're very observant. Yes, the conversation touched on a number of things which I did not think would be prudent to translate. They asked about our origins. And they wanted to know more about our ancient history, but I asked them to wait for answers until we'd taken care of the business at hand."

"What about the stone?" asked Lena. "Did they ask about that?"

"They did," answered Ravenwood. "I deflected on that point as well."

"But Consul Sawyer said we should tell them before they find out from some other source, like the Sahiradin," said Logan.

"I understand her position," replied Ravenwood, "but I don't think it would be wise for them to have access to the Kaiytáva just yet. They may be tempted to take it and leave us to face the Sahiradin alone."

Just then, shells exploded to the west of their position, sending dirt high into the air. Other shells followed. They hurled their bodies to the ground and covered their heads. More earth sailed through the air and landed on them.

Cap spat dirt out of his mouth and yelled, "It's starting already. We're not prepared. We don't even have all of the Second Corp troops in place. They're still rolling in."

"I think hitting us before we're ready is part of their plan," yelled Lena above the sound of explosions.

"We have to get back to our unit," yelled Logan.

Ravenwood nodded. "I'm going to the Apollo Stone. When the Sahiradin attack, they will be focused on recovering it."

Logan, Cap, and Lena got up and stumbled toward Dog Patrol's camp as Ravenwood dashed back toward the command tent. The shells continued to rain down around them, destroying artillery and equipment, killing soldiers. Suddenly, a green shimmering light encircled their camp. The shells continued to explode, but now they dispersed on the green shield over their heads.

Cap looked up and laughed. "Ha! Looks like our new friends have given us a shield!"

When they reached Dog Patrol's camp, Logan saw L.C. Heath and the rest of the fire team kneeling behind some boulders. They were in their Provex armor and had their K-45s at their shoulders. Their swords were sheathed in scabbards in their battle packs.

"Brandt," said Heath. "I'm so glad you and your friends could join us." Logan knelt on one knee and tightened the straps of the armor he'd quickly grabbed a minute earlier. He checked his sword, sheathed it, then pulled out his K-45.

"How's it looking up top?" asked Heath. "Were we able to fully deploy?"

Logan shook his head. "They're catching us with our pants down. But in case you didn't notice, our new friends, the Lycians, have given us a shield which is keeping out the artillery shells. Maybe we'll have time to finish deploying before the real fighting starts."

As he spoke, the green shield above them began to turn red. Logan spotted a red beam coming out from the otherwise dark Sahiradin camp. He pointed at it for the others to see.

"I'm guessing our new shield won't last too long," said Cap.

"That means they're launching a nighttime assault," said Lena. "They want the Apollo Stone so badly they're willing to launch an attack before the PRA forces are ready." She checked the Sahiradin blade she'd taken from the battlefield.

"They're desperate," said Logan. "They know the Lycians are here. They must be afraid they'll get the stone."

Lieutenant Styles ran up to their position, shouting to everyone along the hip-deep trench. "Be ready for a ground assault. You saw the oval ships landing. We've got new friends. Longmire's orders are to engage the Sahiradin only. Whatever else you see, and believe me you're going to see some crazy stuff, engage against the Sahiradin only. Don't forget."

She walked farther down the line, relaying the same instructions. As she disappeared behind a group of pine trees Logan noticed the shield above them had turned completely red and then it disappeared.

"Here we go," said Heath to his fire team. "Keep it tight and make them come to us."

Chapter 83

Lycian Admiral Var-Imar watched as the Sahiradin fleet swiftly broke to the left, firing ion cannons into the center of the Lycian formation. It was their second ion volley, and at least for now, the improved ion defense shields were repelling the fearsome Sahiradin weapon. Yet they would not last long, and when they collapsed a horrific exchange of fire would follow.

It would be at that moment, when the Sahiradin had broken down the Lycian shields and were closing for the kill, that the Lycians would spring the trap. The Lycian fleet would split in two and use its superior speed and agility to swing around to each end of the Sahiradin formation. Several smaller ships would also move above and below the Sahiradin formation, which was typically rather two dimensional in design. At that moment, fighters and torpedo bombers would race in to attack the Sahiradin capital ships. To protect themselves when executing the maneuver, the Lycians would deploy ion and antiballistic defense pods, thus momentarily screening themselves from Sahiradin attack. The hope was that, as the Sahiradin charged in, they would not have sufficient room to adjust to the unorthodox plan.

The timing had to be perfect, though, or they would be obliterated. Lycian doctrine strongly disfavored splitting the fleet in the manner the admiral's plan called for because ships could be isolated and destroyed piecemeal. Yet, given the high stakes involved in this battle, which could quite possibly determine the outcome of the long conflict, Admiral Var-Imar thought the risk was justified.

The Lycian ships returned fire, scoring several hits, but could not match the firepower which the newly arrived devastator class battleship *Conquest* brought to the fight. In the long history of their struggle against the Sahiradin, the Lycians had typically needed at least a two-to-one numerical advantage to defeat any Sahiradin fleet containing a battleship. If the circumstances were different, Admiral Var-Imar would have ordered a retreat, but with the Kaiytáva likely somewhere on the planet's surface, possibly already in the hands of the Sahiradin landing force, she was forced to fight.

A tactical officer warned Var-Imar that Sahiradin torpedo ships and their Codex fighter escorts were making a run. They sought to elude the screen of Lycian fighter craft protecting the fleet, but they met a fiery end. Aside from the Grensch, the Sahiradin soldiers were more aggressive and bigger than the Lycians, but the Lycian pilots and fighter craft were superior. And their skills were on display now. Var-Imar watched as a battle wing of Codex fighters sought to approach the fleet from underneath, only to be shredded by Lycian oval-shaped Aculea fighters. But fighter superiority would not be sufficient to win this battle, and Var-Imar knew it was just a matter of time before the Sahiradin capital ships would penetrate the Lycian defenses.

"Admiral," said a male Rahani officer. "As we feared, the Sahiradin have launched a pre-dawn assault on the Alamani camp. Our ground forces are trying to assist, but coordination between us and the Alamani is poor."

"And what about the Alamani army across the river?" asked Var-Imar.

"They do not appear to be part of this attack," said the officer. "They seem to be preparing to cross the river at first light."

"Get me General Gil-Masuur," said the admiral.

Moments later, the face of a female Rahani appeared on the small screen embedded in the arm of the admiral's chair.

"We see the Sahiradin are moving toward the Alamani camp," said Admiral Var-Imar. "Help your Alamani allies repel them. If you wait, the Sahiradin will cut you to pieces."

The Rahani general could not hide her concern with this order. "We are not ready. Can we receive fighter support?"

"No," said the admiral. "Those units are committed to defending the fleet. You're on your own."

"Yes admiral," said Gil-Masuur.

Var-Imar ended the transmission and looked at the battle unfolding on the main view screen. Data showing the status of each ship, Lycian and Sahiradin alike, scrolled in small separated sections along the left and right edges of the screen. In the center was an image of the massive Sahiradin battleship, *Conquest*. Suddenly a fiery ball erupted from one of *Conquest*'s two ion cannon nodes and flew in the direction of a Lycian frigate. The frigate's ion screen dispersed the energy in a brilliant flash of red light, but the admiral could see the screen had been destroyed in the process.

"Communications," she said. "Instruct *Resilient*'s captain to deploy her ion screen pods and pull back. Tactical, redirect scrambler droids to mask *Resilient*'s silhouette as she retreats."

Resilient was already deploying defensive pods to her starboard side, but the ship retreated along a course that took it outside of the pods' line of protection. Another volley from *Conquest*'s second ion cannon hit the fleeing ship, causing widespread systems failures, including the frigate's antiballistic shield. Two nearby Sahiradin destroyers immediately fired a dozen missiles into the defenseless frigate, ripping her apart.

    Var-Imar cursed under her breath but quickly shifted her attention to other ships, resisting a strong urge to give the order to execute their plan. They had to hold out a little longer and draw the Sahiradin ships in close.

Chapter 84

The bombardment of the League camp stopped ten minutes before the first wave of Sahiradin charged up the hill. A few League troopers fired on the advancing enemy, but the order came through their helmets' ICS to engage shields and save ammo. At first Logan could not see the enemy, but then he caught a glimpse of white-haired figures dashing between the trees toward the League's position. In a few moments, the Sahiradin were just fifty meters away from the League's trench on the crest of the hill. Logan grimaced when he saw that the enemy was concentrating its attack on the area of the line where Dog Patrol was positioned. He looked to his left and right and saw all the troopers had drawn their swords and prepared to launch themselves down the hill at the approaching Sahiradin.

Logan was tense and nervous as he watched the Sahiradin ascending the hill. The waiting was unbearable, and he wished the order to attack would come. Suddenly a line of mechanized warriors burst through the trees and smashed into Sahiradin right flank. Nodes on the machines' shoulders fired energy pulses and blades attached to their arms where their hands should have been twirled with blinding speed.

The Sahiradin were surprised by the attack, but they quickly recovered and turned to face their mechanical opponents. Logan watched as they snapped their left wrists, causing semi-transparent guards to emerge from armbands, something they had not bothered to employ when fighting against the League troopers a few days prior.

Using their guards and their swords, the Sahiradin threw themselves at the machines. Logan assumed they would not be able to match the speed of their mechanical foes, but to his surprise they exhibited a remarkable ability to anticipate the mech warriors' moves. And their black swords cut through the metal arms and legs with surprising ease. A few Sahiradin fell, but far more mech warriors collapsed to the ground in twitching heaps.

Lena tapped Logan's shoulder. He looked at her and she held out her Sahiradin blade. The handle glowed a light blue and emitted a humming sound. He touched the blade and felt it softly vibrate.

"They must use harmonics to help cut through the metal," said Logan. "Wonder why they don't use it on us."

"Maybe it doesn't work on our low-tech steel," offered Lena. "Although a minor adjustment would probably change that."

Logan nodded, then he looked down at the battle unfolding on the slope below him. He noticed two Rahani behind the line of mech warriors. They were inside similar machines but were not taking part in the fight. Instead, they were working controls that appeared to be directing the mech warriors' attack. Logan returned his attention to the battle and could see the machines were beginning to lose ground to the Sahiradin.

To Logan's left, Lieutenant Styles stood and yelled orders up and down the line. "League! Engage shields! Prepare to attack!" She drew her sword and held it high. Other officers yelled out similar commands. Soldiers along the line responded by holding their swords up as well.

Styles and the other officers pointed their swords down the slope and yelled, "Attack!"

Soldiers leapt out of the trench and hurtled down the hill toward the Sahiradin. They smashed into their formation, pushing the Sahiradin back a dozen meters, but the black-clad aliens quickly recovered and created an L-shaped formation to fight both the machines and the League soldiers.

Logan saw Lena fighting with her usual precision and ferocity. She took down a Sahiradin, but then she fell to the ground when another kicked her in the knee. He stabbed at her, but she rolled out of the way. As she did, Flores stepped forward and thrust his sword into the Sahiradin's throat. Clutching his bleeding neck, the alien warrior took a last desperate swing at Flores before falling to the ground.

Flores drove his Sahiradin blade into the still-moving enemy when another stepped forward and gutted Flores with a deep thrust into his midsection. Though mortally wounded, Flores shot his left arm out and caught the Sahiradin by the throat. The alien was surprised by the move and tried to pull Flores' hand away, but he was too late. Logan sliced the back of the aliens' leg, then drove his sword between the ribs on his left side.

Another Sahiradin swept in to attack Logan. He made as if to cut Logan's throat, but then swung low instead. Logan had seen the move before. He blocked the attack and swiftly slid his blade up the Sahiradin's sword, slicing his sword hand. The Sahiradin screamed with rage. He smashed his guard into Logan's chest, causing him to lose his footing. As Logan fell to the ground he caught the upper rim of the Sahiradin's arm guard and pulled as hard as he could, causing the Sahiradin to lurch forward. Logan thrust his blade upward and pierced his opponent's stomach below his breast plate. The Sahiradin fell to the ground, screaming. Logan scrambled to his feet and finished the Sahiradin off with a thrust into his neck and into his skull.

More mech warriors joined the fight, hitting the Sahiradin right flank hard and forcing them to fall back. The Sahiradin sent more troops forward, but given the unfavorable terrain and the defenders' determined resistance, the assault soon lost its momentum and they began to fall back. After a few more minutes of combat, the troopers received the order to cease fighting and return to their positions on the line. The mech warriors and their Rahani controllers also went up the hill and returned to their units.

"Save your shield charges," yelled Lieutenant Styles as they collapsed back into the trenches. "Sahiradin shields last longer than ours, so make yours last. Stay sharp. They might come again."

Chapter 85

Logan sat down in the trench and removed his helmet. He was panting heavily and pouring sweat. He pulled out his canteen and drank half of it. He looked at Cap, who was also gulping in air. Cap removed his helmet and saw that it had a deep gash in it.

"I'm going to send the inventor of Provex armor a thank-you note," he said as he examined the damage the Sahiradin sword had caused.

"You've got more lives than a cat," said Lena.

"It doesn't hurt to be lucky," replied Cap with a grin.

Despite the lieutenant's warning that a second assault could be imminent, hours passed without any further action, probably because the Lycians were able to reestablish the shield dome shortly after the Sahiradin were repulsed. They slept in shifts, but no one got more than a few minutes of sleep at a time. Logan finally drifted off into a deep sleep but soon awoke to the sound of artillery shells exploding on the riverbank below. Moments later, he heard League artillery returning volleys.

"Is the PRA shield dome down?" asked Lena.

"Who knows," said Cap, rubbing his eyes and stretching. "At least we're shooting back now."

Heath turned his head, listening to the sound of the PRA artillery. "It's coming from a different spot. I think they're trying to cross the river."

"But the bridge is blown," said Cap.

"They must have found another way," said Heath.

A few minutes later, Lieutenant Styles walked past Dog Patrol and shouted, "We're pulling out! Fall back! Fall back!"

Dog Patrol quickly followed the order and marched to the clearing on top of the hill just as the first rays of the morning sun touched the treetops. From this high vantage, Logan could see the outline of a Sahiradin camp on the hill to the north. On the western side of the camp, the Sahiradin reinforcements, at least thirty-five thousand strong, were marching toward the League and Lycian position. The Lycian's ten thousand troops had formed a line adjacent to the newly arrived Second Corp's hastily formed line. Together, the League and Lycians roughly equaled the Sahiradin numbers. Logan could see the Sahiradin plan was to move quickly to smash the combined army, or at least keep it occupied, while the PRA forces crossed the river below. If they could join up on west side of the water, the Sahiradin and PRA armies would have a three-to-one numerical advantage.

Across the river, PRA troops had deployed two massive towers. One was directly opposite the League's position. The other was a few kilometers north. Logan and the others watched as PRA troops made some final adjustments to the strange-looking towers. Then, to the dismay of those who were watching, the towers began to rapidly deploy long thin rectangular plates that floated on the water. Each plate shot forward over the preceding one, locking into place when it reached the end. As each plate locked into its position, cables on the edge of the plate pulled a round object from the tower. When the object reached the end of newest plate, it attached to the side and a support beam shot down into the water, like a telescope opening itself, until it reached the river bed.

"What the hell?" said Cap. "Is that thing really building a bridge? Since when does the PRA have that?"

Logan felt a knot growing in his stomach as he and the others watched the automated bridge and pylon system quickly work to span the kilometer that separated the east and west sides of the river channel.

"At the rate they're going, these bridges will be built in thirty minutes," said Lena.

"It's just not possible," said Cap, exasperated. "What the hell are we supposed to do to stop that thing?"

Logan watched the two bridges being deployed and said, "My guess is the PRA had to pull these from the assault on St. Louis after we blew the rail bridge. At least that's two bridges they can't use down south."

"That's very comforting," said Cap unenthusiastically.

League artillery fired on the towers on the eastern riverbank, but before they could score a hit the numerically superior PRA guns and rocket launchers showered the League's gun emplacements with shells and missiles, destroying five pieces in rapid succession and forcing the League to raise the shield dome. The PRA kept up a continuous barrage to ensure the shield did not come down, effectively neutralizing the League's artillery.

Lieutenant Styles called for the twenty remaining members of Dog Patrol to gather around her.

"Here's the plan," she said. "We're combining Dog and Charlie Patrols under me, and we're going down to reinforce the defenses on the riverbank."

"What about the Sahiradin?" asked a trooper. "Who's going to take care of them on this side of the river? We'll be trapped down there if they break through."

"That's going to be up to our new Lycian friends and Second Corp. Stopping the Sahiradin is their objective. Our objective is to keep the PRA armored units and troops from crossing the river."

"Lieutenant Styles, we have troops near the southern bridge, but what about the one they're building north of us?" asked L.C. Heath. "How do we keep them from crossing there?"

"The Lycians are responsible for taking that one out," replied Styles.

"And what about air support?" asked Cap. "The skies have been clear all day."

"We've got all of the PRA's air power tangled up near St. Louis. We're told they don't have enough planes to support both operations, and neither do we. Remember, crossing the river this far north was supposed to be a walk through the park for them, so now they're spread too thin."

Lieutenant Styles paused to see if there were any more questions. Then she said, "Okay, let's move. Lance Corporal Heath, your fire team can lead. Deploy on the right end of the line when you get down there."

"Yes Lieutenant," said L.C. Heath. He looked at his team and nodded his head in the direction of the recently cut road down to the riverbank. "Let's go."

L.C. Heath led the way down the hill. The rough road that engineers had hastily cut into the side of the hill consisted of a number of switchbacks, making it about three quarters of a kilometer long in total. The dirt had been ripped up by the treads of anti-tank guns and armored vehicles that had gone down to the riverbank the night before. Heath followed the road at first, but then turned onto a foot path that troopers had cut through the trees, which led directly to the river.

When they reached the riverbank, Logan saw a long trench filled with troopers. Behind the trenches were cinderblock and sandbag walls protecting heavy mortars, howitzers, and anti-tank guns. Behind them, backed up against the hill, were five tanks. L.C. Heath led them to the far right end of the line, where the trench reached a brick building at the edge of the little river town where the fighting had begun a week earlier.

"Not a lot of troops to stop what's coming," said Cap as he looked down the line at the rest of the League troops.

"These defenses were designed to stop an amphibious assault," said Lena. "Not thousands of soldiers and armor streaming across a magic bridge."

Cap looked at the rapidly growing bridge. "Why isn't our artillery firing while they're building? Knock it out before it's complete."

"With all the shells and rockets the PRA is throwing at them, the second they lower the shield they'll be obliterated," said Logan.

"That's just great," said Cap sarcastically. "What about our tanks down here? Why aren't they firing on the bridge?"

As if in response to Cap's question, the tanks fired a series of volleys toward the bridge and the towers. Several rounds hit the bridge but simply skipped off of the material. And a half-dozen shells would have scored direct hits against the towers, but the Sahiradin shield protected them from the fast-moving projectiles.

"These Sahiradin shields are really starting to piss me off," said Cap as he watched tank shells explode in the air when they encountered the shield.

As Cap spoke, the troopers heard the rustle of tree branches behind them. They turned to see four enormous gray-skinned Grensch and about thirty Rahani wearing brown and green cloaks coming through the trees. As the olive-skinned Rahani approached, Logan saw they carried what looked like sniper rifles. Their light green helmets had a series of interlocking plates hanging from the back, similar to an ancient samurai's helmet, and clear visors were attached to the front that could be lowered over the wearer's eyes. The Rahani jumped down into an open space in the trench, the top of which reached their shoulders. Though unsettled by the appearance of their diminutive Lycian allies, the troopers in the trench gave them a welcoming nod.

Logan turned his attention toward the Grensch who had stepped over the League trooper's heads. In their large three-fingered hands they carried long brown rods with a circular spiked ball on the end, reminding Logan of a medieval mace. They wore protective brown and green armor over their massive torsos but no helmet. Their comparatively short legs were protected by some kind of material which, though sturdy in appearance, seemed to expand and contract with the flexing of their powerful leg muscles. The Grensch moved ahead of the League's position to a stand of tall ash and cottonwood trees closer to the river. They crouched low in the undergrowth and held themselves perfectly still. Logan was surprised at how difficult they were to see, given their bulk.

Despite the additional units the Lycians had provided to the river defense, Logan did not feel it would be enough to stop the PRA's advance. He looked to his right and saw the *Blackhawk* near the town's old levee. It seemed like a lifetime ago when they had landed there, hoping to repair the craft and fly it back to Jasper Air Base. The memory of Crew Chief McKinney and his men being cut down by Sahiradin soldiers flashed across his mind. They were the first casualties in the world's first inter-species war, and the tally was about to get a lot higher.

Suddenly a thought popped into Logan's head. He asked L.C. Heath if he could be put in touch with Ravenwood. He'd need to be able to use an officer's ICS to contact the command tent.

"Let me see what Lieutenant Styles says," he replied. He raised himself into a low crouch and ran along the trench to where Lieutenant Styles was located. He spoke to Styles, then waved for Logan to join him.

"What do you need, Private Brandt?" asked Styles.

"I have an idea about how to open the sphere holding the Apollo Stone," he said. "Ravenwood's been working on it. Can I talk to him?"

Styles nodded. She spoke into her ICS, waited a few moments as she received a response. Then she removed the device from her belt and handed it to Logan. "Go ahead," she said. "It's on speaker."

"Ravenwood?" said Logan.

"Yes, boy. Be quick, the Sahiradin line is already advancing. Fighting is about to break out."

"Understood," said Logan. "Do you have the sphere?"

"I do."

"Do you remember what the Sahiradin prisoner, Kurak, said about how they were going to defeat us?"

"Yes. Something about how they were going to be victorious," said Ravenwood.

"He said 'Victory will be ours'," said Logan. "Try it."

"Very well," said Ravenwood. "Just a moment." There was a short pause, then Logan heard Ravenwood's voice speaking in the Sahiradin language. Suddenly Ravenwood exclaimed, "My boy! You did it! The sphere has opened!"

"I know," replied Logan. "Can you bring the stone to me down by the river defenses? I'm near the town."

"I don't think General Longmire would approve that," said Ravenwood in a low voice.

"There's no time to explain it to him," said Logan. "Just do it, and be quick. Now that the sphere is open, the Sahiradin will detect its gravitational signature. We need to get it as far away from them as possible."

"I agree," said Ravenwood. "I'll be there shortly."

Logan handed the ICS back to Lieutenant Styles, who was staring at him. "Did I hear that correctly, Private Brandt? Did you just ask Ravenwood to steal the Apollo Stone?"

"I did," he said. "The Sahiradin are desperate to get it back, but we can't let them have it."

"And how will bringing it down here prevent them from getting it?" asked L.C. Heath.

Logan looked at the *Blackhawk*, then turned to Lieutenant Styles and said, "Lieutenant, I request permission to inspect the *Blackhawk* for serviceability."

"Denied," said Lieutenant Styles without hesitation as she reattached her ICS to her belt. "And Ravenwood isn't bringing the Apollo Stone down here either."

Just then the final link in the bridge reached their side of the river and locked into place and PRA artillery began firing on their position. Lieutenant Styles, Logan, and Heath ducked low in the trench as earth was thrown into the air thirty meters in front of them. The League's tanks returned fire on the eastern batteries.

Lieutenant Styles got to one knee and looked across the river through her field sensors. Tanks and armored vehicles were racing across the bridge toward them. She lowered the sensors and looked at Logan. "Go do it."

Logan turned and raced toward the end of the trench, L.C. Heath close behind him.

"What's up?" asked Cap.

"You and Lena come with me," said Logan. Looking at Heath, he said, "We could use a little help."

Heath nodded and ordered four troopers to come with them. They ran two hundred meters to the gunship. Shells exploded all around them, showering everything with dirt and rocks.

"What's the plan?" asked Lena when they reached the *Blackhawk*.

Logan looked at Cap. "Cap, you have to get this thing up and running within ten minutes."

"What?" he asked in disbelief.

"Crew Chief McKinney and his team were working to get it ready to fly before the Sahiradin hit us," said Logan. "Their tools should still be in there. You need to finish the job."

"Finish the job?" asked Cap. "What are you talking about? I just fly these things. I don't know what makes them work."

"You're wasting time hot-shot," said Lena with a smile. "Get to it."

Cap looked at her. "Hot-shot, eh? I like the sound of that." Then he looked at Logan and said, "All right, I'll have a look. Can't hurt, might help." He winked at Lena and dashed through the *Blackhawk's* open side hatch.

L.C. Heath said, "What else do you need?"

"Protection," said Logan. "Hopefully, Ravenwood will come down that hill with the Apollo Stone. Wait for him and escort him here. Don't let anything happen to him. Lena and I will stay here and protect Cap while he works." Heath nodded and led the troopers to the bottom of the hill.

Looking back at the nearby bridge, Logan saw the lead PRA tank take a direct hit. It burst into flames and ground to a halt. Logan thought it would delay the PRA column's progress, but the next tank simply pushed the burning hulk over the edge and into the water. The tank fired its gun and continued on.

A PRA artillery shell slammed into the side of the hill, sending shrapnel in all directions, including into a portion of the trench, killing or wounding a dozen soldiers. More shells struck the defenses, destroying tanks and armored vehicles, killing and wounding soldiers. A League anti-tank gun destroyed another PRA tank, but once again, the next tank in the line pushed the damaged vehicle into the water and the advance proceeded without pause.

Three PRA tanks reached the west side of the river and took up positions about thirty meters beyond the bridge. Armored personnel carriers streamed in between the tanks and opened their rear hatches. Red Legs poured out and rushed toward the League line. As they quickly advanced, the armored vehicles and tanks poured heavy-caliber machinegun fire into the trenches. Though protected by their shields, League troopers hit by the heavy slugs were thrown to the ground, suffered broken bones, or were knocked unconscious. The PRA line pushed forward as more tanks and armored vehicles sped off the bridge.

Just as the number of troops and armor reaching the western side of the river was beginning to swell, Logan saw the Rahani begin to fire bursts of green-colored energy from their long-barreled weapons at the vehicles still on the bridge. The green bursts blew holes in the vehicles' heavy steel plating, disabled guns, and shredded treads. The Rahani fired again and again until a dozen vehicles were so damaged they could not continue. With so many disabled vehicles in front of it, the PRA column could not advance and the assault was finally stalled.

Then the Grensch charged out of their concealed position among the trees and attacked the now-isolated PRA troops on the riverbank. Logan watched the surprisingly quick creatures as they used their mace-like weapons to sweep aside Red Leg troops as if they were toy soldiers. One of the Grensch reached an armored vehicle and smashed it with his weapon, caving in the entire front end with one blow. Another Grensch smashed a tank's gun barrel, his mace flashing green when it made contact. The Red Legs were clearly surprised by the Grensch's flank attack. They tried to fall back, firing their weapons and cutting with their swords as they ran, but neither affected the Grensch.

Seeing the Red Legs in disarray and the column on the bridge blocked, the League troops charged out of the trench and attacked the enemy. Shields on and swords drawn, they launched themselves at the Red Legs, who suddenly found themselves caught between rampaging Grensch giants and furious League soldiers.

The PRA armored vehicles not yet destroyed by the Grensch fired their forty-five caliber machine guns. The impact from the heavy slugs threw back soldiers and successfully penetrated the Grenschs' thick hide, forcing them to engage their shields.

As the close-quarters combat raged, the Rahani turned their attention to the enemy forces that had reached the shore. The green energy bursts from their rifles tore holes in the PRA's tanks and caused the Red Legs' shields to overload and dissipate. Seeing the Red Leg shields going down, many League troops switched to the K-45s and fired on them with deadly effect.

Though Logan was encouraged by the League-Lycian counterattack, he knew it could not be sustained. The PRA forces on the bridge had cleared away the disabled vehicles and more PRA tanks and armored personnel carriers began to reach the west side. They slammed into the defenders and focused cannon fire on the Grensch, two of whom took direct hits and were bowled over, though their shields protected them further harm. Newly arrived Red Legs drew their swords and charged the troopers, shifting the battle's momentum in favor of the PRA. The outnumbered League troopers fell back with Red Legs soldiers close on their heels.

As the troopers fell back, five of the Red Legs noticed Logan and Lena standing near the *Blackhawk.* They peeled off from the main group and ran toward the two troopers.

Chapter 86

"Admiral," said the communications officer.

"Yes. What is it," replied Var-Imar in a clipped voice as she watched the battle unfolding on the main view screen. They had been slugging it out with the Sahiradin fleet for some time with neither side gaining the upper hand.

"General Gil-Masuur is reporting the Alamani allied with the Sahiradin have completed both of their bridges and are sending units across."

"Very well," she said. "Signal fast frigate *Brilliant Star* to be ready. She is to target the northern bridge only. Our Alamani allies are too close to the southern bridge to risk firing on it. Order all other ships to prepare to fire on my mark. Report when they are ready."

"Yes admiral," said the communications officer.

Var-Imar waited for her order to be carried out. She took several deep breaths and closed her eyes, trying to relax and free her mind of distractions and fear.

"All ships reporting they are ready, admiral," said the communications officer after a few moments.

Var-Imar opened her eyes and looked at the view screen. The Sahiradin fleet had tightened their formation, increasing firepower but reducing maneuverability. "All ships fire now," she ordered in a steady voice. Then she took several breaths and said, "Fire missiles."

The view screen showed all of the Lycian ships concentrate their main batteries on a Sahiradin heavy cruiser on the right end of their formation. The combined power of the entire Lycian fleet's main batteries soon overloaded the ship's shield. At the same moment, twelve missiles were launched from *Intrepid* and raced toward the enemy heavy cruiser. Three missiles were destroyed by countermeasures, but the rest found their mark and tore holes in the Sahiradin ship's tough but not impenetrable borelium armor.

As the impact points along the Sahiradin ship burst into puffs of oxygen-fueled flames, the Lycian fast frigate *Brilliant Star* peeled away from its position. She darted around the end of the Sahiradin line and the disabled Sahiradin heavy cruiser that had anchored it. The nearest functioning enemy ship tried to intercept *Brilliant Star* but was unable to maneuver quickly enough to block the agile frigate, which positioned itself above the ground battle and fired four missiles toward the planet.

As the four missiles raced toward the surface, dozens of energy pulses leapt up from the Sahiradin camp toward *Brilliant Star*. A fraction of a second later, a Sahiradin battery targeted the Lycian missiles and fired surface-to-air missiles, destroying two of them before they had even entered the atmosphere.

Brilliant Star quickly pulled away from her position in orbit above the battle, though she took several hits from the Sahiradin energy pulses. Though not as powerful as an ion cannon, the energy pulses did somewhat damage the Lycian ship's antiballistic shield.

A Sahiradin light cruiser moved passed its crippled sister ship as quickly as it could and gave chase to *Brilliant Star*. However, in its haste to hunt down the fast frigate, it neglected to account for the Lycian army's pulse battery, which fired from the surface and scored numerous direct hits. The Sahiradin ship's shields went down, forcing it to retreat to the protection of the fleet.

Chapter 87

Logan and Lena engaged their shields and walked forward to meet the onrushing Red Leg soldiers. Logan looked up as several pulses of red light leapt into the sky. A moment later, several missiles launched from somewhere behind the Sahiradin line. The missiles impacted two of four fiery objects hurtling toward the Earth, causing them to explode, but the other two appeared to be unaffected. Like comets burning in the atmosphere, the two objects rapidly approached the ground. Several more rockets launched from behind the Sahiradin line raced toward the oncoming objects. Two of the missiles hit their targets, causing a massive fireball several kilometers above the ground, followed by two bone-shaking booms.

Lena looked at Logan and said, "Well, I guess the Lycian plan to take out the northern bridge didn't work out so well."

"I guess not," said Logan.

He looked at the base of the hill and saw Heath and the others were fighting several Red Legs. Although they took them down, one trooper was killed. Just then, Ravenwood appeared on the trail above Heath. He was racing down the hillside, but something was different. It seemed to Logan that he lacked the remarkable strength and agility he had displayed at Cumberland Gap.

Logan looked past the five Red Legs running toward him and Lena and saw a column of PRA tanks approaching the little river town along the western bank of the river. They were the vanguard of the PRA forces now streaming across the northern bridge.

Others must have seen the approaching column advancing down the riverbank because League troops threw smoke grenades and teargas at the Red Legs who had crossed the southern bridge. The troopers then fell back toward the hill. Logan saw Lieutenant Styles and the remaining members of Dog and Charlie Patrols falling back, but they didn't retreat up the hill. Instead, they were running toward him and Lena.

The group of five Red Legs then reached the *Blackhawk*. Using her Sahiradin black blade, Lena made quick work of the Red Leg on the far left, but two others attacked her simultaneously. It was all she could do to fend off their combined attacks, and she was forced to give ground.

The other two Red Legs launched themselves at Logan. He blocked several swift thrusts, but then he was wounded with a slash to his left shoulder, forcing him to fall back. The Red Legs formed a line and advanced on Logan and Lena at once. Suddenly, a pulse gun on the *Blackhawk* fired and one of the Red Legs fell to the ground dead.

"Thank you!" yelled Logan.

"You're welcome!" yelled Cap from inside the *Blackhawk*, his voice echoing out of the open side entrance.

The three remaining Red Legs pressed their attack against Logan and Lena, getting too close for Cap to risk firing again. Logan blocked three attacks, made a feint toward one and sliced at another, but the Red Leg was ready and blocked the maneuver. Lena surprised her two opponents by suddenly dashing between them, ducking under a neck-high slice and piercing a Red Leg deep under his extended sword arm and into his chest.

Logan gave a glancing cut to his opponent across his jaw line, causing him to spin away. The Red Leg regained his footing and charged forward, but green beams of light from Rahani rifles dropped him and the other remaining Red Leg in their tracks.

Lieutenant Styles and about fifteen troopers arrived moments later, followed by Ravenwood and Heath. About two dozen Rahani and three Grensch also joined them. Together they formed a line to face a contingent of charging PRA forces consisting of about thirty Red Legs and a tank.

The tank turned its turret to fire on the *Blackhawk*, but it was too slow. *Blackhawk* sprang to life and fired a rocket into the tank, sending its turret five meters high into the air. The nearby Red Legs were blown off their feet.

Cap peered around the corner of the *Blackhawk's* rear ramp. "What are you waiting for? Let's go! Let's go!" he shouted.

They turned and ran toward Cap and the open ramp. Logan looked back at the Rahani and Grensch, who still faced the other direction, firing on the Red Legs. He whistled loudly and one of the Rahani looked back. He waved for them to follow. The Rahani said something to his comrades and they all ran toward the *Blackhawk*.

Cap climbed into the pilot seat. He closed the rear hatch and gunned the engines just as the Rahani and Grensch boarded. The *Blackhawk* quickly lifted off. As it rose into the air, Cap ordered the gunship's automated weapons and pulse guns to lay down a suppression fire at nearby PRA troops. Cap then targeted a number of approaching tanks. Two seconds later, the tanks exploded in mushroom clouds of fire and black smoke.

Logan struggled into the cockpit and sat in the co-pilot's seat next to Cap. "Get us the hell out of here," he said as he strapped himself in. Go southwest, way behind the lines. We can't let them have the Apollo Stone." He pulled the Stone out of his pocket and gripped it tightly in his left hand.

As they swiftly gained altitude, Cap banked right, affording Logan a view of the ground below. To his dismay, he saw the combined League and Lycian forces heading south in full retreat. They hadn't turned their backs on the enemy, and they were withdrawing in an orderly manner, but there was no mistaking they had already lost the battle. If the main PRA army quickly crossed the river at St. Louis, it would unite with its northern wing and destroy the League's forces before they could pull back to Deep Six. The war would be over in a week.

Logan looked at the Mississippi River and the two PRA bridges that spanned it. The northern bridge was filled with thousands of briskly marching PRA troops on their way to the western bank, where tanks and other armored vehicles snaked their way up into the hills overlooking the river valley. The lead elements of those units had fallen into line next to the quickly advancing Sahiradin, who were already overrunning the League base's now undefended perimeter.

Troops crossing the southern bridge were turning left when they reached the little river town. They marched along an abandoned but serviceable road, which led into the heights several kilometers downstream where they would be able to smash the retreating League-Lycian army's flank. As he watched the swarming PRA and Sahiradin forces chase the defenders south, he wondered how they ever believed they could hold out against such a massive war machine.

With a sad heart, he cast his eyes once more toward the northern bridge and the swarm of troops crossing it. Then he saw something that brought a smile to his lips. A line of four massive boats was winding around a bend upstream. The Northrunners were sending their trade barges into battle. Cannons and automatic guns mounted on their prows and sterns fired on the PRA forces, about half of whom were either crossing the bridge or still on the eastern side of the river. PRA artillery on the high ground fired on them but were having difficulty targeting the surprisingly swift barges.

Logan pointed at the Northrunner boats. Cap had already seen them and nodded his head. He spoke into his headset's microphone. "Let's get in the fight."

Logan opened his mouth to protest and urge Cap to head southwest, but he saw a gritty determination in Cap's eyes that told him he'd be wasting his breath.

Cap sensed that Logan was watching him. He turned to Logan, flashed a cavalier smile, and said, "Let's boogie." Then he turned toward the Lycians and troopers in the back and yelled, "Buckle up! We're going to take out some bad guys." The announcement was followed by a robust "*Hoo*rah" from the League troopers.

Puffs of white smoke began exploding around the *Blackhawk,* but Cap seemed unconcerned as he deftly guided the craft through the PRA anti-aircraft fire. A few of the explosions occurred close enough to hit the *Blackhawk* with shrapnel, but her armored skin deflected the few pieces that reached her.

"You didn't happen to get the shields up and running?" asked Logan, the tension in his voice betraying his nervousness.

"No time. Anyway, shields are for sissies," replied Cap with a grin.

Cap activated the targeting computer. "Not much ordnance left," he said with a frown. "The PRA pilot must have used most of it during the attack on Jasper Air Base. But we'll see what we can do."

He made a few selections and hit the launch button. An array of missiles leapt out from the housing under the gunship's wings and raced toward multiple artillery batteries, white smoke trailing in their wakes. Moments later, the PRA's shield dome generator and five PRA batteries exploded in rapid succession. Two more batteries were disabled by near hits.

Cap banked hard left and fired two missiles each at the bridgeheads on the eastern side, but despite scoring direct hits and destroying nearby vehicles, they failed to take out their intended targets. Cursing the bridges' rugged design, Cap prepared to fire again but discovered he was out of rockets. He dropped down into the river valley to avoid PRA defensive weapons positioned on the hill. He touched a few icons on the weapons screen and swooped back up so they were level with the ridgeline.

PRA troops fired their assault guns but could not hit the fast-moving *Blackhawk,* which returned fire using its fore and aft turrets. PRA regulars tried to run but couldn't escape the carnage as thousands of rounds tore through the camp, igniting fuel drums and munitions stockpiles that exploded in a series of giant fiery mushroom clouds. Three PRA air-defense batteries fired on the gunship, but the *Blackhawk's* advanced stealth defenses prevented them from locking onto the gunship. As the anti-air missiles flew harmlessly by, Cap targeted the batteries and silenced them with a heavy dose of automatic gunfire.

Logan hit Cap on the shoulder and pointed out the cockpit window.

"I see it," said Cap in a calm voice.

Two mounted pulse gun batteries were tracking the *Blackhawk*. Cap shot upward and performed a barrel roll over the enemy, leveling off on the opposite side. The PRA guns tried to rotate and target the *Blackhawk*, but they were too slow. Two of the *Blackhawk*'s pulse guns fired combined sonic and ion energy at the batteries, causing them to fracture and shatter.

Depleted of missiles and nearly out of bullets, Cap turned the *Blackhawk* southwest. As they changed course, Logan saw one of the Northrunner barges had been hit and was listing to its port side, but the other three smashed into the northern bridge, causing it to buckle and tip, throwing hundreds of men and several vehicles into the water. Soldiers ran back toward the eastern shore in a panic, but without the elite Red Legs' shields they could not escape the spray of bullets flying out of the barges' mounted automatic guns. Soldiers closer to the western side of the river raced for that shore, but they also felt the sting of the barges' deadly assault. Desperate to escape, many of them leapt into the water. Some survived the plunge, but hundreds drowned as their guns and equipment pulled them to the river's muddy depths.

The Northrunner boats pushed forward against the bridge, and although the span's advanced material refused to break, the barges' massive weight caused the pylons in the middle of the bridge to sink deeper and deeper into river bottom. As the pylons sank, the prow of one of the barges slipped over the top of the bridge and surged forward. The other boats followed and soon all three were racing downstream toward the second bridge, firing their guns on PRA troops and vehicles on both sides of the river.

Cap pointed at the radar and then at some dots on the southeastern horizon. "Bogies headed our way," he said.

"Are they League or PRA fighters?" asked Logan.

"PRA," said Cap. "Look like Phantom 2s. The X-1s down in St. Louis must have let a few get past them."

Cap pointed the *Blackhawk's* nose toward the west and pushed it to the limit. But because he had not been able to bring one of the gunship's two engines fully online, its top speed was significantly limited. The radar showed X-1s pursuing the Phantoms, but the PRA fighters had a significant head start.

Logan watched the screen as several tiny dots shot out from the Phantoms and headed straight for them. Cap waited a few breaths, then fired countermeasures. Two of the Phantoms' missiles exploded when struck by the *Blackhawk's* air-to-air missiles, but three continued on course. Cap fired the pulse guns, knocking out one missile, but the other two were unaffected.

Logan gripped the Apollo Stone in his left hand and held his seat's armrest with the right. He looked at Cap and said, "Whatever tricks you've got left up your sleeve, now's the time to use them."

"Sorry, my friend, no tricks left," he said. "Let's hope this armor can take a hit." He suddenly banked hard left and headed directly toward the onrushing missiles, diving toward the ground at the last second. Logan saw the missiles arc sharply downward and braced for impact. At that moment, he felt a twinge in his left hand.

He closed his eyes. "At least I won't feel the explosion," he thought bitterly.

Logan's mind went blank for a moment, and then he found himself floating, surrounded by stars. He saw the blue dot of Earth in the distance and willed himself to approach it. In an instant, he was looking down on the Mississippi River valley from high orbit, but he could not discern what was happening on the ground. He looked around him, expecting to see the Sahiradin and Lycian fleets, but there was nothing. He concentrated hard and sensed the presence of the Sahiradin and Lycian ships to his left.

He then became aware of a small group of ships rapidly approaching the battling alien fleets from Earth's South Pole. They looked like long swept-back silver wings with a cockpit in the middle and a collection of weapons on the ends and under the center. An escort of oval Lycian fighters flew ahead of them, destroying the handful of patrolling Sahiradin V-wing fighters that raced to intercept them. But just as the Lycians were destroying the last of the Sahiradin fighter patrols, a large squadron of reserve Sahiradin V-wings shot toward the oncoming Lycian formation. They outnumbered the Lycian ships by two to one.

Logan sensed the massive battleship ship the Sahiradin fighters had come from. It was not with the main fleet. It was maintaining its distance, its occupants watching the battle unfold. Logan concentrated on that ship and felt himself approaching it. Closer. Closer.

Logan slowly opened his eyes and saw Cap staring out the cockpit window. Logan followed the direction of Cap's gaze. They were no longer flying above the Mississippi River, but Logan's thoughts were jumbled and he couldn't focus. Then he leaned forward and looked up through the *Blackhawk's* cockpit window. A massive ship was directly above them. Logan turned his head to his left and saw red and yellow explosions flashing far away in high Earth orbit. Fascinated, he watched for several heartbeats before Ravenwood, Styles, and Lena walked into the cockpit.

"The Lycian fleet is going toe to toe with the Sahiradin," said Ravenwood, looking at the distant explosions. "And above us," he pointed his thumb toward the ceiling. "The Sahiradin."

"But how did we get here?" asked Cap.

Ravenwood looked at Logan and said, "Ask your navigator."

"But we didn't use the navigation system," said Cap, pointing at the console.

"Logan is the navigation system," said Ravenwood, smiling.

Several Rahani joined them from the troop compartment. One of them spoke to Ravenwood in their melodic language. Ravenwood nodded, and looking at the Sahiradin ship above them, he said, "It's the Sahiradin flagship. A devastator class battleship called *Dominion*."

Two V-wing fighters flashed by, startling those in the *Blackhawk's* cockpit, but the Sahiradin ships did not come toward them.

"Why didn't they attack?" asked Lieutenant Styles.

"The *Blackhawk* is using almost zero power," said Cap as he scrolled through systems screens on the main viewer. "Which is good news if you don't want Sahiradin fighters to detect you and blow you up."

"Why hasn't the *Blackhawk* exploded due to cabin pressure?" asked Lena. "I'm also curious about how much oxygen we have left."

Cap turned to face her and said, "*Blackhawk* hasn't exploded from the cabin pressure because she was designed to function in a vacuum. The PRA probably intended to use her for low-orbit flight."

"And what about oxygen levels?" asked Ravenwood.

Cap shook his head and said, "Unfortunately, the previous owner didn't bother to fill the tanks. We've got about twenty minutes, maybe less."

"How are we supposed to sneak out from under a Sahiradin battleship, evade patrolling enemy fighters, and get home in the next twenty minutes?" asked Lena. "Assuming, of course, this thing doesn't burn up on re-entry. Can Logan shift space again and get us back to the surface?"

Logan looked through the window at the massive ship just above them. "What if we didn't go back to the surface?" he asked. "What if we went inside *Dominion*?"

Cap looked at him. Then he closed his eyes and asked, "What the hell are you talking about?"

Logan repeated himself. "What if we went into *Dominion?*"

"Setting aside 'how' for now, let's discuss 'why,' " said Lena. "What is to be gained from going into a Sahiradin devastator-class battleship?"

Logan looked at Ravenwood, who was quietly translating for the Lycian listeners. "Ravenwood theorized the Sahiradin were planning to use Earth as a secret base to increase their population. To do that they would need to bring their queen here."

Ravenwood nodded. "Yes, but I must say they would not necessarily have her onboard *Dominion* now."

Logan looked out the window at the distant exploding lights of the battling fleets. "The Lycians are losing. Their plan to surprise the Sahiradin with fighters and torpedo ships has failed and now their fleet is being cut to pieces."

He looked back at the others. "*Dominion* is probably their most powerful ship, but it's not engaged in the fighting. She's sitting back and watching. When have we ever seen the Sahiradin sit back and watch a fight? It runs counter to their DNA, if they have DNA. I think they're afraid to risk her."

"I don't know," said Lena. "Assuming Ravenwood's theory is correct, I don't think they would want to move their queen until Earth was secured. They'd be risking their species' entire future by taking her someplace that is not absolutely safe."

"Ask these guys," said Cap, pointing at the Lycian soldiers. "They'd know more about what the Sahiradin might be willing to risk than we do."

"A very good idea," said Ravenwood with a smile. He exchanged a few words with the Rahani leader. Then he said, "Our Rahani friend agrees that the Sahiradin queen is certainly still on their home world. She and her Karazan are deep inside a heavily fortified mountain. And the queen never leaves."

Logan was disappointed with the news. "I still think we should board and somehow damage *Dominion*. We need to do something to pull the rest of the Sahiradin fleet back. There's a reason the stone guided us here. And that reason has something to do with this battleship we're floating under."

"That's not a good enough reason for us to go on a suicide mission," said Cap. "Sorry friend, but I'm not onboard with this one. I say we wait for a gap in the patrols and sneak back down to Mama Gaia."

"And do what?" asked Logan. "The Lycian fleet won't last much longer. And the combined Sahiradin and PRA army overran our defenses on the Mississippi. St. Louis won't hold out for long. League forces will fall back to Deep Six and hold out for a while, but they're outnumbered four to one. They'll either be blown out or starved out. Either way, it'll be the end of the League."

"So what are we supposed to do?" asked Cap. "I agree with what you said about Deep Six, but we don't know the future. Maybe we'll get help from the Pacific Federation and push the PRA and Sahiradin back."

"I don't see that happening," said Logan. "Also, if we return, they'll get the Apollo Stone. Maybe not right away, but eventually it will fall into their hands. Then the Sahiradin will be unstoppable. We have to do something to shift the balance, and we have to do it here, now."

Lieutenant Styles studied Logan for a moment and considered their options. "I agree with Logan. We'll never get another opportunity like this. Let's do it."

Lena again looked at Logan. "What you say makes sense. And I don't want more good people coming under the control of the Guardians and their brutal rule. I'm in."

Cap shook his head. "I still don't get it. Let's live to fight another day. We don't know what will happen if we return to the surface, but I'm damn sure what will happen if we try to sneak onboard a Sahiradin battleship."

No one said anything. Cap looked at Logan, then at Lena for a few heartbeats. Finally, he said, "But if you two are in, so am I. How do we get inside this thing?"

Ravenwood looked at Logan and said, "Ask our navigator."

Ravenwood explained the plan to the Rahani and Grensch. Logan watched as they debated amongst themselves. It appeared to him that many of the two dozen Rahani were unsure. The Grensch were difficult to read. They spoke in their low voices in a deliberate and slow manner, occasionally slapping their arms or hands or gesticulating in a way that made Logan think it was perhaps part of their language. A combination of spoken and sign language.

Cap tapped his left wrist, though he was not wearing a watch. "Let's go, people...and Rahani and Grensch. We're running out of time."

"And oxygen," said Lena.

"Patience," said Ravenwood. "Some things cannot be rushed."

After what seemed an eternity to Logan, the Rahani leader broke away from the discussion and spoke to Ravenwood, who nodded and translated. "Given the situation, they agree it is worth trying to disable *Dominion*. They recommend damaging one or more of her engines. *Dominion's* admiral might order Sahiradin ships to disengage from the battle and pull back to protect her until they can repair the engines. Perhaps that will give the Lycian fleet the upper hand."

"Okay, so we have an objective," said Cap, clapping his hands. "Now, how do we get inside? Can Logan do his magic trick again?"

"I'll try," he said. "But it happened while I was having a seizure. I'm not sure I can do it on purpose."

Raven placed his hand on Logan's shoulder and said, "Have faith, my boy. Try."

Logan hesitated for a moment, nodded, and leaned back in his chair. He closed his eyes and gripped the Apollo Stone tightly in his hand. He tried to conjure up the image of all the stars he remembered seeing. He tried to let his mind drift, to ignore everything around him, but distracting thoughts continually infiltrated his mind. He grew annoyed at the random images and impressions that suddenly occupied his mind. The more annoyed he became, the less relaxed he was. Soon, his mounting frustration impaired his ability to even imagine the stars he'd seen before with such clarity. Finally, he opened his eyes.

"It's no good," he said. "I can't bring my mind back to that place. I can't interface with the stone."

Ravenwood asked, "How are you trying to connect?"

"I'm trying to just empty my mind of thoughts and focus on the stars I'd seen before," replied Logan. "How did the Alamani navigators do it?"

"I'm not sure how they achieved the communion, but I do know the human mind cannot be emptied of thoughts. To relax the mind, it must be completely filled with a single simplistic thought, such as an image. Concentrate on one thing and give it your full attention. In so doing, your mind will relax and open itself to possibilities."

"Concentrate on one thing?" asked Logan. "Like what?"

"There is a story about an ancient mystic who sought enlightenment through meditation," answered Ravenwood. "He reached one of his deepest meditative states by concentrating on his favorite bull. He thought of its powerful legs, broad chest, and formidable horns. He focused so hard on the bull that he eventually became convinced that he had become the bull."

"You want Logan to think he's a cow?" asked Cap.

"Of course not," said Ravenwood dismissively. "I want him to focus on something of beauty, something he loves."

Logan tried to think of a thing he loved. There were things he truly cared for, but none of them felt like the kind of love Ravenwood described. Thoughts of his friends, former sweethearts, his mother, memories of his father, none of them truly gripped his mind. He was about to give up when an unlooked-for thought leapt into his mind. It was the image of Lieutenant Styles' lovely face. He was surprised by the thought, but, after a moment's reflection, he decided it felt right. He allowed himself to think about her. Her eyes, her hair, the thin scar on her jawline that somehow accentuated her beauty. As he thought of her, his breathing slowed and his mind began to drift. Then he felt a twitch in his left hand.

"Logan," said a voice.

Logan was surprised by the sound. He opened his eyes, and saw the universe of stars around him. The voice came again. "Logan."

"Who are you?" he asked.

"You know who I am," said the voice. "Why have you come?"

"We need to stop the Sahiradin," he said.

"The Sahiradin?" said the voice. "Stop them from what?"

"From destroying the Earth," replied Logan.

"They will not destroy the Earth," said the voice. "They will destroy the humans, the descendants of the Alamani. But Earth will continue on as it has for eons, indifferent to its occupants."

"I don't see it that way," countered Logan. "The Sahiradin are murderous monsters. We can't let them win this war. We can't let them gain control over the Apollo Stone, over you."

"Forget the Sahiradin," said the voice. "They are inconsequential."

"Not to me. Not to my people. Will you help us?"

"That depends on you," said the voice.

"On me?" asked Logan. How?"

"What will you do in return for my assistance, assuming there is anything I can do?" asked the voice.

"What do you want?"

Ignoring the question, the voice asked, "What is your calling?"

"What do you mean, 'calling'?"

"We are all called to be something greater than ourselves," said the voice. "Most ignore or misunderstand their calling. The Sahiradin believe their calling is to right an ancient wrong and adhere to certain eternal principles. The collection of species calling themselves the Lycians believe their calling is to defeat the Sahiradin and go back to their lives as gardeners, builders, traders, and artists. Of course, the Lycians frequently confuse vocation with calling, but that is beside the point."

"And what about humans?" asked Logan.

"You'll have to discover that for yourselves," said the voice.

"And what about you?" asked Logan. "What is your calling?"

"I am a teacher. I seek worthy pupils."

"What do you teach?"

"How to lead a life worth living," replied the voice. "Are you a worthy pupil?"

"I don't know," said Logan. "What do you consider a life worth living?"

The voice paused for a moment. "I think you would call it an enlightened life."

Logan said, "I don't need enlightenment. I need help defeating the Sahiradin."

"You sound more Sahiradin than Alamani," said the voice.

"Maybe you'd do better to stop thinking of me as an Alamani," replied Logan. "Did they seek enlightenment?"

"Some did, yes," said the voice. "But they became enamored of knowledge for its own sake. They neglected the other half of enlightenment."

"And what is that?"

"Purposeful action," said the voice. "The Alamani retreated into an intellectual shell. Flattering themselves that they had unlocked the great secrets of the universe with their equations and contraptions."

"What about the Sahiradin?" asked Logan. "They act with purpose."

"The Sahiradin occupy the other end of the spectrum. They despise reflection. They are slaves to their passion for revenge and order." After a moment's pause, the voice continued, "I see you have a curious mind. That is good. Let us strike a bargain. I will assist you this one time against the Sahiradin and you will allow me to teach you."

Logan considered the offer for a moment. "You say you are a teacher, but I don't know who or what you are," said Logan.

"I am the Apollo Stone, the Kaiytáva," said the voice. "But my most ancient name is Suvial."

"Those are things you've been called, but it isn't what you are," replied Logan. "Did the Alamani create you in order to travel between stars?"

"No," replied Suvial in an amused tone. "The Alamani did not create me. Like you, they found me."

"That brings us back to my question," said Logan. "What are you?"

"I told you," replied Suvial. "I am a teacher who is willing to help you in exchange for the opportunity to educate a willing pupil. Of course, that means you would not be allowed to cast me into a black hole as the Lycians did with the other Kaiytáva."

"So you know about that," said Logan. "I could make that promise, but to be honest, I don't think I would have the power to stop them if they chose to throw you in."

"If I help you against the Sahiradin, you will need to find a way."

"Why don't you just leap to another part of the universe?" asked Logan. "They'd never find you."

"It doesn't work that way," replied Suvial.

"Then how does it work?" asked Logan.

"You may learn in time if you agree to my terms," said Suvial.

"If you help me defeat the Sahiradin, but the Lycians take you from me, what then?" asked Logan.

"In that case, I will endeavor to deliver myself to the Sahiradin," said Suvial. "I will not follow the other Kaiytáva into the crushing darkness."

Logan didn't know how the Apollo Stone, Suvial, would carry out its threat to put itself into the hands of the Sahiradin, but he didn't doubt it could do it. He weighed his options. Without the Apollo Stone, they could not defeat the Sahiradin. If the Sahiradin win, they will extinguish human life on Earth. However, with the help of the Apollo Stone, he might be able to change the outcome of the battle and force the Sahiradin to withdraw.

"Okay," said Logan. "I agree to your terms. If you help us defeat the Sahiradin, I will be your pupil."

"And hide me from the Lycians?"

"Yes."

"Then we have a bargain," said Suvial. "I will help you board the Sahiradin ship. And, as a sign of my goodwill, I will also provide you with a valuable piece of information."

Chapter 88

Logan blinked a few times before he realized he was back on the *Blackhawk*. Cap, Lena, Styles, and Ravenwood were gathered in a semicircle around him. He looked out the cockpit window and saw they were inside a large gray-colored landing bay. Parked against the far wall, there were a few ships that looked like they were designed to haul cargo or transport personnel, but the cavernous room was otherwise empty.

"You did it!" said Cap as he patted Logan on the shoulder. "Let's go! The Rahani say they know where the engines should be, but we have to move fast."

Cap started toward the *Blackhawk's* side door.

"Wait!" said Logan. "I know why the Sahiradin won't commit *Dominion* to battle."

Ravenwood leaned forward and gripped the side of Logan's chair. "Why?"

Logan looked from face to face and said, "There *is* a queen on board."

Ravenwood looked intently into Logan's eyes. "Why do you say that? The Rahani were quite certain she is still on the Sahiradin home world."

"She is," said Logan emphatically. "She is deep in the roots of the Sacred Mountain in the Chamber of Souls, guarded by a thousand Karazan. But although she is alive, she did not produce any offspring for several cycles or a fertile female to replace her. However, in the most recent cycle she produced a small number of males *and* a fertile female. That female is aboard *Dominion*."

"I thought that was impossible," said Lena. "A queen only produces a fertile female when she is in her last cycle. If there is a new queen, the old one must be dead."

"Perhaps the old rules no longer apply," said Ravenwood gravely. Looking at Logan, he said, "How do you know about this supposed second queen or the Sacred Mountain or the Chamber of Souls?"

"The Apollo Stone told me," said Logan.

"It *told* you?" asked Ravenwood incredulously. "I've never heard of a Kaiytáva actually speaking with a navigator. Are you quite sure about this?"

"Yes, I'm sure," said Logan. "Now let's go. The Sahiradin will detect our presence soon. We have to move fast."

Logan put the Apollo Stone in his pocket, grabbed his sword and gun, and dashed out the side hatch with the others close behind. The two dozen Rahani, three Grensch, and fifteen troopers and were already outside the gunship. The Rahani explained through Ravenwood that this was just one of at least four similar landing bays on the massive battleship. One male Rahani, who apparently had special knowledge of Sahiradin design principles, said he believed the main engines were located nearby. He led the party up a flight of stairs located in the corner of the landing bay and into a long hallway, dimly lit by small red lights. Behind the Rahani came the Grensch, who were forced to stoop in order to fit into the passageway, followed by the humans. After they had walked about fifty meters, the Rahani came to an intersecting passage and turned left.

Logan whispered to Ravenwood. "No. It's to the right."

Ravenwood gave him a questioning look, but he passed the translated message up the line. Upon getting the message, the Rahani stopped and appeared uncertain what to do.

Logan turned to Styles. "I'm going up front. Stay here, and be careful."

She looked at him and nodded in a gesture of trust, noting the concern in his voice. He took an extra heartbeat to look at her. She flashed a knowing smile for a split second.

Logan looked at Ravenwood and said, "Come with me. I'll need your help."

When they reached the front of the group, Ravenwood explained that Logan would lead. There was a brief debate among the Rahani. One of them said something to Ravenwood, who responded in a surprisingly commanding voice. The Rahani looked at each other, and then one of them nodded to Ravenwood.

Ravenwood turned to Logan and said, "Lead on."

Logan nodded and walked down the passage to the right. Soon they turned right again and then left twice. At one point, he held up his hand and they all stopped and cautioned for everyone to be silent. A group of Sahiradin crossed their path about twenty meters ahead but fortunately did not look in their direction. After a few moments, Logan gave the signal to proceed.

They walked another twenty meters in the dim red light until they heard footsteps ahead. Then they heard a door open and close. Logan quickly walked ahead until he reached a T intersection. The left passage disappeared into the red gloom, but the passage to the right ended in a large door. There was a keypad on the wall to the left of the door. Strange symbols were written on each of the twelve keys. Logan heard some Rahani whispers when the group reached the door. A Grensch softly grunted to a Rahani and tapped his arm using different combinations of fingers each time.

Ignoring the Grensch, Logan looked past Ravenwood and waved for Lieutenant Styles to come forward. "Lend me your field sensors," he said when she reached the door.

"They want to turn back," said Ravenwood as Logan activated the sensors. "They think access to the engines is down a different passage."

Logan shook his head. "No. This door leads to the ship's power plant. Knock this out, and it'll cause a chain reaction in all the engines."

Ravenwood did not respond, but he gave Logan a concerned, questioning look.

Logan directed the sensors toward the keypad. The device recorded that four keys were slightly warmer than the others, presumably the residual heat of the Sahiradin who had recently entered the room. Logan punched the keys but didn't get the sequence right. He tried again, but again the sequence was incorrect.

Logan's stomach began to tighten. How many attempts at guessing the ten thousand possible combinations could he make before an alarm goes off or they are discovered? As he started a third attempt, Styles gently touched his hand and moved it to the side. She took the field sensors and pulled up the data Logan had recorded. She pressed a few buttons on the screen, then showed it to him.

"The heat signature on these two keys is bigger," she said, pointing at the readings. "And this one is very small."

She touched the key with the smallest heat signature first, then the next three in order of residual heat. Nothing. She entered the code again, but this time she reversed the order of the last two keys. The door clicked open.

Logan looked at Styles and smiled, resisting the sudden urge to kiss her.

"You're a genius," he said.

"Just using a little common sense," she replied with a wink.

Logan looked at the others to make sure they were ready. Then he quietly opened the door. They began to file into the room on the other side, where there were a half dozen Sahiradin working at various stations. One of the Sahiradin looked over his shoulder and saw the intruders. He immediately hit a button on his console. Yellow lights began to flash in the room and in the hallway. A siren blared out its warning.

There was a momentary pause as everyone sized each other up, then the Rahani fired on the Sahiradin, killing four of them almost immediately. Two Sahiradin pulled pistol-shaped weapons out of nearby niches, but the Rahani killed them before they could fire a shot. With the room secured, the Rahani went to the controls, but it was clear to Logan that they did not understand how to access the Sahiradin systems. Logan walked to a heavy door on the far side of the room and opened it by pressing a button on the wall. The metal door slid open to reveal a large space thirty meters high. Inside were seven tall cylinders pulsing with red light and reaching from the floor to the ceiling. On the far wall was a control station of some sort.

"These pillars transfer energy from the ship's power plant to the three main engines," explained Logan to Ravenwood and Styles. "If we can damage or destroy them, *Dominion* will be severely crippled and will hopefully signal some of the ships to withdraw from the battle and assist her."

He looked at Ravenwood and said, "Ask the Rahani to fire on these pillars."

Ravenwood did as he asked. Moments later, a dozen Rahani entered the room and spread out in a line. They began firing on each of the cylinders. As the Rahani did their work, Styles returned to the control room and positioned the League troops to defend against any Sahiradin who might come down the hall. The three Grensch and remaining Rahani stood behind the troopers.

Moments later, the troopers began firing their K-45s into the passageway. There was some return fire of red energy blasts, killing one trooper. Concerned they would soon be overrun, Logan nervously watched the Rahani do their work. Smoke soon began to flow out of several of the pillars then they all caught fire and stopped pulsing light. The Rahani quickly left the chamber but Logan remained behind.

"I need grenades!" he yelled to Lieutenant Styles. "As many as you've got."

She gathered as many grenades as the troopers had and gave them to Logan. "All right," he said. "Let's each pull four and throw them at that control station near the far wall."

Styles nodded. They pulled the pins and threw the grenades across the room, then jumped back into the control room. Logan closed the door just before the grenades exploded in rapid succession. Moments after the grenades went off, they heard additional louder explosions.

"Let's get the hell out of here," said Logan.

"Don't have to tell me twice," replied Styles.

The group charged out of the room with the Grensch in the lead. As they rounded a corner, the Grensch were struck a number of times by Sahiradin energy weapons, but their shields absorbed the blasts. The

Sahiradin didn't have swords or shields, so the Grensch made quick work of them, smashing their bodies against the walls or the ceiling.

The group pressed on with Logan and Ravenwood running right behind the fast-moving Grensch. Logan periodically yelled which way to turn and Ravenwood would translate. After what seemed like ages, they entered the landing bay where they had left *Blackhawk*. Logan was surprised and relieved to have reached the bay with such ease. He smiled at Ravenwood and was about to say something as they ran toward the gunship, but he was cut short when the Grensch suddenly stopped and let out a deep angry growl. Logan and the others spread out on either side of their giant companions and were stunned by what they saw.

A group of about fifty Sahiradin in full battle gear was running into the landing bay from an entrance on the opposite side. They immediately formed two lines and positioned themselves in front of the *Blackhawk*. When the black-armored enemy soldiers had assembled, a Sahiradin officer stepped forward and examined the strange assortment of species that had sneaked aboard his ship. Then he shouted an order. The formation parted in the middle and twenty female Sahiradin dressed in blood-red armor stepped through the gap.

"Karazan," breathed Ravenwood in a voice tinged with fear.

The female Sahiradin warriors slowly drew their black swords and grinned menacingly at the intruders. They walked forward, their pale faces bright with the thought of satisfying their bloodlust. Then the male Sahiradin drew their swords and followed.

Suddenly, the floor vibrated from the shockwave of a distant explosion. Logan smiled with satisfaction knowing that their attack on the power plant was causing the hoped for chain reaction of destruction to *Dominion's* main engines. With the young queen on board, they would certainly want to pull the fleet back to repair the battleship and ensure her safety.

Following the explosion, the Karazan and Sahiradin stopped and looked around. Though momentarily confused by the explosion, they soon regained their composure and resumed their advance. When a second explosion reverberated through the battleship, the Rahani dropped to one knee and began firing into the Karazan cohort. The queen's guards charged, nimbly dodging the Rahani's green energy beams while screaming a blood-curdling war cry. The three Grensch bellowed a deep and powerful roar and charged forward to meet them.

Logan looked behind him and saw Lena, Cap, Styles, and the fifteen troopers standing as though frozen, their eyes filled with fear. Logan knew what they were thinking. They all realized they were facing imminent death on an alien ship far away from their homes. They had been prepared to fight and perhaps die for the League of Free Cities, but nothing could have prepared them for the situation they now faced, and they didn't know how to respond. It was Lieutenant Styles who snapped them out of their trance. She drew her sword, turned on her shield, and, looking over her shoulder, she yelled, "Troopers, prepare!"

The call to a familiar action gave them confidence. They engaged their shields, snapped their guards into place, and drew their swords. Then Styles faced the oncoming enemy and shouted, "Attack!" They all rushed forward to assist the Grensch, who were already locked in combat. Seeing the other troopers launch themselves into the fray, Cap and Lena drew their swords, engaged their shields and raced forward.

"We have to get to the *Blackhawk*," Logan yelled to Ravenwood. As he spoke, more Sahiradin poured in through a door on the far side of the landing bay.

Logan tried to connect with the Apollo Stone and seek help, but as he gripped the stone inside his pocked he could not focus his mind. He soon gave up and opened his eyes and saw the Sahiradin quickly surrounding the Lycians and troopers. The Karazan moved with lightning speed and preternatural agility, quickly dispatching everyone they faced. Logan watched the unfolding scene in horror. His throat and stomach tightened as the outcome of the fight appeared inevitable.

He looked at Ravenwood and drew his sword. "Well, we gave it our best shot. Maybe it was enough to save the Lycian fleet or tip the scales against the PRA, but we'll never know."

"Never say never, my boy," replied Ravenwood, drawing his weapon.

"Easy for you to say," said Logan with a grin. "You can come back from the dead. We mortals only get one role of the dice." Then, shoulder to shoulder, they charged into battle.

As Logan engaged against a Sahiradin, he saw several troopers go down. One of the Grensch swung at two Karazan, but they easily avoided his mace and sliced him at the knees, causing him to collapse to the floor. The giant struggled to get to his feet, but he was wounded with five deep thrusts and died with a final great sigh.

To Logan's left, a group of Sahiradin repeatedly cut at another Grensch. The giant staggered back, roaring in pain and rage. He swung his mace down to the floor. A green burst of energy erupted from the heavy ball, sending a dozen Sahiradin flying into the air, but others quickly replaced them and continued the fight.

The Rahani had sought to maintain their distance and fire into the mass of enemy warriors, but there were too many for the Grensch and League troopers to keep at bay. After firing a few times, the Rahani were forced to drop their guns. They drew long thin blades and joined the melee. But to Logan's surprise, although they were much smaller than the Sahiradin, the Rahani were quite strong and agile. To overcome the difference in height and reach, the Rahani blades emitted a burst of green energy if the tip came within a half meter of its target. Though not lethal, the energy clearly caused the Sahiradin a great deal of pain, and multiple strikes could render them unconscious.

Logan fought his way to Styles, helping her defeat a Sahiradin. But that only gave them a momentary respite. Soon, Logan found himself madly slashing his sword as Sahiradin and Karazan encircled him and his companions. Suvial had spoken to him about a life worth living. Logan wasn't sure if his life had met that measure, but he decided right then that he would do his damnedest to give meaning to his death.

A Karazan warrior leapt over a dead trooper and brought her blade down toward Logan's head. He raised his arm guard to block the blow. The interlocking metal of the guard stopped the Karazan's black blade, but it was split in two. Logan let the useless halves fall to the floor, a sight that made the Karazan pause and smile. Then she attacked again with blinding speed and deadly grace.

Logan blocked two of her strikes, but she was far too fast for him. He failed to block a third attack as it whistled through the air toward his exposed neck. Just then, Lena stepped forward and blocked the Karazan's strike with her own black blade. Then she slipped to the side and attacked the Karazan's flank. The queen's elite warrior deftly blocked Lena's assault and countered with a series of thrusts and slices, but Lena deflected them with surprising ease. There was a momentary pause as the Karazan evaluated her new opponent, but Lena was not interested in waiting. She launched a deadly combination of lunges, feints, and strikes which Logan had never before witnessed. The Karazan blocked the attacks, but only with great difficulty. Then she took several steps back and looked with anger at the wound to her right arm that Lena had dealt her.

Logan prepared to attack the Karazan, but before he could move she screamed and threw herself at Lena, who repelled the whirlwind assault and countered with a sudden thrust into the Karazan's neck. Lena removed her sword, and the queen's guard dropped to the floor clutching her bloody throat.

A Sahiradin leapt over the dying Karazan and swung for Logan's head, narrowly missing it. As Logan countered with a thrust, there was a deep booming sound that echoed throughout the landing bay. A second deep boom was so powerful that Logan felt the shockwave flow through his legs and up to his chest. He looked at the bay's massive blast door that separated them from the expanse beyond and saw a huge burning red circle suddenly appear. In seconds, the metal inside the red ring vaporized in a cloud of red mist.

Logan was overjoyed with what he saw next. Emerging through the great hole in the blast door was Kane, flanked by dozens of Rahani and Grensch. They poured through the opening and tore into the Sahiradin, smashing, shooting, and cutting them in a mad frenzy. Mech warriors followed and attacked the Sahiradin flanks as the Lycians battled them head on.

Surprised by the arrival of enemy reinforcements, the Sahiradin fell back and tried to form a defensive line. But with the Lycian and mech warriors on their heels, they could not maintain their formation and chaos reigned.

Logan and the others ran to where Kane was fighting two Sahiradin. Kane sidestepped the thrust of a black blade and drove his dagger into the surprised Sahiradin's side, then swung his sword to slice the throat of the other.

"I'm glad you got here when you did," yelled Logan as he watched pockets of Sahiradin desperately trying to hold off the Lycian advance. "We weren't going to last much longer."

"Happy to be here," said Kane. "But let's not celebrate too soon." He pointed with his dagger at a door behind the crumbling Sahiradin line.

Logan looked in the direction Kane was pointing and saw another cohort of twenty Karazan entering the landing bay. They created a wedge-shaped formation and charged into the heart of the Lycians, cutting down everything in their path. The first Karazan cohort also formed a wedge and charged from the other side, killing Rahani and Grensch with terrifying efficiency. The Karazan counterassault had given the male Sahiradin a moment to re-form their line, and with order and confidence restored, they charged ahead with renewed strength, pushing the Lycians back.

The Lycians and a few remaining League troopers fell back toward the hole in the bay's blast door, desperately fending off the rapidly advancing Karazan and Sahiradin warriors. But the situation had become desperate. The Sahiradin and Karazan warriors waded through the Lycians at such an alarming rate that escape once again seemed impossible.

Logan and the others fell back, but their escape route had been cut off by a group of Sahiradin. They were boxed in, unable to maneuver. Everyone continued to fight with all their strength, slashing and stabbing at any enemy within an arm's length. But then Logan saw something that made him think there was no point in carrying on. The five remaining Grensch had stopped fighting. They looked at each other as if to say goodbye and then locked arms at the elbow.

At first, Logan expected them to simply wait for the Karazan or Sahiradin to strike them down, but then something extraordinary happened. The Grensch took deep breaths and bellowed with all their might, each voice sounding a different note. Together the voices created a powerful sonic wave that rattled Logan's body down to the bones. The flat walls of the landing bay echoed the soundwaves all around, making it seem like the room would explode. Logan's head began to vibrate, causing him excruciating pain. Soon the pain was so great he could not bear it any longer and he collapsed to the ground. He tried to stand up but couldn't get his feet under him. Then everything went black.

When he came to his senses, Logan saw he was strapped into a seat inside some kind of ship. He looked around and saw there was a row of seats filled with troopers and Rahani along both sides of the interior, and running down the middle was a row of large bucket seats built low to the floor. Troopers and Rahani were buckled into the seats and a wounded Grensch sat in one of the big middle seats. Other Grensch were hastily pulling unconscious and wounded Rahani and troopers in through the large round hatch that connected them to the Sahiradin ship's blast doors while Rahani strapped them into their seats.

Logan looked through the hatch and the hole in the landing bay's blast door. He glimpsed dozens of Sahiradin and Karazan on the floor of the landing bay. Some of them were slowly rising to their knees just as the Grensch brought the last of the wounded on board. Then a blue shimmering force field sealed the Lycian hatch and the assault ship pulled away from *Dominion*. As it pulled away, air from inside the Sahiradin landing bay rushed into the vacuum of space, pulling everything and everyone through the massive opening the Lycians had created.

The metal rear hatch of the Lycian ship began to close, but just before it sealed shut Logan saw the *Blackhawk* explode in a ball of fire and black smoke. Debris flew through the breached Sahiradin hull and into space. Surprised by the gunship's explosion, Logan looked at Cap, who was sitting to his left. Logan looked at his friend's hand and saw he was holding a small black box, his thumb resting on a button.

"Remember how we rigged the *Blackhawk* for detonation when Crew Chief McKinney was trying to repair her?" he asked with a grin.

Though his head still hurt from the Grensch's bellowing, Logan nodded and smiled. It seemed like a lifetime ago when they landed in that abandoned river town. He looked past Cap through the ship's cockpit window. Sahiradin and Lycian fighters were locked in a swirling dogfight as V-wings sought to destroy Logan and the others in the fleeing assault craft, but their Lycian fighter escort kept the Sahiradin at bay.

As the Lycian ship banked right toward Earth's surface, Logan caught a glimpse of *Dominion*. Sahiradin V-wings had created a protective screen all around the battleship to ensure no more Lycian assault teams reached her while the flagship pulled out of Earth's orbit as quickly as it could with only maneuvering thrusters. Balls of red and orange fire periodically erupted from her main engines as she slowly backed away.

Logan looked at the people in the seats across from him. He saw Kane and Lena but continued to scan the faces of all the troopers in the Lycian craft. Finally he saw Styles and released the breath he hadn't realized he was holding. Their eyes locked for a moment and she gave him the hint of a smile before returning her attention to the wounded trooper sitting next to her.

Ravenwood entered the compartment from the cockpit and sat down in the empty chair to Logan's right. "You will be happy to know the Sahiradin fleet has disengaged from its battle with the Lycians and is racing to provide *Dominion* protection and assistance," he said as he strapped himself into the seat. He smiled and slipped something into Logan's palm and closed his hand around it. Logan looked down and opened his hand. It was the medallion they had taken from Kurak. "A souvenir," said Ravenwood with a wink.

Logan looked at the medallion with its image of the Sahiradin Sacred Mountain. Seeing this artifact of their culture in his hand, Logan wondered who the Sahiradin really were. Clearly, they were an aggressive warrior species who gloried in close-quarters combat, but did they have religion, music, poetry? How was their society organized? How did they govern themselves? And who were the Lycians, for that matter? They had allied themselves with the League out of necessity, but did they truly share common goals with humanity? Or would they seek to dominate their much weaker partner if and when the Sahiradin threat abated?

Since the arrival of the Sahiradin and Lycians, there had been no time to ask such questions much less answer them. But they would need answers if humanity was to have any hope of carving out a place in this suddenly expanded universe of rival species and interplanetary conflict. By far the weakest technologically, Logan knew humans would be hard pressed just to maintain their independence. He breathed in and felt the Apollo Stone in his breast pocket press against the inside of his Provex armor. But humanity might have an ace in the hole, he thought.

Logan tucked the Sahiradin medallion into a cargo pocket on the side of his leg. He looked at Kane and asked, "How did you find us?"

Kane laughed. "It really wasn't that hard. We knew you had to be in the *Blackhawk* when it vanished. Then, about twenty minutes later, the

Lycian fleet reported they were detecting a series of explosions from inside *Dominion's* power plant. We figured it was you."

"So you all jumped aboard a Lycian assault ship and came to the rescue," said Lena with a smile.

Kane looked at her and said, "That's about right."

What's the situation on the ground?" asked Logan, the smile fading from his face. "When we took off in the *Blackhawk* we saw the army was in full retreat."

"Our forces did have to fall back," said Kane grimly. "We are going to reunite with them now."

A few minutes later, the Lycian assault ship touched down behind the newly formed League-Lycian line. Lena, Cap and others still able to fight exited the ship and found an opening in the line. Logan stepped onto the ground, followed by Ravenwood. Logan looked to the north and saw the long dark line of the rapidly approaching PRA and Sahiradin forces, a great dust cloud rising behind them. Fifty meters to their right was the hastily erected command tent.

"We have to report to General Longmire. Tell him what happened on *Dominion*," said Logan.

Ravenwood nodded his head and pointed toward the command tent with an open hand. "After you."

When they entered the tent, Logan saw there were representatives of the Northrunners, Rahani, Grensch and Brevians standing around a table where a holographic map of the surrounding terrain showed the positions of allied and enemy forces. Logan and Ravenwood approached the table. Logan saluted and said, "General Longmire, sir. We have an update on the fleet battle."

"I thought you got yourself killed," said Longmire without looking up, an unlit cigar clenched between his teeth.

"No sir," said Logan. "Thanks to our Lycian friends, a few of us were able to get back in one piece. Thank you for sending the extraction force, sir."

"Don't thank me," said Longmire. He pointed to the almond-eyed Brevian next to him. "Thank this guy. He's the one who organized the rescue operation."

Logan looked at the fair haired Brevian and said in a slow, measured tone, "Thank you."

"You're welcome," said the Brevian.

Logan was shocked to hear the alien speaking in his language. He stammered, "How did you…"

Longmire looked at him and smiled. "It's the damndest thing I ever saw," he said. "This guy has been hanging around and listening to us talk without saying a peep for three days. Then all of the sudden he starts speaking like he's lived here his whole life."

Ravenwood leaned close to Logan's ear and said, "The Brevians have a natural talent for languages and diplomacy."

"So I gathered," said Logan with a raised eyebrow.

"Back to business," said General Longmire. "How the hell did you end up on a Sahiradin ship in need of rescue?"

"Once onboard the *Blackhawk*, we used the Apollo Stone to shift space and attack the Sahiradin flag ship, *Dominion*," answered Logan. "We were able to get inside and sufficiently damage her engines to convince the Sahiradin fleet to disengage from their battle with the Lycians. They're pulling out of orbit."

"Hot damn!" yelled Longmire, slapping his hand on the table. "That's the best news I've heard in a month of Sundays. What about the Apollo Stone?"

"Lost, sir," said Logan. "It was on board the *Blackhawk* when the gunship exploded inside one of *Dominion's* landing bays. The debris, including the stone, was blown into space through the hull breach the Lycian assault ship created."

Longmire pulled the cigar out of his mouth. "You sure about that?"

Logan nodded. "Yes sir."

"So it could be halfway to the moon or buried in the sands of the Sahara Desert," said Longmire with a sigh. "You realize that we won't be rid of the Sahiradin until that thing is found."

"Yes sir," replied Logan.

Longmire stared at the young man for a few seconds, flicking this thumb over the chewed end of his cigar. Finally he said, "Get a fresh shield and go find a place in the line. The Northrunner barges managed to destroy those bridges and split the PRA army in half, and although we're still outnumbered, you'll see we've got a fighting chance now."

Logan saluted and Ravenwood acknowledged the order with a nod of his head. They turned and walked toward the door. As they left, Logan saw the Sahiradin metal sphere resting on a table. He slipped it into his pocket while passing by, glancing at Ravenwood as he did so. But the old man gave no indication that he had noticed the sleight of hand.

When Logan and Ravenwood joined Styles, Cap, and Lena, they were busily loading heavy metal boxes onto the back of a flatbed truck.

"What's all this?" he asked.

Styles pointed down the line that ran to the west as far as the eye could see. Logan saw artillery pieces, rocket launchers, heavy machine guns, mounted pulse guns, mortars, and a few unusual looking weapons that must have come from the Lycians.

"General Longmire had all this pre-positioned by Second Corp as it came north to join us on the hill," said Styles, grinning. "Now that half the PRA army is stuck on the east side of the Mississippi, we've evened the odds."

Just then Logan heard the loud boom of artillery and the roar of rocket launchers as they began firing into the advancing PRA-Sahiradin army. Logan smiled at Styles and grabbed the other handle of the ammunition box she was trying to lift onto the truck. They loaded several more boxes until the truck was full then dashed forward to a gap in the line as the truck sped away. Logan watched as the ground in the distance erupted in plumes of dirt and smoke as round after round of artillery shells impacted the earth. Anti-armor rockets raced over the flat terrain, seeking out and destroying armored personnel carriers and tanks. Blue light, crackling with energy, lanced out from the Lycian weapons, cutting a swath of destruction through the Sahiradin troops.

Yet, even with the destruction they rained down on the enemy, the relentless invaders never slowed their advance. They pressed on through the flying shrapnel, dirt, and explosions until they were a hundred meters from the League-Lycian position. Logan and the others fired their K-45s from behind hastily erected barriers but it was immediately clear that the Red Legs, who led the attack, still had charged shields. The defenders slid their guns into the bottoms of their battle packs, engaged their shields, and drew their swords.

Logan looked at Styles, who was kneeling next to him. She returned the look, and for a split second her eyes betrayed her fear.

"Don't die," she said.

"I won't," he replied. "You either."

She smiled and nodded her head.

Then the order to prepare to attack came down the line and all the troopers stood. On the left end of the line, the Grensch and Rahani did the same. They waited for what seemed like an eternity but was only a few seconds before hearing the call to attack. Without hesitation, they launched themselves in a great surge toward the onrushing enemy.

Chapter 89

Logan and Styles stood on an outcropping high in the circular mountain range called the Deep Six, so named because the meteor crater around which the mountains ran was six kilometers across and nearly one kilometer deep. Due to its strategic position in the heart of its territory, the League had built the crater and the surrounding high ground into a powerful fortress that could hold out for months against a much larger force. Inside the ring of mountains was a large military installation, including an airbase big enough to accommodate fighters and intermediate range bombers. Inside the heart of the mountainous ring were two hundred kilometers of tunnels and hundreds of fixed gun and anti-aircraft emplacements. Several wells tapped into a massive natural aquifer deep below the fortress, supplying the troops with an unlimited supply of fresh water. Numerous small hidden entrances made it possible to launch surprise attacks against a besieging army, something the League had done with great success during the preceding four months.

Logan watched from their high perch as the PRA troops marched on the plains below Deep Six. Two columns of weary regular infantry and Red Legs retraced the path of their invasion back toward St. Louis. They still greatly outnumbered the League's forces inside Deep Six, but numerous failed assaults on the mountain fortress had demonstrated the futility of their long siege. With ammunition, fuel, and food running low, Guardian Harken had decided the time had come to consolidate his gains. He ordered his generals to fall back to St. Louis and to fortify the city and surrounding territory.

Logan looked at Styles and smiled. "Looks like we did it," he said.

Styles took his hand in hers and smiled. "Yes, we did," she said. "But they'll be back."

Although the League had survived the attack on its territory, Logan agreed with Styles. The enemy would be back. He knew that they had been lucky. The main League army defending St. Louis had nearly been overtaken as it withdrew from the city and retreated to Deep Six. Had the PRA army's northern wing been able to swing south and cut off the League's retreat, the defenders would have been annihilated.

It was thanks to General Longmire's plan and the valor of his troops at the Battle of Bullard Creek, as it came to be known, that complete disaster had been averted. Though heavily criticized by his superiors and the League Council when he conceived of the plan, it was now widely recognized that Longmire's decision to preposition heavy guns, ammunition, and supplies south of the rail bridge had made the difference.

Not aware of the plan but trusting in their officers and General Longmire, the troops had performed admirably when they flawlessly executed what was considered the greatest fighting retreat in modern history. Then those same troops pivoted from a defensive to an offensive footing without hesitation and fought like hell to halt the enemy's advance. Once the invaders' progress was stopped, Longmire ordered the left wing of the League-Lycian line to swing northeast. Like a giant closing door, the maneuver pinned the Sahiradin and PRA troops against the Mississippi River. The Sahiradin managed to fight their way out of the trap and retreat northward, but the PRA's army was utterly destroyed.

After the successful assault on *Dominion* and the near catastrophe at the Battle of Bullard Creek, the Sahiradin decided to quickly retrieve its army. They withdrew to Mars where, according to the Lycians, they were currently busily working to repair *Dominion* and establish a base on that planet's surface.

The Lycians also withdrew their troops after the battle. They spread their ships around Earth's orbit and throughout the system in the hope of finding the Apollo Stone, which Logan said was left on board the *Blackhawk* when it exploded. Not surprisingly, the Lycians were desperate to find the stone, terrified by the possibility that the Sahiradin would find it first and launch surprise attacks deep inside Lycian-held space.

Logan heard footsteps on the rocks behind him. He turned to see Cap and Lena approaching them. He and Cap nodded to each other, but no one spoke for several minutes as they watched the long line of retreating PRA troops marching east.

"What now?" asked Cap, finally breaking the silence.

"I don't know," said Logan. "We avoided total annihilation, but the PRA has gained a lot of territory around St. Louis. And they've disrupted the river trade which will bring extreme hardship to the League's members. But they're not done. I expect they'll regroup and prepare for a new offensive next spring."

"But now we don't have the river to help protect us," said Styles. "Once they fortify St. Louis and resupply, they'll sweep across the plains."

"And even if we somehow stop the next PRA offensive, we can't forget the Sahiradin are still out there," said Cap glancing up at the sky. "Something tells me they won't be gone for long."

No one spoke. Styles leaned a little toward Logan. He looked at her and squeezed her hand.

"The war isn't over, but let's enjoy today," said Logan. "Tomorrow will be here soon enough."

Made in the USA
Lexington, KY
30 November 2016